THREE NIGHTS WITH A SCOUNDREL

Tessa Dare

WINDSOR
PARAGON

First published 2012
by Ebury Publishing
This Large Print edition published 2012
by AudioGO Ltd
by arrangement with
Ebury Publishing

Hardcover ISBN: 978 1 4458 2364 5
Softcover ISBN: 978 1 4458 2365 2

British Library Cataloguing in Publication Data available

Printed and bound in Great Britain by
MPG Books Group Limited

WITH A SCOUNDREL

Elyssa, this stud's for you.
Thanks for being his fan from the very beginning.

So many people helped me as I wrote this trilogy. My wonderful husband, children, and extended family have been so supportive—I can't thank them enough. In particular, this manuscript benefited from the advice and perspective of Courtney Milan, Amy Baldwin, Elyssa Papa, Jennifer Haymore, Janga Brannon, Sara Lindsey, Terri Osburn, Diana Chung, Lindsey Faber, and Manda Collins. To Maili, thanks for patiently answering so many questions, and apologies for any mistakes I made despite your generous help. Thanks to Kim Castillo and Frauke Spanuth for lending their expertise behind the scenes.

I'm so grateful to everyone at Random House, including my editor, Kate Collins, and her assistant, Kelli Fillingim, my publicist, Alison Masiovecchio, copy editor, Martha Trachtenberg, and Lynn Andreozzi, for my gorgeous cover. And many thanks to my fabulous agent, Helen Breitwieser, for always going above and beyond.

Chapter One

London, October 1817

Lily awoke to a rough shake on her arm. A searing ball of light hovered before her face.

She winced, and the light quickly receded. With caution, she opened her eyes. Blinking furiously, Lily strained to make out the lamp-bearer's identity. It was Holling, the house keeper.

Good Lord. She bolted upright in bed. Something dreadful had occurred. The servants would never shake her awake unless it was a matter of extreme urgency.

She pressed a hand to her throat. 'What is it?'

Yellow lamplight illuminated an apologetic face. 'Downstairs, my lady. You're needed downstairs at once. Begging your pardon.'

With a nod of assent, Lily rose from bed. She shoved her toes intonight-chilled slippers and accepted assistance in donning a violet silk wrap.

Her sense of dread only mounted as she descended the stairs. And the feeling was all too familiar.

Nearly five months had passed since the last time she'd been summoned downstairs in the dark. No one had needed to wake her then; she'd been unable to sleep for an insistent sense of foreboding. Her fears were confirmed when she opened the door to find gentlemen crowding her doorstep—three men with nothing in common save their membership in the Stud Club, an exclusive horse-breeding society her brother Leo had founded. They were the reclusive Duke of Morland, scarred war hero Rhys St. Maur, and Julian Bellamy—the London *ton*'s favorite hell-raiser and Leo's closest friend.

One look at their grave faces that night, and there'd been no need for words. Lily had known instantly what they'd come to tell her.

Leo was dead.

At the age of eight-and-twenty, her twin brother was dead. Leo Chatwick, the Marquess of Harcliffe. Young, handsome, wealthy, universally admired— beaten to death in a Whitechapel alleyway, the victim of footpads.

The last time she'd been summoned down these stairs at night, her existence had been torn in half.

Lily's knees buckled as she reached the foot of the staircase. She clutched the banister for support, then drew a shaky breath as a footman waved her toward the door.

Holling thrust her lamp over the threshold. Gathering all her available bravery, Lily moved toward the door and peeked out.

As there was no one on the doorstep, her view went straight to the square. The first gray insinuation of daylight hovered over the manicured hedges and paths. The streets were still largely empty, but here and there she saw servants on their way to market.

At the housekeeper's insistent gesturing, she looked down. There, on the pavement at the bottom of the steps, lodged a costermonger's wheelbarrow. The wooden cart was heaped with carrots, turnips, vegetable marrows . . . and the body of an unconscious man.

She clutched the doorjamb. *Oh, no.*

2

It was Julian Bellamy.

Lily recognized the red cuff of his coat before she even saw his face. She clapped a palm to her mouth, smothering a cry of alarm.

There'd been one consolation in mourning Leo: the knowledge that she could never endure such a devastating loss again. He was her twin, her best friend from birth and, since their parents' deaths, her only remaining close kin. She would never love anyone so dearly as she'd loved him. Once Leo had left this world . . . pain could not touch her now.

Or so she'd thought.

Staring down at Julian's senseless form, it was hard to believe she'd ever felt this frantic. She sensed her throat emitting sounds—ugly, croaking sounds, she feared. But she couldn't make herself stop. Even when Leo had died, Julian had been there to stand by her. Devilish rake he might be, he was her brother's steadfast friend, and hers as well. Over the years, they'd come to think of him as family. If Julian left her . . .

She would truly be alone.

For the second time that morning, Holling gave her arm a shake. Lily looked to the house keeper.

'He's alive,' the older woman said. 'Still breathing.'

Tears of relief rushed past Lily's defenses. 'Bring him in.'

The footmen scrambled to obey, lifting his sprawled body from the wheelbarrow and hefting it up the steps.

'To the kitchen.'

They all filed down the narrow corridor, heading for the rear of the house. Holling first with her lamp, then the footmen bearing Julian. Lily brought

3

up the rear as they descended the short flight of steps to the kitchen.

Even at this early hour, the kitchen staff was hard at work. A toasty fire warmed the room, and a yeasty aroma filled the air. A scullery maid lifted floury hands from the breadboard and stepped back in alarm, making room for the footmen to pass.

They placed Julian by the hearth, propping his head on a sack of meal.

'Send for the doctor,' she said. When no one sprang into action, she repeated herself at the top of her lungs. 'Doctor. *Now*.'

With a hasty bow, one of the footmen hurried from the room.

Lily knelt at Julian's side. Heavens, he was filthy. Dirt streaked his face, and the smell of the gutter clung to his clothes. She put a hand to his forehead, finding it clammy and cool to the touch. Perhaps he needed air. Her fingers flew to his cravat, and she tugged at it, unwinding the starched linen from his throat. A day's growth of whiskers scraped her fingertips. She turned her cheek to his face, rejoicing at the warm puff of breath against her skin.

He suddenly convulsed, as if coughing.

She ceased her tussle with his cravat and pulled back to stare at him, not wanting to miss any word he might speak.

His eyes went in and out of focus as his gaze meandered over her form. 'Hullo, Lily.'

Relief washed through her. 'Julian. Are you well?'

He blinked several times, in rapid succession. Then again, slowly. Finally he said, 'Violet always was your color.'

4

He slumped back, eyes closed.

Was he drunk? She leaned forward, sniffing cautiously at his exposed throat. No liquor. No gutter smells here, either. Just hints of starch and soap, mingled with the metallic, pungent odor of . . .

Oh, God.

She grabbed his arm, shook it hard. 'Julian. Julian, wake up.'

When he failed to respond, she withdrew her trembling hand and looked down at it. Just as she'd feared. Her fingers came away wet with blood.

*   *   *

Julian Bellamy had died sometime during the night.

That could be the only explanation. He'd perished, and there'd been some sort of divine mistake. Because this morning, he'd woken up in heaven. The sheer purity of it blanked his senses.

All was light. Fragrant. Lush. Clean.

The qualities of Paradise, as his boyhood self would have imagined it. The antithesis of everything he'd known from birth to the age of nine years: squalor, dirt, darkness, hunger.

Come to mention it, he still felt a faint pang of hunger. Odd.

His bare arms glided between layers of crisp linen and quilted silk as he stretched, idly wondering if the dead felt hunger. And if so, what mead-and-manna banquet awaited him here?

'At last. There you are.' A feminine voice. Husky and warm, like honey. A *familiar* voice.

His pulse stuttered.

His pulse? Bloody hell. To the devil with hunger.

5

Dead men definitely did not have pulses.

Julian shot up on one elbow and forced his bleary gaze to sharpen. 'Lily? Surely that's not you.'

The elegant oval of her face came into focus. Dark eyes, anchored by a straight, slim nose. The rosy curve of her mouth. 'Of course it's me.'

Holy God. He was not in heaven; he was damned. He was in a bed—presumably a bed somewhere in Harcliffe House. And Lady Lily Chatwick sat on the edge of the bed, entirely too close. Within arm's length. And he knew this couldn't be a dream, because he never dreamed of Lily. He'd *tried* to dream of her, on a few occasions when he was feeling especially maudlin. It had never worked. Even in sleep, he couldn't fool himself. Every part of him, conscious and unconscious, knew he didn't deserve this woman.

Damn. He scrambled to remember the events of the night previous. What the devil had he done? What had he caused *her* to do?

'Lily.' His tongue felt thick, felted. He swallowed with difficulty. 'Tell me this isn't your room.'

Her lips quirked in a half-smile. 'This isn't my room.'

He released the breath he'd been holding. Now that he flashed a quick glance about him, he could see that the bedchamber was decorated in masculine shades. Rich greens, dark blues.

A worse thought struck him. He sat up further. 'Lily. Tell me this isn't *his* room.'

Her smile faded, and sadness melted the laugh lines at the corners of her eyes. 'No. This isn't Leo's room.'

With a muttered curse of thanksgiving, he fell back against the pillows. It was one thing to

6

disgrace his dead friend's memory. Another thing entirely to do it in his dead friend's own bed.

'It's just a spare bedchamber. How is your arm?' she asked.

In answer, the limb gave a fierce throb. The wave of pain pushed memories to the fore. The dusty storehouse. The panicked crowd. The escaped bull, smashing him against the rail.

With his right hand, he touched the bandage tightly wound about his biceps.

'The doctor's come and gone,' she said. 'He seemed to think you'll survive.'

'Blast.' He threw his wrist over his eyes. 'How on earth did I get here?'

She clucked her tongue. 'So dramatic. I should think this is a common occurrence for you, waking up naked in a strange bed.'

Naked? Had she truly just said . . . ?

Julian lifted the sheet and glanced downward. Thank God. Though he was undressed to the waist, the pewter buttons of his trouser fall winked up at him. And they were lying flat and obedient in a tame row. At the moment. If she kept hovering over him, they wouldn't stay that way for long.

'Minx.' When she only laughed harder at her own joke, he lowered the sheet and chided her, 'You are an unforgivable tease.'

'And you are an unmitigated ass.'

When he shifted onto his side, she laid a hand to his bare shoulder. Her touch was a brand against his skin. 'Lily . . . '

'No, I mean it. You know I don't normally use such words.'

She never used such words at all. Oh, she often *thought* them, he knew. But she never *said*

7

them. And the scoundrel in Julian was perversely delighted that he'd provoked her into speaking her mind. Lily had a lot of thoughts worth sharing, and all too often she kept them to herself.

She handed him a glass of barley water, and he accepted it gratefully.

'You are making an ass of yourself, Julian, and I don't mean just this morning.' Her eyes narrowed to angry slits. 'But while whe're on the subject, let's start with this morning.'

'Must we?' Tucking the sheets close to his chest—to guard her modesty, not his—Julian sat up in bed. He drank as she continued, downing the barley water in greedy gulps.

'Yes. Do you have any idea what a fright you gave me? A costermonger found you in the street before dawn. Lying in the gutter, bleeding.'

Ah, yes. The blood. That was what had done him in. Jagged shards of memory began to piece themselves together.

'Fortunately, Cook recognized you when the costermonger brought you by in his barrow, tumbled in amongst the turnips and celery root.' Her voice rose. 'Really, Julian. Can you imagine?'

Yes, he could. He had a vague recollection of celery root. The night came back to him now, in a hot, sweaty rush. Setting aside the glass, he massaged away a sharp pain in his temple. 'I can explain.'

'Please do.'

'There was a boxing match in Southwark.'

She shook her head. 'Not another boxing match. That's all you care about these past few months.'

'I don't attend for love of the sport.'

Julian had never shared the popular fascination

8

with pugilism. He'd tasted too much of real danger in his life to take amusement from contrived imitations. But he wished to God he *did* enjoy blood sport. If so, a good man would still be alive. Months ago, Julian had agreed to attend a boxing match at Leo's suggestion. At the last minute, he'd begged off, preferring to pass the evening in a woman's embrace instead.

Worst decision he'd ever made. And not just because Carnelia was uninspired in bed.

Leo had attended the fight without him. And afterward, he'd been attacked and beaten in a Whitechapel alleyway—murdered in the street by a pair of footpads. A random act of thievery, it was concluded by most.

Julian knew better. That attack had been meant for him. In recent months, he'd attended every boxing match, cockfight, dogfight, and bear-baiting within a day's travel of London. If the scent of blood hung in the air, he followed it—no matter how the spectacle turned his stomach. He could not rest until he reckoned with Leo's murderers, lest they become his killers, too.

'Do you really think attending these matches will lead you to them?' she asked. 'You have scarcely any description of the men. They could be standing next to you on the street, and you would never know.'

'You don't understand.' Though he had a better description of the men than Lily supposed, it was vague at best. He knew well how ineffectual the search was. It didn't matter. Giving up was unthinkable.

'No, I don't understand. I don't understand a great many things you do lately. For example, just

9

how do you get from a boxing match in Southwark to a costermonger's wheelbarrow in Mayfair?'

'After the bout, there was a bull-baiting. The beast snapped its tether, and the crowd panicked.' Julian closed his eyes and pinched the bridge of his nose, his thoughts crowded out by memories of noise. The men shouting, the dogs' frenzied barks, the thunder of footfalls as everyone rushed for the exits at once.

He raised both hands between them—one balled in a fist, the other extended as an open palm. 'The bull charged.' In illustration, he drove the fist into his palm. 'I was in the way.'

'I don't suppose you were doing something noble, like diving in front of the beast to save a hobbling grandfather.' She put a hand under his chin and tipped his face to the light, examining his cheek. Her finger traced a slanting line toward his mouth—he must have a scratch there, he supposed. He licked his cracked lips.

Her touch skipped to the bandage encircling his arm. She ran her fingers over the binding, tucked a raw edge under the fold.

The casual intimacy of her touch was affecting. Too affecting.

Shaking his head, he pulled her hand away. 'Nothing noble. I was just the one stupid enough to be wearing red.'

'Julian.' Her dark eyes glimmered with emotion as she squeezed his fingers. 'You must stop making yourself a target.'

'I was only squashed. No real injury, save the pain in my arm. I decided to walk home to shake it off.'

'*Walk* home? From Southwark?'

He shrugged his good shoulder, easing his hand from her grip. 'It's not so far.' Not for him. Lately he spent most nights wandering all quadrants of the city.

Last night, he'd made his way back so far as the square where Harcliffe House was situated. This house was always the last stop on his nightly rounds. He would pause on the corner down the street. If he stood half on the pavement, half on the green . . . then craned his neck . . . he could *just* glimpse the fourth rightmost window on the second floor. The one he knew belonged to Lily's bedchamber. If the window was dark, she was sleeping and at peace. He, too, could relax. On the nights he found a lamp burning, he ached for her sorrow. And he simply stood there, quietly sharing her grief, until that light went dark or the sun came up—whichever occurred first.

In the weeks after Leo's death, he'd found that lamp burning more often than not. As the months passed, however, her bad nights had grown less frequent. Last night, he'd been comforted to see the window dark. And just as Julian had turned to seek his own home, that faint pain in his arm shifted to a deep, persistent throb.

He said, 'I was passing nearby. I stopped under the streetlamp to have a look at my arm. Just a flesh wound, but I hadn't noticed it earlier. Something was caught . . . a shard of glass, I think.' He touched his ban daged arm in demonstration. 'I grasped it and pulled it out, and there was a fair amount of blood. Quite startled me, and I . . .'

'And you fainted.'

'*Fainted?* No.'

'You swooned.'

11

'No,' he said stoutly, jamming his hand under his arm. 'Absolutely not. I didn't swoon, Lily. Men do not swoon.'

'You slumped to the pavement unconscious, for the costermonger to find. Sounds like a fainting spell to me. What else could it have been?'

'I don't know. Something different. Apoplexy. Malaria.' Anything more masculine than *swooning*.

Her eyes rolled toward the ceiling. 'You don't have apoplexy or malaria. Aside from your wound and a few bruises, the doctor could find nothing wrong with you. Not physically, at any rate. You're simply exhausted. When was the last time you slept through the night?'

'Can't recall, honestly.'

'Hm. And when's the last time you had a proper meal?'

'Ah, now *that* I remember. I had a very fine steak at the Stoat's Head.'

'Yesterday?'

He hedged, pushing a hand through his hair. 'Not precisely.'

One dark eyebrow arched in disbelief. 'You fainted, Julian.'

'And what if I did? What would you have me do, start carrying a vinaigrette?' He chuckled to himself. That would be a good joke. Within a week, every young buck in London would be carrying the same. Like Beau Brummel before him, Julian was the trendsetter of his day. His clothing, hair, even mannerisms were meticulously copied by the impressionable young gentlemen of the *ton*. Just as he'd planned from the start.

'Don't be ridiculous. I want you to start taking care of yourself, that's all. Sleep. Eat. Avoid scenes

12

of violence and mayhem. Is it really so difficult?'

'*Yes*. It's impossible.'

She winced, absorbing the force of his reply. He regretted his vehemence, but not the sentiment.

She said quietly, 'I want you safe. I care about you. What's so impossible about that?'

Everything.

He yanked the coverlet about himself, scanning the room for his clothes. He had to get out of this bed, this house . . . before this conversation went places it shouldn't. He planted one foot on the floor and transferred his weight to it.

Dizziness swamped him. The room made a violent twirl, and he found himself pitched straight back to the mattress.

'Malaria,' he muttered. His arms felt wooden at his sides.

'It's not malaria. Nor even a fainting spell this time. The doctor left a sleeping powder, and I put some in your barley water.'

She pushed him back on the bed, arranging the coverlet about him. Her hands . . . they were everywhere. As she leaned forward to arrange the pillows beneath his head, he got an intoxicating lungful of her sweet warmth. The swell of her breast brushed against his wounded arm. Soft. God, so soft. His heart gave a wild kick. Now *this* was perilous.

He said, 'I thought you wanted me to avoid danger.'

'I do. That's why you're going to sleep. When you wake up, you're going to eat. And then we're going to talk.'

Her words seemed wrapped in cotton. It took him a moment to unravel their meaning. 'Just how

13

much sleeping powder did you give me?'

'Two doses, and an extra pinch for good measure. You're a large man, Julian Bellamy.'

'Ah, Lily. You noticed.' The flirtatious retort slipped out by accident. Damn. He was so sleepy, drunken with it. He couldn't censor his replies.

'You're also an ass.'

'You know me so well.'

'Do I?' She laid a hand to his cheek. 'Sometimes I wonder. Sometimes I think I don't know you at all.'

'Don't say that.'

Her dark eyes searched his. So beautiful, those eyes. He wanted to keep staring into them for hours—forever—but some devil's imp had tied lead weights to his eyelashes. He couldn't hold them up much longer.

'Go to sleep.' Her soft form receded.

'No, wait. Don't go. I'm sorry.'

A spike of clarity pierced his drugged haze. He struggled up on one elbow. With his other hand, he reached for her, curling his hand around the back of her slender neck. He wove his fingers into the thick silk of her hair, holding her tight. Leaving her nowhere to look but at him. He needed to say this. Nothing in the world was more important than saying these words, right now. And he needed to know she understood.

He twisted his grip in her hair, and she gave a little gasp. He waited until her gaze fell to his lips. There. Now he knew she was listening.

'I'm so sorry, Lily. So damn sorry, and I wish to God . . . It's my fault, you know. Leo's murder. My fault. But I'm going to make it right. Not right. Can't be put right. But better. I swear to you,

14

I'll . . .'

Damn it, he was rambling like a bedlamite. From the furrowed set of her brow, he could tell he'd lost her some ways back.

'Please,' she said. 'Don't distress yourself so.'

'I'm sorry,' he repeated, his voice breaking into a hoarse whisper. He began again, forcing his lips to shape the words clearly, even if no sound came out. 'You must know I'd do anything for you. For you. You and I . . . I wish . . .'

She shushed him, tapping her thumb against his jaw. 'Rest, Julian.'

Julian. The name echoed through his skull until he scarcely recognized it as his own. Perhaps because it wasn't.

'You should sleep,' she said.

His chin concurred, nodding in agreement. He should sleep. He should.

No. His eyes snapped open. He couldn't let her go, not yet. And if he couldn't reach her with words, he'd have to try something else. With his last bit of consciousness, he pushed up on one arm, pulled her close with the other—

And kissed her. God damn his soul, he kissed Lady Lily Chatwick for all he was worth. Which, unfortunately, wasn't much at the moment.

Beneath his palm, her neck went rigid with shock. Her lips were warm, but firm. Resistant. Sealed.

Still he held her fast, pressing his mouth to hers with artless desperation. All his seductive techniques—clever caresses, murmured endearments, nimble flicks of the tongue—they'd deserted him utterly. After all these years, so many fantasies of this moment . . . Bloody hell. This was

15

not going well, not at all.

He tilted his head, hoping a different angle might help. A panicked sound creaked from her throat.

Julian cursed himself. *Really,* he wanted to pull back and insist, *I'm a much better kisser than this.*

But what was the use? He'd never have another chance to prove it.

Then, suddenly, something happened. Or nothing happened.

Because in that moment, neither of them moved. Neither of them breathed. They just . . . existed together. The tension melted away. And the kiss was still artless, still desperate—but only because it was real. The most honest, truthful moment they'd ever shared.

The sheer power of it was a lightning strike, jolting them apart.

He stared at her, unable to speak as the room contracted to a dark, narrow tunnel. He at one end, and she at the other. Sleep tugged at him with its clumsy grasp, stealing the edges from his vision and the strength from his limbs. His grip slipped from her neck. Strands of her hair slid through his fingers like water. Cool and abundant and vital.

Impossible to hold.

He fell back to the bed, and knew no more.

Chapter Two

There had been a time, not so very long ago, when Julian had counted few regrets in his life. The night of Leo's murder, those 'few' regrets multiplied to 'many.'

16

And he faced today with the unhappy knowledge that at some point overnight, 'many' had been revised to 'innumerable.'

From the tangled nest of bed linens, he peered at the mantel clock. His head throbbed with pain as he struggled to focus. Noon already. He'd lost half the day.

Bugger half the day, his pounding brain insisted. *You've lost your wits. You kissed Lily, you unmitigated ass. And you didn't even do it well.*

God. He couldn't conceive of how to remedy the circumstance now. If it could be remedied at all. He had to get out of here.

Taking care with his wounded arm, he rose from the bed and staggered to the washstand. Unwilling to wait for a proper bath to be drawn, he made good use of the pitcher of water and cake of soap. After he'd sponged his face and torso clean, he dried his body with a small towel and cast about for something to wear. To the side, a set of clean garments was laid out. Crisp shirt and cravat, dun trousers, dark blue coat.

Julian didn't recognize the clothes as his own. Which meant they were likely Leo's.

Suppressing a morbid shudder, he rang for a servant. 'I want my own clothing,' he said to the footman who promptly appeared.

'But sir, they're soiled. The laundress hasn't yet—'

'I don't care. Just bring them.'

The liveried youth bowed. 'Yes, sir.'

While he waited, Julian turned his attention to a tray of covered dishes on the side table. He lifted a silver dome to find an array of food: cold meats, cheeses, pickle, bread and butter, a dish of grapes

17

and apricots. His stomach churned. Much as he hated to admit it, Lily had been right in this respect. He needed to make more effort to take sustenance, even when he didn't feel like eating. Brandy and fury could only fuel a man for so long.

He forced himself to choke down some cold ham, a small hunk of bread, and a wedge of hard cheese. By the time he'd washed the food down with a cup of tea, the footman had reappeared with his clothing.

The shirt and cravat had been washed out and hastily ironed. The left sleeve still showed a jagged rent, of course, and some faded bloodstains spotted the fabric. But the unstarched linen felt warm and fresh against his skin. The silk front of his waistcoat was largely unblemished.

His topcoat, however . . . the thing was beyond saving, but someone had made a valiant attempt. The garment had been carefully hung and brushed, and, he judged with a sniff, steamed with a light perfume. The tear on the sleeve was not so obvious to the observer, but inside, the lining was streaked with dried blood.

Julian's nose wrinkled as he slid his arms into the sleeves. He would have to burn the thing as soon as he returned home. Underneath that misting of *eau de cologne,* the wool retained the faint odor of filth.

Much the same, his detractors would doubtless say, as Julian Bellamy himself.

Tugging violently on his cuffs, he cursed his stupidity. Of all the places to collapse—on the street in front of Harcliffe House? He was no stranger to the gutter, but he'd sworn he would never return. And for Lily to see him like that . . .

He rubbed his temples. Time to make his escape.

18

'If you please, sir.' Swift, the butler, appeared in the doorway. 'Lady Lily requests that you join her downstairs, once you are feeling quite'—the silver-haired man gave him an assaying look—'restored.' He bowed and left.

Restored. Julian mused on the word. *Was* he feeling quite restored? With a full belly and a ban daged arm, perhaps he approached that definition. But feeling restored was a different matter from feeling redeemed. The latter sensation would continue to elude him, he feared.

Couldn't he just sneak out of the house? Send her a note of apology later, perhaps with a flower arrangement of outrageous size?

He sighed heavily. No, he couldn't.

He took the stairs slowly, then ducked his head into each open room in turn, searching for Lily. She wasn't in the salon. Nor the morning room, nor the parlor. The music room seemed an unlikely spot, but he crossed the corridor and tried it anyway.

No Lily.

Leo's library was next. He breezed by it, not expecting to find her there. When he glimpsed a flash of muslin inside, he pulled up short, stumbling against the doorjamb and banging his injured arm.

'Blast. Bugger. Bloody hell.'

The string of oaths—even so violently uttered—was spoken without consequence, swallowed whole by the stillness of the room.

Lily sat at the desk, quill in hand, her dark head bent over an open ledger. From the doorway, Julian observed her closely. The plume of her quill continued its slow, stately promenade across the page. He could just make out the gentle scratch of her script over the fierce drumming of his heart.

He leaned against the doorframe—on his good shoulder this time. 'I've mucked it right well this time, haven't I? Tell me, Lily. How do I make this right?'

The pen stilled. Her slender, elegant hand slowly replaced the quill in the inkwell. She raised her head a few degrees, giving him her exquisite profile. Midday sunlight streamed in from the window behind her, gilding the soft features of her face and dusting her eyelashes with bronze. She had the loveliest ears he'd ever seen, each one a delicate porcelain spiral, like the handle of a teacup. So perfect.

So fragile.

'Do you know,' he said, 'there are men who would like very much to see me dead. Powerful men. Obscenely wealthy men. Men who can afford to be patient and engage the services of large, ruthless brutes. I've managed to evade them all. But you . . . God's truth, I think you'll be the very death of me.'

She frowned at the ledger, then flipped it closed. Sliding the book aside with a graceful turn of her wrist, she withdrew a neat stack of letters from a drawer.

While she unfolded the topmost missive, Julian reached for the mirror. As was the case in every room of the Chatwicks' graciously appointed Mayfair town house, a small mirror dangled from the doorjamb, affixed there by means of a length of ribbon and a tack. He twisted it, angling the reflective surface to face the window. Catching a ray of sunlight, he flicked his wrist back and forth until the flutter of bright flashes drew her attention.

Blinking with surprise, Lily lifted her face to the

doorway. As she took in his appearance, her lips curved in a welcoming smile. 'Oh, Julian. Forgive me, I didn't notice you there.'

'Good afternoon.' He made a gallant bow, crossed the room to her, and took her outstretched hand in his, giving it a light squeeze, nothing more. When he released her fingers, her expression was puzzled, perhaps even hurt. But today he didn't trust himself with a kiss.

She gave the cuff of his sleeve a smart twist. 'You needn't use the mirrors. They're for servants, not friends or family. You're both.'

'I didn't want to startle you.'

Julian wondered if it would ever cease to startle *him,* the boundless generosity of the Chatwicks. Ever since he'd formed an acquaintance with Lily's twin brother, Leo, the late Marquess of Harcliffe, Julian had been welcomed into this house. First as a friend, then as honorary family. They knew nothing of him. Not his ancestry, not his origins. Not even his true name. But never once had they treated him like one who ought to use the mirrors rather than tap a noblewoman's shoulder to draw her attention.

Leo and Lily Chatwick were, without question, a singular example of goodness among the social elite. Now Leo was dead, and it was Julian's fault. And Lily was left alone, and that was his fault, too.

'You look lovely,' he told her, as if a feeble compliment could make everything right.

'Thank you. You look dreadful.' Her dark brown eyes scanned his appearance. 'Just look at that coat. Once it fit you to perfection, and now it hangs loose on your frame.'

'I'm making it the new fashion. Next Season, they'll all be wearing ill-fitting coats with ripped sleeves. The tailors will despise me.'

Lily gave him a chastening look. 'We need to talk.'

Here it was. The moment he'd been dreading. 'Very well.' He took a straight-backed armchair and placed it just a few feet from hers, positioning it to facilitate lipreading. 'Let's talk.'

'No, not here.' She replaced the bundle of letters in the drawer, then shut and locked it with a small key. Reaching for her gloves, she said, 'Let's go out to the square. It's a lovely afternoon.'

Julian hesitated. 'Really, I'm not fit for public view. And I ought to be—'

Ignoring his protest, she threaded her arm through his. He promptly misplaced any will to argue.

It truly was a lovely afternoon, Julian thought as they stepped out into the crisp late October air. This was that rare time of year when the London air could actually *be* crisp, rather than wavy with humidity or fuzzy with soot. A clear sky capped the rows of lavish town homes and the square they framed. The sun floated bright and yellow overhead, and the world was sharp beneath it. Every edge glinted; each pane of glass reflected blue. And he had Lily on his arm.

Yes, indeed. A lovely afternoon. Goddamned heartbreakingly beautiful.

As they crossed into the square, Julian decided to face the matter head-on. They found a vacant bench and sat on opposite ends, turning to face one another.

'I'm sorry for last night,' he began. 'Or rather, for this morning.'

'You should be.'

'What I did was . . . unconscionable. You have my word it will never happen again.'

'I should hope not.'

In some other circumstance, with some other lady, his pride might have taken a knock or two, simply from the sheer alacrity of her agreement. But then, they were often of one mind, he and Lily. He told himself this quick consensus was a good thing. A humbling thing, but a good thing.

He went on, 'I don't know what possessed me to take such liberties. I can only blame the sleeping powder, combined with my state of extreme exhaustion, and I—'

She held up a hand. 'Wait. What are you talking about?'

He paused, suddenly unsure. 'What are *you* talking about?'

'You can't possibly be apologizing for that kiss?'

'I . . . I can't?' Did she not want him to apologize for that kiss? She couldn't possibly have *desired* it. Much less enjoyed it. Could she have? The mere possibility sent stupid, irrational hope blazing through him.

She made a dismissive gesture. 'It was scarcely worth mentioning, let alone deserving of apology.'

Right. Just to confirm: The hope was both stupid *and* irrational.

After briefly pressing his lips together to seal his humiliation, he said, 'I apologize for my behavior nonetheless. It was wrong of me.'

'You weren't yourself. You were drugged and barely conscious.' Smiling, she added, 'And considering you swooned again in the middle of it, I'm not certain that kiss reflected favorably on me, either.'

23

'For the last time, I did not swoon.'

'You did.' Her eyes went grave. 'You fainted dead away, Julian. And you do owe me an apology. Can you imagine what you put me through? Roused from bed in the dark of night, summoned to the door to view your senseless body in a heap? It was like Leo all over again. I can't endure another scene like that.'

Guilt twisted his heart. 'Lily . . .'

'How much time has passed since Leo died?'

He gave her a look, one that spoke without words. *You, of all people, should not have to ask.*

And she didn't. Leo had been loved by many, but by no one so much as the two of them. They shared a moment of silent grief.

'Five months,' she said. 'Almost.'

'Four months, three weeks, and a day.'

'As you say. And to look at you, one would think five years have passed. Haunting the streets at all hours, developing a sudden fascination with blood sport, chasing shadows down dark alleyways. And you've grown so thin and pale.'

She suddenly tilted her head and narrowed her eyes at him. 'I've just formed a suspicion. I think I know who . . . or rather, *what,* you truly are.'

His pulse quickened. Sweat beaded at the back of his neck. Despite the mad upheaval in his chest, he strove to look bored. 'Oh yes?'

With a glance to either side, she inched closer. Her eyes gleamed with humor. 'You're a vampire. Aren't you?'

A relieved chuckle escaped him. He made a show of stretching his arm along the back of the bench— not coincidentally toward her—and defiantly tilting his face to the sun. After a long moment, he cocked an eyebrow. 'Here I am, sitting in broad daylight. I haven't disintegrated to ashes yet.'

'No. Not yet.' Her voice went serious. 'You must stop. You must give up this search before it kills you, too.'

Julian rubbed his eyes briefly, then dropped his hand. 'Impossible.'

'Not impossible. Merely difficult. Believe me, I do understand. I've buried myself in ledgers and papers, putting things in order for the transfer of the estate. I could leave the duty to others, but I don't. Because as much effort as it is, I need the distraction. Grieving is work in its own right. A harsh, relentless sort of labor.'

He would not have thought to phrase it so, but she was right. Julian felt as though he'd been spending recent months digging trenches with a teaspoon. But there was more to this than Lily supposed.

'It's not just a distraction,' he said, trying to explain as best he could without revealing details. 'I need answers. Leo deserves answers.'

'Sometimes there are no answers.'

Before he could argue back, a pair of beribboned young girls in white pinafores bounced past, hand in hand. A round-faced nursemaid followed them, tugging a miniature terrier by the leash. The dog gave Julian's boot a low growl.

Lily cleared her throat. 'I had an unexpected caller the other day. Lady Norwich. You remember her.'

The abrupt change of subject set his brain spinning. 'Do I?'

'I should hope so. You had an affair with her two summers ago. *Before* her husband passed away.'

'Oh.' An awkward pause. '*That* Lady Norwich.' With false nonchalance, he asked, 'And what did she have to say?'

'She wants me to marry her brother, Mr. Burton.'

He sputtered. Damn that Maria Norwich. She wasn't supposed to be so obvious. But then, subtlety never had been Maria's forte. 'She *said* that?'

'No, of course she didn't say it. But there is no other reason she should have called, except to pave the way for her brother. She had nothing whatsoever to talk about. Just sat there like a stick, sipping tea.'

'I didn't know sticks could sip tea.'

She cut him a stern look. He could tell she meant that glare to have teeth. The problem was, when Lily was near, Julian's thoughts fixated on lips and tongue.

'Stop making fun,' she said. 'I know you sent her, or at least put the thought in her head. You're matchmaking again.'

'Burton will inherit an earldom.'

'I am not interested in Mr. Burton, or his earldom.'

Leaning forward, he reached into her lap and took her hands in his. She cast an apprehensive glance to the side, and he ignored it. Etiquette be damned, he had to convince her of this.

He squeezed her gloved fingers tight. 'You must marry, and soon.'

'I don't intend to marry at all.'

'Leo's heir will arrive from Egypt in a matter of weeks.'

'Yes, and the new marquess is my cousin. We haven't seen one another since childhood, but I doubt the man will cast me out of my home.

26

He may be perfectly happy for me to manage the household until he marries, as I did for Leo. And if such an arrangement is not agreeable to us both, I will find living quarters of my own.'

'Alone? You cannot live alone.'

'I most certainly can. I am a single woman in possession of good fortune. Why should I be in want of a husband?'

'Lily . . .' He released her hands. There was no way to talk around it. 'You cannot hear.'

'I am deaf, yes, and have been so these past nine years. And . . . ?'

And there were innumerable obstacles for a deaf single woman setting up a household of her own, and well she knew it. She was simply being difficult. 'The merchants will cheat you, for one.'

'Holling and Swift look out for me. And I can hire a companion.'

He made an exasperated gesture. 'The companion will cheat you.'

'I'm safer in the hands of a cheating companion than saddled with a grasping fortune-hunter husband. Even if a servant siphons ten percent of my fortune, I still retain the greater part. If I marry, I lose control of everything. And really, Julian. Malachi *Burton*?' A laugh caught in her throat. 'When we were younger, he lacked the temerity to ask me for a dance. Now marriage? He must presume me desperate indeed.'

Her gaze wandered to the center of the square. A little smile touched the corners of her lips. 'You never knew me before my illness. I had so many suitors in my first season.'

Julian blinked at her. Unbelievable. She spoke the words as though they should come as a surprise.

27

'As many as there were eligible gentlemen in London, I'd wager. You could have just as many now. Show your face at a party now and then, and the men would flock to you.'

'Please.' Her cheeks flushed. 'I'm eight-and-twenty, not a debutante.'

'Were you eight-and-forty, any man would be lucky to marry you.'

'Any man would be lucky to attach himself to my money and connections, do you mean?'

He tsked. 'Don't fish for compliments, Lily. It's unbecoming.'

'I'm not fishing for anything. I'm stating facts. Even ignoring my impairment—which most find difficult to ignore—by the *ton*'s standards, I'm a dried-up spinster.'

'Nonsense.' He brushed her cheek, then held up his thumb to mock inspection and pronounced, 'Glistening with the dew of youth.'

With another woman, he might have put that same thumb in his mouth, lightly sucked it in lascivious suggestion. He would not do that with Lily. He would *not*. No matter how much he wished to savor the sweet essence of her skin.

She gave him an arch look, one eyebrow rising in reproof.

He returned the expression, mirroring her primness with such success that she laughed despite herself. He loved the sound of her laugh. It wasn't musical or affected, just honest and real.

'I've missed this,' she said suddenly. 'I've missed our friendship so much.'

Julian didn't know what to say. Of course he'd missed her friendship, too. But did she have to graze his wrist when she said that, sit forward on

28

the bench . . . tugging his eyes down the bodice of her dress, giving rise to desires that strayed well beyond the bounds of friendly discourse?

She said, 'The house is so empty with Leo gone.'

God, yes. Speak of Leo. Help me smother this inappropriate yearning under a thick blanket of guilt and grief.

'I haven't bothered with parties in years. The house was always full of his friends. I never felt deprived of companionship, but now . . .'—she straightened her glove—'those friends don't come around so often as they might.'

He was unable to look at her for a moment. 'I've been busy.'

In just how many ways was it possible to betray a friend? Julian had lied to Leo for the duration of their acquaintance, lusted after his sister for almost as long, and then sent the man alone to a violent death that had been meant for him instead. It galled and shamed him, to look back on the record of this 'friendship' and feel how acutely, how catastrophically he'd failed. He'd vowed to prove a truer friend now, even as the poor man shivered in the grave. Justice for Leo's murder and a suitable husband for Lily: These were now his guiding aims in life.

She noted his solemnity. 'I know how hard it will be for you to let this investigation go. The senseless nature of it all offends you deeply. You're so like Leo that way. He never could tolerate injustice. That's why the two of you were such fast friends.' She framed his jaw with one hand, lifting his face until his eyes met hers. 'He knew, as I do, that beneath all that scandal and devilry . . . you're a good man, Julian Bellamy.'

29

A good man? Good Lord. She had no idea.

Just that slight, innocent touch—the curve of her palm, the scattered pressure of three fingertips against his cheek. Sensation rioted in his blood, incited by multiplying possibilities. They all started with a kiss. He wanted to kiss her again, right now, and do a proper job of it. Slide down the bench until their bodies met, steady her with a light touch, tilt her face to his . . . This time he would learn the taste of her.

This constant war between his base male instincts and what remained of his conscience—he'd been waging it for years. And by the gods, it was an epic struggle. Worthy of lutes and Homeric poetry. More. He deserved his own damned constellation.

You're a good man, Julian Bellamy.

No, he really wasn't a good man. Nor was he even Julian Bellamy. But he would pretend to be both, for a little bit longer.

'Leo was a good man.' He cleared his throat. 'And you're right. It's the injustice I can't abide. Good men should not be killed in alleyways. Brutal murders should not go unpunished. And,' he said with a meaningful look, 'bright, beautiful ladies of marriageable age should not live vulnerable and alone.'

Her eyes went serious, unblinking. She leaned closer still. The epic battle, it would seem, was only beginning.

'Then don't leave me.'

30

Chapter Three

It wasn't easy for Lily, holding Julian's gaze. His eyes were a bold, piercing blue. And the face they were set within . . . well, those fine features were unsettling indeed.

After years of friendship, Lily would have thought she'd be inured to his good looks. But no. She suspected there was something instinctual about it, something elementally female. Obviously, he had a certain effect on women. For a lady to look upon Julian Bellamy and *not* feel herself heat from within . . . well, it would be rather like a hare calmly staring into the eyes of a wolf. Improbable—and even if it could be achieved, imprudent.

But no matter how her heart bounded in her chest, Lily held his gaze, hoping to sink home the import of her words.

Don't leave me. I can't lose you, too.

Could she even explain what his friendship meant to her? Their connection was both open and secret at once; in some ways freely admitted and in others never discussed. While she and Leo had almost known each other *too* well, every interaction with Julian felt fresh and exciting. He made her think, laugh, debate.

Lately, however, he just had her terrified. Since Leo's death, each time she saw him, he looked a little more gaunt, a little less alive. And then that scare today in the early morning hours . . .

Even now, she felt the slick warmth of his blood on her fingertips, the strength of his grip tangled in her hair.

31

The taste of desperation still lingered on her lips.

That kiss . . . botched and meaningless as it was, it had changed everything. It was the kiss of a soldier marching off to war, or a man on his way to the gallows. The kiss of a man who expected to die, and soon.

She would not allow it. She couldn't.

'Losing my brother was the most horrid thing to ever happen to me,' she told him. 'I can't lose you, too. I just want you to be safe.'

'Can't you understand? I feel the same. I want you safe, and you only refuse my attempts to secure your future.'

'That's not the same at all.'

'Isn't it?' His frustration was obvious. 'If you don't like my matchmaking, by all means, go into society and choose a husband yourself.'

She stared at him for a long moment. Within her, a decision dovetailed into place. 'Very well, then. Perhaps I will.'

He shook his head. 'Lily, sooner or later you'll have to . . . '

She could tell the instant her meaning sank in. Julian froze from the tips of his boots to the roots of his hair, his mouth hanging open a fraction. To his credit, he did not quite fall off the bench.

'What did you say?' he asked. 'Repeat it for me, slowly.'

She couldn't help but laugh. 'I thought that's my line.'

He was not amused.

'I said, very well. I'll offer you a bargain. I will reenter society. But only if you come with me.'

His expression went from displeasure to confusion.

32

'Come now. This is a bright, clear autumn afternoon.' She gestured at the bare-branched trees above them, so starkly outlined against the blue sky. 'A perfect day to come out of mourning.'

'Come out of mourning? But . . .'

'Don't misunderstand. We will never *forget* Leo. That would be impossible. But he would want us to move forward with our lives. We are both of us healthy and reasonably young, and we reside in one of the largest, grandest cities in Christendom. Let's go out, see our friends. Have fun.'

'Fun?' His expression was incredulous. 'The two of us?'

'Yes, fun. Amusement. Good cheer. I know it's been awhile, but surely you remember the concept? You were always the life of a party before.'

'Yes, *before*. This is after.'

She gentled her demeanor. 'It won't come naturally. Not at first. But we simply cannot go on as we are. We must push ourselves to seek amusement and company. If we pretend to be happy convincingly enough, perhaps we will succeed in convincing ourselves.'

In truth, going to parties was the last thing in the world Lily felt like doing. But she could think of no other way to divert Julian from his reckless, pointless search. She had to do *something*.

He pushed a hand through his unruly black hair. 'You just said you don't want to marry.'

'I don't. But since you insist . . . I'm willing to give a few gentlemen the opportunity to change my mind.'

'A *few* gentlemen? You'll be besieged. Attend one party, and they'll be milling three-deep on your doorstep the next morning.'

33

'Then I should think you'd be pleased.'

Oddly enough, Julian did not look especially pleased. He gave no answer, except to feint at a cluster of nearby pigeons, setting the creatures aflutter.

'Settle your feathers,' she said, trying to lighten the mood. 'If you want me to attract suitors, I need the company of a trusted friend. I need *you*. In social settings, Leo helped me manage in a hundred small ways. It will be difficult without him.'

'Difficult' did not begin to describe the prospect of facing society without her brother. Over the years, they'd developed a system for large gatherings. He helped her follow the conversation, let her know if she was speaking too softly or too loudly. Without him, Lily wasn't sure how she'd manage at all. But she would find a way, if it meant saving Julian. He insisted it would only take a few events to have suitors thronging her doorstep. Well, perhaps it would take just a few events to remind him of his zest for life, pull him out of this deep well of sorrow. She could only pray.

'Lily, I cannot be your escort. It's not appropriate. You're aware of my reputation.'

'Yes. I'm aware of it.'

'I seduce women. It's what I do. I enter into illicit *affaires* with what's become quite tedious regularity. At one of my clubs, there's a garland stretching the length of the billiard room, fashioned solely from the garters of my paramours.'

'I *said*, I'm aware of your reputation.' Lily's mouth twisted. 'But thank you so much for that vivid illustration.'

'It's revolting, I know. It wasn't my idea. They aren't even truly the garters of my paramours,' he

34

explained, scratching the back of his neck. 'The fellows just string a new one up whenever I've—'

'*Really*. No further explanation is necessary.' She fought the blush creeping up her face. Men, and their tasteless displays of virility. 'At any rate, you needn't worry. I promise not to hamper your amatory pursuits.'

'No, that's not it.' He made an impatient gesture. 'You'll be ruined. That's the problem. If you're seen with me too often, you'll be tainted by association.'

'Ah, but only an impoverished lady must guard her reputation. People overlook those things where rank and fortune are involved.' She smiled. 'Everyone will understand we are only friends. And even if they don't . . . I must admit, it might give me a little thrill to be assumed one of your many conquests. Better than being thought an invalid. I may send one of my garters to your club.'

'Don't even joke like that.' His face clouded, and he shifted his long limbs with restless vigor. She feared for the pigeons again.

He went on, 'There are other reasons.'

'Such as . . . ?'

'I simply haven't the time. I'm busy. There are still places I haven't searched, men I haven't interviewed. I don't have time for parties. For God's sake, I haven't even been round to the club in months.'

Precisely my point.

'Julian, it's a few evenings of your time. I'm not asking for forever.' When he set his jaw and looked away, she sighed. 'Leo was killed. His murderers may never be found. It was a devastating tragedy. We have grieved and mourned and suffered. But now I have accepted the reality and decided to

35

move forward. Don't I deserve a chance to enjoy life again?'

'Of course you do, but I—' He bit off his reply.

'But *you* don't. That's what you were going to say.' He made no attempt to deny it.

'That's the source of your hesitance,' she said, scanning his face. 'You don't think you deserve to be happy. You're still blaming yourself for Leo's death. Risking your health, seeking out danger, starving yourself . . . ' She grabbed for his hand and held it tight. 'Julian, it wasn't your fault. No one blames you, least of all me. Leo would hate to see you like this. You have to—'

'No.' He stood, shaking off her grip. 'I can't do as you ask.' He spoke down at her as he straightened his coat sleeves. 'If you want a social chaperone, find someone else.'

Lily stared up at him. His cold refusal hurt beyond expression. 'This morning,' she said carefully, 'you said you would do anything for me.'

He flinched, almost imperceptibly, and pretended not to hear. A cruel trick, that. He knew she couldn't always be sure of her voice's volume. By ignoring her, he hoped she'd conclude that he'd missed her words entirely.

She thrust her hand into her pocket and pulled out a small tablet and pencil. She always carried these items, in case she needed to make certain she was understood. The tablet came in handy with shop keepers and such. The fact that she had to resort to this with Julian was a sad comment on the state of their friendship.

Anything for me?

36

After underscoring the first word, she shoved the scrawled phrase into his hand.

'I was drugged and exhausted, Lily. Not myself, as you said. Now I'm sorry, but I really must be going.' The paper crumpled in his fist. 'Come, I'll see you back home.'

'Thank you, no.' She folded her hands in her lap. 'I believe I'll stay here and enjoy the fine afternoon.' It was the tiniest act of rebellion, and hardly a satisfying setdown. But she had to assert herself somehow.

'Lily . . .'

She averted her eyes and stared at the fountain, effectively ending the conversation. If he would pretend not to hear her, she would pretend not to see him. After a moment, she caught the sight of him leaving out of the corner of her eye.

Lily remained on that bench for some minutes. Frustration surged through her veins, hot and angry. What an impossible situation. How could Julian be so protective of her, to the point of bullying men into proposing marriage—yet completely negligent when it came to his own well-being? Couldn't he see that taking care of himself was the surest way to safeguard her happiness? As for his guilt . . . she was at a loss for new reassurances. There was nothing to say that she hadn't repeated time and again, over the past several months. He always dismissed her words.

For the first time, she began to see this obsessive investigation as selfish, and worthy of some resentment. Which made her angrier with him still, because she didn't want to resent Julian. She just wanted her friend back.

And then, suddenly, she got her wish. Her friend

37

was back.

He towered over her. 'Three,' he said, holding up the same number of fingers. 'If you agree to consider marriage, I'll escort you to three events. No more.'

A wave of relief lifted her to her feet. 'Thank you, Julian. This is wonderful. We can start with dinner tonight, at Amelia and Morland's.'

'What?'

'They're back in London, since Friday last. Hadn't you heard the good news?'

'Morland in London.' He scowled. 'How can that be good news?'

'I know you and the duke don't get on. But Amelia is my friend, and I'm glad to have her near.'

To say Julian and the Duke of Morland didn't get on was rather like calling the Thames an insignificant trickle. The two men had nothing in common, save that ridiculous club Leo had started. Membership in the Stud Club was represented by ten brass tokens, and anyone holding a token was afforded breeding rights to Osiris, a valuable race horse now retired to stud. In the wake of Leo's murder, Julian had first insisted that Lily should marry Morland. When the duke married Amelia instead, Julian interrupted the wedding to accuse the duke of murdering Leo just to gain ownership of the horse. That too had proved a groundless accusation, but even once the duke was exonerated of any involvement, the enmity between the two men continued to grow.

They resented one another, actively. Sometimes violently.

And absurdly, in Lily's opinion, for two men who had nothing to fight about, save shares in a horse.

38

'Amelia has already invited me to dinner tonight,' she said. 'I'll see that she invites you, too. A small party amongst friends will be the ideal way to ease my reintroduction to society. From there, we can go anywhere. Everywhere. Balls, the theater, the opera, assemblies.'

He shook his head. 'From there, Amelia and Morland can be your social guides. If they're in Town, you don't need me.'

'Oh, no. Not so fast. You've promised me three nights, and I mean to hold you to your word.'

'Don't you know? I'm an inveterate scoundrel. My word is worthless. Always has been.'

She smiled. 'Not with me.'

He paused. Their gazes locked, and the moment stretched. Stretched into something of uncertain shape; a pocket of time that held more awkwardness than it logically should. Lily felt the uneasiness swirling around them, pooling in her belly. She didn't understand its source and wasn't sure she wished to.

'I really must go,' he finally said. 'I'm late for an appointment with my tailors.'

Her uneasiness dissipated as he made a dashing bow in retreat. His spirits must be improved, if he was meeting with his tailors.

Julian was known for having the smartest clothes, setting the current fashion. The young men of his set had their tailors and valets working day and night to copy the cut of his coats, the jet-black color of his hair. But no matter how faithfully they reproduced his look, they remained pale imitations of the original. It wasn't Julian's clothes they coveted; it was his devilish appeal, his incisive wit. His shoulders filled out a topcoat quite nicely, but

39

his presence filled rooms.

He would know that feeling again soon—the admiration of a crowd. And if her gamble worked, it just might be his saving grace.

Lily hurried across the square, then the street, and up the steps of Harcliffe House. She stopped in the entry to address the butler. 'I'd like the carriage readied, Swift. Quickly, please. I intend to pay a call.'

Swift masked his surprise quite well. Normally, she never paid calls, not on her own. But this was life after Leo—a series of tiny, halting steps toward independence.

While she waited for the carriage, she went back to Leo's study. Just thinking of her conversation with Julian, not to mention the urgent pleas she must make to Amelia . . . her mind was awhirl. She sat down at the desk and flipped open the ledger she'd abandoned, hoping to gather some composure from the orderly columns and rows. Leo had never possessed any head for sums or figures, and he couldn't be bothered to keep watch over the various estate accounts. Rather than trust it all to the stewards, Lily had gladly assumed the responsibility. She adored ledgers. Loved the precise, elegant pen strokes they required, the neat rows of columns and tables, the satisfaction of balancing a month's expenses and income to the last penny.

Just as she and Leo had balanced each other. From childhood, it had always been this way. Where one of them was weak, the other was strong. His personality was affable and outgoing, while hers was reserved, reflective. After her fever and resulting deafness, they'd settled even further into

40

those roles. Leo handled the social obligations of the marquessate, while she kept the accounts and papers in line. Lily had always been proud of how well they worked as a team. Two halves of a whole; the sum greater than its parts.

But now Leo had died. And she was left with only half a life. She hadn't cultivated her social side for many years, having apportioned that duty to her brother. His acquaintances were hers; his social circle defined her own. Lily's own friendships—such as the one she'd shared with Amelia—had withered from neglect.

As for Leo . . . who could imagine what regrets he might have had? Their lives might have unfolded very differently, had they not depended on each other so much.

From the corner of her eye, she caught the gleam of curving brass. The handle of the topmost desk drawer taunted her.

With impulsive speed, she rose from her chair and closed the door. Retaking her seat, she fished a small, flat key from her chatelaine and unlocked the drawer. She tugged it open, stared into it for a moment. After a pause to draw breath and gather her courage, she removed the packet of letters.

Even though she'd just shut the door not a minute ago, she cast another glance at it now to assure herself of her privacy. It had been a close call, earlier, when Julian had interrupted her. Fortunately, she'd been able to cache the letters and her emotions away without drawing his comment or concern.

She made no attempt to hide those emotions now. With trembling fingers and a hammering pulse, she opened the time-faded paper and read.

41

Salutations are forbidden me. Closing words are a thing I refuse to contemplate, let alone pen. This is therefore a letter without beginning, without end. A fitting reflection of my love.

My love, my love.

Come soon. I am in torment.

*   *   *

Julian did indeed have an appointment with his tailors—just not the ones Lily might have supposed, and he took a circuitous route to meet with them.

He bypassed the corners of Bond and Regent Streets, with their many mercers and haberdashers and tailors. On another day he might have stopped in to order a new waistcoat with contrasting embroidery, or a coat with an extra button on the cuff. These small modifications to accepted style were the way he'd harnessed the allegiance of England's young aristocrats. He now pulled them along on a worsted thread, to the point that the bucks of the *ton* would wear undyed homespun, if Julian Bellamy declared it the latest thing.

It took him twenty minutes to walk to his relatively modest home, just over the boundary into Bloomsbury. He could have afforded a larger dwelling in a showier part of Town, but this house suited his needs. Its common rooms were unremarkable, cramped, and unsuitable for parties, which absolved him from repaying invitations. The third floor, however, was one vast, lavish bedroom suite, ideal for entertaining female guests singly. Most usefully, at the rear it backed against a busy merchant street.

Upon entering, he followed his habit of proceeding directly to his library. A young man dozed in an armchair by the window, wide-brimmed hat pulled low over his eyes. Julian recognized him as Levi Harris, one of the runners he'd hired to investigate Leo's murder. Harris was young but hungry—and reputed to be the best. Leo deserved no less than the best.

The best, however, needed to look alive. Julian slammed the library door.

Harris woke with a start. As his boots hit the floor, he blurted out, 'Good morning, Mr. Bellamy.'

'It's afternoon. News?'

'Nothing much of interest.'

'Tell me everything. I'll determine what's of interest.'

Harris told Julian nothing he didn't already know. He'd also attended the boxing match in Southwark last night. The bout had featured one of the same pugilists who'd fought the night of Leo's death. The investigator and his men were supposed to be stationed at every exit, watching for anyone who matched the description of Leo's killers.

'I'm sorry, sir,' Harris said. 'After that mishap with the bull-baiting, the crowd got away from us. My men and I lingered well after the melee, traced all the nearby streets. We didn't see any suspicious activity, other than the usual. And no pair of men matching the description.'

Julian nodded his understanding. What description they had was pitiful indeed. The prostitute who'd witnessed the attack could only describe Leo's killers as two large men in rough clothing; one bald, the other with a Scots accent.

He sank into the rich, tufted leather of his desk

43

chair, deflating with fatigue and frustration. Almost five months since Leo's death, and despite the discovery of new information and witnesses, he was no closer to the killers now than he had been the day his friend was buried. And so long as the attackers themselves went free, the name of their employer remained secret. Julian had no way of knowing just which of his many enemies had discovered his true identity and ordered his death. He'd been going at it from the wrong angle—trying to ferret out the brutes, rather than the man or men who'd hired them.

'Very well,' he told Harris. 'That will be all.'

'Until tomorrow then?'

Julian shook his head. 'No. I mean, that will be all. We're finished with this.'

'Finished?' Harris rose to his feet. 'Sir, you mean to abandon the investigation? Leave the murder unsolved?'

He obviously didn't like the idea, and Julian respected the man's dedication. But they couldn't go on in this manner any longer when it yielded no meaningful results. And he most certainly couldn't give Harris the information necessary to pursue a different tack. From here, Julian proceeded alone.

'I mean,' he said, 'your services will no longer be required. Send me an accounting of your charges and expenses, and I'll see that you're compensated with all due speed.'

Harris opened and shut his mouth a few times, as if he wanted to argue back. He ultimately decided against it. 'As you wish, Mr. Bellamy.' With a perfunctory bow, he left.

Alone, Julian sorted through the correspondence that had amassed atop his desk. Invitations, of various kinds, comprised the bulk of the missives. Everything from 'Your presence is cordially requested . . .' to 'Darling, my husband will be away . . .' No matter that he hadn't accepted an invitation of either sort in months, they still heaped his blotter daily.

With a weary sigh, he tossed them all into the grate. He never had answered the things anyway. He simply appeared at events where and when the mood struck. Ironically, this complete disregard for etiquette had only enhanced his popularity. For when he did make an appearance, he did so in grand style, whether playing to a crowd of hundreds or entertaining an audience of one.

An appearance by Julian Bellamy, he strove to ensure, ranked among a certain class of delights. Rather like roasted chestnuts at Christmas, or simultaneous orgasms. Not so rare as to be mythical, never so commonplace as to become boring. Dependably satisfying, occasionally transcendent. In sum, an experience to which no one could pretend ambivalence.

Save Julian himself, of course. He pretended ambivalence very well indeed.

It was a talent shared by his house staff. As Julian entered his bedroom suite, his valet greeted him from behind a sporting newspaper. 'Good morning, sir.'

'Good morning, Dillard,' Julian greeted him dryly. 'Oh, please. Don't get up.'

A soft grunt was his only reply.

'Is my bath drawn?'

The newspaper rustled. 'I reckon it is.'

Dillard was the most spoiled, useless valet in all London. Normally, Julian demanded competence

45

and efficiency from all people in his employ, but he made an exception for his personal servants. In this house, indolence and a marked lack of curiosity were desirable traits. Julian only kept Dillard on for appearances. Or rather, *not* for appearances. That was a valet's usual post, of course—tending his gentleman employer's appearance in all particulars: bathing, shaving, attire, and more. But where his own appearance was concerned, Julian attended to every detail on his own, save the laundering, pressing, and boot-blacking.

He lowered his weight to a bench and removed his boots. 'I'm off to bed,' he told Dillard, setting the boots neatly to one side. 'Not to be disturbed. See that these are polished by tonight.'

Another grunt.

Julian left the man to his paper and crossed into his dressing room. It was a large space, formerly a bedchamber in its own right, but he'd had it fitted with custom shelving and mirrors. He tossed his befouled topcoat in the grate and stripped to his skin. After a hasty bath and a close shave, he wrapped an Oriental-patterned silk banyan about his torso.

With grave deliberation, he selected a set of clothing for that evening. He had a new waistcoat in pigeon's blood red, and this he laid aside for pressing, along with a royal blue topcoat with brass trim and charcoal-gray pantaloons. From his row of sixteen hats, he selected a jaunty blue felt with a red band. The color combination was revolting. But he needed to draw notice tonight, even more so than usual.

Though he'd opposed the idea initially, on reflection he saw the potential in this social scheme of Lily's. His investigative efforts were going nowhere. By withdrawing from public life, he'd given his enemy a sense of complacency.

These were the inescapable facts: In trying to kill Julian, someone had killed Leo instead. If Julian wanted justice for Leo's murder, he would have to draw the cowardly rat out of hiding—by making himself the bait.

He'd start with dinner tonight, then a genial round of the clubs. All very friendly, all very tame—even if he had to sit on his hands when Morland drew near, just to keep it so. He would remain on good behavior through a few scattered, sedate appearances—the three evenings he'd promised Lily. Once he'd reestablished his place at the top of every guest list and Lily's marital prospects were assured . . . only then would Julian Bellamy lay his trap.

At the moment, however, Julian Bellamy was retiring to bed.

Once inside the richly appointed bedchamber, he locked the door behind him. And then he waited. When a few minutes had passed and he was certain no one was listening, he followed the golden path of the carpet's Greek maze border, skirting the four-poster bed with its crimson velvet hangings, until he stood before a bookcase in the room's farthest corner. He pulled a lever in the hidden recesses of the third shelf, then stepped back to let the panel swing out on its hinges.

On the other side of the false wall was a narrow, humble closet that belonged to the mercantile building in the rear.

The small space held a shelf of starched white shirts and cravats, a few folded pairs of trousers in

47

neutral shades. Plain brass hooks supported a row of four coats: dun, gray, black, and dark blue. Two hats.

Tossing his banyan aside, he stepped through the hidden passageway and closed the panel behind him. His night as Julian Bellamy was over.

He was very late for his day as James Bell.

Chapter Four

Mr. James Bell did not employ a valet. Nor a cook, nor a butler, nor indeed a single footman. Just a charwoman to come in and sweep twice a week. She was an illiterate and perpetually harried woman, unlikely to snoop.

Mr. Bell was, however, a generous employer. He compensated said charwoman thrice the normal amount, and he treated his clerks well. Paid wages promptly, with annual rises in pay and bonuses at Christmas. Well-paid employees did not question or complain.

Mr. Bell lived in rooms above his business offices, and he kept eccentric hours. Though his dedication was above question, the clerks never knew at what time he might appear belowstairs. He'd let spread a vague rumor that he suffered from recurrent bouts of headache. Some mornings, they found him already behind his desk at eight, cravat-deep in accounting ledgers. Other days, like today, he didn't appear until well after noon. This inconsistent schedule kept his clerks on constant alert.

Mr. Bell dressed in unremarkable though

well-tailored attire. He parted his black hair severely and combed it with pomade until it lay flat against his scalp. 'Fastidious,' some might have described him. The less charitable might have said, 'Dull as toast.' Rarely was he observed going out-of-doors without a hat, and he wore spectacles at all times.

There was only plain glass in the lenses, of course. Julian didn't wear them to see. He wore them so he would not be *seen*.

And the disguise had worked quite well for several years.

It was midafternoon when he came down the back stairs today and entered the offices from the rear. As usual, he found his eight clerks hunched over two neat rows of desks that ran the length of the room. They all hastened to their feet with a chorus of 'Good day, Mr. Bell.'

He nodded in reply.

The errand boys threw him guilty looks from a corner, where they no doubt had been dicing until a few moments ago. Julian decided to overlook the infraction. For now. He'd provide tasks enough to keep them hopping the rest of the day.

'As you were,' he said, retreating into his office—a partitioned section at the back with a glass window for supervisory purposes and drapes he could pull when privacy was desired. The frosted pane set in the door was lettered in gilt: 'J. Bell. Manager, Aegis Investments.'

So far as his employees understood, Mr. Bell managed the interests of several wealthy investors. These unnamed investors—aristocrats, it was presumed, who could not be seen sullying their hands with trade—had pooled their money toward

49

various business endeavors: in particular, several wool and linen mills to the North, and commercial real estate holdings in most of England's larger cities. Mr. Bell oversaw the operations and management of these investments with the assistance of his clerks and a personal secretary, and he reported to his superiors regularly.

In reality, Mr. Bell had no superiors, and there was but one investor: Julian himself. He not only owned the mills in the North and the buildings in Bristol, Oxford, York, and beyond—but he in fact owned most of this very block, including the mercantile building that housed the Aegis Investments offices and the residential row to the rear. He was, by any standard, a man of great wealth. And key to all of this was maintaining his status as a man of many secrets.

If certain powerful men learned just how he'd amassed this fortune and just what he intended to do with it . . .

Well, he already knew the completion of that thought, didn't he? Those certain men would arrange to have him waylaid in a darkened alleyway, pummeled to death.

He shuddered, thinking of Leo and his broken face.

His secretary, Thatcher, followed him into his private office, waving a clutch of papers. 'The morning post, sir.'

'What's in it?'

Thatcher riffled through the papers. 'A report on the fluctuating price of indigo. A letter from the Benevolence Society for the Deserving Poor, requesting the renewal of the investors' generous subscription. The contract for lease of the Dover

50

property. Your express from the mills.'

'Give it here. The express, I mean. Leave the rest on the blotter, and you may go.'

Thatcher did as asked, as always.

Julian broke the wax seal and quickly scanned the letter in his hands. He now demanded twice-weekly expresses from the mills, and he always read them first thing. Worker morale remained high, his agent reported, and production was steady.

Good, all good. After the flare of labor riots earlier that year, he'd been keeping close watch on his mills. Outside efforts to mobilize dissent amongst his workers had so far met with little success. And little wonder—his laborers were the best paid of any textile workers in the region, and he took pains to make them feel secure in their posts. He'd even gone so far as to visit each mill personally and assure the workers no jobs would be lost to the new machines.

It wasn't such a radical formula to Julian: Invest a measure of good will in the workers, reap benefits in the form of steady production. He'd never understand why the other mill owners didn't grasp the concept. But then, their loss was his gain. His mills' reputation for consistent, high-quality production was the source of many lucrative military contracts. Over the course of the past decade, more than half the enlisted men in the British Army had marched into the fray wearing Aegis wool on their backs. When they fell in battle, their wounds were bound with Aegis flannel.

Now, with the wars over, England's economy was depressed. But the wealthy still had coin to spend. Mr. James Bell made certain the country's finest mercers, drapers, and upholsterers all carried Aegis cloth in their shops. Meanwhile, Julian Bellamy set the fashions, assuring those shops of a steady trade.

He called Thatcher back in. 'Here,' he said, hastily scrawling his signature on the lease before passing it across the desk. 'This is done. Tell the Benevolence Society we'll renew the subscription, and direct the warehouse to send over any surplus bolts of cloth for their use.'

'Yes, sir. And if you please, sir, the tailors are here.'

'Send them in.'

Schwartz and Cobb filed into the office, laden with patterns and samples. With a curt nod of greeting, Julian waved the latest sketches to his desk. He had not lied to Lily on this count, at least. He *was* late for this meeting with his tailors. Unconscionably late. The drawings and samples before him represented the culmination of a year's preparation and strategy, and his men had teetered on the brink of action for months. The plans wanted only his final approval before a production schedule could be set. But something always held him back. The patterns weren't right, or the dyes were inferior, or the price of wool too dear . . . Again and again, he'd found himself delaying, for one reason and another.

Strike that.

He'd been delaying for *one* reason. No other. Lily.

Her sweet rosemary scent bloomed in his memory, and his thoughts tangled in the lush fringe of her eyelashes. He forced down the tide of emotion in his chest. Not here. He could not allow himself to think of her here. Whatever nocturnal exploits Julian Bellamy enjoyed, Mr. James Bell did not have time for women.

And neither man could afford to contemplate love.

*   *   *

'I told a dreadful lie today,' Lily said, even before the greetings were out. Standing in the entry of the Duke of Morland's drawing room, she hugged her hostess tightly and confessed, 'Several lies, as a matter of fact.'

Amelia pulled back from the embrace. 'Really? That seems unlike you.'

'It is.' With a fretful shake of her head, Lily squeezed her friend's arm in supplication. 'I'm here to beg your assistance, Amelia. I have to make those lies the truth. At least some of them.'

'Well, I am all anticipation to hear what this is about. It's not often I'm recruited into clandestine schemes, you know. But please, do sit down first and take some tea.'

Lily's racing pulse insisted there wasn't a moment to waste. But she would win no favors by being rude. And today she needed to ask a very big favor indeed.

Amelia steered her toward a pair of French armchairs situated beneath a tall, lace-draped window. A small table between the two chairs held a tea service and refreshments. In accordance with Amelia's talent for homemaking, all was the picture of refinement and good taste. When Lily sat down, she found the striped silk upholstery to be so smooth and taut, it took some effort to keep from sliding off the seat.

53

'What's brought you to Town?' Lily asked, as her friend poured tea. 'I thought you and the duke would remain in Cambridgeshire until the babe is born.'

Amelia nipped a lump of sugar into the teacup and stirred. 'Oh, it was Spencer's wish to return to London. He wanted us closer to specialists and physicians when my time draws near.' She shrugged, extending the cup and saucer to Lily. 'Never mind that the man owns England's largest stud farm and has attended hundreds of equine births. When it comes to his own child, he's suddenly a bundle of nerves.'

'It only proves how much he adores you.'

Despite the duke's terse, autocratic nature, Lily had suspected from the first he'd make Amelia a surprisingly tender husband. It would seem she'd been right.

'I am no specialist,' Lily said. 'But to my untrained eye, you look the picture of robust health. Not only health, but true contentment.'

From her radiant complexion to her gently rounded belly, Amelia *embodied* domestic bliss. And despite herself, Lily knew a brief moment of envy. Perhaps this was the real reason she'd let her friendships with women fall by the wayside over the years. One by one, they'd all become wives, then mothers. Much as she'd loved Leo and valued her financial independence, Lily found it hard sometimes, not to want what they had, too.

'I do feel well,' Amelia replied modestly, lifting her own teacup. 'No sickness anymore. I'm more fortunate than many women in my condition.'

They each sipped their tea.

After they lowered their cups, Lily looked to her

friend expectantly, waiting for her cue to begin. A long moment passed. She threw an anxious glance toward the clock, growing increasingly concerned with every swing of the pendulum.

Lily cleared her throat. 'Well.'

Amelia raised her eyebrows and gave a benign smile. 'Yes?'

Had she forgotten Lily's confession, or was she simply playing coy? Just when Lily was beginning to wonder whether she needed to start at the beginning again, recognition snapped in Amelia's eyes.

'Oh, yes!' she said, setting down her teacup to frantically churn the air with her hands. 'You told a lie, or several of them, and you desperately need my help.' She slid forward on her chair. 'I'm so sorry dear, it's an effect of breeding, it seems. Strong fingernails, weak memory. Please, tell me what I can do.'

Relieved, Lily said, 'It's Julian. He's still obsessed with finding Leo's killers, to the exclusion of all else. He wanders the streets at all hours of the night. He scarcely eats or sleeps. He's neglected all his friendships, declines every invitation. He's on course to join Leo in the grave, and I don't know what to do. Perhaps it's naïve, but I can't help thinking . . . if only I could nudge him out into society, you know? Then perhaps he would return to his old, carefree self.'

Amelia nodded in encouragement. 'Go on.'

'This morning, we . . . argued. In the end, I extracted a promise from him. He agreed to escort me to three social events. I gave him some flummery about wanting to enjoy life again and considering taking a husband, but in truth, I just

55

want to keep Julian out of harm's way. And I didn't want to delay, so I told him the first event would be tonight.'

'I see,' said Amelia.

Not yet, she didn't.

Lily bit her lip. 'Here is the lie. I told him you and Spencer were hosting a dinner party.'

'A dinner party? Tonight?' Now Amelia looked to the clock. 'Oh, dear. Already half two.'

Lily grabbed her friend's hands. 'I know it's a tremendous imposition, and here you are in such a delicate state. But believe me—nothing less than the truest fear for Julian's life would drive me to suggest it. It needn't be anything too grand, and I'd help you however I could with supplies, kitchen staff . . .'

'Menus and servants are no problem. I have both in ample supply. But inviting guests, on this short notice . . . ' The corner of Amelia's mouth twisted. 'And then there's Spencer to contend with. He abhors parties of every sort.'

'Perhaps if you explain to him what's at stake.'

'Tell him he must host a party to save Julian Bellamy's hide?' Amelia shook her head. 'Forgive me, but I don't think that argument will work. There's no love lost between Spencer and Mr. Bellamy.'

Lily's heart sank. 'Is there no way to convince him?'

'Oh, I have my ways of convincing Spencer.' Amelia's brow made a flirtatious quirk. 'But it's not only him I must worry about, unfortunately.' Her demeanor grew serious, and she drew her chair closer to speak in confidence. 'I'm sorry, Lily. I wish I could help you, I truly do. But there

56

are more obstacles here than the late hour and my husband's reluctance. This isn't to be repeated, you understand.'

Lily nodded, encouraging her to continue. She focused intently on her friend's lips. 'Slowly, if you please.'

'We're not alone here in Town. Do you recall last summer, when we were all at Briarbank and my—' Amelia's head suddenly jerked, as though she were heeding a call from somewhere behind her.

Lily looked over Amelia's shoulder. A young woman stood in the door. It was Claudia Dumarque, the Duke of Morland's cousin and ward. Claudia was a rather strange girl—a fractious mix of rebellion and sensitivity—but Lily attributed the awkwardness to her age. She was fifteen, or at least she had been the past summer, when they'd all been together at Amelia's family home in Gloucestershire. Perhaps the girl had turned sixteen by now. Regardless, she was very young.

And she was pregnant. Hugely so.

Lily's mouth fell open in shock.

Claudia said something to Amelia as she moved into the room. The loose smocking of her dress billowed and stretched as she walked. Her time of delivery must be fast approaching.

'I didn't realize you were entertaining a guest,' the girl said, stopping before them. 'I was just looking for my . . .' She paused when her eyes met Lily's. A self-conscious smile dimpled her cheeks. 'Goodness, Lady Lily, I'm not a ghost. I'm only breeding.'

Lily snapped her mouth shut, feeling a blush work up her throat. She'd been staring at the poor girl like something that crawled out from a crack in the plaster.

To Amelia, Claudia said, 'You hadn't told her?'

'Not yet,' Amelia replied. She cast an apologetic glance in Lily's direction.

At last, Lily recovered herself. 'It's so good to see you, Claudia.' She embraced the girl as best she could around her massive belly, planting a light kiss on her cheek. 'I hope you're well?'

Stupid question. What possible answer could the girl give? Pregnant and unmarried, and sixteen at the most—she could not be feeling entirely well.

'As well as can be expected, I suppose.'

'Will you join us for some tea?' Lily gestured toward the chairs.

'No, thank you. I'm on my way to have a rest. I was looking for my book, but I must have left it upstairs. If you'll excuse me, Lady Lily.' She nodded in lieu of a curtsy and moved to leave.

'One moment,' Amelia told Lily, extending a hand in the universal gesture for *wait*.

Lily resumed her seat as Amelia rushed to her young ward's side. Together they ascended the grand staircase, Claudia with one hand on the railing and the other arm on Amelia's shoulder.

Tearing her gaze away, Lily busied herself pouring yet more tea. She didn't want to be caught gawking again.

After a minute, Amelia dropped into the chair opposite. 'So,' she said.

'So . . . ?' Lily prompted.

As Amelia began to tell the tale, her strength of emotion was evident. Unfortunately, it also made her speech difficult to follow. Her story was a rapid stream of words, twisting in several directions as it flowed from beginning to end. Though Lily couldn't catch everything her friend said, she gathered that Claudia had been seduced by one of her tutors. Her pregnancy was to blame for her strange behavior at Briarbank that summer, it seemed. The poor girl had hidden her condition from everyone.

At last, Amelia's words slowed. 'We *are* in Town to be close to specialists, but not for me. My own pregnancy has gone easily, but Claudia has had episodes of bleeding and pain. At least here we're closer to the best physicians.'

'My goodness,' Lily said, trying to absorb it all. 'What a difficult situation.'

'Claudia is confined to the house. We've kept the pregnancy secret for now. It only seems the prudent thing, since we're still uncertain whether she'll keep the child.'

Lily briefly wondered whether Amelia referred to the option of fostering the baby with another family, or the possibility of a stillbirth. Both, she supposed. 'I thought you said you're not often recruited into clandestine schemes.'

Amelia shrugged. 'It *has* been occurring with more frequency of late. Poor Spencer was going mad with worry in Cambridgeshire, but the stables were always his refuge. Now he's away from all that, trapped in a London house with two breeding women, one of whom is ill . . . It's understandably trying. So you see, a dinner party may not be the best idea.'

'Of course. I see.'

'You're disappointed.' Amelia laced her hands together and squeezed.

'No, not at all,' Lily lied brightly. 'It was only an idea, and a flawed one at that. We'll do it another time. I'll just send Julian a note to tell him tonight's

59

dinner is canceled.'

And hope he doesn't turn up dead by morning.

She shut her eyes, and red dots swam behind her eyelids. The same bright crimson shade as his blood.

When Amelia leaned closer and put a comforting hand on her arm, Lily couldn't help it. The tears welled in her eyes and overflowed. Soon she was sobbing on Amelia's shoulder.

'I'm sorry,' she said. 'I'm just so worried for him. This morning the costermonger delivered him to our doorstep before dawn. He'd collapsed on the street, and he was bleeding, and for a moment . . . '

All the fears she'd battled in those predawn hours came rushing back, assailing her with double force. This time, she let herself feel them, surrendering to the comfort of her friend's embrace as the tears fell.

Once she'd mastered her emotion, Lily said, 'For a moment, I was so certain he was dead. Just like Leo.'

Amelia pulled back. Her own eyes were moist with sympathy as she offered a handkerchief. 'You poor dear. Is he well now? Mr. Bellamy, I mean.'

'Yes.' Lily wiped her eyes with the square of linen. 'It was only a small injury, sustained when the crowd panicked at a boxing match. He won't stop attending the things, you know. Wherever there's fighting—man or beast—he goes there, hoping to find Leo's killers. But I fear he's just going to get himself killed. It's been five months now. I don't understand why he can't let it go.'

'He feels responsible. That's what he told us that night. He was supposed to be with Leo, and he thinks he could have prevented the murder if he'd been there.'

Lily sniffed. 'Does he think he has some exclusive claim on regret? Doesn't he realize I've felt the same guilt, every day since Leo died? If only I'd asked him to stay home, I tell myself. If only I'd insisted he take the family carriage instead of a hack. If only *I'd* been with him that night. Never mind that I'm a woman and a slightly built one at that. If I'd been in that alleyway with Leo, I would have fought those men with everything I had. Strength, fury, nails, teeth. I would have done anything in my power to save my brother's life, even if it meant giving my own.'

A little sob escaped her, and Amelia clasped her wrist.

'And now,' Lily went on, 'it's like I'm watching Julian wander into that same alleyway that claimed Leo's life. The only difference is, it's all happening at a slower pace. I'm forced to watch from a distance, standing helplessly by as each step brings him closer and closer to danger. No matter how I call out to him, he doesn't respond. Then this morning . . .'

Then this morning had changed everything. She'd held his senseless body in her arms, felt his blood on her fingertips. Atop it all, that desperate kiss . . . It made the danger so real. She refused to stand by and watch Julian stumble toward his own doom. This time, she would fight.

In her lap, her hands curled into fists. 'Before Leo died, Julian lived to amuse and be amused. He loved balls, the theater, his friends, and his clubs. Somehow I have to force him back into that world, so he'll remember what he's been missing. Since the dinner party won't work tonight—'

61

'Wait,' Amelia said, her chin firming. 'The dinner party will work. We'll make it work.'

'Truly?' Her heart leapt. 'But what about the duke? What about Claudia?'

'Leave everything to me. Claudia will remain upstairs. Though I warn you, the menu will be simple, and I can't promise Spencer will be the most gracious of hosts.'

'That doesn't matter. It's probably for the best if he and Julian stay in separate rooms, anyhow.' She squeezed her friend's hand. 'I can't tell you what this means to me.'

'It's my pleasure, truly. I love to give parties but have little opportunity. What about other guests? Is there anyone you'd like me to invite?'

Lily paused. 'I know this may be difficult at such short notice,' she said, 'but do you by any chance know where we might find a sizable group of eligible bachelors?'

'What's this?' Amelia broke into laughter. 'You do realize you're talking to a woman who was, as recently as five months ago, a confirmed spinster with no suitors at all?'

'It's just that I promised Julian. If he would be my escort to social events, I told him I'd consider marrying. I have no real intention of marrying at all, and no desire to inspire the hopes or attentions of gentlemen I actually . . . . Oh, this is sounding horrible, isn't it?'

'Rather.' Amelia's eyes widened with amusement. 'Let me be certain I understand. You'd like me to find some warm male bodies to fill chairs at the dinner table. All of these men must be presentable and feasibly marriageable, yet hungry or lonely enough to show up for dinner on a few hours' notice?'

'Well . . . ' Lily shrugged. 'Yes?'

Amelia smiled as she patted Lily's shoulder. 'My dear, it just so happens, today you are in luck.'

Chapter Five

Blue was the color of the evening.

As she surveyed the Morland drawing room, Lily noted that each person present was wearing that color, in one shade or another. Her own simple gown was fashioned of indigo silk, a dark shade suitable for mourning. Amelia wore a lovely periwinkle satin. The glimmering hue did wonderful things for her eyes. From where he stood beside his wife, lightly touching her waist, the duke's impeccable tailcoat looked black. But up close, Lily would have guessed it to be a very deep blue.

And then, rounding out the party, there were five officers of the Royal Navy, each attired in formal uniform. Everywhere she turned, gold braiding and buttons caught the candlelight, sparkling like stars against a navy blue sky.

Unfortunately, the scene was lacking one particular shade of blue—the intense cobalt hue of Julian's eyes. They'd delayed dinner half an hour already, and still he hadn't appeared. Lily oscillated between fear for his health and a desire to cause him personal injury. How could he abandon her like this? Didn't he understand what a challenge this night would be for her? She hadn't attended a dinner party with strangers present in months.

63

And never without Leo. All around her, discussion bloomed, branched, wilted and died, germinated entirely new topics of debate. She was lost in the thick jungle of conversation. From the apologetic looks Amelia kept sending her, Lily knew her friend would have liked to be more help. Unfortunately, her duties as hostess kept claiming her attention.

Lily was on her own.

Well, wasn't this exactly what she kept insisting to Julian she could handle? And handle it she would.

Squaring her shoulders and readying a polite smile, Lily sought out a familiar face. The fair-haired officer standing by the window was Michael d'Orsay, one of Amelia's five brothers. Lily had known him as a cowlicked boy in Gloucestershire, and now he was Lieutenant-Commander d'Orsay.

'It's so lovely to see you again,' she said. 'What great fortune that your ship has just returned. And how good of you to bring your friends.' How resourceful of Amelia to invite them, she added to herself. What better place to find a group of clean-shaven, respectable, eligible men desperate for a dinner invitation, than naval officers just returned from six months at sea?

'It's good to see you, too.' His expression went grave. 'I was so sorry to hear the news of Leo.'

'Thank you. I know you can understand the pain of losing a brother.' Hugh d'Orsay had been killed at Waterloo.

'Yes. But Leo's death . . . so unexpected. Tragic.' Sadness etched his face, making him look far older than his eight-and-twenty years. Of all the d'Orsay brothers, she and Leo had been closest to Michael, since they all three were of an age. He and Leo had gone off to Eton together.

She didn't want to ignore Michael's feelings, but she couldn't bear to talk about Leo right now. As rarely as she went out in society, this happened too often for her comfort. Whenever Lily began to feel that her own wounds had scabbed over, along would come an acquaintance for whom Leo's death was a new development. And that person would want to talk of him and mourn him—as was only natural, for her brother had been loved by many— but once again Lily would feel ripped apart. She couldn't cope with that tonight, not atop everything else.

She looked around the room, casting about for diversion. And she found it. All thoughts were promptly driven from her head by a flirtatious smile. The smile belonged to a tall, well-formed officer plastered with insignia and gold braid. He was not an especially handsome man, but neither was he ill-favored. He had intelligent, playful eyes.

And he was headed straight for her.

Nerves danced in the crooks of her elbows. To Michael, she whispered, 'Did you tell your friends about my impairment?'

He shook his head in apology. 'Should I have? I wasn't certain if . . .'

Before she could answer, the officer had joined them.

'Come, d'Orsay,' he said, eyeing Lily. 'I can see you mean to keep this enchanting lady to yourself all night. I shall have to pull rank and command an introduction.'

Lily kept her eyes glued to Michael's mouth. Names were especially hard to catch, as they came

65

without context.

'Lady Lily Chatwick, may I introduce my superior officer, Commander . . .'

Oh, drat. She missed it. Was it Merriman? Or perhaps Barryman? Lily's eyes flickered over the man's attire as he bowed. Maybe his name was engraved on a buckle or his scabbard. But then, wouldn't it seem worse to be caught boldly ogling a man's person than to simply have missed the name?

She offered her hand. 'I'm delighted to make your acquaintance, Commander.' She had that, at least. Thank heaven for military ranks.

And thank heaven for Amelia, who came to her rescue moments later, when she and the duke approached the group.

Amelia touched Lily's arm, drawing her aside. 'I'm not certain I can delay dinner much longer. Shall we continue to wait for Mr. Bellamy?'

'No.' Lily sighed with disappointment. 'Don't delay.'

The Duke of Morland's mien was, as usual, censorious. 'I loathe that man,' he said, just before tipping a glass of whiskey.

Lily felt horrible. She knew the duke hated parties, and here she'd forced him to host one on ridiculously short notice. And now the guest of honor—or rather, *dis*honor—had not even bothered to show his face.

Amelia called for her guests' attention, inviting them into dinner. Suddenly the commander was at Lily's side, offering his arm along with a quick salvo of words that soared straight past her. She merely smiled and nodded by way of response, sending up a fervent prayer he hadn't just confided he had a wasting illness, or remarked on the culinary skill of

66

cannibals in Lesser God-Knows-Where.

They filed into the dining room, and Amelia indicated the place for each guest. The duke, of course, took the head of the table, and Amelia sat at his left hand, with Michael at his sister's other side. On the duke's right, the commander took the place of honor. Lily sat at his right, directly across from Michael.

Amelia said, 'Six gentlemen and only two ladies . . . what an unbalanced group. A poor reflection on me as a hostess, I'm afraid.'

Michael replied, 'Certainly a more favorable ratio than we're accustomed to having at sea.'

To Lily's left, the commander said something in reply. However, she turned her head too late. Once again, she missed his words entirely.

Michael noted her puzzlement and explained, 'The good commander says you and my sister are uncommonly lovely. So lovely, you're each worth three of other ladies, and therefore the balance is exact.'

Lily smiled. 'Only until Mr. Bellamy arrives.'

If Mr. Bellamy arrived. She slid a glance toward the empty chair at her right. His absence was upsetting her own balance, greatly. She stared at the vacant seat with angry desperation, as though Julian might materialize on the striped damask if only she willed it fiercely enough. He'd promised to come. He'd given his word.

Looking beyond his empty chair, she flashed a half-hearted smile at the three young lieutenants holding down the far end of the table. They immediately ceased casting doleful looks at their empty plates and grinned in return. So young, so hungry. If any of them were older than twenty, Lily would be astounded. When she'd been introduced to them earlier, they'd practically tumbled over one another to take her hand. Now she gave them a polite nod of greeting, and they all replied at once, speaking and laughing amongst themselves.

Hopeless.

Beneath the table, she balled her hands in frustration. This never happened to her with Julian. He was much easier to lip-read than most people, simply because he was so expressive. She didn't catch his every word, but she could always gather his meaning. He seemed to intuit how to make it easier. He rarely forgot to face her when they conversed, never spoke too quickly or in confusing circles, repeated himself before she even had to ask.

But then, Julian did have one advantage over these men. He knew she was deaf.

She acted on the decision swiftly, before she could reconsider. Placing her hands on the table, she rose to her feet. The men looked to one another, then began to push back their own chairs and stand, in accordance with etiquette.

'No, please.' Lily motioned for them to stay seated. 'I have something to say, and it will only take a moment.' She resisted the urge to put a hand to her throat, hoping those years of work with speech tutors would serve her well. 'My old friends know this, but just so my new friends are equally aware . . . I lost my hearing several years ago, while stricken with fever. I'm deaf.'

The mood of the guests altered instantly. In the space of a moment, they'd gone from casually admiring her to examining her with keen curiosity. Rather like garden show attendees who'd moved

68

on from a pleasing clump of pink tea roses to an exhibit of carnivorous spotwort from the Amazon. All around the table, heads tilted and jaws went slack.

She breathed in, then out. 'I do read lips, but it's difficult for me to follow conversation in a group. All I ask is, if you mean to talk *to* me, please face me and speak clearly. If you merely wish to talk *about* me, well . . . Now you know, you may do so with impunity.'

A ginger-haired lieutenant chuckled, then smothered the laugh with his palm. A horrified expression overtook his eyes.

'It's all right,' she assured him as she took her seat. 'Please do laugh. I meant it as a joke. There's no need to mince around my feelings.'

The commander drew her attention with a light tap on her wrist. 'But we are officers of the Royal Navy, my lady. Your protection is our duty. It would be the height of rudeness for any of our number to speak over or around you.' To his lieutenants, he said, 'If any one of you wishes to speak—to anyone, for any reason—you will stand and face Lady Lily. One at a time, mind you.'

'Really, Commander,' Lily said, 'that isn't necessary.'

'Perhaps not. But it should prove amusing.' He gave her a little wink as he reached for his empty wineglass. 'We shall put these new officers to the test.' He tilted his head and called around her, 'Lieutenants! Who among you will take wine?'

Lily swiveled her head in time to catch the three young men exchanging frantic glances. Finally, the ginger-haired one rose to his feet, faced Lily directly, and said, 'I will take wine, sir. And be glad

69

of it.'

The second one stood. 'Sir, if it please you and our esteemed hosts, I, too, will take wine.'

The youngest of the three, a pup who wore his dark hair in the ruffled style Julian had made popular, stood, grinned, and said simply, 'Me!' before retaking his seat.

Lily laughed, more from nerves than amusement.

The commander touched his sleeve to hers, giving her a merry look before barking out, 'Lieutenants! Red or white?'

The ginger-haired one took the lead again. 'Red.' He smiled at Lily. 'Naturally.'

'White,' said the second.

The third shot to his feet. 'Both, if I may.'

The table and plateware shook with the officers' laughter. At the head of the table, Lily thought she saw the duke frown.

Amelia caught her eye. *Do you mind?* her expression tacitly asked.

Lily shook her head in the negative. The game was a bit theatrical, she supposed, and no doubt the commander was flaunting his authority to impress. But she would choose to interpret his idea as considerate, not crass. Perhaps he meant to sacrifice his lieutenants' pride to make her feel more comfortable, so any laughter or embarrassment in the course of the meal would be at their expense, not hers.

Once the wine had been poured, the servants began covering the table with soup tureens and domed platters.

'I hope no one minds if we dine *en famille*,' Amelia said. 'It seems we are all close friends or family, in one way or another.'

70

From every corner of the table, the guests nodded their approval. But no one spoke. Lily worried that the commander's 'stand and declaim' order would quell all meaningful conversation.

As the footmen shook out the napkins and laid them in each guest's lap, she screwed up her courage and turned to her dinner partner. 'May I ask where your family resides, Commander?'

'In Somersetshire, my lady. My father is a baronet. I'm the third son. The ne'er-do-well, I'm afraid, sent off to the Navy at the tender age of seventeen.'

'You must have distinguished yourself very quickly, to have reached such an elevated rank.'

Michael said, 'The commander is being modest. He proved his mettle during the action in Chesapeake Bay three years past. He was there for the burning of the city of Washington.'

'Is that so?'

But no answer was forthcoming. Amelia rose from her chair, and all the gentleman shot to their feet as well. This prompted a giddy ripple of laughter at the lieutenants' end of the table, but as Lily watched, the amusement vacated their faces to make way for awe.

A darting glance toward the doorway confirmed her suspicion.

Julian had arrived. And arrived in *style*. He was always well-dressed, but tonight he'd outdone himself. Every detail of his appearance—each button, cuff, or twist of his cravat—had been arranged with such precision, the military uniforms in the room looked like paupers' rags by comparison.

He bowed deeply to their hosts. 'I apologize for

my tardiness. I was'—he cast Lily a brief, cryptic look—'detained.'

The duke inclined his head with thinly veiled irritation. Amelia made hasty introductions, and everyone settled back to the table.

Lily indicated the empty seat next to her. 'You're just in time.'

So strange. Julian's arrival ought to have heralded a deep surge of relief in her soul. If he was here, that meant he was not out chasing danger. And if he was here, it meant she had an ally to facilitate communication. She'd been waiting for him all night.

But when he approached, took her hand, and bowed over it—his intense blue eyes never leaving hers—it wasn't relief she felt, but a prickling awareness that seemed some distant cousin to fear. The ground beneath her narrowed, coiled round and round on itself until she balanced on a taut, thin cable stretched between this moment and the next. Dizzying.

As Julian took his place at the table and the footman poured his wine, Lily found her attention drawn to parts of him she wasn't in the habit of noticing. The neat, blunt edges of his fingernails. The freshly clipped fringe of hair just behind his ear. The red, razor-thin score on the underside of his jaw—the result of overzealous shaving, perhaps. The faint sandalwood aroma of shaving soap hovered about him, elusive and masculine, and with every breath her lungs expanded greedily, determined to catch more of it.

Had his earlobes always been that square-ish shape? Why had she never noticed it before?

Why was she noticing *now*?

Julian suddenly turned his head, and his gaze crashed straight into hers. She startled, embarrassed to have been caught staring. His eyebrow quirked in question. She didn't have an answer.

'Commander,' she blurted out, swallowing hard as she turned. 'You were telling us about the burning of Washington.'

'Yes,' the commander replied, his chest puffing a bit. 'We occupied the American capitol for all of six-and-twenty hours before we were forced to retreat. But I was part of the group who burned the White House. When we entered, we found supper waiting on the table. Hospitable of them, wasn't it?'

'Truly?' Amelia asked.

'Oh, yes. We walked in, and there was a meal laid for forty. So before we set fire to the house, we sat down and ate Madison's supper.' He smiled. 'But I must say, Your Grace, that meal was nothing to touch the feast you've laid before us tonight.' He gestured toward the array of roasts and delicately sauced vegetables.

Amelia blushed her thanks.

At the head of the table, the duke gave his wife a look of admiration and pride. He raised his glass. 'A drink to her health. Her Grace, the Duchess of Morland.'

In unison, the lieutenants bolted to their feet with a chorus of 'Hear, hear!' before sitting and gulping wine.

Julian's brow creased with annoyance. 'Such enthusiasm. Is that a naval tradition?'

Lily took it upon herself to explain. 'The commander has requested his lieutenants stand when they speak, so that I may better follow the

73

conversation. Isn't that considerate of him?' With her eyes, she pleaded for his agreement.

She didn't receive it.

'"Considerate" isn't the word.'

The lieutenant in the middle rose from his chair. 'If I may say it, Mr. Bellamy, it's an honor to meet you, sir.'

Lily smiled at his earnestness. These officers were a perfect audience for Julian's charm. Like so many men of their generation, they clearly idolized him.

As the first sat, the ginger one rose. 'At sea, we're always telling jokes and amusing stories. All the best ones trace back to you.'

'All the bawdiest, you mean.' With a riffle of his short dark hair, the youngest ignored the one-at-a-time proviso and fairly exploded from his seat. 'Do Prinny! Or Byron, if you will.'

Lily knew Julian had dined for years on the popularity of his imitations. Supposedly, he had the uncanny ability to reproduce a voice faithfully after hearing it just once. Leo's friends never tired of the amusement, but it was a talent wholly lost on her.

Reaching for the platter of broiled trout before him, Julian demurred with a shake of his head. 'Not now.'

But the young lieutenant would not be deterred. He leapt to his feet again. 'Please, sir. I saw you a year ago, when my uncle took me by Boodles before I shipped out. And I've been telling my mates about it ever since—'

'Sit down.' Julian leveled the fillet knife at him. 'And stay seated. All of you. You're insulting the lady.'

The youth's face blazed crimson as he sank

74

to his chair. Lily felt her own cheeks heat. Well. That was the last they'd hear from any of the lieutenants at this table. They would not disobey their commander by speaking without standing, and neither would they dare to cross Julian.

She passed a dish of potatoes in his direction, taking the opportunity to murmur, 'What are you doing?'

'I'—he accepted the dish with an angry motion—'am truly standing up for you.'

She bit back a response.

For several minutes, they all busied themselves with eating rather than conversing. But even with Amelia's excellent fare, the diversion could only last so long.

The commander touched her wrist. 'Will you flee to the country soon, my lady? Or do you winter in Town?'

'I will remain here in London,' she told him. 'I expect my cousin—the new marquess—to arrive from Egypt soon. And you? How long will your ship be in dock?'

'A few months at least.' He gave her a solicitous smile. 'Perhaps we will cross paths again.'

'Perhaps.' She turned to Julian for agreement, only to find his gaze trained fiercely on the commander's hand where it still touched Lily's wrist.

Yes, it was rather a liberty on the commander's part. But really, nothing to demand that level of outrage. Julian glared at the man's hand as though he were planning to take it joint from joint, cleaving muscle from sinew with a butcher's efficiency—and perhaps a butcher's implements, as well.

Lily gently withdrew her hand and reached for

75

her glass, taking a long, leisurely sip of wine as a means of changing the subject. As she drank, she felt a palpable tension radiating from Julian's quarter. She wanted to weep for despair. Why was he so angry all the time? Would they never be able to simply be friends again?

After the dishes and plates had been cleared, Amelia asked, 'Since we are so uneven in our numbers this evening, shall we all adjourn directly to the drawing room? The gentlemen may enjoy their port in mixed company without fear of offending any delicate feminine sensibilities. Don't you agree, Lily?'

'Yes, of course.'

'Excellent. What a lively group we'll have for parlor games.'

They all rose, the chastened lieutenants apparently buoyed by the prospect of quality port. And though the duke looked faintly horrified by the prospect of parlor games, Lily held out hope that the group's general humor would improve.

Unfortunately, as they departed the dining room, the commander was hasty in offering his arm. Lily had no polite way to refuse. She cast a beseeching look at Julian.

'Go on,' he said, eschewing her company for the duke's. 'Morland and I need to chat. Privately.'

The duke nodded his agreement, no doubt eager to escape the parlor games. He and Julian fell behind, then ducked into a side room.

Lily sighed. She hoped that by 'chat,' Julian meant . . . an actual discussion. Not an exchange of insults and blows. But no matter how much she wished for the former, she knew the latter was a distinct possibility.

76

*   *   *

One minute in Morland's study, and Julian already wanted to hit the man.

'Well, Bellamy.' The duke unstopped a decanter of brandy, timing the loud pop for dramatic emphasis. 'It's been awhile.'

Julian endeavored to remain calm. He concentrated on the amber flow of brandy as it swirled and tumbled into his glass. 'Not nearly long enough for me.'

'I would be inclined to agree'—the duke filled his own glass—'if you didn't owe me a great many explanations.'

Julian clenched his jaw. He owed this man nothing. 'I assume you refer to the search for Leo's murderers?'

'I fronted the money for that investigation. Several thousand pounds. So yes, I think that entitles me to some explanations. But first'— Morland indicated two chairs, and they sat down— 'let's talk horses.'

'Oh, yes. Forget our murdered friend. Horses always come first with you.'

The duke ignored the remark. 'When I returned to Town, I went first thing to look in on Osiris. Imagine my shock when I did not find him at the same mews.'

'I had him moved,' Julian said testily. 'Wasn't that what you wanted? You had such a litany of complaints about his stabling.'

'I did.'

'And . . . ?'

'And the current arrangements are improved.'

77

Before Julian could respond, the duke added, 'But still not what they should be.'

Arrogant ass. No doubt Morland would watch a pint of blue blood let from his veins before he'd spare Julian a word of concession.

'I still want to take the stallion to Cambridgeshire,' Morland said. 'This is a priceless race horse we're discussing. My stables are the best. Osiris belongs there.'

Julian tipped his brandy. Of course. The duke would never deem any barn fit for that horse, other than his own. The purebred man deserves the purebred horse—that was Morland's thinking. Well, Julian despised the man and his air of aristocratic entitlement. This was the very reason he'd charmed his way into the *ton*. To personally see overblown lords of Morland's ilk mocked, humbled, ruined. Or most enjoyably of all, cuckolded.

Luckily for Morland, even Julian wouldn't sink so low as to seduce the good-natured Amelia. Even if he had the heart for seduction lately, which he hadn't.

'Need I remind you,' Spencer asked, 'that my share of the horse exceeds yours by sevenfold?'

'No. You needn't remind me.'

The ten brass tokens that signified membership in the Stud Club could never be bought or sold, only won or lost in a game of chance. It was the crowning example of Leo's fair-minded nature. What other marquess would devise a club open to anyone with luck, regardless of his wealth or circumstance? Because, though noble-born, Leo had never thought himself the superior of any man.

And ironically, he had been. Certainly worth

ten of this duke. The club had been a source of amusement for years, until Morland ruined it with his ruthless quest to win all ten tokens and own the stallion outright. The duke currently held seven of the ten brass coins. Julian and Lord Ashworth were the only other surviving members.

'Your arithmetic needs adjustment.' Julian set aside his brandy and reached into his coat. 'Because I currently hold two.' From his breast pocket, he withdrew a thin disc of brass. On one side was stamped a horse's head, and on the other, a horse's tail. 'This one was Leo's,' he said, holding up the token between thumb and forefinger. 'I won it back from Ashworth, in Devonshire.'

'What took you to Devonshire?'

'You'll remember last summer, the whore who found Leo's body was tracked down?'

The duke nodded. 'When we last saw each other, you were planning to question her.'

'And so I did. I found her, questioned her, and then took her to Ashworth's backwater village in Devonshire for safekeeping.'

'Safekeeping? Why did she need safekeeping?'

After a brief hesitation, Julian decided to tell Morland everything. Much as he detested the man, he also needed him. Or rather, Lily needed him. And whatever Lily needed, Julian also required.

'The night of his death, Leo picked up the harlot in Covent Garden, asked her to go with him to the boxing match. Afterward, they lingered in the street . . . negotiating where to . . . you know.'

'I can imagine.' Morland grimaced. 'Just skip that bit.'

Julian did, and happily. He didn't like thinking about Leo spending his last night on earth with a whore. Truthfully, Julian had been shocked to hear he'd picked up the girl at all. Common light-skirts weren't Leo's usual way.

'Anyhow,' he went on, 'before they could proceed, a man appeared.'

'The one who resembled you?'

'Yes. And according to the harlot, Leo seemed to know him. The two went round a corner. The girl heard an argument, then silence. Then a fight. She turned the corner and saw two footpads pummeling Leo and this stranger.' Julian reached for his brandy and downed the remainder. It burned going down, but it wasn't nearly so hard to swallow as the truth.

He cleared his throat and forged ahead. 'She didn't see the attackers clearly. Could only describe them as two large brutes in rough clothing. One was bald, she said, and the other sounded like a Scotsman. She managed to scare them off with a scream, but both Leo and his companion were left severely injured. The whore went for help, but by the time she returned with a hackney driver, this mystery fellow had disappeared. Only Leo was there. She brought him to my house, and you know the rest. He died en route.'

'So who was this other man?'

'That would be the question, wouldn't it? I searched for weeks, made inquiries.' Finding the man had been a harder task than one might think. Since Julian set the trends for fashion, a great many young gentlemen resembled him. 'I finally learned his name. You should know it. Peter Faraday. He's a former member of the Stud Club.'

'I remember,' the duke said, refilling both glasses. 'I won his token just a few nights before

Leo's murder.'

'And just *after* the murder, Faraday fled Town for a remote cottage in Cornwall. I thought I had the answer. Faraday was disgruntled over losing, or desperate for funds, perhaps. I thought he must have lured Leo into an ambush. Ashworth and I went to Cornwall, bringing along this prostitute to identify him. But when we arrived at Faraday's hideaway . . . ' Julian expelled a rough sigh. 'The man was an invalid. Could barely walk, even two months after the attack. He claims he and Leo were merely talking, and then these two brutes fell on them without warning.'

'And you believe him?'

He shrugged. 'Ashworth does. Says he must be innocent—that no man would willingly incur injuries that severe, even to cover up his involvement in a murder plot. But I still say Faraday's hiding something. Whether ambush or accident, there's more he's not telling us.' He reached for the token again and tapped its edge against the arm of his chair, beating a steady rhythm. 'Now the investigation is stalled.'

Morland's gaze trained on the token in Julian's hand. 'That should be mine, you know. I wrote you a bank draft to fund this investigation, on the understanding that token would come to me.'

'You are unbeliev—'

'Save it.' The duke waved off the remainder of Julian's protest. 'I don't give a damn what you think of me. But I truly do want what's best for that animal. You *could* make this easy and agree that Osiris deserves a comfortable retirement at my estate. But since you won't, I'm forced to call in debts.'

'There are no debts.' Julian put away the token and withdrew the other item he'd secured in the breast pocket of his coat. He unfolded the rectangle of heavy paper and extended it to Morland.

The duke took it, frowning. 'Is this . . .'

'Your bank draft, yes. I never drew the funds.' Morland blinked at him.

'Oh, I performed a thorough search. Hired runners, investigators, crawled over every inch of this city. But I used my own money.'

'Then why did you accept this?' The duke held up the bank draft.

'As a bond, of sorts. To certify your good faith and innocence. I'm convinced of those things now.' Albeit grudgingly.

'Well,' Morland said dryly. 'And here it only took five months. I thought I said the remainder of the amount was supposed to go to Lily.'

'She won't take it. Believe me, I've tried.'

'Well, then.' The duke folded the paper and ripped it in quarters before casting it into the fire.

'You still owe her your assistance.' Julian leaned forward to confront the duke, bracing his elbows on his knees.

'I assume you have something specific in mind.'

He nodded. 'There's more to the story. Faraday had a theory as to why those men attacked him and Leo. And the evidence supports his conclusion.'

'Which is . . . ?' Morland leaned forward with interest.

Julian hesitated. He hadn't spoken of this to anyone since Cornwall. 'The attack was meant for me. Someone wants me dead.'

As he spoke the words, he felt the tension in his shoulders melt. Strange, that an admission of imminent danger and possible pursuant death would be accompanied by the sensation of relief. But it was. It helped to talk, and there were few people with whom he could discuss this openly. His usual confidants were Leo and Lily. One was dead, and the other must never know anything of this.

'Just one person?' Morland scoffed. 'I would have wagered many.'

'God damn it. This is serious.' Julian rose from his chair and paced the carpet's antique gold fringe. 'Leo's dead, and—'

His voice broke at the sudden memory of Leo's battered face. That image haunted him, even now. Leo had died too quickly for much bruising to occur. His features had been not so much swollen as . . . misshapen. Broken beyond repair.

'Leo's dead, and it's my fault. You're right, my enemies are plentiful. That's the bloody problem. If there were only one person, I'd know where to go. But there are too many men with a grievance against me, and some incidents are decades in the past.' He couldn't just go knocking on doors and ask, *Beg pardon, but are* you *the one who's discovered my true identity and wants me dead?* He massaged his temple with one hand. 'If I want to find Leo's killers, I'll have to find the man who hired them. Which means I'll have to provoke him, draw him out.'

'Draw him *out*? None of this makes sense. It's been five months since Leo died. If someone truly wanted to kill you and failed, one would think by now he'd have taken a second stab at it.' To Julian's affronted silence, Morland half-shrugged in apology. 'Poor choice of words.'

'Yes. I've noticed you have that problem.'

83

The duke went on, 'Have there been any other direct attempts on your life?'

'No,' Julian admitted. 'Not that I'm aware.'

'Then why are you so convinced it was a planned attack meant for you?'

'It only makes sense. The timing, the method, the resemblance between me and Faraday. He even said Leo's last words were "Tell Julian."'

He turned away, swearing softly. 'The man lay wounded and dying, and his last thought was to warn *me*.'

Leo was decent and selfless to the last, and what had Julian offered in return? Lies. Lies, and improper lust for the man's only sister. What a miserable excuse for a friend he'd been.

'That proves nothing. He was wounded, and you were his closest friend. In any scrape, wouldn't his first thought be, "Tell Julian"?' Morland approached, raising his hands in a gesture of peace. 'Listen. Leo was murdered by footpads. It was a random attack by petty criminals, not paid assassins. This was the simplest explanation from the first, and it remains the most credible theory now. It's a tragedy. But you need to let it go and move on.'

'I *can't*. You don't understand.' And neither could Julian explain it. He surmised that Morland had some notion of his less-than-illustrious origins. But the duke didn't know the particulars.

Someone out there did. And that someone wanted him dead, eventually. Five months were an insignificant delay, after so many years.

'There will come a time,' he said, 'perhaps quite soon, when I will disappear. Whether voluntarily or not, I dare not guess. When that happens, you must promise me you'll look after Lily.'

Morland looked surprised. 'Certainly. Amelia is very close to Lily. We'll offer her any assistance she might require.'

'Damn your offers of assistance. I need you to *protect* her.' Julian gestured angrily in the direction of the dining room. 'Better than you did in there just now.'

'What do you mean?'

'You know what I mean. That row of trained porpoises at the dinner table.'

The duke raised an eyebrow. 'That was not—'

'The devil it wasn't. And then that odious Commander Merriwin, taking every opportunity to fondle her wrist.'

'*Fondle?* I scarcely think—'

'Exactly. You scarcely thought.' Julian leveled a finger at Morland, leaving him with a tenuous grasp on his emotions. 'This is your house. Lily is your guest. How could you allow those . . . those seafaring apes to make a mockery of her, right to her face?'

'No one was mocking Lily,' Morland replied evenly. 'You're the one who insulted her.'

'Me? *I* insulted her?'

'Yes, by treating her like a child who needs tending. Lily is an intelligent woman, and not nearly so fragile as you make her out to be. She can handle herself. She was doing so this evening, quite capably. Until you arrived. That's the moment she began to look miserable.'

The truth silenced Julian. Morland was right. She'd worn a broad smile when he entered, but she'd visibly tensed as he slid into the chair beside hers. She certainly hadn't spurned the slimy

85

advances of that Merriwin slug—a fact that *should* have filled him with hope for her marital prospects but instead left him hollow with rage. And the wounded look she'd sent him when he barked at the lieutenants to sit down . . .

Dagger, meet heart.

He knew, rationally, that Lily was a capable, clever woman who didn't need his help. But when he was around her, rational thought grew wings and flew out the nearest window. In its place, protective jealousy reigned supreme.

He scrubbed his face with one hand. 'Well. At least she won't have to put up with me much longer.' He rose and moved to quit the room.

The duke asked, 'Just how much does Lily know?'

'About what? About her brother's dalliance with a low-class whore? About Faraday? My enemies?'

'About your feelings for her.'

That dagger piercing his heart twisted, grinding against his solar plexus. He was too stunned to dissemble. Morland knew?

'Of course I know,' the duke said. 'And if even I've noticed, it's the worst-kept secret in England. When it comes to matters of the heart, I'm not especially perceptive.'

'You don't say.' Julian stopped, hand and gaze fixed on the doorjamb. For years, he'd kept so many secrets. Why was he failing so miserably at hiding this? If even Morland could tell, did Lily suspect? How could she not, after that stupid, disastrous kiss?

Three nights, he told himself. He just had to make it through three nights. Somehow.

'Nothing,' he said flatly. 'Lily knows nothing about any of it. Nor will she.'

86

Chapter Six

'A louse!'

The ginger-haired lieutenant shook his head and tried again, dragging his fingers through his hair in affected swoops and every so often tossing his head.

'A milkmaid!' the youngest shouted, leaping to his feet.

In response to this, the lieutenant shot a death glare toward his young compatriot. He adopted a new strategy now, tucking his thumbs into his armpits, puffing out his chest, and beginning to strut about the room. As he walked, his head jerked forward and back.

Michael raised his hand to guess. 'A bantam?'

The lieutenant gestured his encouragement. *Not quite right,* his motions said, *but getting closer.* He thrust his fingers into his hair again, ruffling it with vigor until it stood straight up in the middle. He pointed to his smart ripple of carrot-colored hair. It could not escape anyone's notice that he resembled a cross between Julian Bellamy and a rooster.

Ah. But of course.

Lily called out the obvious. 'A coxcomb.'

With a wide grin, the ginger-haired lieutenant touched a finger to his nose, then bowed and left the circle. Everyone laughed—but the three young lieutenants laughed most gleefully. Lily supposed it must be some balm to their pride, to have a hearty chortle at the expense of the man who'd given them such a rude and literal setdown at dinner. Had Julian been out of circulation so long that his polished charm had lost its luster? Or did he simply not care anymore?

From his seat beside hers, the commander touched her wrist again. 'Well done, my lady. Will you favor us with a turn?'

She shook her head. 'To be truthful, charades really aren't my forte.'

'Then name your amusement.'

She hedged. Honestly, she'd never been much for parlor games of any sort. 'Cards?'

The commander stood and immediately ordered the younger officers to set the room for cards.

Lily rose from her chair and moved to the window seat, taking a moment's amusement from the heated discussion a simple rearrangement of furniture could cause, where five men were involved. And then, in the next moment, she wondered—*again*—about Julian. She couldn't stop thinking about him. Ever since this morning, her heart seemed to alternate pulses between her own life and his. If only he'd stay in the same room for a while, she might be saved from developing palpitations.

A sober-faced Michael joined her at the window. 'I can't stop thinking of him.'

'Truly?' she answered, briefly wondering what cause Michael would have to be obsessively thinking of Julian.

'It's just . . . so hard to believe he's gone.'

Leo. He means Leo, you fool. Strange. For the first time in months, Lily *hadn't* been thinking of her brother.

'I wish I'd been able to attend the burial,' Michael said. 'I hadn't seen him in above two years.'

'Didn't you see him the summer before last? Oh,

but perhaps you were at sea that July.'

'Two summers ago?' Michael shook his head. 'I wasn't at sea. I was in Plymouth. But no, I didn't have a chance to see Leo. Wasn't he with you in Gloucestershire?'

'Not for July. He went . . . ' Lily bit her tongue. 'Oh, I'm sorry. I must be remembering it wrong.'

That July, Leo had spent the month at a reunion of his old Eton friends. She didn't want to make Michael feel poorly for having been excluded. But then, why *should* Michael have been excluded? He'd been Leo's closest friend at school. It made no sense, unless . . .

Unless Leo *hadn't* attended a reunion with his old Eton friends. Unless he'd spent a month somewhere else.

The room went fuzzy around her. Fragments of those letters floated to the surface of her memory.

When I close my eyes at night, I imagine we're there again. We lie still in the tall grass. A clear sky hangs over us. The sun's warmth bakes the dew from our skin. Your fingers lace with mine. Like children, we laugh at the skylarks mating overhead.

Then you turn to me slowly, brush a lock of hair from my brow.

We kiss, and childish thoughts are put away.

Lily jolted back into the present. The commander stood before her.

'Shall we?' He extended a hand and tilted his head toward the card tables.

'Oh!' She rose to her feet. 'Yes, of course.'

They sat down to whist. She, Amelia, Michael, and the commander occupied the first table, whilst the three younger lieutenants were left to play shorthanded at the other, with the empty fourth seat designated 'dummy.'

Lily was partnered with Michael, and the commander seated himself to her left. As Amelia shuffled the deck, Lily tried to focus. She was good at cards, and especially skilled at whist. She looked forward to displaying proficiency in *something* this evening.

But she couldn't. Her concentration was so scattered. Several times, she had to be prompted to play her turn. At her left, she felt the commander growing impatient. The testy set of his jaw told her what his words did not. He was bored with her. It happened. People like the commander started out solicitous and enthusiastic, treating conversation with a deaf woman as some sort of parlor game in its own right. But once they realized the game had no end, and furthermore, no prizes would be awarded . . . they sometimes grew weary of the effort and ceased trying.

To be fair, Lily was poor company. Her mind kept circling back to her conversation with Michael and that stack of letters she'd found hidden in Leo's desk drawer. She'd always thought there'd been no secrets between her and her brother. Evidently she'd been wrong.

What had he been hiding from her? Or more to the point, whom?

And where in the world was Julian? He promised to *escort* her to three events, not make an appearance just long enough to humiliate her before fleeing the scene and leaving her all alone to deal with Leo's grief-stricken friends. Not to mention commanders of the Royal Navy who were short on patience and entirely too free with their hands.

Even though she knew it to be unfair, she wanted to take her every moment of uncertainty, awkwardness, and undiluted fear in this endless day and heap the blame squarely at Julian's feet. She was so very tired, and tired of being angry with him. Between the unshed tears blurring her vision and the trembling of her fingers, she could barely make out the figures on her cards.

'I beg your pardon,' she said, laying down her cards and rising from the table. 'I believe I need some air.' When the other men began to rise, she motioned for them to remain in place. Amelia's eyes flashed concern, and Lily tried to reassure her with a smile. 'Don't get up, please. I'll return momentarily.' *Just as soon as I find Julian and drag him back, too.*

As she smoothed her skirts, she tried not to feel defeated. Yes, she *could* handle these settings alone. But given the choice, she would prefer to handle them with Julian.

When had he become so essential to her?

She turned away from the card table and moved to quit the room.

Then she stopped. Because Julian was there in the doorway, headed toward her.

When their eyes met, they each stumbled to a halt. He smiled at the coincidence. She pressed her lips together. In unison, they exchanged brief nods, followed by matching expressions of suppressed laughter. A whole conversation, crammed into the space of a moment, with nary a word exchanged. The understanding and patience she craved . . . it was all there, waiting in his eyes. Strange impulses tugged at her. The strongest of which being the desire to run at the man, fling both arms around his neck, and hope—just breathe and wait and hope, with her pulse thundering in her ears—that his arms would naturally wrap around her, too.

But before she could embarrass them both, Julian's gaze cut away, darting to the card players behind her. Lily watched his face blanch, then flush crimson with fury. His lips formed crisp, distinct words. Words not intended for her, but for someone beyond her right shoulder.

'What the devil did you just say?'

Oh, dear. The commander must have made some remark when she'd turned away. Something insensitive, when she couldn't overhear. And of course, Julian was incapable of letting such remarks pass. His mouth thinned to a tight, angry line. At his sides, his hands balled into formidable fists.

He was going to hurt someone. Soon.

Lily stepped in front of him. The scene wasn't disastrous yet. If she pretended to be oblivious to the whole situation, everyone else could act the same. 'Mr. Bellamy,' she said lightly. 'I . . . I was just on my way to get some air. Would you take me for a turn about the garden?'

She took his hand. Or rather, his wrist, since his hand was a solid lump of knuckles and thumb.

He glared past her, at the commander. 'You're a bastard. Don't think she doesn't know it.'

'Julian,' she whispered, frantic. 'Take me for a turn in the garden. Now.'

This time, she did not wait for his agreement. Mining a reserve of strength she hadn't known she possessed, Lily yanked him by the wrist until he did an about-face. She thrust her arm through his, linking him securely at her side. He stiffened for a moment, as though his mind and muscles were at odds over how to respond. But when she stepped forward, he did too. Thank heaven. Together, they left the drawing room and the card tables and the commander behind.

But they never made it anywhere near the garden.

Lily tugged him into the first available space—a room just across the corridor—and, with a quick glance about for servants, carefully shut the door behind them. This must be Amelia's day room. The room was thick with overstuffed furniture designed for comfort, not fashion, and needlework baskets and homely curios occupied the tables. The windows were hung with plush velvet draperies. It was the perfect place for a private conversation.

Just the same, she strove to keep her voice low as she turned to Julian. 'What was all that, then?'

His face shuttered. 'Nothing.'

'For pity's sake, you can tell me. I gather the commander made some jesting remark, one he knew I couldn't hear. It must have been quite ill-mannered, to turn you that particular shade of red.'

Julian just shook his head, refusing to answer. He took a few paces, swinging the tension from his arms as he walked.

Lily crossed her arms over her chest. Because the room was cold, and because she needed a hug— and it seemed Julian would not offer one. 'Will you make me guess? Let me see . . . We were playing whist, and I left them short-handed. Ah. It must have been something about having to play with a dummy hand, hm?' She smiled to herself. 'Yes, that

93

would make sense. "Trading one dumb player for another." Was it something like that?'

When Julian made no motion to deny it, Lily supposed her guess to be near the mark. A nervous chuckle escaped her control.

'How can you laugh?' he demanded.

She threw up a hand. 'How can I not? I mean, it's a terrible pun. I'm only deaf, not dumb at all. But there's no denying I've played abominably all evening.'

He blinked at her, incredulous.

She felt her own face heat. Her tongue stumbled against her teeth as she tried to explain. 'It's easier to laugh. One must have a sense of humor about such things, or life becomes unbearable. And if you're going to be my escort in society, you'll need to gird yourself against these little slights, too. People don't understand. Some assume my mind went with my hearing. Others shout themselves red, as if increased volume will help. Still others are just so flummoxed by the whole idea, they ignore me entirely. The commander may be a self-important boor, I'll grant you. But you can't fly into a rage every time one of those fresh-faced lieutenants makes an honest attempt at conversation.'

'They were insulting you.'

'That's mine to decide, not yours. I'm so tired of you thinking for me. First I can't live alone. Then I can't hold a simple dinner conversation without a knifepoint intervention. Now I can't even know my own mind? I thought you were my friend, Julian, but a true friend wouldn't keep reminding me of my limitations. He'd believe in me, and help *me* believe I can do anything I choose.'

His expression softened. 'Lily, of course I believe

94

in you, but—'

'But what? There's no room for "but" in that sentence. You can't say you believe in me, *"but."* Either you believe in someone, full stop—or you don't.'

Sighing heavily, she took a few paces about the room, trying to master her emotions and revive some faith in herself. If there was one thing worse than being the object of others' pity, it was succumbing to self-pity. After nine years, the deafness itself rarely caused her a moment's lamentation. Only the thoughtlessness of others sometimes dragged her spirits low.

'You have no idea, Julian. These little slights this evening—they're nothing.' Pausing by a side table, she gave the porcelain beagle squatting there a pensive tap on the head. 'Once,' she said, smoothing her fingertip down one floppy ear, 'the year after my illness, I received a letter from my mother's Aunt Beatrice. In it, she expressed her very deep distress about my affliction, as she called it. She felt it her Christian duty to point out that my deafness was a judgment from God. My punishment for being too beautiful and too proud. She prayed I would be more mindful of my spiritual health, now that my physical well-being had been compromised.'

Lily hadn't thought about that letter in years, not consciously. But obviously the paper-thin score on her heart had never quite healed, festering all this time. Had people thought her too proud in her debut season? She hadn't been, not excessively. Only shy. But some had obviously mistaken her natural reserve for vanity, and in a fashion, Lily must have felt shamed by Aunt Beatrice's rebuke—

for she'd never spoken of that letter to anyone, not even Leo. Why she was telling Julian about it now, she had no idea.

Julian's hand fell on hers, warm and strong. When she lifted her face, he spoke slowly and distinctly. 'Your mother's Aunt Beatrice was an unforgivable, imbecilic, self-righteous bitch.'

And with that, he gave her exactly what she'd been needing. This was why she'd told Julian. Leo never could have said *that*. He was far too congenial, and besides—Aunt Beatrice had given him his first pony.

'Yes.' Lily nodded, feeling years of resentment uncoil within her. 'Yes, she was.'

'As if an illness could somehow be your fault, or God's will.'

Sensing an opportunity in this vein of conversation, Lily asked, 'If not mine or God's, whose fault was it? The doctor's? My parents'?'

'No one's, of course.'

He pried her fingers from the ceramic dog and held her hand in his. Strange, confusing sparks of sensation traveled from her wrist to her elbow.

'It wasn't anyone's fault,' he went on. 'Sometimes bad things just happen, and there's nowhere to point the finger of blame.'

'Exactly.' The current of electricity buzzed through her whole body now. 'Just like with Leo. Sometimes bad things just happen, and there's no one to blame.'

'That's different. That's different, and you know it. Where there's murder, there's blame. By definition.'

'But—'

He dropped her hand and stalked to the unused

96

hearth, propping one boot on the grate and leaning his forearm on the mantel, glaring hard into his fist.

She crossed to him. 'We have to talk.'

'We've been talking.'

'No, I mean . . .'

Curse him, she'd been hoping to avoid this conversation. Ever since Leo's death, Julian had become so protective of her, so intense in their every interaction. And now it would seem she'd caught the same contagion. Unable to put him out of her mind, ascribing strange tingles to his casual touch. Perhaps if they discussed this tension between them, it would dissipate.

'Ever since my brother died,' she began, 'I've been struggling to answer this question: Without Leo, who am I? He was such a large part of my life, and in many ways I defined my existence in relationship to his. In *too* many ways, I fear. I'm sorting out the tangle, slowly. But as if that weren't hard enough, there's this other question. It comes to the fore whenever we're together. I can only imagine it's the reason we're always quarreling of late.'

He stared at her, impassive. 'What question would that be?'

Anxiety prickled in her throat. Using all available willpower, she blunted her nerves and met his gaze. 'Without Leo . . . who are *we*?'

A glimmer of some inscrutable emotion lit his eyes, but she didn't dare focus on it too long. Instead, she dropped her gaze and concentrated on his mouth, awaiting his reply. As much time as she'd spent staring at him, she couldn't help notice that his lips were so well-shaped. Wide and sensual, curved at the edges just a bit. The faintest pull of

97

his jaw muscle could tweak that curve into a playful smirk or a genuine smile or a wicked suggestion. He must be a very good kisser, when he wasn't under the influence of pain and sleeping powder.

Her own tongue darted out to moisten her lips. Oh, this was terrible.

Words, Lily. Concentrate on his words.

'I mean,' she continued nervously, 'we became friends through Leo, and now that he's gone, it's only natural that we would be forced to . . . ask ourselves that.'

'And have you arrived at an answer?'

'I know what we aren't. You can't be Leo's replacement. I don't need a substitute brother, watching over everything I do.'

A little tug of his jaw tipped his mouth. 'I don't want to be your brother.'

'I don't need a guardian, either. I'm eight-and-twenty, not a girl.'

'I'm well aware of that, too.'

'Then why have you become so protective and overbearing? Always demanding that I marry, then chasing off any man who so much as dares to touch my hand?' Even as she asked the question, Lily knew the heat building between their bodies was a very good clue.

Still she prattled on, hoping more words would dispel it. 'You . . .' She touched a hand to his chest. A mistake. Too solid, too strong. Those sparks again. 'You feel guilty and bound to protect me, and I . . .' She withdrew her touch and pressed the same hand to her own breast. Softer, uncertain. Quivering with each pounding beat of her heart. 'I feel lonely and unmoored. We're both emotional and searching for answers, and I just wish . . .'

98

She dropped her gaze, because she couldn't bear to be interrupted. She had to get these words out. 'I just wish our friendship could be the one thing that's never in question. Can you understand? It pains me so much, to always be arguing with you, worrying about you. Just because Leo died, it doesn't mean everything between us must change. I want to go back to the way we were before.'

She paused, eyes lowered and breath bated, wondering why those words tasted false on her tongue.

He seized her by the shoulders, forcing her gaze to meet his. 'We can't, Lily. We can't go back. Too much has changed.'

'I don't want things to change. Why can't we just stay friends forever?'

'Because . . .' His grip tightened on her shoulders, and excitement rippled through her veins. 'Lily, you can't tell me you don't know.'

No, she couldn't. A hidden, deeply feminine part of her understood him perfectly. And yet . . . 'I want you to say it.'

He pulled her to him, bringing her body flush against his. 'Because I want you, Lily, the way a man wants a woman. I always have.'

He held her fast, and she stood breathless, slowly becoming aware of his body. Then, slowly, growing aware of her own. She had a thin, willowy build. People always teased that there was scarcely anything to her. But here in his arms, she felt her own substance. Her weight, her heat, her curves.

'There's always been a tension between us,' he said. 'I know you must feel it. Tell me you feel it, too.'

She nodded. Oh, yes. The tension, the attraction,

99

the force of his ardor. She felt all those things. But she could also feel *it*—a firm ridge, swelling against her belly. The physical manifestation of male desire, and yet she wasn't made timid by the display. To the contrary, for the first time in months, she felt powerful and strong.

His eyes searched hers, then dropped to linger on her lips. She watched his mouth as he formed the unmistakable syllables of her name. 'Lily.'

So prescient of her parents, giving her that name. L-sounds were among the easiest to lip-read. The trouble was, the shape of her name always looked a bit silly to her. Especially with her honorific attached: 'Lady Lily.' Two l's were bad enough, but three were ridiculous. All that tongue-flapping made her want to giggle.

But when Julian spoke her name, it never looked like a joke to her. No, it looked vaguely . . . *naughty*. Sensual, not silly. She'd always loved watching her name on his lips.

Always.

The word seeped down into her bones, into her soul, where it simply . . . fell into place. Like the moment of triumph she felt after scouring a ledger a dozen times and finally finding the six shillings unaccounted for, in the column where she'd mistaken a seven for a one. At last, it all made sense—all the quarreling and worrying and strange tingling that resulted from his touch. This explained why he'd grown so inordinately protective of her, and why the sight of his blood on her fingertips had thrown her into absolute panic. Because he'd always wanted her this way. And deep down—so far deep down she hadn't even been fully aware of it until this moment—she'd always desired him, too.

Here was the answer. Who were they, without Leo? They were two people who *wanted* each other.

And right now, they were two people who were just about to kiss.

Chapter Seven

Lily leaned into his embrace, needing to touch him. Wanting him to know that she craved this, too. She knew she ought to close her eyes for the kiss, but she just couldn't. So she watched, restless with anticipation, as his mouth lowered to hers. And just as his breath caressed her lips . . .

He startled. And leapt back.

Left with nothing to lean against, Lily pitched forward. She barely managed to catch the mantel's edge before tumbling to the floor. She shook herself, confused and gasping and uncertain where to look. Had she merely misread his words, or the entire situation? How much mortification could fit into one evening, anyway?

Finally, unable to do otherwise, she looked to Julian for an explanation.

He said, 'My God. You're pregnant.'

What? Her mind rattled in her skull, shaken by the utter impossibility of that statement. To be sure, she'd just felt the tangible proof of his virility pressed against the general vicinity of her womb . . . But no man was so potent as *that*.

Then she realized Julian wasn't speaking to her.

Lily turned, pressing a hand to her chest. In the corner of the room she spied Claudia, the duke's young ward, shyly emerging from behind a fold of

101

velvet drapery.

'You're pregnant,' Julian repeated, moving toward the girl.

Claudia placed a hand on her belly. 'So the doctors tell me.'

He turned to Lily. 'Did you know about this?'

She shook her head. 'They've kept it very quiet. I only learned of it this afternoon. Claudia's condition, I mean. Believe me, I had no idea she was hiding in the draperies.' She turned to the girl. 'I thought you were to remain upstairs.'

'I was,' she said, biting her lip. 'I was supposed to stay upstairs. I only wanted a look in at the party.'

And at the naval officers, Lily imagined. Claudia was nothing if not curious about handsome young men.

'Then you came in,' she went on, 'and so I hid. I meant to simply wait until you left the room, but . . .' Her cheeks colored. 'Eventually, it seemed better to reveal my presence than conceal it.'

Claudia cast a wary look at Julian, causing Lily to wonder if the girl believed herself to be protecting Lily with her interruption. It would have been almost sweet of her, if it weren't so wholly unnecessary. Not to mention unwanted. She looked to Julian, but he was studiously avoiding her gaze, frowning at the carpet instead. She doubted his frustration was meant for the interlocking rings of cream and gold. No, he was angry with himself. He regretted what had just occurred between them. Or rather, what had *almost* occurred.

'You'd best slip upstairs now,' Lily prompted the girl.

Claudia nodded and turned to leave. 'Please,' she said, pausing on her way to the door. 'Don't tell the duke I was downstairs. And kindly don't tell anyone about . . . ' Her hand circled her belly. ' . . . this. I promise not to speak a word of what happened here.'

Julian caught the girl by the elbow. 'Nothing happened here.'

'Exactly.' Claudia smiled, looking from Lily to Julian. 'You needn't be concerned. I'm very good at keeping secrets.'

The girl left the room, and Julian flopped into an armchair and buried his face in his hands. With that disappeared Lily's last bit of hope that they might resume where they'd left off.

He dropped his hands. 'God only knows what that child thinks she saw.'

'What *did* she see?' Lily wasn't certain herself. 'Julian, can we—'

He shot to his feet. 'I have to leave. There are places I need to be.'

'No.' She moved toward him. 'No, please don't go. I won't sleep at all, if I know you're out wandering the streets alone.'

'You shouldn't lose sleep over me.'

'I can't help it.' She couldn't help but lie awake at night and wonder where he was. Because she wanted him there, in bed with her. How could she not have understood it before now?

As she neared his side, she could actually *see* his breath come faster, in the accelerated rise and fall of his chest. If she laid a hand to that spot just beneath his cravat, slid her fingers under the edge of his waistcoat . . . she sensed she'd feel his heart pounding every bit as fiercely as hers. But there the similarities would end. She would find hard muscles there, and the masculine heat of his skin. Did he have hair on his chest, she wondered? How strange, to think that she didn't know. Of course, she'd always known he was a man, and a fine-looking one, at that. But she'd heretofore focused on their commonalities, their affinity.

Now she looked at Julian and saw . . . *otherness.* Differences. New contrasts to explore. With each passing moment, she grew exponentially aware of the essential, primitive masculinity raging beneath those fine clothes and flip expressions. And her own essential womanhood asserted itself in response, plumping her flesh to a feverish pink in all the obvious places—and a few surprising ones, as well. Lips, breasts, mons—she understood the significance of these. But what the backs of her knees had to do with anything, she could not possibly have guessed.

She reached for him, hoping he might help her understand. 'Julian . . . '

He intercepted her touch, grasping her fingers in his and pressing them briefly—chastely—to his lips.

'We'll be missed,' he said, releasing her hand. 'And it's growing late. I'll speak with Morland. He'll see you home in his carriage.'

'But can't we—'

'You were right, I was an ass to the lieutenants earlier. I'll make it up to them, take them round to the clubs and such.' In an apparent effort to collect himself—or avoid her—he tugged down the front of his waistcoat and ran both hands through his tousled black hair. 'No boxing or bull-baiting, I promise.'

Disappointment twanged in her chest, but Lily didn't know how to argue. Hadn't this been her aim when arranging this party? To push Julian back into the social life he'd once loved—the clubs, the theater, the company of friends? She should count this a tremendous success.

Except there were still so many questions churning in her mind, so many emotions coursing through her blood. Julian wanted something more than friendship, he'd said. What more did he want, precisely? Her body? Her affection?

What more did *she* want from him?

'Will you call on me tomorrow?' she asked.

After a brief pause, he nodded. 'If you wish.'

'I do. I do wish it.' For that, and for something more.

*   *   *

When Julian arrived at Harcliffe House the following morning, he again found Lily seated at the desk in Leo's library. Her neck was curved white and graceful as a swan's as she bent over an open ledger. Something about the contrast between that elegant sweep of her neck and the precise point of her elbow as she dipped her quill . . . A tide of longing pushed through him, laying waste to everything in its path.

Bypassing the signal mirror this time, he entered the room and approached her from the side. She was so absorbed in her work, she didn't notice him until he stood nearly beside her, just at her right shoulder. Even then, she did not look up. She simply went still, holding her quill at attention. Only the slight change in her breathing let him know she'd realized he was there.

She was waiting. Waiting to see if he would touch her. So he did. He laid a hand on her shoulder

105

where her thin fichu met her gown.

'Good morning,' she said distractedly, taking a moment to finish her notation before replacing her quill in the inkwell. With a breathy sigh, she tipped her head to the left, stretching the slender column of her neck. Then back to the right. 'I've been sitting here too long. I've gone all stiff.'

How could he resist an invitation like that? Julian pushed aside the frail, gauzy fichu and squeezed her shoulder gently, running his thumb along the tense ridge of muscle and sinew at the base of her neck. She had indeed been working too hard. Her muscles were drawn taut, resistant to his touch. As he kneaded her shoulder, the tension melted beneath his fingertips.

She moaned low in her throat.

Lust rocked him in his boots.

'Yes,' she sighed. 'Just there.'

Suffice it to say, now Lily wasn't the only one contending with uncomfortable stiffness. He slid his hand forward, over the ridge of her collarbone. Excitement surged to his fingertips. Mere inches below, the snowy expanse of her décolletage tempted.

Here was a perilous slope.

He did what any man approaching a precipice would do. He inched forward and peered over the edge.

What a breathtaking view. The gentle mounds of her breasts cradled a steep, luscious valley. She looked so soft. Julian had seen and touched and held to his cheek the finest textiles the world had to offer—velvets, silks, luxurious furs from every corner of every continent. And yet he knew instinctively, none of them could approach the sleek perfection of Lily Chatwick's bosom. There would simply be no apt comparisons. Just as the terms 'oak,' 'granite,' and 'tempered steel' failed to describe the current state of his arousal.

'You can't have her,' he told himself aloud. 'Not like that.' Before he could second-guess himself, he jerked his hand from her body.

She circled her head, stretching. 'Mm, thank you.' Then she looked to him, eyebrows rising in expectation. 'Well . . . ?'

'Well.' Eager to conceal his own expectant, rising parts, Julian pulled up a chair and seated himself across the desk from her. 'Good morning. I brought you something.' He carefully lifted his offering onto the desk. He'd been holding it in one hand all this while, and the parcel's contents had grown noticeably agitated.

She was having none of it. 'Julian. Do you honestly mean to pretend last night didn't happen?'

He froze. He'd been asking himself that very thing. If he wished, he could deny everything. With a bit of bluster and diversion, he could lead her to believe she'd misunderstood his words and actions. He could convince her that no, he actually *hadn't* lost his wits and impulsively confessed to harboring years of lust for her. With luck, he could have her believing that whatever he'd planned on doing instants before they were interrupted, it most certainly had *not* been kissing her for the second time in one day.

But today, looking into her lovely face, he found he simply couldn't stomach more lies.

'No,' he said. 'I don't mean to pretend anything.'

Why shouldn't she understand that since the day they'd met, he'd been seized by a powerful attraction to her? Lily was no fool. She would understand, as he did, that nothing could ever come of it. So many factors prevented him from acting on his desire—her mourning, the inequity of their rank, the recent resurrection of his innate sense of decency. Not to mention the fact that within a fortnight, Julian Bellamy would permanently disappear from London society. One way or another.

Let her know. Let her know what she did to him.

'So.' She drummed her fingers on the desk. 'You desire me.'

'Yes.'

'Always have.'

'From the first.'

Her drumming fingers stilled. 'And last night, when you flew into a rage with that Commander . . .'

'Merriwin. Commander Merriwin.'

'Yes, him. It wasn't because you thought I was weak, or in need of protection.'

'No. It was jealousy. An instinctive male reaction, and one I should have suppressed.' He leaned forward. 'I do believe in you, Lily. I know you could handle that man, or ten just like him. The weakness was mine.'

'Well.' Leather creaked as she sat back in her chair. 'This is all so very enlightening.'

'It is?'

'Yes, of course. It explains so much.' Her cheeks went pink. 'I mean, it's undeniably flattering. Or at least, reassuring. I was beginning to feel like the only woman in London who *didn't* catch your eye.'

His heart sank. Nothing—in all his life, absolutely *nothing*—could have made Julian regret

108

his history of debauchery more than this: for him to finally confess his desire for Lily, and for her to conclude that his admiration simply made her one of a crowd. So utterly wrong that she should believe that, and yet . . . so convenient.

'As long as we are being honest,' she continued, her gaze sliding to the side, 'I have to admit that I find you attractive, too. Not that it should be surprising. Again, I seem to be in the female majority.' She smiled.

'So,' he said, groping his way down the escape hatch she'd opened. 'We've established that we are two attractive people.'

She nodded.

'And that each of us, logically, finds the other attractive.'

'As is only natural.' She stacked her arms on the desk and leaned against them. 'It makes perfect sense. I'm so glad we've had this discussion, aren't you?'

Julian was stunned silent for a moment. That was it? Truly? He admitted to wanting her, and she confessed to harboring a few innocent fancies of her own, and then they just . . . moved on from the topic entirely? Could it really be so simple? She wouldn't think so, if she could have seen him arching on his toes for a glimpse of her breasts just now.

'Er . . . yes,' he finally said. 'I'm glad, too.'

'Excellent. Now, what's this you've brought me?' Her brow wrinkled as she studied the canvas-covered dome he'd placed atop the desk.

'A gift. Every dried-up spinster should have one.' With a flourish, he removed the canvas drape.

'You didn't.' Her eyes went wide. 'Oh, Julian.'

'Oh, Julian,' the parrot sang, bobbing its crimson head in agreement. 'Oh, Julian.'

'Is he speaking?' Lily asked. 'What does he say?'

'He seems to have taken a liking to my name. Or at least your pronunciation of it.'

'Oh, Julian,' the garish creature sang, rustling its blue-and-green wings. 'Oh, Juuuulian.'

Oh, lovely. What an idea this had been.

He reached into his coat and retrieved a packet of shelled walnuts. 'Here,' he said, pushing the packet at Lily. 'He's likely hungry.'

She shook some of the nuts into her palm and pinched one between thumb and forefinger, offering it to the parrot through a gap in the bars. She laughed as the bird swiveled its head nearly upside down to grasp the nut in its dark, hooked beak. 'Wherever did you get him?'

'I lost a bet.'

'*Lost* a bet?'

'Yes. This fellow's ancient, been passed around for years. He's long outlived his original owner. A barrister supposedly brought him home from Jamaica ages ago.'

The parrot bristled. 'Guilty, guilty!' it trilled. Its round, red head tilted, then righted itself. 'Thank you, that will be all.'

'What does he say now?' Lily asked, offering the creature another walnut.

'He's pronounced judgment on me, I believe. And I've come up wanting. No death sentence as yet.'

Clever bird. Truthfully, Julian had felt sorry for the poor feathered beast. It had been passed from gentleman to gentleman for years. Usually as the forfeit in some wager—loser gets the bird. No one

110

seemed to want the thing, and he was beginning to understand why. The parrot's vocal antics would be amusing at the outset but could quickly become a source of aggravation.

'You don't have to keep him,' he told Lily. 'I only brought him by because . . . Well, I felt I owed you some sort of peace offering. And I guessed you'd be drowning in flowers this morning.'

'Drowning in flowers? What do you mean?'

'Haven't you seen the drawing room?'

She shook her head. 'I've been working in here all morning. I told Swift I wasn't at home to anyone but you.'

A genuine grin stretched his cheeks. Oh, he was going to enjoy this. He rose, lifted the parrot's cage in one hand and offered the other to Lily. 'Come.'

He led her down the corridor and into the drawing room.

'Oh,' she said upon entering. 'Oh, my.'

From his cage, even the bird gave a whistle of admiration.

The Harcliffe House drawing room was, as drawing rooms went, a large one. Near palatial, really. And today it was full to bursting with grandiose flower arrangements. Roses, orchids, delphiniums in abundance—but overwhelming all of these, lilies. Lilies of every possible variety, covering every available surface and filling every niche.

'Between the parrot and the flowers, it's a veritable jungle,' Lily said. She turned to regard the bird hopping madly in its cage. 'Oh, do let him out. He must feel as though he's home.'

Julian obliged, setting the birdcage on the floor and opening the door. The bird didn't move.

111

Lily kneeled before the open cage, beckoning the reluctant bird. 'Come now, pet. Take a turn about the room.'

'Guilty, guilty!' the agitated parrot squawked. 'Thank you, that will be all!'

'Perhaps he's timid in a new place,' Julian suggested, helping Lily to her feet.

'Perhaps. We'll give him time.' She turned a slow circle in place, surveying the exotic flora. A laugh bubbled from her throat. 'All these lilies. They don't have much imagination, do they?'

'Perhaps not. But they do have unquestionably good taste.' Julian reached for a salver heaped with calling cards and hand-delivered notes.

She sifted through the correspondence. 'I can't imagine how word got around so quickly.'

'Can't you?'

Julian knew how word had got around so quickly. He'd spread it. After leaving Morland House last night, he'd taken those lieutenants to every gentlemen's club, gaming hall, and opera house in London, all the while leading them in a voluble discourse on the inexhaustible topic of Lady Lily Chatwick. Her beauty, elegance, virtue, good humor, and, most important of all, sudden availability. 'It's just as I said. The gentlemen are falling over one another to court you.'

'I'm not sure they're truly interested in that. After so much time out of circulation, I suspect I'm more of a curiosity at this point.'

Julian didn't know how to argue, because he suspected it was partly true. But once everyone had the chance to see how intelligent, lovely, and personable Lily was, idle curiosity would become keen pursuit.

112

'You should give some thought to the invitations.' He plucked a familiar-looking envelope from the heap. 'Start with this one.'

She opened it and scanned the contents quickly. 'An assembly next week at the Shelton rooms, hosted by Lord and Lady Ainsley. You've already heard of it?'

He nodded. His own invitation had arrived weeks ago. The assembly would be the last major social event before most families adjourned to the countryside for Christmas. Everyone who was anyone in London would be there, and it was unquestionably Lily's best opportunity to encourage suitors before the end of the year.

'You should attend,' he said. 'Most definitely.'

Her eyebrows arched. '*I* should attend? Don't you mean to say "we"?'

'Yes,' he forced himself to say. 'Yes, of course. *We* should attend.' Why was it so hard to say that word? Putting the two of them in one syllable . . . it just seemed imprudent, somehow. In the same way he should avoid being mashed together with Lily in a small, dark, enclosed space. No telling what would happen.

'Oh, Julian, look out!'

He ducked instinctively, an instant before the parrot swooped over his head.

'Oh, Julian,' the bird squawked, coming to land on an unused candelabra. 'Oh, Juuuuuulian.'

He glared at it. 'Don't "Oh, Julian" me.'

Lily laughed. 'I think I will keep him, if I may. He reminds me of you. Handsome, ruffled. Decked out in bright colors. A mimic.' Her eyes shone with merriment. 'Perhaps I'll name him after you, since he likes the sound of it so much.'

Julian couldn't even form a response to that. No polite response, at least.

'The assembly,' he said, reaching out to tap the invitation. 'We should attend.'

Her expression went pensive. 'It's been so long since I've danced. I don't know if I remember the steps.'

'You needn't dance at all if you don't care to. You can always use mourning as an excuse. I'll ward off anyone who pressures you.'

'There you go again. I don't want to be excused, or guarded. I want to dance.' Her chin took on a decisive set. 'Even if only for a few sets. Last night, I was unprepared for that party. So overwhelmed. This time, I want to show everyone I'm equal to the occasion.'

'So I see.' More than that, he sensed, she wanted to prove it to herself.

Of course she did. And why shouldn't she? Just like the bird currently swooping from candelabra to chandelier, Lily had too long been caged by habit and grief.

She had a loving, generous soul, and she was not a woman formed for a life of solitude. But by pressing the idea of matrimony so strenuously, Julian had only given her more reason to build up a defense. If he truly wanted to be her friend, to see her settled in a happy, healthy future—to see her *married*—he needed to stop shielding her and start empowering her. Lily didn't need protection from him. What she needed was confidence. Her chance to soar.

If he could give her that, Julian thought it just might be the truest accomplishment of his life.

She put her hands on her hips, scolding the

114

parrot through a smile. 'Come down from there, you cheeky thing!' Turning to Julian, she asked, 'Did I leave the walnuts in the study?'

He nodded. 'Shall I send a servant for them?'

'No. No, don't. Let him fly.'

Yes, he thought as he watched her flirt with the errant bird, what Lily needed was confidence. And oddly enough, confessing his attraction had been a first step. He should have thought of it long ago. Nothing made a woman more desirable than an awareness of her own desirability. He could note the difference already. A saucy cock of the hip, a mischievous crook of the finger. The subtle drop of her shoulders that emphasized her bosom. She was aware of her body in ways she hadn't been this time yesterday. With progress like this in a day's time, by next week she'd have the men of London at her feet.

And yes, the reality of that would turn Julian into a snarling, jealous beast. But for Lily's sake, he would take his turn in the cage.

'So will you help me?' she asked him suddenly. 'Practice dancing for the assembly, just a bit? Perhaps tomorrow, or—'

'No.'

She blinked.

'Not tomorrow, and not just a bit.' Smiling, he moved forward to take her hand. 'We'll start right now. We'll practice for as long as it takes. And then, at the assembly—Lily, you will show them all.'

Chapter Eight

Damn, it was good to have a direction. Real, physical work he could do for her. Even if that work was just shoving aside some furniture and rolling up the carpet while a parrot taunted from above.

Julian led her to the pianoforte in the corner. After removing an arrangement of lilies from the top, he ran one hand over the polished wood veneer. This was a remarkably fne instrument. Far superior to any he'd learned on in his youth. He'd never had a single lesson, nor even much opportunity to practice. But after a few hours sitting down to the thing—testing the keys and experimenting with intervals, learning how the contraption worked—he'd understood it and had simply been able to play. He could hear a tune with his ears, and his fngers just knew how to translate it into the proper sequence of keys.

Some said God had given him a gift. To Julian, it was much the same as his ability to reproduce voices—just one more function of having acutely trained ears. From the earliest days of his life, listening had always been his paramount task. He'd always been alert, *always* been listening. Their lives had depended on it.

'Julian,' she teased as he sat down to the instrument, 'you know actual music isn't required. Not for me, anyhow.'

'Humor me,' he said, shaking his fingers loose. 'How shall we begin?'

'The quadrille? Surely balls still begin with the quadrille?'

He nodded in confirmation. 'Place your hands flat atop the pianoforte. Lean against it, if you will.'

She complied.

'Now close your eyes.'

She did so, smiling.

His breath caught in his chest. 'God, Lily. You're so damned beautiful it hurts.'

She didn't react, of course. He'd known she wouldn't. But for whatever reason, he couldn't help testing her. It was the strangest thing. He'd been that way with his mother, too. Always testing her with outlandish comments made to her back: 'Look sharp, it's an elephant!' and such.

Setting the memory aside and placing his fingers to the keys, Julian played several bars of Le Pantalon, the first figure of the quadrille. When he stopped, Lily opened her eyes.

'How does it feel?' he asked.

'A bit unpleasant. It tickles all along my teeth.'

'But the rhythm. Did you recognize it? Can you visualize the steps?'

She nodded.

'Again,' he said. She closed her eyes, and he played through the same section, taking it a few bars further this time. Her fingers tapped along with the beat.

'Once more,' he directed at the end. 'This time, eyes open.' He played straight through to the end of the figure, holding eye contact with Lily as together they recited the steps. 'One, two, turn . . . ,' 'Now to the corner,' and so forth. At the conclusion of the sequence, he rose and offered his hand. 'Are you ready to try?'

Nodding her agreement, she took his hand. Together they moved to the center of the room and

117

queued up facing one another.

Their first attempt was over before it even began. They started with a deep, stately curtsy and bow, but when they lifted their heads, they found the parrot sitting on the floor between them, cocking his head and blinking a perplexed, beady eye. Lily dissolved into helpless laughter while Julian shooed the creature away.

They tried again, this time making it through a small section of the dance.

As they practiced the figure, the occasional feathered interruption overrode any awkwardness. For the most part. One particular segment of the pattern required them to link hands and circle one another, maintaining eye contact all the while. On each attempt, Julian lost his rhythm in those lovely eyes and stumbled over his feet. It took a half-dozen tries before they executed that turn successfully.

But they did eventually succeed, and Lily's pleasure in their mastery of the figure was clear. Using this method, they worked their way through each section of the quadrille. First, Julian would sit at the pianoforte and play the rhythm, and Lily would 'listen' with her hands. Then they would attempt the steps with varying success, avian antics depending.

The quadrille conquered, he suggested a particular country dance, one that had climbed to a new apex of popularity just this season past.

'It's all the rage,' he said. 'They're certain to include it at the assembly.'

'I never learned that one.' Lily worried her bottom lip with her teeth. 'But let's have a go.'

It was a disaster. Though the rhythm was simple,

118

the dance's pattern was lively and complex. Julian attempted to demonstrate both the lady's and gentleman's parts, but he could only be in one place at a time.

When Lily missed her entrance cue for the fourth time running, she threw up her hands in defeat. 'I'm sorry. I'll never learn this. I'm wasting your time.'

'No, you're not.'

She shook her head, obviously discouraged. 'I just can't seem to catch it. Popular or no, I'll have to sit this dance out.'

'Don't be distressed,' he said, grasping her by the elbows to prevent her from turning away. 'We'll try again later, or tomorrow. Every day until the assembly, if that's what's required. And it will go so much easier in a group, you'll see. With dancers on either side, you can take your cue from them.'

Her chin quavered, and frustration rose in his chest. It wasn't frustration with her, but with his inability to fix this for her. To fix everything for her.

'Lily,' he said. 'It's just a dance. You *can* do this. You can do anything.'

She sighed, shrugging away from his touch. 'There's not enough time. I shall have to stick to the dances I remember, never mind that they're a decade out of fashion. If only I could recognize each dance by the music, that is. This is hopeless.'

'No, it's not. I'll learn the order of dances ahead of time and write it down.'

'How will you do that?'

'Easily.' Simple matter of slipping a coin or two to the orchestra leader. 'You can keep the list folded in your glove. And we'll strategize, when it comes to arranging partners.'

119

'There's always waltzing,' she added. 'Surely I can manage a waltz with any competent partner. I needn't do anything but follow his lead.'

'True,' he agreed. 'We can make certain you're paired with someone you know. A good dancer. Morland would do.'

'Or you.'

He paused, momentarily struck mute by the thought of holding her in his arms, close and tight, while the entire *ton* looked on. 'Or me.'

'Can we try?' She looked to the pianoforte.

'But of course.'

He sat down to the instrument once again. This time, he allowed his fingers to linger, skimming over the tops of the ivory keys as he deliberated just what to play. Finally, he positioned his hands, closed his eyes, and simply let his fingertips decide. They coaxed from the instrument a slow, melodic waltz. He couldn't even remember where he'd heard it. Perhaps in one of those Austrian snuffboxes, with clockwork that produced tinkling tunes? The melody did have a Viennese lilt. As the progression built, he allowed the music to take over and surrendered to the beauty and haunting romance of the tune.

When he finally looked up, some moments after the final chord, he found Lily draped over the instrument, staring rapt at his hands. 'I've always loved watching you play,' she said. 'So much passion.'

He couldn't respond to that. So, wordlessly, he stood and offered her his hand.

They moved to the center of the room, and she tentatively placed her hand on his shoulder. His palm fit perfectly into the notch between her shoulder blades. She smelled of fresh dusting powder, and her eyes were a rich, deep brown. If it wouldn't sound so puppyish to say it, he might have compared them to burnt sugar. Dark, and all the sweeter for it.

In lieu of compliments, he gave her an appreciative smile. Then, without warning, he spun her into the waltz. Her little gasp of surprise thrilled him more than it ought. He loved the feel of her body, lithe and warm. The way they fit together, moved as one. She trusted his lead, and he swept her in confident turns about the floor.

'You waltz beautifully,' he told her, after they'd completed a few circuits of the room. 'You have nothing to fear. At the assembly, you'll be the object of admiration from every quarter.' He would make certain of it.

She pressed against his lead. 'That's enough, I think.'

He twirled her to a halt, but she didn't move away. Instead, she pulled their clasped hands closer, into the space between their chests.

Good. He needed that extra barrier. She was too close, and he was tempted to pull her closer still. His heart pounded a rhythm three times faster than the one their feet had so recently obeyed.

'Do you remember the night we first met?' she asked.

He bit back a laugh. Did he remember the night they met? Of course he remembered. He could have cited the date, the occasion, the warmth of the evening, the ruby-red shade of his waistcoat that night. The double twist of her pinned-up hair, the fourteen silk-covered buttons down the back of her gown. The precise moment he'd first seen Lily

Chatwick smile. He remembered *everything*.

He said, 'Remind me.'

'It was here, of course, at the house. Leo's birthday dinner.'

'Your birthday dinner, too.'

'Yes, but the guests were his. It was the night he started that ridiculous club with the stud horse, Osiris. Do you recall it now?'

He nodded.

'You watched me all that night. Through our conversations, at the dinner table, then over drinks afterward . . . You never took your eyes from me.'

'I was attracted to you. Haven't I confessed as much? You're a beautiful woman, Lily. I've always been attracted to you.'

'It seemed more than that.' She tilted her head, looking at him from a new angle. 'There was something almost predatory in your gaze that first night. I think you were forming designs on me.'

'Wh—?' His breath left him, and with it went any hope of denying the truth.

'Oh yes,' she said, her mouth curving in a subtle smile. 'I knew it. You followed me from the room, remember? Before we went into dinner, I excused myself to check on the place settings, and you followed me. Most brazenly.' Her cheeks colored with a blush, and her gaze flirted with his lapel. 'You've forgotten it, I'm sure. To you, it was just another idle flirtation. But it wasn't an everyday occurrence for me.'

'It should have been.'

'Yes. Yes, that's precisely what you said. I asked you if there was something you needed, and you said no.' She smiled. 'I was flustered by that arrogant smirk you wore, however well I know the

122

expression now. I asked you directly, "Why are you following me?" And you said . . .'

He gave in. 'I said, "Why are you surprised? When a beautiful woman leaves a room, she hopes a man like me will follow her."'

She gave his shoulder a playful smack. 'Exactly! And I was so angry with you.'

'No, you weren't. You were pleased.'

'I was not.' She gave him a coy glance through lowered lashes. 'Perhaps a little. I thought you would try to kiss me, but you didn't.'

'No.'

Julian never kissed a lady upon first flirtation. He preferred to let her simmer with the possibilities a little bit longer, imagine what *might* have occurred. He found it made her all the more receptive on second approach.

'I shouldn't admit this,' she said, 'but I felt certain you meant to seduce me.'

'Perhaps I did.' He said carefully, 'I've set out to seduce a great many women.'

'I know that. I *knew* that, and yet—somehow that only made it more thrilling. I lay awake all that night. I didn't know how I would react when I saw you again. I rehearsed polite demurrals and cutting setdowns, and . . .' She swallowed. 'And there was a part of me that didn't want to refuse.'

'Lily . . . ' He stepped back.

She held his hand fast, keeping him close. 'But I didn't need to refuse. The situation never arose. When I saw you next, you were friendly and polite. Even charming. But you never pursued me that way again. What changed?'

'Nothing changed.'

'Something must have changed. Was it you? Or

me?'

'Neither.' How could he explain? It was one thing for her to be generally aware of his reputation, and quite another for him to openly admit he'd spent those years methodically bedding his way through the wives of the English aristocracy, simply out of spite. And since the Marquess of Harcliffe had no wife, Julian had decided seducing his twin sister would suffice. But then he'd spent an evening in this house, where he'd been welcomed as an equal and a friend. Before the night was out, he was a charter member of London's newest, strangest, and most elite society: the Stud Club.

For those few precious hours, they'd made him feel he *belonged* here. In a way that Julian—a bastard child raised on the streets—couldn't remember feeling he'd ever belonged, anywhere.

'I suppose,' he said honestly, 'I decided I liked you too well to seduce you.'

She laughed with self-effacing charm. 'There's a compliment to me in there somewhere. If I think on it long enough, perhaps I'll make it out.'

Julian hated to offend her, but he could see no good way to end this conversation. A blunt exit was his only hope. 'I'm sorry, but I have business that requires my attention.' That wasn't prevarication. He was horribly late to his office, again. 'We'll practice again tomorrow.'

'Wait.'

What could he do? He waited.

'If I really intend to do this,' she said, picking at an invisible bit of fluff on his sleeve, ' . . . attend this assembly, invite the attention of suitors . . . I need practice with more than just dancing.'

He frowned, waiting for her to explain.

'I've lost all talent for flirtation. What little I possessed to begin with. I can't even remember the last time I was kissed.' She threw him a quick, guilty glance. 'Well . . . er . . . aside from the other morning, but that hardly counts.'

'Right.' Good Lord, would he never live that down?

Her words tumbled out in a breathy rush. 'Anyway, I just thought perhaps, since there was once a time when you actually meant to pursue me . . . and since you say you've always found me attractive . . . that maybe you wouldn't mind . . . kissing me now.'

He could only stare at her. Somewhere in that great chain of words, had she just asked him to kiss her?

'I'm sorry,' she said. 'I'm being ridiculous.'

He nodded. Yes, ridiculous.

She took a deep breath and began again, looking him full in the eye as she spoke. Her whole demeanor had changed. No girlish nervousness now, just direct communication, woman to man. 'Julian, let me be perfectly clear. In an embarrassing, utterly juvenile way, I am offering you the chance to kiss me. Just this once, without promise or penalty attached. Without the influence of sleeping powder.' Her voice dropped to a sultry whisper. 'Without interruption.'

She stared at his mouth, awaiting his response. Which made him stare at hers. Her lips were so pink and so plump and so alluring. And trembling, just a little, because despite the forthrightness of her request, she was frightened of what came next.

She was wise to be afraid. She wanted a kiss? He wanted more. So many impulses buffeted him. Not

125

just the tickling breeze of fancies, but full-force, catastrophic monsoons of desire. If she could see the images whipping through his mind, she would turn on her heel and run. In one instant, he wanted to hold her, wrap his body around hers, and protect her from the world. In the next, he wanted to strip her bare and ravish her completely. Possess her, lay waste to her, have her naked and quivering right here on the floor.

Truly, man? On the floor?

Yes, devil take it. He was that depraved. He wanted this elegant, noble lady who was thirteenth in line for the Crown, and he wanted her bared and panting on the waxed parquet. A kiss was what she asked, but for him—a kiss would not be enough.

And now Julian trembled, because he was a little scared, too.

At some point, he'd released her hand. Her touch had slid from his shoulder. They stood facing one another, arms dangling at their sides. They weren't even touching anymore. It ought to be easy to walk away.

Just like waltzing. Slide one foot back . . .

'A kiss, Julian. Just this once.' As his hesitation stretched, her brown eyes glimmered with hurt. 'Are you truly going to refuse?'

He closed his eyes. Sighed. Opened them again. And spoke the only word he could.

'No.'

The decision made itself. He lashed one arm around her waist, cinching her close. With his other hand he cradled her neck, tilting her lips to just the perfect angle.

Because this time, damn it—he was going to do this right.

126

Chapter Nine

Lily knew all about Julian Bellamy. He was a profligate seducer, an infamous rake, a devil-may-care scoundrel.

Who could have guessed the man would be so difficult to kiss?

First that disastrous lip-lock in the early morning yesterday, then their interrupted embrace at Morland House . . . Lily was hoping the third time would prove the charm. All morning, she'd been waiting for him to make the advance. She'd all but begged him to dance with her. She'd nudged the conversation down suggestive paths.

Finally, she'd decided to take matters into her own hands. And she'd juggled those matters clumsily, nearly dashing them to bits on the floor. But none of it mattered now. Because now his arm was around her, holding her fast, and his strong hand cupped the back of her neck. She'd just read that thrilling 'no' on his sensuous lips, and his eyes were full of affirmation. He wanted her, that intense blue gaze said. And this time, he meant to have her.

His lips met hers, and her eyes fluttered closed.

Yes, the third time was a charm.

The third time was pure *magic*.

He kissed her firmly, then softly. A bit too chastely for her preference. Lily felt herself growing impatient for more. But he refused to hurry, wouldn't heed the plaintive whimpers tickling the back of her throat.

No, he took the kiss slowly, leading the way with

127

tender, masterful care. Sipping first at her lower lip, then the upper. Teasing the corner of her mouth with his tongue, until her lips parted to release a sigh of pure delight.

His tongue slid inside her mouth, and she welcomed the gentle invasion. At first she tried to hold still, as it only seemed the hospitable thing. She'd invited him in, and the least she could do was facilitate his exploration. But as his tongue rubbed hers again and again, she found herself moving helplessly against him. Snaking her arms around his neck, nestling closer into his embrace.

Lily didn't have a great deal of experience to judge by, but from where she was standing . . . he was very, very good at this.

There was spice and a hint of sweetness in his kiss, and she curled one hand into his hair, drawing him close so she could savor it. How was it possible she could know a man so well, but only now be learning his taste? He thrust his tongue deeper, and she closed her lips around it, suckling lightly.

He groaned. She felt the sound rumbling from his chest. The low vibration played her ribs like piano keys, and the tune was a slow, sensual burlesque. They were dancing to it, the two of them, moving mouths and hips in a steady rhythm.

Her whole body sparked and snapped with sensation. Another lady might have thought to herself, *I can't wait to tell my friends how wonderful this is*. But instead Lily thought to herself, *I can't wait to tell Julian how wonderful this is*. She almost laughed at the irony. But she didn't dare let him in on her joke or pay him any pride-swelling compliments just yet. She was too afraid of breaking the spell, because . . .

Oh, because.

His hand had begun a slow, steady descent from the small of her back, down the curve of her hip, all the way to the bottom of her . . . well, of her bottom. He palmed one cheek of her backside and squeezed, lifting her up on her toes and pulling her flush against him. Taking the kiss to a whole new level.

His chest was hard; his abdomen, flat. She loved pressing against him, feeling her pliant, feminine contours mold around his solid male physique. And, wedged against her soft belly, the stiff ridge of his manhood made quite the impression. His obvious arousal only inflamed her own desire. Her nipples puckered to tight darts, jutting against the restrictive confines of her bodice. She imagined how they must look—red, puckered nubs standing out, desperate for attention. *His* attention. Because he would understand just how to soothe them.

As he claimed her mouth over and over, she writhed in his arms, trying to ease the ache in her breasts. The friction only stoked a different flame of need. One that burned deeper, darker. Distinctly lower, down between her legs.

This . . . this was true desire. This was animal lust.

This was never going to end. Not if Lily could help it.

She might be inexperienced, but she was hardly a ninny or a prude. She understood the sensation of arousal. She'd felt, many times, physical attraction to a man. But never before had she found herself in this kind of situation, where proximity and possibility worked their strange alchemy, transforming vague desire into urgent, undeniable *need*.

Her breathing, her hunger, even the beating of her heart . . . her every primal instinct centered on one goal. And Lily clung to it—to him—with both hands.

Until he let her go. Lifted his mouth from hers and released her with no warning whatsoever.

She swayed, unsteady on her feet. He grasped her by the shoulders and braced her with outstretched arms, holding her up. But also holding her away. Stunned, she blinked hard at his cravat, gasping for breath.

He dipped his head to catch her attention. 'Lily . . . ' His gaze was steeped with regret. 'Lily, I'm—'

'Don't.' She closed her eyes in defiance. At her sides, she clenched her hands in fists. 'Don't tell me you're sorry. I'm not sorry. I could never regret what just happened between us. It was wonderful, Julian. I haven't felt so alive in months. *Years*. And if you mean to apologize for it . . . to give me some nonsense about liking me too much to spare me the attentions you've lavished on half the female population of the *ton* . . . ' She sniffed. 'Please, just don't.'

Another, more prudent lady would be grateful he'd showed restraint. It *was* a true compliment, that Julian liked and respected her too much to seduce her. That he'd been attracted to her all this time, but he valued their friendship too much to act on that desire. He didn't want Lily to be just another garter decorating the club's billiard room. She understood. It was decent of him. She'd always known him to be a decent man, at heart. It was only . . . she'd just had her first taste of his *indecent* side.

And she'd liked it, a great deal.

Finally, she opened her eyes. Only to find him wearing a sheepish grin.

'Lily, I only meant to say . . . I'm sorry, but there's a damned parrot on my shoulder.'

She jerked her gaze to the right. There, from its perch on Julian's impeccably tailored sleeve, the bird in question swiveled its head and stretched its beak in a squawk.

Lily put a hand over her mouth, laughing into it until tears streaked her face. Tears of relief, more than amusement. 'Dratted bird,' she finally managed. 'What a nuisance you are.'

'Shall I take him away?'

'No, no. Just one more way he reminds me of you.'

'Brilliant.' With a gentle touch and soothing words, he coaxed the bird from his arm to his outstretched finger. He returned the parrot to its cage and latched the door.

When he came back to Lily, Julian's expression was serious. 'All joking aside, Lily. You know nothing can happen between us.'

'Something's already happened between us.'

He sighed. 'Nothing more.'

'Julian, please. I asked for one kiss. We shared one kiss. If it can never go further than that, I understand. All I'm asking is . . . don't dismiss what happened. Don't wish it away.' She reached for his hand. 'And don't leave. Or if you must go, take me with you. I don't want to be alone. I've been spending far too much time alone. We could go somewhere, anywhere . . . What about the theater?'

His surprise was evident. 'The theater?'

'Yes.' The idea took form as she spoke. 'Yes,

131

I want to go to the theater. I read in the paper they're doing something of Molière's at Drury Lane. I should like to see it. I haven't been to the theater in years.'

'Then why do you want to go now?'

'I just do. And you must take me. We made a bargain, Julian. You promised me three nights.'

'I promised three social events.'

'The theater *is* a social event,' she countered. 'One I thought you typically enjoy.'

To be truthful, the theater had never held a great deal of fascination for Lily, and even less after she'd lost her hearing. But she just knew she couldn't sit at home alone tonight, wondering where Julian was and whether he was safe . . . and now, when she slept, dreaming of his kiss. Since she didn't suppose she could conjure up a second last-minute dinner party in two days, the theater it must be.

At length, he said, 'Leo always had a box at Drury Lane. Unless you've loaned it out, I suppose it's been sitting empty.'

'Oh, dear.' Her stomach knotted. 'No. I can't go sit in Leo's box. It's just not right. Everyone will be staring and whispering about him, about me. I can't abide the thought of it.'

'Shall I find another box?'

'No, no. Everyone will still be staring. And they'll still be whispering. About Leo, about me, about why I'm not in Leo's box.' She blew out her breath. This hadn't been such a brilliant idea after all. 'Besides, I can't follow anything from his box. It's at an odd angle, and much too far above the stage. That's the reason I stopped attending years ago. I wish I could just go and sit on benches in the pit, the way the common people do.'

'Lily, you're the daughter of a marquess. You are not common people.'

'Sometimes I wish I were.'

He turned a meaningful glance around the room. Marking the expensive pianoforte, the silver-framed portraits on the wall, the gilt chandelier overhead. 'No, you don't.'

Her cheeks heated as she absorbed his gentle rebuke. Though he pointedly never discussed his past, she suspected that Julian had not always lived so affluently as he did now. She, by contrast, had always enjoyed a life of wealth and privilege. From an early age, she and Leo had been taught to be mindful of their advantages. She could hear Mother's litany in her ears: *Be grateful to God, humble before friends, charitable to those less fortunate.*

'I'm sorry,' she said, feeling churlish and small. Her eyes stung with frustration. 'I didn't mean to sound petulant.'

He caught her chin and tilted her face to his. 'You didn't. Just disappointed.' His gaze searched hers. 'This is really that important to you? A night at the theater?'

She nodded. It *was* that important to her, for reasons she didn't quite comprehend. 'If you'll take me.'

'I'm going to leave.' Releasing her chin, he warded off her protest with an open palm. 'But I will come back for you at seven. Be ready. Do something simple with your hair, and wear your plainest gown.'

'That's not how I would dress for the theater.'

'Precisely.'

She clapped her hands together. 'Oh, Julian. Are

133

we going to the theater in disguise?'

'No. Absolutely not. You're not attending the theater at all, Lady Lily Chatwick.' He gave her a crafty wink as he backed toward the door. 'A common woman is going in your place.'

He bowed. And then he was gone, leaving Lily alone with the thrill of anticipation, a full afternoon to dress, and one very interesting question. If a common woman was attending the theater tonight . . .

Just who would her escort be?

*   *   *

'Mr. James Bell. At your service, ma'am.'

When Julian returned to Harcliffe House that evening, Lily met him in the entry. He doffed his hat and made a deep bow. So deep that his rain-misted spectacles slid to the end of his nose, and when he straightened, he had to push them back up with a fingertip. An appropriately clerkish touch, he thought.

Lily clapped a hand over her laughter. 'No. It isn't you.'

'I don't know what you mean.' He pulled a serious face. 'I'm a lowly clerk, as you see. An overworked one, in desperate need of an evening's diversion at the theater.'

There was more truth to the guise than fiction, and exposing even this much made him nervous. It was an unpre ce dented risk, coming straight from his offices without even changing his attire. But this was important to Lily. Over the course of their friendship, he'd heard Leo lament many times that he couldn't coax Lily to the theater anymore.

134

Today, for the first time in years, she'd *asked* to go. And she wanted to watch from the seat that would best allow her to enjoy the performance. She deserved that much. As Julian Bellamy, he could never escort Lady Lily Chatwick to the pit of Drury Lane, where she would sit front and center, brushing sleeves with working men and their mistresses. They would draw too much notice. Her reputation would suffer, at best.

But as James Bell . . . he just might pull this off.

He cleared his throat. 'If you'd care to join me, miss, I've two seats reserved at Drury Lane, in the second row of the pit.'

'You don't say.' Wonderingly, she shook her head. 'I can scarcely credit the transformation. Your hair's so tame, and those clothes . . .' She gestured at his buff trousers and brown coat, his simple, unadorned boots. No buttons or tassels to be found. Her gaze made the slow climb back up to his face. 'Those spectacles!'

He wrinkled his nose and squinted up his eyes. 'Don't I look like a nondescript mole of a man?'

'Not at all. You're more handsome than ever.'

He waved off the remark, stepping over the threshold and into the entrance hall.

'No, I'm serious,' she said, her eyes still laughing. 'Have I never told you what a penchant I have for men wearing spectacles?'

He couldn't answer her. For he'd just peered at her through said spectacles, and the twin discs of glass might as well have been air, for all the protection they afforded him against her appearance.

Lily looked stunning. And not in an 'Oh, what a pleasant surprise' sort of way, but in a 'Help,

135

I've been clubbed with a mallet and am suffering visions' sort of way. She wore a diaphanous creation of peach gauze, held together with . . . with strands of ether, apparently, and seeded with an alarming number of brilliants and pearls. And the cut of the gown . . . If that squared neckline edged but a half-inch lower, Julian felt certain he—and any ogling passersby—would be treated to a tawny glimpse of areola.

The prospect left him breathless.

'That,' he finally managed to croak, 'is *not* your plainest gown. In fact, I don't think I have ever seen you wear a gown that so completely failed to approach the definition of plain.'

'I know,' she said. 'That's the point. *All* my gowns are plain. The only dresses anyone's seen me wear for months are black or gray or dark blue. Even before I entered mourning, my tastes were modest. That's why this is the perfect disguise.' She twisted in place, and the gown threw an audacious shimmer about the room. 'It's horrid, isn't it? It's been in my closet for years. I never wore it anywhere.'

'This will never work. Everyone in the theater will be staring at you.'

'They might stare at the dress, but they won't see *me* in it.' She ficked open an ivory fan, obscuring the lower half of her face. The mischievous quirk of her brow drew his attention up, to the cluster of overwrought ringlets piled high atop her head and tumbling loose around her ears.

'What have you done to your hair?' he asked. 'Lily, you were meant to look like a common*er,* not like a common—'

'Trollop? Why not?' She raised her eyebrows coquettishly. 'Surely a lowly, overworked clerk like

136

Mr. Bell deserves a treat for himself now and then?'

Oh, no. They would not play this game. They would *not*.

'Go upstairs and change,' he told her.

She lowered the fan, and her face fell. 'Do you know how long it took me to dress? We'd miss half the play.'

Julian bent his head and raised a hand to his brow. 'Holling!' he barked.

The stout, middle-aged house keeper took her time shuffling out—presumably to belie the fact that she'd been standing just on the other side of the door.

'Yes, Mr. Bellamy? Can I help you, sir?'

'Holling, have you a winter cloak? Something drab and utilitarian?'

'No, sir. My winter cloak is ermine, lined with silk.' The corner of her mouth twitched.

He cut her a droll look. 'Why, Holling. It's your annual fare of personality.' He tsked. 'Subdue it, please, and just fetch the cloak. Her ladyship requires loan of it.'

'Yes, sir.' The house keeper curtsied and left. A minute later she returned with an armful of heavy wool in a dark shade, the ideal hue between charcoal gray and beef-drippings brown.

'Perfect,' he said, taking the cloak from Holling and promptly swinging it around Lily's slender shoulders. Thanks to the disparity in the two women's body shape, he could nearly wrap the thing around her twice.

As he fastened the ties and tucked in the edges, wrapping her tight as an Egyptian mummy, Lily's bottom lip protruded in a pout.

When he yanked the hood up over her curls, she

137

frowned down at her shapeless woolen cocoon. 'I look like a charred potato.'

'Ah, yes. Wholesome.'

'Lumpy.'

'Come along, then. I have the costermonger's wheelbarrow waiting just outside.'

Despite herself, his charred potato quivered with laughter. As he could not offer her his arm, Julian gave her a stiff thump on the shoulder, prodding her into motion. She turned her back to him and shuffled toward the door.

'I'll repay you for this,' he heard her growl.

'No doubt.' He smiled, and was further amused to catch Holling smiling, as well. 'What is it, Holling? Are you ill?'

She shook her head.

'It's the bird, isn't it? You're vexed about the bird.'

'No, sir. Well, perhaps a bit, but . . . ' The older woman sniffed and wiped her eye. 'I'm sorry, Mr. Bellamy. It's been too long since her ladyship enjoyed herself, that's all.'

Dear devoted Holling. Julian was glad Lily had her. And now, he was mildly regretful about the bird.

'She'll enjoy tonight,' he assured the house keeper. 'I'll see to it.' If there was one thing he knew well, it was how to keep a lady entertained. His challenge would be ensuring that *he* didn't enjoy the evening too much. Memories of their kiss had haunted his every thought that day. They would likely do so for years to come. And good Lord, that gown . . .

Holling helped the cause of restraint by sending him out the door with a pocketful of guilt. 'Thank

138

you, sir,' she said. 'It's an unconventional outing, but I believe the late Lord Harcliffe—God rest his soul—would approve.'

With a grim sigh, Julian tugged down the brim of his hat. Leo, approve of this? He sincerely doubted it.

Chapter Ten

They were late for the curtain, just as Julian had planned. Much better to enter the theater during the preliminary entertainment, when most eyes were hopefully fixed on the stage instead of idly roaming the crowd.

The hack let them out near the side entrance. Here was another helpful factor in maintaining their disguise—the theater had separate entrances for separate classes of ticket-holders. Members of the gentry and nobility occupied the boxes and entered through the grandest, most central way. Their servants climbed a steep, humble staircase to the shilling seats in the gallery. And those with three bob to purchase a seat in the pit—tradesmen, scholars, occasionally their wives and more often their mistresses—entered through this passageway.

He paid their entrance at the door. Halfway down the tunnel, Lily pulled up and refused to budge.

'Not until you un-truss me,' she insisted, screwing up her lips to send a burst of breath upward, toward a stray ringlet dangling between her eyebrows like a sausage link. Her huff briefly lifted the curl but failed to dislodge it. 'This is ridiculous,' she said. 'I

139

need the use of my arms.'

After a moment's pause, during which he considered the inherent dangers of removing his glove, putting a hand to her fair, lovely brow, and tending to the stray lock himself . . . Julian capitulated. He released all but the uppermost ties. Immediately, she reached up with one elegant, white-gloved hand to brush the impertinent ringlet aside. A ray of peach iridescence burst from the brown-gray wrap.

'You must keep it on,' he admonished, tugging the garment tight around her shoulders in case the tunnel's dim lighting prevented her from understanding his words. 'The hood as well.'

She signaled agreement with a nod.

When they reached the house, Julian scanned for the two boys he'd paid to reserve their seats. There they were, in the center of the second row, staring slack-jawed as a mustachioed man led a trio of trained poodles through their paces on stage. Just viewing their wide-eyed expressions, Julian paused, reluctant to disrupt the boys' enjoyment. But then the younger one caught sight of him, elbowed his friend, and together they rushed to vacate the seats, hungry for their promised shillings. Much as they liked the entertainment, they wanted the coin—and the food it would purchase—more.

Julian slipped each boy a crown instead. He could well remember that hunger. At their age, he would have waded through molten lava to retrieve a sixpence. A sixpence was a true windfall—it meant three trips through the soup line for him and Mother, *each*. More like four for him and two for her, because she always spooned some of her portion into his bowl. They could have dined on a crown for weeks.

As the trained poodles departed the stage, Julian shook off those cold, hungry memories and laid a hand to Lily's back. He ushered her to their place on the velvet-padded bench. A juggler in classic harlequin garb took the stage for a few minutes. After his routine, the lights dimmed a touch.

As the curtain rose on the play proper, Lily leaned close. Her warm breath stirred against his ear. *'Thank you.'*

Just as quickly as she'd come, she slid away. But her arm lingered, grazing his. Suddenly, Julian was reliving a different part of his youth—those heady adolescent years when he'd lived for the slightest brush of female skin, a whiff of sweet perfume, or a furtive glimpse of stocking-clad ankle. That exhilaration of first contact was hard to recapture now. As a consequence of his exploits over recent years, he'd grown jaded, and precariously close to bored, when it came to women on the whole.

But Lily was different. A mere glance from her could be a thorn to his side or a balm to his soul, depending. She could voice but a syllable, and it was like silk sliding over his skin. And nothing thrilled him more than simply seeing her content. That whispered thanks against his ear made the whole night worthwhile. Honestly, it probably redeemed the better part of his year.

Absurdly choked with emotion, he slid his gaze toward her. She sat with her head tilted up, staring at the actors on stage. Her eyes were bright with reflected stage lamps, and the hood of her cloak had slipped back, revealing a mass of dark curls and her dusky, parted lips. She was lost in the performance, utterly absorbed.

For his part, Julian didn't hear a word of the play.

*   *   *

'My goodness,' Lily said, 'did you not hear a word of the play?' She took Julian's arm as they moved to exit the theater. Departing guests crushed on all sides, forcing them closer together. 'How could you fail to have an opinion?'

'What opinion can one have on a comedy? Either it amuses or it doesn't.'

'But that's not true. A comedy can have all manner of themes and meanings. Take the character of Tartuffe, for example, and his disguise of false—'

Lily's remark was cut short when a theatergoer jostled her from behind. She stumbled, but Julian pulled her up and steadied her elbow with his free hand. When she'd regained her balance, he pivoted her to face him.

'Are you well?' he asked.

She wasn't sure. The look in his eyes—blue and brimming with intense concern—made her weak in the knees all over again. Goodness. This must be the look he used to seduce women. That look said, *If you are hurt, I am hurt. If something is broken, I will fix it. Tell me your great toe is sore, and I will walk to Shropshire to gather herbs for a poultice.* Sir Walter Raleigh had made these eyes at the queen before throwing his cape over that mud puddle. Lily was sure of it.

At length, she nodded. 'I'm fine. Thank you.'

He frowned and gestured in the vicinity of his brow. 'Your hair is showing.'

142

With an exasperated tug, Lily drew the woolen hood up and over her curls. Really, if there were people of her acquaintance in attendance, they were not likely to be scanning the crush of humanity in the pit. And, even if there were, the chances of one of them marking Lily out in the crowd were slim indeed.

They exited through the same tunnel by which they'd entered. When they emerged, they found the night cold and dark. Moisture fizzled in the air—not quite rain, not quite fog. Now and then, a knife-edged gust of wind cut straight through the protection of Holling's thick cloak.

'We'll find a hack just up here,' he said.

Despite the stinging mist, Lily kept her face up and her eyes open wide. The stream of people exiting the pit flowed through an entirely different channel than the route she was accustomed to following. They turned onto a narrow street, lined with little shops. Street vendors waved to them from both sides—standing under burning oil lamps, hawking roasted nuts and steaming pies, snuff for the gentlemen, flowers for the ladies, ballads for lovers.

Her eye was drawn to a Romany woman dressed in vibrant silks and carrying a basket of cut flowers. Her smoky eyes promised intrigue and romance. As Lily passed, the old gypsy woman held out her palm and raised a brow.

Lily tugged Julian's arm, pulling him to a halt. 'Let's have our fortunes told.'

He gave her a disbelieving look as people streamed around them.

'Come on,' she said. 'Why not?'

'Because it's late and cold and raining, and if we

stand about chatting with shady street merchants, I predict with certainty you'll catch a chill.'

She smiled patiently. 'Fortunately, I do have a rather formidable cloak.'

Lily knew it was late, and the weather was harsh. Truth be told, she was shivering violently in this gray woolen cocoon. But she just couldn't bear the thought of the evening being over. After this night, he'd only promised one more.

She shook herself, unwilling to dwell on that thought. It neighbored too close to desolation.

Working beneath her cloak, she tugged one hand from its glove and stretched it toward the fortune-teller. 'Give her a coin, won't you?'

Julian grabbed for Lily's hand instead. He turned it palm-side-up in his gloved grip and said, 'If it's a fortune you want, I'll read it.'

The sudden contact left her breathless. 'Oh.'

A fingertip clad in warm, close-fitting kid leather slid over the lines of her palm. Suddenly, the night didn't seem so chilled anymore.

'A long life,' he said, tracing a line from the crook of her thumb to the outer edge of her palm. 'Good health and happiness.' He lifted her hand and pretended to peer at it. 'Ten . . . No, eleven.'

'Years?'

'Children.'

'Eleven children?' A burst of laughter escaped her. 'Goodness. By whom?'

'By your husband, of course. In your future, I see you taking a very dependable, respectable, faithful husband.' Droplets of moisture dotted the glass in his spectacles. She couldn't make out the expression in his eyes.

'He sounds terribly dull.' She couldn't help but

144

tease. 'Is he perchance a clerk?'

He dropped her hand, and the air between them was suddenly heavy with awkwardness.

'At least buy me a flower?' she said.

He fished a coin from his pocket and tossed it in the gypsy woman's basket, withdrawing a single mist-glazed rose. 'Here,' he said, presenting it to her wrapped in a ribbon of irony. 'Because the hundreds of blooms in your drawing room are growing lonely.'

'I like this one best.' She took it in her ungloved hand, and together they continued on.

Lily glimpsed a row of hackney cabs waiting up ahead. Too close. She couldn't bear to let him go just yet. She stopped abruptly.

Again, he turned to her, plainly confused. 'Lily, is there something you want?'

Words failed her. What could she say? She hardly knew what she wanted, much less how to ask for it. Time. She just wanted time. Time spent with him, exploring this delicious, palpable attraction and the meaning of it all.

'Julian, when you were staring into my palm . . .'

He nodded, swallowing hard.

'Did you perchance see dinner in our future? I'm positively famished.'

'I'm certain Holling will have—'

'No, no. I don't want to wait that long. I'm hungry now. Surely there are shops hereabouts that cater to theatergoers.'

'There are, I'm certain. None of them are fit for you to visit.'

'Me?' She smiled. 'But you forget, I'm a common woman, sir. I dine in these establishments all the time.' To her left, a leaded glass window threw diamonds of yellow light onto the pavement. Lily peered through the open door. A greasy aroma wafted out, mingled with the sharp tang of spirits. 'What about this place? Is it a cook-shop? Or an ale house?'

Julian frowned. 'A bit of both, and then some other things besides. If it's a label you're looking for, "Den of Iniquity" would likely cover it.'

'Excellent. I'm absolutely starved for some iniquity.' She dropped his arm and walked through the open door, knowing he would follow.

Chapter Eleven

Julian followed her, of course. What choice did he have?

Catching up to her in the entryway, he grasped her by the elbow and wheeled her around. She tottered on her heels. For a brief moment, he considered throwing her over his shoulder and carrying her straight out the door. Then he found himself enjoying that image, far too much.

'No,' he said simply. To her or to himself, he didn't know.

'It doesn't look so bad,' she said, darting a glance about the place. 'Let's stay.'

Julian surveyed the place. She was right; it didn't look so bad. The room was crowded with a number of tables, stools, benches and the occasional straight-backed chair. About half of the tables were occupied with couples or chatty groups of men, many of whom clutched playbills in their hands.

'Very well,' he said, resigned. 'Just dinner.'

Because truthfully, he didn't want to take her home. In the theater, with the peerage hovering above them, he'd suffered the constant fear of discovery. But in a place like this, it was so easy to imagine that there was nothing to fear. That she was just his sweetheart, and he was simply . . . himself. He wanted to revel in the illusion of honesty, if only for a while.

He chose a small table in the furthest, most isolated corner of the room. Once they were seated, a serving girl made her way to them.

'Have you beefsteak?' Julian asked her.

'Yes, sir. Also joints of mutton, and a very fine fish pie.'

'Is the beefsteak truly beef? You know, from an actual cow?'

'Julian!' Lily chided.

He raised a brow. 'You never know in these places.' To the girl, he said, 'Two of the steak, then. Ale for me, and spruce beer for the lady.'

'Spruce beer,' Lily muttered. 'What am I, twelve years of age?' She motioned for the serving girl's attention. 'That'll be wine for me, thank you.'

They waited in hungry silence. Looking around the room, looking at each other. Their gazes collided, and his face warmed with an unaccountable blush. God, he truly was like a youth again.

'I've just decided something,' she said. 'What to name the parrot.'

Please, not 'Julian.' Please, not 'Julian.' He couldn't bear to think that once he was gone from her life, his legacy wore feathers. Better to be forgotten entirely.

'I'm going to call it Tartuffe.'

147

He chuckled with relief. 'Excellent choice. Very clever.'

After another minute, their food and drink arrived.

'There's something I've been meaning to ask you,' she said, sawing away at her steak. 'I've been putting the subject off, but I suppose I feel emboldened tonight. There's no one in this place to overhear.' She gulped her wine, then stared into it. 'This helps, too.'

Julian wondered what in the world she was on about. He was a little afraid to find out.

'Did my brother have a . . . Well, did he have someone special?'

'What do you mean?'

'You know, a . . . ' Her cheeks colored. 'I truly don't mean to be nosy, and I don't want details. It's just that if Leo had a longstanding . . . you know. Someone who perhaps depended on him financially? I would like to set aside a legacy from the estate, but it must be done before my cousin arrives in England.'

Julian shook his head slowly. 'I don't know.' It was the truth, and he'd never been more blissful in ignorance. Of all the conversations he wouldn't want to have with Lily.

To be sure, there'd been many nights when he and Leo met for drinks at the club and then pointedly went their separate ways. But they'd never discussed details. Julian had always avoided asking about Leo's *affaires* because he'd rather not open the topic of his own. Leo was a principled, loyal sort. While Julian had his reasons for pursuing the women he did, he wasn't especially proud of himself for it. He would have felt downright

148

shabby discussing his conquests with Leo. Though he'd never explicitly asked, he'd always assumed Leo had a regular mistress whom he kept housed and comfortable somewhere in Town. That was why Julian had been surprised to hear of Leo approaching a Covent Garden prostitute on the night of his death. It seemed so out of character, and now Julian wasn't sure of anything.

'I'm sorry,' he said. 'If he did have someone, I don't know her name.'

'Oh. Well, I had to ask.' She reached for her wine again.

As she drank, Julian relaxed, pleased to escape this topic of conversation unscathed. He cut a large bite of steak and stuffed it into his mouth, just to preclude further inquiry.

Lily gave her own meat a thoughtful jab with her fork. 'I'm thinking of taking a lover.'

He choked on his steak.

Her eyebrows lifted. 'What? People do it all the time. *You* do it all the time. Why shouldn't I?'

Julian could think of a hundred reasons, but they were all currently dammed behind an unchewed hunk of beef. For the moment, he couldn't speak— only listen.

'I know what you'll say,' she went on. 'You're so convinced I should marry. But I don't want to settle down, Julian. I want to *live*. When we kissed this afternoon, it was magical. I feel awakened now. And not roused by the first rays of dawn, either. It's like my eyes have snapped open to greet the full light of noon. Everyone else is out there living, and I've been sleeping the day away.'

She put down her knife and fork. The edge of her cloak slipped back, exposing her pale, perfect

149

shoulder and a wispy peach-colored sleeve. With her fingertip, she traced the edge of her wineglass, circling round and round in a seductive manner.

'Yes,' she said. 'I think taking a lover will be just the thing.'

Good Lord. What had he done?

Lily was a sensual woman. Julian had always been exquisitely aware of it. Now he'd made *her* exquisitely aware of it. That awareness should have been a good thing, when properly directed toward eligible suitors who might make suitable husbands. But instead of placing her in company with those sorts of gentlemen, he'd brought her alone to the theater. And now to dinner in a seedy ale house, amidst a clientele that was growing rougher by the minute.

He was an idiot. He needed to get her out of here. Just as soon as he managed to swallow this damned piece of steak. Bloody hell. Had the beast been raised on India rubber? His eyes watered as he furiously chewed.

'You can't do that,' he managed to croak around the remainder of his bite, shaking his head for emphasis.

'I don't believe I asked your permission.' She propped her chin on her hand and gave him a coy smile. 'What's the matter? Don't you think gentlemen will find me attractive enough?'

He rolled his eyes and reached for his ale. She knew very well that wasn't his objection.

She looked at him through lush, lowered lashes. Her wine-stained lips made a silky, sulky pout. 'God only gives us one life, Julian. From this point forward, I intend to make the most of every minute.'

With a long draught of ale, he washed down the last of the steak. Finally.

'Good *Lord*,' he said, slamming the mug to the table. Empowerment be damned, he was taking control. 'First, no more wine for you. Second, you are not taking a lover. Third, fix that cloak. We're leaving. Now.'

But she hadn't understood him. Her attention had turned. To the wall, of all things.

'Do you feel that?' she said, placing her hand to the flat surface. 'It's music, isn't it?'

He nodded. It *was* music, emanating from the establishment next door. The fiddling had begun some time ago, but the intensity and volume had suddenly increased. Now a thunder of footfalls joined the instruments, rattling the silver on their plates.

'Dancing,' she said, lighting up with surprise. 'They're dancing.' She looked to him, all but leaping from her seat. 'Let's go.'

Once again, she fled before he could argue against the wisdom of such an activity. Swearing to himself, Julian threw a few coins on the table and gave chase. He followed as she dashed into the street and hurried on to the next shopfront. He caught her by the waist.

'Lily, no. We're not dancing here.'

'Can't you see?' she said brightly, staring past him into the tavern. 'It's the same country dance. The one you tried to teach me earlier.'

Julian followed her gaze. Inside, a dozen couples lined the narrow floor, stomping and twirling and clapping as they danced a lively pattern. It was indeed the same country dance they'd tried—and failed—to work through in the drawing room.

151

'I can *feel* it, Julian.' She placed her hand to the windowpane, which shivered in time to the beat. 'The rhythm's bouncing all through my bones. You have to let me try.'

'This is no place for a lady.'

'No one knows I'm a lady.'

She grasped his hand and tugged, catching him off-balance. His boot skidded on the damp cobblestone of the lane, and he stumbled to regain his footing without losing her hand. By the time Julian stood solidly upright again, they were inside. Dancing.

And Lily danced beautifully. Just as he'd predicted during their practice session, she had a much easier time following the steps with ladies lined up beside her. They joined the dance at the end of the line, and Lily threw back the hood of her cloak. She watched the other dancers carefully, taking her cues from them and copying their movements. Which allowed Julian to stare openly at her. He loved watching her unabashed enjoyment, almost as much as he admired the fearless spirit with which she embraced the challenge. When she made the inevitable misstep, she made a breathless, laughing apology to the green-clad man at her corner—and Julian could tell, that green-clad man would be delighted for Lily to tromp on his boots all night. In fact, he could sense every man in the room strategizing how to engage her for the next dance.

But when the music stopped, Lily gave them no opportunity. She flew to Julian's side, as if she belonged to him. Meaningless as the gesture was, it swelled him with triumphant pride.

She pressed against him, panting for breath.

152

'There now. Did I do well?'

'You were magnificent.'

A look of satisfaction graced her face. A bright flush painted her cheeks and her brow glistened with perspiration. 'I can't remember the last time I had so much fun.'

'Neither can I.' And what a surprise that was. He'd promised Holling that Lily would enjoy tonight, but what Julian hadn't realized was how much he would enjoy it, too. While they were dancing, he'd felt almost . . . carefree. He couldn't recall that word describing his emotional state, ever.

And God, she was so beautiful. He wanted to touch her so damn badly. He compromised by reaching up to tease an errant curl. The ringlet gave a voluptuous, undulating bounce. Her gaze softened, and her mouth . . . her mouth was the shape of a kiss. Not a chaste pucker, but a lush, pouting kiss a man could sink into for days.

The moment slowed. Stilled.

Shattered.

A voice behind him sent chills down his spine, freezing him where he stood.

'Mr. Bell?' the unseen someone called, from a distance of mere paces away. 'Mr. Bell, is that you?'

Bloody hell.

The instinct of self-preservation was a powerful force. Julian didn't stop to wonder which of his employees or business associates had recognized him. He didn't ponder the implications of his two lives colliding in this crowded tavern, or even pause to think of some witty, deflective remark that might have fixed everything.

He didn't think at all. He acted.

153

'Let's get out of here.' He slid an arm around Lily's waist, whirled her around, and pulled her straight into the thickest knot of dancers, weaving through the crowd.

'Mr. Bell!' the voice called again, closer this time. 'Mr. Bell, it's me!'

Deuce it all. It was Thatcher, his secretary at Aegis Investments. He would know that voice anywhere, and of course the man would recognize him in any crowd. Here Julian had been so concerned about Lily being recognized, he hadn't thought to conceal himself. So bloody stupid. He briefly cursed himself for paying his employees such generous wages that they had coin to toss away on ale and dancing. Thatcher would be on starvation pay, from this day on.

A hand touched his shoulder.

Julian swiveled his head.

Thatcher grinned. 'Mr. Bell, it *is* you. We've a table just there. Come join us, if you will. Can I buy you and your lady a—'

Julian gritted his teeth and shook his arm free. 'Thatcher, damn you. Not now.'

Then he pressed ahead in the opposite direction. Lily hadn't heard Thatcher, she hadn't heard him. She knew nothing, and he was determined to keep it so.

'This way,' he said, tugging her to the back of the room and through a narrow corridor. They passed by a small, crowded kitchen and through a storeroom, where Julian located a back exit through a narrow door.

They emerged into the alleyway. It was a step down to the pavement, and Lily stumbled a bit as he hurried her into the street. Julian tightened his arms about her delicate form, and together they reeled to a stop just before colliding with a brick wall.

He gasped for breath, looking over his shoulder to make sure they hadn't been followed. Light shone through the open door, casting a cone of illumination into the dark alleyway. With his heart drumming in his ears, Julian scanned the surroundings.

No one, thank God.

'Did that man in the brown suit know you?' she asked, twisting in his arms. 'Is he a friend of yours?'

'No.' Damn it. Wrong answer. The correct one would have been, *What man? I didn't see any man. There was no man.*

'Then why did he follow us? And why have you brought me out here?' She looked to the sky and shivered. 'Perhaps we should go back inside.'

'No.' He cinched his arms about her waist, pinning her close. 'We can't.'

'Why not?' In the dark, her pupils were wide and inquisitive.

He had to do it. He had to supply some reason for dragging her out here, and he had to stop the flow of questions from her lips. Really, it was the only way.

He dipped his head and brushed his lips against hers. 'Kiss me. Just kiss me.'

Again and again, he feathered light, teasing caresses of his lips against her mouth. Just the merest suggestions of a kiss. She went soft in his arms, releasing a sigh of pleasure.

'Kiss me, Lily,' he whispered, teasing the seam of her lips with a flick of his tongue. Telling her what he wanted in clearer terms than spoken words. 'Let

155

me know that you want this. Kiss me.'

He stopped, pressing his brow to hers. Their breath mingled in the ribbon-thin gap between their lips. He wanted to kiss her again. He wanted so much more than that. God, how he *wanted*. But if this went any further, it had to be because she wanted it, too.

Kiss me, he silently pleaded. *The* real *me. The man who cares nothing for clubs or parties or the current style. The man who spends all day thinking of you, wondering where you are and what you're doing and what it is you're thinking. The man who wants nothing more in this life than to come home to you after a day's honest work and listen to anything and everything you have to say before sweeping you off to bed.*

Kiss me.

Arching her neck, she pressed her lips to his, just softly. Then retreated. Teasing him as she'd been teased.

'That's it,' he murmured, nearly mad with the effort of holding back. He nuzzled closer, letting his breath warm her cheek and lips. 'More.'

And there came an instant—a blissful instant—where the air around them took on an electric charge, or the night warmed a degree with revelation. Somehow, he just knew it was going to happen.

Still, he wasn't prepared for it to happen so *fast*.

She flung her arms around his neck. Caught off-balance, Julian stumbled a step in reverse. She tightened her arms around his shoulders, stretched up on her toes, and gifted him with a warm, passionate, open-mouthed kiss. His lips fell apart, and she slid her tongue between them, exploring his

156

mouth with an innocent, fearless passion.

He was, honestly, more than a little surprised. But he was not complaining.

He let her have her way, forcing himself to be patient as she tentatively swept her tongue against his, over and over again. So delicious. She tasted of wine and that essential Lily sweetness he'd sampled earlier that day. But there was something new in this kiss. Determination had replaced curiosity. She kissed him not only to satisfy needs of her own, but to incite need in him.

And damn, was it working. He craved her like nothing he'd ever known. That mad rush of blood and energy that had fueled their escape—rather than dissipate, it took new purpose, surging all through his body and centering in his groin. Julian couldn't think; he could only act. He kissed her back, taking control of the embrace by fisting his hands in the heavy wool of her cloak and pulling her tight against his chest.

'Wait,' she said, tearing her mouth from his and stepping back. Her fingers went to the ties of her cloak. 'This thing is unbearable.'

'Don't. You'll catch a chill.' He turned his palm to the heavens in demonstration, and a few droplets of rain collected in his hand.

'You'll keep me warm.'

The cloak fell to the wet, filthy ground. The instant it hit the cobblestones, Julian knew the garment was irretrievable. *Deepest apologies, Holling.*

'There's no one to see,' she said. 'No one but you.' The brilliants and pearls sewn into her gown sparkled and flashed. 'I want you to see. I only wore it for you.'

157

He groaned as she ran her hands down the bodice, smoothing her palms over her slight breasts and hips.

'Well? How do I look?'

Stupefying. Words failed him for a moment. Until at last, he peeled his tongue from the roof of his mouth. 'Like the most brilliant, beautiful star in the heavens, fallen to earth.'

She laughed, drawing closer. 'It's too dark. I have no idea what you're saying, but I love the way you're looking at me. As if you're not even seeing the dress, but what's beneath it.' She picked up his hand where it dangled at his side, then pulled it to her waist. 'Put your hands on me.'

He did. Devil take him, he put his hands all over her. Skimming her trim waist and gently rounded hips, reaching up to cup one pert, perfect handful of breast.

And he kissed her, hard. So hard, her head recoiled with the force of it, and for a terrible moment he feared he'd hurt her. But then she moaned eagerly around his tongue, renewing her own efforts with vigor. Giving him back as good as he gave. She wound her fingers into his hair. Her fingernail scraped the flesh behind his ear, sending a sharp burst of pain to sweeten the pleasure. He would find a mark there tomorrow. Proof he hadn't imagined it all.

Good Lord, this was happening. Really, truly, disastrously . . . *finally* . . . happening.

He bent his head and pressed his lips to her exposed throat, reveling in the heat and scent of her skin. His tongue flicked over her pulse as he murmured her name. 'Lily. *Lily.*'

'I lied to you earlier,' she whispered, between

158

arousing gasps and sighs of pleasure. 'I haven't been thinking of taking a lover. I've been thinking of you.'

'I can't do this,' he murmured, even as he traced her jaw with his tongue. Bollocks. He was already doing this, and he was primed to do far more on the slightest encouragement.

And encouragement was what she gave. Nothing slight about it.

'I can't stop thinking of you. All day long, all yesterday for that matter. Ever since that first kiss. I can't concentrate. I'm so restless in my own skin. When I close my eyes, all I see is you. All I feel is this.' She kissed his temple, his cheek. 'I don't know what's happened to me, but I *need* this, Julian. I need you.'

Sweet heaven. He felt like he'd been waiting his whole life to hear those words. A fount of bliss and lust opened up inside him. He couldn't dam it now. It just wasn't in his power. Perhaps he juggled two identities, but he was only a man, at the base of both. A man who went after what he wanted—and he'd wanted her for so damned long. What restraint he possessed had been exhausted earlier that afternoon, walking away from her in the drawing room—and there, he'd had the added inducements of servants about, full daylight to reveal them, Leo's ghost, and a judgmental parrot dangling from the gilt chandelier. Here, in this alley, they were just a man and a woman, stripped down to essentials. Anonymous. Libidinous.

Nothing could stop him here.

Possibilities churned furiously in his mind. He could have her, just for one night. Satisfy her curiosity, slake his own need. Just this once. He

159

could protect her from consequences; he was expert at preventatives. If he experienced a sudden attack of conscience, they could simply refrain from actual intercourse. He needn't physically join with her to give her pleasure.

God, the vivid images that thought inspired . . . A groan scraped from his throat.

But where? There was no good place. This was *Lily*. He could not take her to Julian Bellamy's house, the scene of so many illicit liaisons. He would never allow her near James Bell's humble rooms. A hotel? Too public. A carriage? So sordid.

'Take me home,' she said, intuiting his dilemma. 'Just see me home, then stay. No one will notice. No one will care.'

Her house. Leo's house. Inconceivable. He might as well dig up the man's coffin and spit on it. 'Swift would murder me.'

She launched herself into his arms, sending him back against the brick wall. He landed with her straddling his leg, the luscious swell of her thigh rubbing against his arousal. Pleasure blanked his brain. He grasped her backside, rocking her pelvis against his. How could something feel so unbelievably good, but still be not nearly enough? He needed more from her. He needed all of her. There had to be somewhere they could go.

She licked his ear, and he bit back a growl.

Here. There was here.

'Greedy bastard!'

The shout from the end of the alley froze him in place. Lily, oblivious to the interruption, kept right on tracing the contours of his ear with her tongue, greatly impeding his ability to think. Had a man from inside followed them? Or was this someone

160

new?

' 'Ere now, lass,' the man called. 'Give us some o' that, eh?'

Julian's stomach turned. Not only from the quite deserved implication that he was about to use Lily like a cheap whore in the street, but because the accent marked the man a Scot.

There were thousands of Scotsmen in London. Thousands.

Still, Julian couldn't help but wrench Lily away and crane his neck for a glimpse of the shadowy figures disappearing into the mist. Two large, densely muscled men. As they moved around the corner and through the feeble illumination of a lamp, Julian thought he caught the light glinting off a smooth, hairless head.

Two men. Large brutes, the both of them. One a Scot, the other bald.

Jesus Christ. After all his futile searching . . . Could it be Leo's murderers had finally found *him*?

Chapter Twelve

Lily hardly knew what was happening. One moment, she and Julian were entangled in a passionate embrace. The next, he'd set her on her feet and dashed off down the alley.

Her kiss couldn't have been *that* bad. Could it?

She hurried after him, catching up to him at the end of the block. 'Julian—'

He motioned for quiet, peering around the corner.

'What is it?' she whispered. 'What's going on?'

161

Pointless to ask. In the dark, it wasn't as though she could see to read his answer. He knew it, too, so he didn't stop to give her one. He just grabbed her by the wrist and tugged her around the corner, pulling her down the street. They walked quickly, clinging to the shadows that edged the narrow lane. Lily spied two men some distance in front of them, lumbering down the street with the unhurried arrogance of men who've had too much to drink. Julian seemed to be following them. For what reason, she couldn't imagine.

She struggled to keep pace with him, skidding and sliding over the wet cobblestones in her impractical evening slippers. She would have been better off barefoot. Her heel caught in a narrow gap in the pavement, and her ankle turned. Surprised by the sharp twist of pain, she cried out.

Ahead of them, the two men stopped in the street. Then, they began to turn.

For all that Lily did not comprehend who these men were, or why on earth they were following them, her viscera intuited one thing: She and Julian must not be seen.

Julian's gut evidently agreed. His arm shot around her waist. Yanking her off her feet altogether, he whisked her to the side of the street, pressing her into the darkened doorway of a shop. He anchored her to the far corner of the alcove with his hips, putting his body between her and any threat. His free hand clapped over her mouth to silence her.

Hot tears sprang to her eyes as she adjusted to breathing through her nose. The aroma of his glove leather overwhelmed her senses, pungent and sharp. She couldn't seem to draw enough air. The

162

instinct to struggle was strong.

Lily fought back panic by reminding herself this was Julian. She *knew* this hand that muffled her. She'd watched him use those long, dexterous fingers to play the pianoforte, shuffle cards, pen letters with graceful ease. But never, until this moment, had she realized just how much strength they had.

Long, agonizing moments passed. It was the worst sort of torture. She had no idea what was happening in the street. She couldn't detect any footfalls or voices to let her know if the men were leaving or coming in pursuit. She didn't even know what sort of men they might be. Harmless drunkards? Dangerous footpads? Julian could tell her nothing. She couldn't even make out his facial expression, much less any words he might speak. But the frantic thumping of his heart and the labored huffs of his breath against her cheek were not very reassuring signs. They were in true peril, or so he believed. What in the world was going on?

Finally, after an agonizing minute, Julian's brow met hers. Butter-soft leather caressed her cheek as he cautiously slid his fingers from her mouth, then replaced them with his lips.

A kiss. *I'm sorry*.

Tearing his lips from hers, he pressed hard against her shoulders, pinning her to the shuttered door.

A demand. *Stay here*.

Keeping one gloved hand on her sleeve, he stepped back and turned, looking into the street.

'Did they see us?' she whispered. 'Are they gone?'

He tapped her shoulder, warning her to stay

163

back. Then he took two steps into the street. A distant streetlamp traced his handsome profile in gold. As she stared at him, Lily felt her breathing slow to a steady, calmer rate. She was still terrified. But she was also strangely relieved to be here, sharing the fear with him. No more sitting up alone at night, worrying about Julian's whereabouts. His whereabouts were hers. If some grave misfortune befell him, it would befall them both.

Julian's chest deflated with apparent relief. For the moment, fortune seemed to be on their side.

He turned to her and stretched out a hand. She took it.

He led her into the street, immediately turning her in the opposite direction of the way they had been walking. Julian set a slow, falsely casual pace, and he kept her close, tucked securely under one arm. They walked about a block before he stopped, directly under a street lamp, and turned to her.

'Are you well? Your leg . . . It's not hurt?' As he spoke, he shrugged out of his coat.

'I'm fine.'

'Good. Come quickly, then. And be silent.' He settled his coat about her shoulders and resumed walking.

She stopped him short, keeping him in the light. 'Julian, what's going on? Where are you taking me?'

'Someplace safe.'

That was all he would say. Together they walked swiftly for another block or two, then turned down a narrow lane . . . emerged into a larger street . . . and then made a series of twisting turns. Lily didn't recognize any of these streets or landmarks, and due to the circuitous nature of their journey, she no longer had any idea in which direction they were walking. She tried to take comfort from the warmth and scent of his coat, for she was well and thoroughly lost.

Finally, they approached a coffee house. The door was open, but the windows were dark. A woman in a white-lace cap was shooing a man out the door and into the street, sweeping him along with a broom as if he were a heap of ale-soaked rushes.

'Oy!' the man protested, jumping at another prod of the broom. 'I'm on my way. No call to be rough.'

With her broom handle, the woman tapped a sign on the window. Lily squinted at it. It read, 'Closed.'

As she and Julian approached, the woman caught sight of them. Her brow wrinkled with displeasure, and again she tapped the broom to the sign. *Closed*.

Julian was undeterred. Releasing Lily, he approached the landlady. As he moved toward her, he made a gesture with both hands.

The older woman stopped, peered at him.

Julian removed his hat to aid her examination.

The landlady froze. Then she threw down the broom in the street and flew at him. Julian reeled from the collision, disappearing into a mass of doughy bosom and starched lace.

Lily gasped, suddenly alarmed. Who would have guessed Julian would escape those two brutes, only to be smothered by an aged matron in a lace cap? She darted forward. Perhaps she could grab up the broom, use it as a weapon . . .

But as she neared them, it became apparent

165

that Julian was not being attacked. He was being hugged. When the landlady finally released him, Julian gestured to indicate Lily. Lily nodded her head in greeting, and the older woman returned the gesture with a tearful smile. After wiping her eyes with a corner of her apron, she opened the coffee house door and waved them both inside.

So curious, Lily thought to herself. Julian and the landlady clearly knew each other well. And in the course of that whole broom-and-bosom interchange—so far as Lily could tell—they'd neither of them spoken a single word.

Even inside the coffee house, they continued this way. Neither speaking a word. Not with lips or tongue, at any rate. No, Julian and the landlady were communicating solely with their hands. Rapid, precise, two-handed movements that Julian only belatedly—after sending Lily an apologetic glance—began pairing with speech.

'She's my friend,' he said to the older woman, matching his words with hand signals that Lily could marvel at, but not understand. 'I need you to keep her here. Keep her safe.'

The landlady made a motion, and her eyebrows lifted in query.

'Not long,' Julian answered. 'A few hours, perhaps.'

'A few hours?' Lily claimed his attention. 'Julian, what do you mean? You can't leave me.'

'I must.' He drew her aside. 'Those men . . . I have to go back and try to find them.'

'Why?'

'Because those might be the men who killed Leo.'

'What? How can you possibly believe—'

166

He shook his head, impatient. 'They match a witness's description. I don't have time to explain it further than that. But I can't let them get away. This is the closest I've come in months, Lily. Five. Long. Months.' He shaped each word distinctly. She'd never seen his eyes such a dark, intense shade of blue. 'Stay here, no matter what occurs. Here, you'll be protected.'

Oh, certainly. *She* would be protected. But what about him? Chasing strange brutes down dark alleys in the night . . .

'Don't go.' She rushed to him and grabbed hold of his arm. 'Don't leave me here alone.'

'Lily, I can't take you with me. It's too dangerous. You'll be safe here.'

'But . . . but how can you know that?'

He paused. Then said simply, 'I was raised here.' Stunned, she released his arm.

'Stay,' he commanded. His hand shot to her face, roughly cupping her cheek. His gaze bored into hers—as though with a forceful look, he could bolt her to the wall. 'Stay. No matter how long it takes. I will come back for you. Do you understand?'

She nodded numbly. He left her no choice. 'Wait. Your coat.' She slid the garment from her shoulders and thrust it at him. 'It's cold out there.'

A word fell from his lips. Judging by the sharp crease of his brow, she guessed it to be a vicious curse. His hand slid back into her hair, and he gripped tight. Then, with those same blasphemous lips, he kissed her full on the mouth.

The kiss was bruising, potent. Far too brief.

By the time she recalled how to breathe, he and his coat were gone.

A teapot appeared before her face.

Lily looked up, into the round face of the woman holding it. Thick, hoary eyebrows rose, disappearing under the brim of a white lace cap. *More tea?* the landlady's expression silently inquired.

Gathering a borrowed blanket about her shoulders, Lily smiled politely and shook her head. She'd scarcely sipped from her first cup. At her elbow, a plate of food remained untouched. Since it had been served to her, the edge of a freshly pared bit of cheese had already gone crusty and dry.

How many hours had she been here? Morning could not be long coming. To stave off panic, Lily pressed one hand flat to the planks of the tabletop, worn glassy-smooth by decades of use. The cool, solid surface calmed her pulse.

Julian would come for her. He'd promised.

Dear God. What would she do if he didn't?

She'd never felt more helpless in her life. She didn't even know where she was. If she could decide where to go—out in search of Julian, back home to wait—how would she get there? Walk out on the street and hail a hackney cab? She'd never hailed a hack in her life, ever. There'd always been a servant or friend to do it for her. Perhaps she could send word to Amelia. But what would the message even say?

The older woman sat down across the table from her. Did she mean to attempt conversation? This would be a challenge, unless the landlady could read lips, too.

Lily said, 'Thank you. For everything.'

168

The woman gestured rapidly in response, and Lily shook her head. 'I'm afraid I don't understand the hand signs. You see, I never learned.'

The woman's amazement was obvious. As if Lily had just confessed to being illiterate, or unable to count.

She knew such a manual language existed, of course. In the first year following her illness, her tutor had shown her an alphabet formed with the fingers. But Leo didn't take to it especially well, and after that failed experiment, Lily had declined to learn any more signs. With whom would she use them?

Except—apparently, she could have been using them with Julian all this while. How did he know this language? Why had he never told her? She was so confused.

From a nearby shelf, her hostess gathered a slate and nub of chalk, then resumed her seat and applied herself to the use of both. When she held up her work, Lily read aloud from the slate.

'Anna.' She looked up. 'That's you? You're Anna?' At the woman's nod, Lily extended an open hand. 'May I?'

Anna passed her the slate and chalk, and Lily carefully inscribed her name on the small square of slate. Beneath it, she wrote, *Thank you.*

Smiling, Anna moved her hand back and forth in the universal gesture of 'no thanks are necessary.' She took back the slate and worked over it for a few minutes. While she did so, Lily managed a sip of cold, too-sweet tea.

After a minute, Anna handed her the slate.

'"Friend of Jamie welcome,"' Lily read aloud. Puzzled, she frowned at the slate. She knew Anna

169

could not hear her. The question escaped her lips anyway. 'But . . . but who is Jamie?'

A sudden vibration jarred her focus. Her teacup did a frantic dance on its saucer. Something heavy had fallen, or perhaps a door had slammed shut? She looked up, and there was Julian. His clothes were sodden, and he'd lost his hat. Dark hair clung to his brow in wet, matted locks. He looked like hell, and not himself at all. But he was here, and he was standing, and he was—so far as Lily could see—all of a piece. *Alive.*

'Me,' he said. 'I'm Jamie. She means me.'

*   *   *

'We can talk up here.' Julian took Lily by the hand and led her up the narrow staircase. 'Mind your head,' he said, adding a palm-to-pate smack for emphasis.

He knew Lily wanted some explanation. And after the night she'd just passed, he couldn't deny her that. But they couldn't discuss matters downstairs in the kitchen. Dawn was already breaking, and soon the milkmaid would be coming round, the day's baking would commence . . . For this conversation, they needed privacy.

It was time to tell her the truth. Or at least part of it. He knew Lily understood they came from different places on the map of English society. What she didn't comprehend was the vast dimension of the gulf between them. This morning, he would acquaint her with its insurmountable nature, in no uncertain terms.

They emerged into a cramped garret, occupied by only a narrow slice of window under the eaves

170

and a wobbly cane chair.

'Sit here,' he told her, stripping off his wet coat. For himself, he extricated an old crate from the furthest reaches of the eaves, overturned it, and sat down—squarely within the shaft of sunlight thrown by the window, and as far away from Lily as the space would permit. Which amounted to a distance of about four feet. Less than ideal, but it would have to suffice. Whatever follies he'd contemplated last night, he could never allow them to become reality. He'd exposed her to people and places she should never have encountered in her life. Worst of all, he'd put her in true danger. Leo had paid with his life, just for calling Julian friend. He could not allow Lily to suffer for the same dubious privilege.

'Come closer,' she said. 'I want a proper look at you. I haven't yet satisfied myself on the state of your health.'

He shook his head. *Absolutely not.* It had been proven to him, several times in the past few days, that he was incapable of resisting her whenever she came within reach. 'I'm not injured. Just wet.'

'Wonderful. So now you'll catch your death of pneumonia.' She slid the blanket from her shoulders. 'At least take this.'

His teeth chattered. 'You keep it.'

'Julian, I expect this conversation won't be brief. I can't watch you shiver through it. Unless'—she tipped her head—'you'd care to share the blanket.'

He accepted the thing with no small twinge of pride. He'd passed a damned cold night, and it wasn't much warmer up here in the garret.

'So what happened?' she asked. 'Weren't you able to find them?'

'I found them. But they weren't Leo's killers.'

171

Julian sighed with fatigue. He'd followed those men for hours. Watched them drink, eat, piss in the alley, drink some more. Then take turns tupping the same apathetic whore. Finally he'd overheard enough to gather they'd only recently arrived in London. It was their first adventure in the fair city, as evidenced by the fact they'd lost their way in St. Giles, and only much later realized the apathetic whore had made off with their purses. He didn't expect it would console the two Scots when they learned she'd left them with the clap in recompense.

So much for his hope of stumbling onto Leo's murderers. He would have to return to the other plan: drawing out the man, or men, who hired them.

Lily shucked her slippers and curled her feet up, tucking them under her flimsy excuse for a skirt. Despite his chilled state, he knew a warm, buzzing current of desire. Parts of him heated beneath the rough blanket.

'Thank goodness,' she said. 'I'm glad it wasn't them.'

'Don't you want your brother's killers found?'

'I do, I do. But I don't want *you* to find them. Not alone and unarmed in the dark. If the solution to Leo's murder comes at the cost of your life, I don't want it. I will live with the mystery, thank you very much.'

She looked close to tears. He hated the fact that he'd put her through another night of anxiety, but it thrilled him that she cared so much whether he lived or died.

'Now, then,' she said, sniffing. 'Speaking of mysteries. What is this place? What do you mean,

172

you grew up here? Why does Anna call you Jamie, and how do you know her sign language?'

'It's a long story.'

'Then do begin.' She leaned forward, focusing intently on his mouth. 'But slowly, please.'

'My mother . . .' He swallowed hard. 'My mother was born completely deaf. She came from a very rural, isolated area of Kent where deafness is common. Her cousin was likewise without hearing.'

'How strange. All in one place? I wonder why that is.'

'You, and many scholars. It seems to pass through family lines. It's so common, signing is like a second language there. For everyone, even the hearing.' He propped an elbow on the windowsill, relaxing into the tale. 'Anyway, when my mother was a child, charity toward the deaf was all the rage. You've heard of Braidwood and his school?'

She nodded. 'My own speech tutors were trained there.'

'His efforts were famous. He made it the fashionable thing to show charity toward the deaf and mute. My mother and her cousin were recruited for employment, offered posts in service here in Town as chambermaids to a wealthy lord's family. The promised wages were an untold sum for two girls from the weald.'

'So they accepted?' Lily prompted.

'Yes. They took the posts. They were young and afraid, but they had each other's company. At first. My mother's cousin took ill and died within a few months of their arrival in London.'

'Oh, no. How tragic.'

'My mother's lot was worse. She'd never learned to speak or write, knew no one in London. Her

173

employers were older and decent enough, but there was a son and he . . . Well, he took advantage.' Bile rose in his throat. 'Chambermaids are misused by their masters every day, but imagine her situation. She couldn't fight him off. She couldn't ask for help. Even if she had, it was doubtful she would have received it.'

Lily hugged herself. 'What did she do?'

'She survived, as best she could. When the house keeper finally saw she was pregnant, she was sacked without reference and tossed to the street. I came into the world a few months later. My mother gave birth to me in a vacant warehouse.'

'Alone?'

'She was afraid of asking for help. Thought her baby would be taken from her, and she'd end up in the workhouse or Bedlam. It wasn't an unrealistic fear.'

'That was very brave of her.'

'Yes. Yes, it was.' He'd been a help to his mother when he grew older. But Julian knew at any time in his infancy, she could have made life a great deal easier on herself by dropping him on the doorstep of a foundling hospital. She hadn't. They'd always had each other. Most times, that was all they'd had.

'Why didn't she go home to her family?'

'She had no money, no means of travel. And she felt disgraced. Ashamed.' He took a slow, deep breath to calm himself. 'That's who I am, Lily. The product of fear, violence, and shame. The bastard son of a lecherous nobleman. Born on the wrong side of the blanket, on the wrong side of Town. Raised in conditions a gutter rat would fancy himself a cut above. We had nothing. No food. No home. No proper clothing. My mother worked

174

when she could; I begged and stole when she couldn't. The rest of the time, we starved.'

Like an ancient echo, hunger rumbled in his stomach. He'd eaten nothing since those few bites of beefsteak last night. Even before Leo's murder, he'd done this often—skipping meals, sometimes for a day or more. He didn't plan it so, but it was almost like he couldn't allow himself to forget the sensation of hunger. That bitter, gnawing emptiness that had shadowed all his early years.

'When I was about nine years of age,' he went on, 'I heard word of this place. A coffee house owned and entirely staffed by the deaf. I brought my mother around, and the owner—Anna's late husband—gave her work as a scullery maid. I ran messages, shoveled coal.' His eyes went to the sloping ceiling. 'They gave us this garret for our lodgings. I had a little cot, just there.' He pointed at the floorboards beneath her chair. 'First real bed in my life. And at night, I lay down to it with a full belly. For the first time in years, my mother had steady work and friends with whom she could converse. She was happy. I was happy.

'It was only later, as I grew older, that I realized what advantages we should have had from the first, and what a toll those years of dire poverty had taken on my mother's health. I finally came to understand the magnitude of suffering my fa—' He couldn't use that word. '. . . the man who sired me had inflicted on her.'

'And on you, as well. Do you know who he was?'

He shook his head. 'He's dead. She told me that much, when I grew old enough to ask. The son died first, not long after I was born, leaving his father without an heir. When the old man died a few years

175

later, the title passed to a distant relation. I gather my mother took me to the executor of the estate, hoping for a settlement.'

'I suppose she was denied one.'

He nodded.

'Julian . . .' Lily inched forward on her chair.

'Noblemen,' he said, ignoring her proffered sympathy, 'came in to this coffee house every day. It was quite the fashionable meeting house, in its time. For years, I smoothed the creases from their newspapers, polished the buckles on their shoes, wiped their spit from the floor. And I watched my mother grow a little weaker every winter.'

'Until she died?'

With a curt nod, he slanted his gaze away.

'How old were you then?'

'Fourteen.' Fourteen. Half a man, and a total fool. 'And I wasn't even there for her. I was in jail when she fell ill.'

'In jail?' Her eyes widened. 'At fourteen? For what?'

He shook his head. There was so much Lily didn't know. Could never know. 'I ran afoul of the wrong aristocrat. The details aren't important now. What mattered was, I wasn't there for my mother. There was no money saved. She was given an unmarked pauper's grave.' Determined to prevent an outburst of emotion, he pressed a fist to his mouth. 'She gave me life in a dusty storehouse, and I let her die alone.'

Beneath the blanket, he began to shake. Not with cold or hunger, but with fury. He'd been living with this anger all his days, like some sort of phantom twin. The fury had life of its own: guts and memory and corporeal strength. It made demands.

176

Lily rose from her chair and crossed to him, sinking to her knees before the crate. With a light, tentative motion, she curled her fingers over his trembling fist. At that first jolt of contact, he sucked in a gasp. He couldn't bring himself to spurn her touch. So generous and warm.

Gently, she pulled his hand away from his mouth, so his lips—and his words—would not be concealed. 'Please don't hide,' she said. 'I need to understand.'

The blanket slipped from his shoulders, and the room's bracing chill gave him a moment of cold composure.

'After she was gone,' he said, 'I found work here and there. Spent some time as a table monkey, cutting patterns in the back of a tailor's shop. It was there I first glimpsed Beau Brummel. He's the son of a secretary, do you know? And he had the cream of English society all clamoring to lighten his tea. One day, I decided, that would be me. I would have everything the lords had. Everything that should have been mine, by rights. I would take it from them. Their money. Their status. Their women. I would reverse the scales, make them envy *me*.' He swallowed a hot, bitter lump of rage. 'I hated them so much, Lily. I hated them all.'

She moved closer still. He could smell the light fragrance of her hair. It smelled expensive, and far too refined for this humble place.

'Don't pity me,' he said. 'I'm talking about your friends. Your family, your peers. I've devoted all the years of my adulthood to taking what I could. I've joined their clubs, fleeced them of their gold, tupped their wives, mocked them to their faces. Forced them to dress in hideous colors. All out of

177

spite and a thirst for revenge.'

'And you kept all this from Leo, and from me.'

'Yes. For years.'

Her bottom lip folded under her teeth, and her gaze sharpened with concentration. She had an aim in mind, and he didn't know what it was.

Her hand slowly stretched toward his face. Julian held his breath. With her fingertip, she dabbed a spot high on his cheekbone, just beneath the corner of his eye. His eyelids fluttered, partly out of instinct and partly out of sheer, sweet torment at the sensation of her touch.

Then she drew back her hand, stared at it. He stared, too, and discerned something glistening on her fingertip.

Oh, devil take it. He was weeping?

She pinched her thumb against her forefinger, rubbing the evidence into her skin. There, it was gone. Just one tear. One tear wasn't weeping. After a night of such extraordinary events, and a morning of such heartfelt confession, limiting himself to a single tear was a formidable display of restraint. Manful, even. Wasn't it?

And really, this garret was dusty as hell. It might have been a case of simple ocular irritation. Anyway, it was over now. He blinked, and no more tears fell. Excellent.

Tragic story told. Tears contained. Crisis averted.

Until Lily sniffed and began to blink furiously. Perhaps the dust bothered her, too.

'I'm sorry,' she said, her tone one of dismay. 'I'm so sorry, but I'm going to cry.'

'No.' Panic seized him. 'No, don't. Please.' With a finger, he propped up her quivering chin. 'Lily, I'm not worth your tears.'

The words squeaked from her throat. 'I can't help it.'

Oh Lord, here they came. Tears, in abundance. Streaking her cheeks, tracing down to her chin. Her shoulders lurched with violent sobs, and she leaned forward, slumping inexorably toward him until her brow rested against his chest.

He raised his hands in defense, or perhaps surrender. What should he do? He could bring himself to refuse her comfort, but he couldn't refuse to comfort her.

So he did the only thing he could. Which was, to be honest, exactly what he'd been wanting to do for a very, very long time. Ever since the night Leo died.

He wrapped his arms around her, drawing her into the protection of his body.

And he held her tight.

Chapter Thirteen

Lily loved him. She loved Julian.

There was no denying it, and at the moment, no classifying it. She didn't know whether it made them friends or lovers or something altogether different and new. She just knew that no matter what his origins, no matter what his sins, no matter how many lies he'd told, she cared for this man— *loved* him—and she could not remain a spectator while he spoke of being born in shame, raised in squalor, and losing his mother while he was still no more than a boy. Her heart could not remain unmoved, and her body would not be still.

She trembled with all the fear he would not admit. She cried the tears he refused to shed. His arms were steel bands about her chest, and she pulled him closer still, crushing her ribcage to his— as if she could draw the pain from his heart and take it into hers.

When she brought her hands to his shoulders and pushed him away, she hated to release him. But he was speaking, and she needed to understand.

'Wait,' she said, touching the backs of her fingers to his cheek. 'Go slowly. You're losing me.'

'Yes.' Sighing, he closed his eyes. 'Yes, I know. And you were never even mine.'

'Julian, please.' How should she take such words? She looked for clues in the features of his face, scanning for an ironic quirk of his brow or a serious set to his jaw.

He joined her on the floor. They both sat, legs folded and hands doing the things hands did when left at loose ends. Picking at seams, tracing cracks on the floor. Light crept up the paneled wall. The new day was gaining strength, taking shape. It could no longer be ignored.

'What happens now?' she asked. Where did they go from here? So long as they went together, Lily wasn't sure she cared.

He said, 'I'm leaving London.'

The air left her lungs. 'You're . . . you're *leaving*? But when?'

'I don't know precisely. Soon.'

Inwardly, she told herself not to panic. Men left London all the time. They had things to do, people to see. Horses to purchase and investments to look after. She said casually, 'When will you return?'

'I won't be returning.'

Cruel, cruel man. She'd just shed a basin's worth of tears for him, and now he told her he was leaving forever?

'This is why you must marry,' he said. 'I can't stay around to look out for you, and I can't bear the thought of you alone.'

'And I'm supposed to rejoice at the thought of never seeing you again?'

'Yes, if you know what's best for you.' He gestured with one hand, stirring the cloud of dust motes between them. 'You're always saying what a decent man I am, beneath the devilry. But it's not the truth. It only seems that way, Lily. It only seems that way because I'm a better man when I'm near you.'

Perhaps he meant those words to be flattering or romantic, but they didn't land that way. A horrid notion wormed in her stomach. 'Does this have to do with your mother? Because she was deaf, and I am too? Is that why you feel so . . .' She hardly knew the word to say. '. . . attached to me, but unwilling to act on it?'

'*No.* No, it's not like that. Trust me when I say this.' His eyes wandered her body, and his mouth quirked with sensual mischief. 'When you're close to me, I'm not thinking of my mother. At all.'

Lily pressed her lips together, hoping he was being truthful. She shuddered at the thought of being some sort of maternal figure to him.

'You do share certain of her attributes,' he went on. 'Kindness, loyalty, courage. Naturally I admire those qualities in you. But you look nothing like her, I promise. And when it comes to the hearing, or lack of it—if anything, I'm more poised to see the differences. My mother was born deaf. You

181

were deafened by illness. It's an entirely separate thing. I can say to you, the pianoforte is out of tune, and though you don't hear it, you understand exactly what I mean. Not so with my mother. But she and Anna and the others downstairs, they notice things—little subtleties of sights and smells and textures—that you and I would never think to heed.' He smiled. 'If it helps, they don't see you as one of them either. They'll be gracious to you, but that's because you're with me.'

She thought of Anna's bewildered expression when Lily confessed she couldn't sign, and her message on the slate: *Friend of Jamie welcome.*

'Is that your name, then? Jamie?'

He shook his head. 'Not really. It's just what they've always called me here. As an adult, I began going by Julian.'

'So it is your real name. Julian.'

He shook his head again. 'No. I don't think so.'

'I'm so confused.'

'My mother was illiterate. She could barely recognize the letters of the alphabet. When she took me to be christened, she and the priest couldn't make one another out. He grew frustrated and just picked a name. Wrote it in the register and pointed, but all my mother could catch was the first letter, J.'

'So you don't even know your given name?'

'Of course I do. It's this.' Bringing both hands together, he made the sign for the letter J and tapped it twice against his heart. 'That's my given name.'

The tears pressed again at the corners of her eyes. With every minute that passed in this cramped attic, she realized how little she truly knew about

182

him. And now she might never have the chance to learn. 'I wish I could have known your mother.'

'I wish you could have, too.' He pushed a hand through his hair. 'I wish a great many things were different.'

'So let's change them. Tell me everything. Whatever your difficulty, we'll work together to find a solution.'

'We can't change the world, Lily. And the difficulty is here, between us. You're a lady of noble birth, and I have you crouched on the floor of a dusty garret, chilled through and weeping. Last night, I was a minute away from deflowering you in a damp, reeking alleyway.'

Really? He would have taken her virtue last night, there in the street? The thought both repulsed and thrilled her.

'If you'd come to harm last night . . . I couldn't have lived with myself today. I don't need to remind you how I put Leo in danger, or what happened as a result.'

Not this *again*. 'Julian, I asked for everything we did last night. And then some. I'm responsible for my own choices. Leo wanted to attend that boxing match, and he did so of his own accord. You are not to blame for what happened to him afterward.'

His eyes flashed. 'How do you know that? I was supposed to be with him that night. I have enemies, Lily. Perhaps the men who killed him were really hoping to kill me.'

'That's madness. I can't imagine why anyone would want to kill you.'

'Of course you can't. I've been very careful to keep those reasons from you. I'll be damned if I'll expose you to them now.'

She shook her head. 'I can't believe this. You admit you're a lowborn, unrepentant scoundrel with a criminal history and an insatiable taste for women and revenge. But *I'm* where you draw the line?'

'Yes. If I have it in me to do one truly decent thing in my life, it's going to be this. Leaving you be.'

'Then you really are a bastard. Can you possibly understand how patronizing that is?' She gave a bitter sniff. 'You're so very careful with me. Because I'm so pure and delicate and deaf, you're a better person around me. I'm the lucky object of your scruples. Meanwhile, you'll blithely dally with any number of women you don't respect. Perhaps I *should* take your advice and marry. If I married one of these lords you hate so fondly, maybe then you'd tup me too.'

Oh, God. Had she truly just spoken those words? Color rose on his cheeks. He angled his gaze to the corner.

Yes. She had.

'Julian, I'm sorry. I shouldn't have said that.'

'No, don't apologize. It was absolutely deserved. I *am* a bastard, Lily, in more ways than one. I'm glad you're starting to see it. It makes this easier on us both.'

'Makes what easier? What is it we're doing here?'

'We're saying farewell.'

She choked back a sob, then buried her face in one hand.

His eyes pleaded with her as he pulled her hand away. 'Try to understand. I have exactly two goals in my life right now. Justice for Leo, and security

184

for you. And after last night, I must face facts. The first may always elude me. As for the second . . . It's been proved beyond doubt, I can no longer be near you without endangering your health, your virtue, or both.'

Wiping her tears, she protested, 'No one gives a fig for my virtue.'

'I give a fig for it. A great many figs. Several puddings' worth. You should, too.'

How unforgivable of him, to make her laugh at a moment like this.

He went on, 'You may say you want a lover—but you don't, Lily. Not really. Take it from someone who knows, and who knows you. The slinking around to avoid discovery, the gossip and scorn if we were found out . . . it would weigh heavily on you. It wouldn't end well.'

Drat it all. She knew in her heart he was probably right. She just wasn't made for illicit *affaires*.

He rose, brushing the dust from his trousers as he stood. 'Speaking of avoiding discovery, we should be going. Come, I'll see you home.' He extended a hand.

She stared at it. A future without Julian stretched out before her like a bleak, endless wasteland. 'Lord and Lady Ainsley's assembly is next week. You said you'd attend. You made me a promise, Julian. Three nights. We've only had two. You owe me the one. You *promised*.' It was a stupid, contrived line of argument, but it was what she had. She just couldn't leave here without knowing she'd see him again.

'So I did,' he said, looking thoughtful. 'Very well.'

With a sigh of relief, she took his hand. 'You'll

come?'

'I'll come.' He pulled her to her feet. 'I can't escort you, but I promise you will see me there. In fact, it's perfect. That night will be your second London debut. And it will be my grand farewell.'

*   *   *

Several days later, Lily sat once again at Leo's desk. October had become November. She turned a fresh page in the ledger that lay open on the blotter. A blank slate.

She dipped her quill and drew a vertical slash down the center of the page, dividing it in two columns. At the top, she headed one 'Arguments For,' and atop the other column, she wrote, 'Arguments Against.' Lily felt like a schoolgirl, but she didn't know what else to do. Ledgers always helped her see things clear.

The second list was by far the easier of the two.
He's a liar, she wrote.
And a criminal, of unknown sort.
He has enemies, also of unknown sort. Possibly dangerous.
He's bedded half the ladies of the ton.

Well, that was hyperbole. Setting aside all the young girls and elderly matrons . . . and taking into account the sheer difficulties of scheduling, and the fact that some never even came to Town . . . How many garters did it take to span a billiard room, anyway? She crossed through 'half' and inked 'one-tenth' in its place as an estimate.

It was small consolation.
He's illegitimate, and of low birth.
She felt horrid even penning that last, but it was

186

an inescapable fact. No one in the *ton* was under any illusions that the man came from royalty. But they had never truly accepted Julian into their ranks—they'd merely tolerated his shadowy origins, because he was amusing to have around. If the particulars of Julian's childhood and social ascendancy were ever made common knowledge, he would be cut by most good families. If she were linked with him, Lily would be cut as well. She would like to have said that didn't matter to her—but it might, a little. Her parents and Leo had been so highly respected. She would hate to besmirch their good name.

Neither could Julian's history of poverty be overlooked. Not because it lowered him in Lily's estimation, but because he seemed so unlikely to ever forget it himself.

She looked at the list, and even with all those items, it felt far too short. She could have listed each instance of deceit, named each of his lovers . . . In the end, she added one more line:

Untold secrets yet to be revealed. Most likely unpleasant.

Now she turned her attention to the other column. Her quill hovered over the page. It wasn't that she didn't know how to begin. It was more that once she'd begun, she doubted she would be able to stop. She couldn't possibly write down every occasion on which he'd made her smile or laugh or reconsider her opinions, feel comforted or confident. And then there were other sensations, ones too indecent to be penned.

I love him, she wrote. Because she did. With every day that passed, she grew more certain, more aware of what had been there all along. After a

187

moment, she added, *And I believe he may love me.*

She stared at the word, *love.* Four rather unassuming letters, for such a vast, boundless thing. But did love balance the ledger? She wasn't sure. Poetry would argue that love conquers all. And perhaps it did, at the outset. But in the long-term accounting, Lily knew it didn't always tally that way.

Julian understood love. He wasn't some lackwit rake, perpetually groping for acceptance in a woman's bosom because as a child he'd been denied a mother's affection. No, he knew very well what love was—what it could mean to a person— and with his looks, intelligence, and charm, he surely would have no difficulty finding women to love him. Nevertheless, he'd chosen not to seek that sort of attachment for himself, preferring to chase revenge instead.

Evidently, love hadn't been enough for Leo, either.

Once again, she succumbed to the temptation and reached for her chatelaine, searching through the keys for the slender finger of brass that opened the locked drawer. She felt guilty every time she fitted the key in the lock—first for spying on something so private, and second because of the heartbreak contained within.

She withdrew the stack of aging correspondence. By now, she was in a fair way of knowing these letters by heart. There was one missive that haunted her in particular—the last in the bundle. She smoothed it with uncertain fingers, and her eyes went to a familiar paragraph.

I've been thinking of your eyes a great deal

of late, and wondering if you can understand how extraordinary they are. I doubt any looking glass could faithfully reflect their depth. But then, perhaps you can see their true mirror in your sister. I can't say how much her eyes resemble yours, and I don't suppose I shall ever have the chance to judge. Such close inspection would require an introduction, and that will never come to pass.

Would she like me, do you think? I know she and I would find at least one thing in common. But I'm teasing now, and that's not fair.

I'm sorry for the things I said last time.

How I despise even writing those words, 'last time.' But it was the last time, wasn't it? This emptiness inside me tells me so. Curse that sterling sense of honor, so deeply embedded in your soul. Excise it somehow, will you? Then you can come to me.

But then—if you came to me without it, perhaps I would not love you as I do.

And I do. I do. Do not forget.

Every time. This letter brought tears to her eyes, every blessed time.

Her brother had been in love, with someone unsuitable or unattainable, and he'd hidden that love from everyone. Even from her. Somewhere, the author of these letters was grieving, mourning Leo all alone—because her brother hadn't seen fit to make the introduction. Would he have made the same decisions, if he had known how few his days would be?

What would he advise Lily to do now?

She laughed to herself. Did it even matter what she decided? She might make all the tables and

189

lists she pleased, but if Julian was determined to leave, he would leave. She could throw herself at him shamelessly, make herself utterly vulnerable to public scorn, only to be rewarded with ruination *and* solitude.

Here was one more item for the ledger. However, Lily wasn't certain in which column it belonged.

I am afraid of ending up alone.

She'd been insisting for months now that she didn't want to marry. But the reality of the alternative—decades of spinsterhood—was beginning to firm in her mind, like drying mortar. She could all too easily see herself years in the future, passing day after day in a gray drawing room with a gray-haired companion and a dozen gray cats. Even adding a rainbow-hued parrot, the picture was unbearably grim.

With a brisk shake of her head, she tore the sheet from her ledger and crumpled it into the grate. Really, she could ruminate all she liked. Nothing could be certain until she saw Julian again.

Tomorrow. She would see him *tomorrow*. The word had little wings, and it beat a joyous rhythm in her chest.

Or, wait—perhaps that was just Tartuffe, fussing on his perch. The bird did make an excellent door knocker. Much more effective than the mirrors had ever been. Lily turned to find Swift standing in the entryway.

The butler bowed. 'If you please, my lady. A delivery.'

From behind him, a footman entered bearing a large, rectangular box. Atop the box was a sealed envelope. Lily dismissed the servants with her

190

thanks and reached for the note. She knew it had to be from Julian. She hadn't seen him since that morning in the coffee house, but he'd been sending little missives every day. That first afternoon, he'd sent a note asking after her health. She'd replied with assurances and asked for the same in kind. He sent them the following morning, along with an inquiry as to the color of her gown for the assembly. She wrote him she had not decided yet but would keep him informed when she did. And on and on, the notes went to and fro, addressing everything but matters of true consequence. He might as well have signed them all, 'Your besotted correspondent, Julian.'

Then yesterday, Amelia and the Duke of Morland had come to call, professing a wish to help her practice dancing. Lily had no doubt that they came at Julian's prodding. She would have been hard pressed to say which had been more awkward—dancing with the taciturn, imposing duke, or dancing with the pregnant Amelia taking the gentleman's part. But despite the discomfort, Lily *had* practiced, and industriously so. There was pride at stake.

And now, it would seem Julian had progressed from sending her notes and visitors to sending her gifts. For a man so determined *not* to woo her, his behavior was curious indeed.

She opened the envelope first and found a neatly ordered list, divided in two columns. In general appearance, it was uncomfortably similar to the paper she'd just tossed into the fire. Her heart skipped a beat. Upon perusing it, however, she learned it was not a list of Arguments For or Against anything—but rather a list of dances in

191

the first column, and on the other side, a list of names. A quick scan revealed them to belong to quite wealthy, mostly titled, and entirely eligible gentlemen. With a few notable exceptions. Near the end, Morland's name was listed next to a waltz, and Amelia's older brother Laurent, the Earl of Beauvale, was down for the opening quadrille.

One name was noticeably missing from the list. Julian's.

Frowning, she opened and read aloud the note he had enclosed. Silly, perhaps, reading aloud for no one's ears—not even her own. But she liked the feel of his words on her tongue.

'"Dear Lily, as promised, I have learned the list of dances for Lord and Lady Ainsley's assembly. I have also taken the liberty of engaging your partners in advance." ' She muttered to herself, 'Yes, a liberty indeed. How very generous of you, Julian.' She returned to the letter. ' "As for the contents of the package, I trust you will know for whom they are intended. For fear of offending propriety, I dare not send the gift direct." '

Now this was a true mystery. What could he mean? Lily untied the twine binding the package and removed the top of the box. In it, she found a cloud of white tissue and a small note card that read,

With apologies. No ermine was in stock.

She lifted from the box a heavy winter cloak. The black wool was of the finest quality, soft as kittens to the touch. The entire garment was lined in velvet, and the collar was edged with sable. It was a cloak fit for—not a queen, perhaps, but a well-heeled

192

member of her court—and its proportions were far and away too large for Lily's frame.

Smiling to herself, she flung the cloak over her arms and went in search of her house keeper. 'Holling,' she sang out down the corridor. 'I believe you have an admirer.'

Chapter Fourteen

Julian prepared for the ball in the same way a pugilist prepared for a prizefight. He rested well, ate well, marshaled his powers of concentration. He readied his jabs and his evasive maneuvers. Tonight was the night he learned the truth—the truth of his enemy, the truth of Leo's death. Anticipation resonated in his bones. By God, he was ready to deal some blows.

But first, there would be dancing. Merriment before the fall. By the time he arrived at Lord and Lady Ainsley's assembly (late, of course; it would not do to be punctual), he'd amassed a long mental list of activities designed to help him avoid standing about, gawping at Lily.

The problem was, he had a difficult time finding any gamblers eager for a brisk game of dice, or gentlemen desiring a good, lengthy chat on the aesthetic merits of Covent Garden's newest Parisian actress. Because, it seemed, every other man at the assembly was perfectly happy to stand about, gawping at Lily.

Within five minutes of entering the assembly rooms, Julian admitted defeat and joined them.

She looked astoundingly well tonight. To Julian,

193

she looked well every night, but on this particular occasion, she'd attained a new pinnacle of elegance. Her gown of shimmering bronze moiré wasn't the most *au courant,* nor the most expensive in the room. The simple upsweep of her dark, thick locks wasn't a new or innovative coiffure. And she did have a few true contenders for the honor of loveliest lady in attendance. But those ladies could go stew in their own beauty. All eyes were on Lily, and her name was on every tongue. In the gentlemen, she inspired open admiration. In the ladies, she inspired rumor and envy. As he passed one knot of besotted young bucks, Julian felt sure he heard her inspiring some shockingly bad poetry.

Julian, on the other hand, could not credit her with any particular inspiration. In fact, he blamed Lily for his difficulty with respiration.

She took his breath away. Oh, she eventually let him have it back, because she was hardly a thief. But she made him work for it, Lily did. To have her within his line of view was to feel the simple act of drawing air had suddenly become a privilege, rather than an instinctive act.

Speaking of bad poetry.

For this dance, she was paired with Mr. George 'Denny' Denton, a stalwart and jovial sort of fellow, if lacking in subtlety, and heir to a sizable fortune and estate. He was also an appallingly bad dancer. He made so many mistakes that Lily's own missteps either went unnoticed or could be blamed on his clumsy lead. Despite the muddle they made of the pattern, they laughed their way through the dance and appeared to be having a high time indeed.

She would do well with a husband like Denny. He would support her, give her children, and be

194

unlikely to ever forget his ridiculous good fortune in securing such a lady's hand. Denny was an affable, uncomplicated man, well liked by his peers.

Julian, of course, had never despised a man so much in his life.

He forced down the red swell of envy, through no insignificant force of will. Jealousy was a distraction he couldn't afford this evening. This was Lily's night to shine, and his night to find answers, at long last.

He drifted into a connecting room, where he found no answers—but he did locate and down a cup of weak punch. He would have liked something stronger, but he needed to keep his wits about him. With Lily's intoxicating presence already proving a dangerous distraction, he couldn't afford to blunt his mind further with spirits. He had to be ready for anything. Fists, pistols, knives.

When he returned to the ballroom, a waltz was just getting underway. Dancers thronged to the floor.

Lily wasn't among them.

*   *   *

'Isn't this dance Morland's? Where the hell has he gone?'

Lily tamped down her defensive reaction and gave him a polite smile. 'And good evening to you too, Mr. Bellamy. You look dashing, as usual.' That wasn't quite true. Despite his angry fuming, Julian looked more dashing than ever. But she didn't suppose he would heed the compliment right now.

'Where is the duke, blast him?'

'He and Amelia already went home.' Lest his anger spike, she added quickly, 'I urged them to go.

195

They don't like to be away from Claudia so late at night, and who can blame them?'

In truth, once she'd seen that list of partners Julian sent her, she'd written immediately to Amelia. Together, they'd worked out matters in advance, ensuring she and the duke would leave before this set. And if Amelia hadn't agreed to help her, Lily would have resorted to pouring sleeping powder in the duke's punch. That's how determined she was to seize this time with Julian.

'I can't believe they would desert you like that and leave you here alone.'

'I'm not alone. I'm with you. And if you'll claim it, this dance is yours.' She offered her hand.

He took it. 'How can I refuse?'

As they moved to the dance floor, Lily should have known a surge of triumph. Except she didn't feel triumphant, she felt exhausted. Even before her illness, she'd found events like these wearying. The dancing, the conversation, the constant effort it required to be aware of her every movement, word, smile, and breath and meld them into a flawless portrait of genteel breeding. Even when she enjoyed herself, it left her feeling drained. And tonight, the ordeal was multiplied tenfold. Atop all those challenges were the strain of following conversation and keeping in step with the dance. Sometimes both at once.

By the time Julian took her in his arms, she wanted nothing but to collapse in his embrace and beg him to take her home. But then, years from now, she didn't want to look back on this evening and remember dancing with every gentleman in the room *except* Julian. She wanted to remember this night as theirs.

196

So they waltzed.

'You're looking at me very queerly,' she said. At least, his stare was making her feel very queer inside.

'Am I?'

She nodded. 'So serious and intent. It is a party, you know.'

'I know it's a party, Lily. If I do look serious, it's not displeasure. It's awe. You are radiant, and this moment is . . . too much to be believed. It's like I've stumbled upon a bit of reality that exceeds all my wildest imaginings, and I don't know where I'll go from here.' His gaze deepened, pulling on hers with the promise of raw truth. 'I'm so damned proud to be the man dancing with you.'

She had to look away. It was that, or dissolve into tears. He could have no idea how deeply those words affected her. Coming from anyone else, they would be pleasant flattery. Coming from Julian, they were manna in the desert.

Still, she tried to keep the conversation light. 'I'll admit to being rather proud of myself. Let's hope no one tells my mother's Aunt Beatrice.'

'Aunt Beatrice can have her moral, miserable corner of heaven, and welcome to it. I'll take tonight.' He cast a glance about the ballroom. 'Truly, this is my perfect exit from the *ton*. It would be impossible to ever top this triumph. Everyone's staring at us. Staring at you. I wish you could see the envy on their faces.'

She wished *he* would stop talking about leaving forever.

'Are you certain it's envy?' she asked. Julian was right that they were being closely watched. But to Lily's eye, the expressions of the onlookers read as

197

fascination, rather than jealousy.

'Oh, yes. It's envy. Admiration for you, tinged with loathing for me.' An ironic half-smile pulled at his lips. 'I think they know, Lily. I think they finally see me for who I am. For years, I've been able to bluff my way into good company, but now that they see me paired with you . . . The truth must be obvious. They all see an illegitimate guttersnipe, daring to waltz with a lady.'

'I don't think that's what they see.'

They were silent for a moment.

'Have you enjoyed tonight?' he finally asked.

'I suppose I have. I've done as you asked, Julian. I've danced with every gentleman on your list, conversed with several more besides.'

'Excellent. Has any man distinguished himself in your regard?'

'Yes. One has.'

His jaw tightened. 'Can I ask his name?'

'I'm not sure of his given name, to be honest.'

'Really? Describe him, then. I know everyone in the room.'

Lily smiled to herself. Were they really playing this game? 'Very well,' she said. 'He's tall. Strong. Dressed to perfection, in a black topcoat and'—she shot a glance downward—'black trousers as well.' She dragged her gaze back up to his face. 'He has hair dark as midnight, and a deceptively light wit. Brilliant blue eyes that make my heart skip beats. A smile that warms me in secret places. He's my dearest friend in the world. And he's a lovely dancer.'

As they swept into a brisk turn, she took the opportunity to ease closer in his arms and speak directly into his ear. She could only hope she struck the right volume—loud enough to be understood, not so loud as to be overheard. An uncertain tenor, for this most risky of declarations.

'Of course it's you,' she whispered. 'There's only you. And if you're determined to see me wed, you'll have to do the duty yourself, Julian. Because I won't have any other man. No one else makes me feel the way you do. No one ever will.'

Beneath her hand, his shoulder muscles bunched and tensed. A defensive reaction, but one that only spurred her on. She gazed over his shoulder at the colorful whirl of dancers. 'You're right. Everyone in this room is staring at us. They're watching us with unguarded envy, and it's all because they see the truth. We're so obviously in love.'

He tripped over his own foot, landing firmly on hers. Lily suppressed a sharp cry of pain. At least she needn't wonder whether or not he'd heard her words. They managed to cover the misstep with a quick turn, but it was a close thing.

He tried to pull back, presumably to speak with her. But she held him tight. 'Not now. Please, let's just enjoy the dance.'

He struggled for a moment more, leading with an erratic rhythm. But before long, he gave in. Their steps fell into a sympathetic cadence. The tension in his shoulders released, and his gloved hand warmed where it gripped hers. And although they were already dancing indecently close, he spread his fingers over her back and drew her closer still.

His thumb caressed her just between the shoulder blades, stroking a current of pleasure down her spine. It was the gentlest of touches, but it was deliberate and true. An admission. *I love you, too.* He could have stopped the music, called

199

everyone's attention, and declared mad, passionate, everlasting adoration for her—in rhyming couplets—and this would still be better. *Now,* she felt triumph. His was the only re sis tance she sought to conquer.

Lily allowed her head to tilt, just slightly, until her temple came to rest against his jaw. She felt his sigh stir her hair, and it roused her deep inside.

When this dance ended, there would be a reckoning. Julian might refuse to admit to his feelings, or refuse to acknowledge hers. Even these sweetest of emotions might not overcome the bitterness and guilt entrenched in his soul.

But while they danced like this, holding each other with such tenderness, he could not deny their bond. So long as this waltz lasted, they were in love—for everyone to see.

It ended far too soon.

They came to a stop. Lily was aware that all around them, people were moving. Couples were separating and re-forming for the next set. For the first time all evening, she pretended deaf ignorance. She couldn't bring herself to let him go.

With one last surreptitious caress, Julian released her. She was afraid to even look at him, because she knew his eyes alone would spell their fate. Would they be filled with love? Hope? Regret? Sadness?

Finally, she braved a glance.

All of the above.

'Lily,' he began. Then he stopped, looking uncertain how to continue. He tilted his head, as though an idea might shake loose, and began again. 'Lily . . .' His gaze cut to the side. 'Lord Weston is approaching. He has the country dance.'

200

Lily wanted to growl. To the devil with Lord Weston and the country dance. She mentally rifled through the stocking drawer of acceptable feminine excuses—fatigue, dizziness, the need for refreshment . . . Why hadn't she thought to turn an ankle during the waltz?

But before she could seize on a way to demur, Julian passed her hand to Lord Weston, bowed, and disappeared. Lily found herself making a numb circuit of the room—a circular promenade in prelude to the dance. As they walked, she searched the borders of the room for Julian. Her heart leapt every time she glimpsed a shock of dark, ruffled hair, but they all belonged to imitators, not the man she sought.

She queued up with the ladies, and then her attention was consumed with following the steps and paying the minimum of polite attention to her partner. Lord Weston was a nice enough man—she didn't wish to be rude, but her concentration was obviously elsewhere. She missed her cue to move diagonally and curtsy to her corner, leaving poor Mr. Barnaby bowing to thin air.

But in the crowd behind him, Lily spied a cluster of gentlemen gathered in a corner, and amongst them—

There was Julian. The breath she'd been holding rushed out of her. Thank goodness.

Mr. Barnaby moved back into place, blocking her view, but at least she knew Julian was *there*. He hadn't left, and that meant her battle was more than half won. After this dance, she would plead a headache or similar and beg Julian to see her home. From there, she just needed to entice him to stay. Desire danced over her skin, raising the little hairs on her arms. She would hold him tonight, and nothing—not even clothing—would come between them.

But first, she had to last through this dance. Fortunately, this particular dance was a pattern designed to showcase a single couple at a time. There were long periods of standing still, interspersed with brief interludes of circling one's partner, then returning to one's place while the couple at the top of the dance traveled the length of the floor, joining the queue at the opposite end.

As she and Lord Weston made their inchworm-like progress toward the head of the line, Lily strained her neck for glimpses of Julian. It became more and more difficult, as he seemed to have drawn a crowd. This must happen at every party—she had seen it happen at Leo's own gatherings. All of the gentlemen, and the bolder of the ladies, would throng around Julian just to hear what amusing thing he'd say next, and to see whether he could be coaxed into doing one of his popular imitations.

She wasn't sure how she felt about watching it now. Seeing him at the center of attention did give her a sense of satisfaction. Much the same, she would imagine, as it made him proud to see her admired. But she knew there was so much more to Julian than cheap party tricks. She wished he would allow people to know that side of him—the real, genuine man inside. If he knew the regard he engendered was sincere, he might have a better sense of his own worth.

Lord Weston moved toward her, and Lily circled him with a dutiful smile. As they parted, another couple moved down the row, and they made

202

another sidestep closer to Julian's end of the room. Again, she found her gaze wandering to him.

On closer inspection, Lily didn't like the scene at all. Julian was still surrounded by guests, but the look on their faces did not signal laughter or amusement. No, they looked shocked and affronted. A few of them appeared to be flat enraged. There must have been an argument, because Lily saw heads turning in Julian's direction. Despite the ire of those around him, his mien remained smug and insouciant. As if he was enjoying the fact that he'd made a scene.

Almost as if he'd *tried* to make a scene.

Drat it all. Lily and Lord Weston had reached the top of the queue, and here came their turn to run the gauntlet. She advanced to the center of the floor, took Weston's hands, and allowed him to sweep her down the aisle, all the way to the other end of the floor. And there she was stuck. An eternity passed before the pattern shifted and allowed her a chance to glance toward Julian's corner again.

By the time it did, the knot of gentlemen had dispersed. Julian was nowhere to be seen.

Curse etiquette. She walked away from the dance, pushing her way toward the area where she'd seen him last. Clustered around, small groups of guests talked and grumbled amongst themselves. At least, she assumed they were grumbling, given the stormy sets of their brows and the heightened color of their complexions. She caught words here and there—distressing phrases like 'insufferable upstart' and 'never again' and 'cut direct.' Even their hosts, Lord and Lady Ainsley, stood beside one another, red-faced and pointedly avoiding one

203

another's gaze.

Lily spied Amelia's oldest brother in the crowd. 'Laurent,' she said, urging him aside. 'Have you seen Mr. Bellamy?'

He made a chagrined face. 'I believe he's left. Or was made to leave.'

'Why would he do that?' she wondered aloud, more to herself than to Laurent.

'To avoid a duel, perhaps?' Laurent shook his head. 'The fool just rattled through the list of men in this room he's cuckolded.'

'But . . .' Lily felt as though she'd taken a punch to the stomach. 'But it's not as though his dalliances are a great secret.'

'Everyone knows about them, but they're never discussed. It's one thing to entertain ladies in private and quite another to boast of it in company, you know. He's unleashed a veritable plague of marital disharmony. And if he values his own health, Bellamy won't dare to show his face anytime soon. Even if he were invited, which is doubtful. Can you believe the man even said—'

Lily turned away, muttering her thanks to Laurent for the information. It really mattered little what, precisely, Julian had said—she understood *why* he'd said it.

That night will be your second London debut. And my own grand farewell.

Laurent's reaction was exactly what Julian had desired. He meant to leave fashionable London society and cut ties, irrevocably.

Including ties with her.

Chapter Fifteen

Well, Julian thought to himself, that ought to have done it.

Pausing just long enough to remove his gloves and retrieve the pistol he'd stashed behind a loose stone, Julian jammed the weapon in his trouser waistband and set off down the street. He kept his steps light, forced himself to maintain a steady, deliberate pace. He didn't want to be too hard to catch. Being caught was rather the point, after all.

He'd been preparing for this night all week. Astonishing—and rather lowering—to realize how little he'd needed to arrange at his home. His offices had presented a greater challenge. He'd led his employees to understand he'd be taking a journey to inspect the mills. That bought him a few weeks' time. If he didn't manage to return, in a few weeks' time or ever . . . well, he'd left instructions with his solicitor. Someone would eventually find them.

As for Lily . . .

He couldn't think about Lily now. And so long as he lived with the specter of murder hovering over him, he would never be able to think about her. After that waltz and her words—those miraculous words; so incomprehensible, he could have mistaken them for phrases in a foreign language, or the utterances of a mystic speaking in tongues— he'd been tempted to reconsider the whole plan. But it was too late. Events had been set in motion. He had to resolve this, for good or ill, if he had any hope of a future at all, much less a future that

205

included Lily.

He *would* do it, Julian vowed. If Lily offered him love, he would give his all. He *would* solve this mystery. He would somehow fix everything, find the answers, redeem his every stupid mistake. He'd crawl through an ocean of broken glass just to hold her again, and hear her speak those words against his ear.

His ear caught a less pleasing sound just now. He'd nearly reached the end of the block, and a burst of noise arrested him where he stood. Footsteps clattered on the pavement, accelerating with purpose as they neared.

That hadn't taken long.

He steeled himself, putting one hand to the pistol at his hip. The thing wasn't even loaded. He needed answers, not a murder charge. He had no intention of shooting his would-be assassin. Yet.

'Julian! Julian, wait.'

No. By everything holy, no.

His heart crashed to his boots as he wheeled around to find not an assailant, but Lily rushing to his side.

'Lily, what the devil are you doing?'

'I'm coming with you,' she said, breathless. 'If you're determined to commit social suicide, I can't stop you. But I'm coming with you. You're not leaving me behind.'

Jesus. What did he do now? Julian grasped her by both shoulders and moved her to one side, looking past her to see if anyone had watched her leave.

'Have we been spotted?' she asked, intuiting his purpose. 'I hope so.' She threw herself at him, flinging her arms around his neck. The pistol clattered to the pavement. 'Compromise me. Leave no doubt. Let them see us together, and no one will think to object.'

He pushed her away to ask, 'Lily, have you gone mad?'

'Mad for you.' With that, she planted a kiss on his mouth, ripe and bold and sensual. Julian's head spun, and his knees went weak. She wanted him. Lily wanted *him*. More than that, she wanted to be his.

'A kiss won't be enough.' She disentangled her arms from his neck. 'We need more.'

Her hands went to her bodice. 'There's a fraying seam,' she said, running her fingers over her bosom in tantalizing fashion. 'Ah—just here.' She worked her finger into a little gap and pulled, ripping the bodice and exposing one corseted breast to the night. 'There. Now you've ravished me, you beast.' Smiling, she turned to look over her shoulder. 'Are they coming yet?'

God. To her, this was all a game. 'You have no idea what you're doing. You're in danger, every moment we stand here.'

'What, because of that scene you caused inside?'

Yes, because of that scene he'd caused inside. And because of the scenes he'd been inspiring all week long, in different venues. He'd made pointed remarks at the clubs, hinting at all his past sins. He'd taken jokes too far, beyond every boundary of well-meant humor. He'd even arranged for newspaper articles in which he claimed to be writing a salacious memoir. All his secrets would be revealed, he'd said, lamenting that he had but one thrilling experience missing from his life's tale—a daybreak duel in St. James Park.

And though he doubted his would-be killer to be one of his paramours' husbands, tonight he'd taken the extra step of enraging them as well. He'd done everything he could think of to provoke his enemy to action, and then he'd provided the perfect opportunity for him to strike. All London knew he would be attending this assembly tonight, and when he left it, he would be walking home alone. He'd all but painted a target on his waistcoat.

And now Lily had attached herself to his chest.

His eyes scanned the street. Everywhere he looked, darkness menaced. Shadows took creeping, malevolent shapes. His ears made a threat of every rustle and snap.

Cold sweat broke out on the back of his neck. He had to get her out of here.

Like a chariot sent from heaven above, a hackney cab turned the corner and started down their block. Julian hailed it and, without conversation, hefted Lily inside before the thing had even fully come to a stop. For an instant, he considered giving her address to the driver and sending her home alone—but then she might demand to be let out God-knows-where and return to this very spot again. In the past few days, Lily seemed to have added a few extra vertebrae to her already formidable spine.

Clearly, the only way to make sure this new, audacious version of Lily arrived home safe was to take her there himself. So regardless of who might be following him—following *them*—Julian barked the address at the driver and climbed into the cab.

The cab's interior was dark and cold as a tomb. He'd barely settled himself on the seat when Lily landed in his lap. The coach lurched into motion, throwing them together. He reflexively grabbed her

208

bared arms to steady her. His fingers slid over skin dotted with gooseflesh. It was cold, and she'd left her wrap behind. He slid his palms up and down her arms, trying to warm her. He needed to warm her, and desperately. Because now that he'd noted the little bumps on her arms, he could not help but notice the twin darts of her hardened nipples pressing against his chest. As the carriage rumbled over the cobbled streets, too many enticing parts of her jounced and rubbed against frantic parts of him.

'Julian,' she said huskily, 'you were right the other morning. You know me so well. I'm not made for illicit *affaires,* all that sneaking around to avoid discovery.' In the dark, her hands crept up his shoulders, then his face. Her fingers teased through his hair. 'Why should we hide at all? Let all London see us together. I don't care what anyone says or thinks. I love you, and I want the world to know.'

He wanted to weep. For joy, for frustration. She was so brave, his beautiful Lily, and the situation was so damned unfair. It wasn't her fault that she made these heartrending declarations at a moment when their lives were probably in danger and he couldn't possibly reciprocate. That fault was his, for choosing to live the way he had and making the decisions he'd made. He didn't deserve her, didn't deserve her love. He most certainly didn't merit these warm brushes of her lips against his skin. But damned if he could bring himself to stop them.

'We're in *love,* Julian. Isn't it wonderful?'

'No,' he murmured as she kissed him again. 'It's not wonderful. It's a disaster.'

Her lips grazed his jaw, then his throat. 'I can feel you speaking, and I know you're probably making some valiant protest. But you know I can't hear those words. Your body is making an altogether different argument, and I'm listening to it.' Her fingers crept inside his waistcoat, splaying over the thin lawn of his shirt. 'Take your heart, for example.'

Yes, take it. Take it and keep it, always.

'It's pounding so fiercely. Just battering my hand. What a wonder it is. I worry that your ribs may not contain all that vigor and emotion. And your breath . . .' She raised her fingers to his mouth, tracing his lips with a slow, gentle touch. He fought the urge to nip at her fingers, suck their silk-gloved tips into his mouth. 'Your breath is coming so fast.' She put a hand to his voice box. 'Was that a groan?'

Of course it was. She was driving him fair insane with desire. His erection swelled against her thigh.

'And your hands . . .' She slid one hand down his arm, until her gloved fingers covered his bare ones where they clutched the edge of the seat. 'They're trembling, just a little bit. Because you're just a little bit frightened. It's all right, Julian. I'm scared, too. I'm not fond of the dark. I hate not being able to hear *or* see. But I know I'm safe with you.'

'No, you aren't, Lily. You're not safe with me, not tonight. Even now, there could be someone following—'

Insensible to his objection, she spoke over him. 'And I'm beginning to appreciate, in the absence of sight, a heightened sense of touch is exquisite compensation. I want to touch you everywhere.'

She smoothed her hands over his shoulders and chest, exploring every ridge and plane, skimming down to the rippled surface of his tensed abdomen.

Lower, his basest instincts urged her. *Lower. Put*

your hands on me there.

She did him one better. Taking leverage from the seat back, she repositioned herself so that she straddled his lap. As she nestled snug against his groin, her breath tickled his ear. 'I should have cornered you in a darkened space years ago. I know you want me, Julian. Your body's telling me so, in no uncertain terms.'

She didn't know. She couldn't possibly know how long and how fiercely he'd wanted her. How crudely, and in how many strange contortions of limbs. To demonstrate, he slid both hands to her hips and rocked her pelvis against his, stroking delicious friction over his rampant arousal. She gasped. He moaned, desperate for more. More pleasure from her body, more sweet promises from her lips. More Lily.

She caught his hand and brought it to her breast, now popped free of her corset entirely, positioning his thumb directly over the puckered knot of her nipple. Her tone was coy, seductive. 'What does my body tell you, I wonder?'

Her breast molded to the shape of his hand. The soft globe warmed in his palm. Still, her nipple protruded against his thumb, tangible proof of her arousal.

'It tells me I'm lost,' he muttered, lowering his head to her breast. 'It tells me I'm weak and shameless and completely, utterly damned.'

*   *   *

His mouth closed around her nipple, and the darkness exploded with stars. Lily's mouth fell open in shock and delight. He kneaded the soft weight of her breast with his fingers, pulling the peak deeper into his mouth. She curled one hand into his hair, holding him to her as he licked and loved the sensitive tip.

'Yes,' she said. 'Julian, yes. Don't stop.'

He moaned. She could *feel* the sound, humming tight around her nipple. The vibrations sent joy shimmering through her veins. Then he pursed his lips and suckled hard, tugging on a cord that seemed to start at her nipple and end right between her thighs. Little bursts of pleasure detonated with every flickering swipe of his tongue. Oh, it was true whateveryone said. He was wicked with that mouth. Depraved, and she loved it.

The firm ridge of his manhood pressed against her inner thigh, and she wriggled in his lap to center herself. Now when she ground her hips, his hard length rubbed against her sex—*there*. Just there, in the perfect place. That perfect, beautiful, necessary place.

His hand tightened on her backside, and he guided her into a rhythm. His hips rode the swaying motions of the cab, lifting and thrusting against her as the wheels rumbled over cobbled streets.

Lily was soaring. Rocketing higher and higher with every wave of delicious sensation.

Oh, dear. Oh, God. She was going to—Right here in the hack, she was going to—

'Julian—'

He gave her no escape. He bucked faster, pressed tighter, suckled harder. Pleasure consumed her. It was too much, too much. Then not quite enough.

And then suddenly, it was *everything*.

She did not come softly. The climax hit with

a spectacular crash of pleasure, receded, then returned with greater power than before. Through it all, he moved against her, relentless, wringing pulse after pulse of ecstasy from her body. For long moments afterward she shuddered with pleasure, then finally went soft with bliss, slumping against his chest.

'Julian, that was . . .' The mental search for superlatives exhausted her. 'I have no words.' She felt certain she must have cried out something as she'd reached her peak, but she couldn't even muster the energy to blush.

He gathered her in his arms, kissing his way from her breast to her throat. His lips covered hers, and he took her mouth hungrily, thrusting deep with his tongue. Reminding her that while *her* needs had been satisfied, his had not.

One strong, deft hand went to her thigh, rucking up the heavy folds of her skirts and sliding beneath to skim her stockinged leg and then her bared, still-quivering thigh. She rose up on her knees a little bit, giving him better access. His fingers went straight to her sex. He cupped her mound, petting lightly. His thumb stroked over her engorged, still-sensitive bud, and she trembled with a delicious aftershock. She was flushed with heat and oh-so-damp down there, and his fingers slipped easily between her folds. He slid a finger inside her.

This time, he was the one shuddering. Her intimate muscles embraced the tender invasion, clasping eagerly and drawing him deeper still. The thought flitted across her mind to be embarrassed, but from the increased vigor of his kisses and the throbbing pulse of his arousal against her thigh, she could tell he liked what he felt.

She wanted to feel him, too. She tugged off her gloves and let them fall where they would. Scooting back on his thigh, she reached for the thick bulge tenting his trousers. She stroked him through the fabric with one hand while she sought the buttons of his fall with the other, eager to touch and explore. He'd given her such indescribable pleasure. She wasn't certain she had the expertise to return the favor in any commensurate magnitude, but she was determined to try. If it took several go-rounds, so be it. It would be no sacrifice.

He kissed her feverishly, delving deeper with his fingers while she set her own shaking hands to the task of working loose buttons. She managed two, then three. Enough to slide her fingers into the gap. Her first impression was that of scorching heat, radiating from his body. She pushed aside the wadded fabric of his tucked shirt. Beneath, she found only skin, sleek and taut. Did he always go without smallclothes? So very naughty. She nipped at his bottom lip, smiling in the dark.

He flinched a little—ticklish, perhaps—when she traced the crease between his thigh and torso. She followed that vulnerable curve to a springy thatch of hair, which felt much like hers. And then a thick, ridged column of heat that was completely different from anything she'd ever touched. She skimmed one fingertip along his length. So curious, how the skin moved with her touch. Like a swatch of rumpled velvet, stretched over steel. She marveled at the idea that this belonged *inside* her, this hot, intriguing combination of softness and strength.

Suddenly, he tore his mouth from hers. His head dropped back against the seat. His breath came as great clouds of vapor that caught what meager light

214

filtered into the cab.

Yes, this was strength. Not just the quite-evident potency beneath her fingertips, but her feminine power over him. With the restrictive cut of his trouser fall and the fact that she hadn't loosed all the closures, she couldn't quite curl her hand around his girth. But she stroked up and down, just lightly, and leaned forward to kiss his neck. And he simply lay there, helpless to resist.

Until the coach stopped, calling a halt to everything.

Lily pressed her forehead to his chest, laughing a little. Well, perhaps it was best they continued from here inside. In a bed.

He withdrew his fingers from her cleft and re-draped the folds of her skirts down over her legs. Then he pulled her hand from his trousers and brought it to his lips for a kiss.

There was a little light now, filtering in from the street lamps. She could just make out her name on his lips, and a few mystery words besides. Sliding off his lap, she fixed her gown as best she could, tucking her well-loved breast back into the cup of her stays. She plucked a hairpin from her upsweep and used it to gather the torn edges of her bodice before Julian alighted and handed her down.

Arm in arm, they hurried up the steps. Lily floated, scarcely feeling the stone beneath her slippers. She couldn't wait to get upstairs and continue where they'd left off.

When they reached the landing, she paused before rapping on the door. 'Why doesn't the hack driver leave?'

Julian held back. 'He's waiting for me. I asked him to stay.'

215

Suddenly, she wasn't floating any longer, just . . . hollow inside. Surely those words were just a trick of the flickering lamplight. He couldn't mean to leave her. Not considering what had just happened in that carriage—and more to the point, what *hadn't* happened yet, for him.

'I have to go,' he said. 'You don't understand. Someone wants to kill me.'

'Someone wants to kill you?' she repeated. 'Well, I want to make love to you. My goodness, Julian. With two such compelling alternatives, however will you choose?'

'I can't be seen going into your house. I must leave you here, at the door.'

She took a deep breath and forced herself to be calm. 'Julian, look around you.' She turned a pointed, slow gaze around the deserted square. 'There is no one following us. No threat to your life or mine. No danger, unless you go in search of it. Don't leave me tonight. Come to my bed, make love to me, and stay safe the whole night through.'

'I can't do that. I've already done too much. I can't engage you in a sordid *affaire*.'

'This is love. Love isn't sordid. And I've already told you, I want more than just an *affaire*.'

'What, marriage?' He seemed to choke on the word. 'To me? Lily, we are from completely different worlds. I shouldn't have to remind you of that. You saw my childhood—the best part of it, mind—with your own eyes, just the other day.'

'I don't care.'

'I've eaten scraps you would not throw to dogs. I spent a month picking oakum in Bridewell. For Christ's sake, I didn't even learn to read properly until I was nineteen years old.'

216

'I. Don't. Care. About any of it.'

'Others will. Your relations, your friends.'

'Then I don't care about them.'

He pushed a hand through his hair. 'You make it sound so simple, but it's not. Not for you, and not for me. I've spent my life hating the very notion of the aristocracy. The *ton* and I . . . we hold one another in mutual contempt. You would ask me to become a permanent part of it?'

She blinked. For a moment, she found it difficult to speak. 'Oh,' she managed. 'I see. So the problem isn't that I'm too good for you. It's that you're too good for me.'

'No, Lily. Never. That's not it at all. The problem is that someone murdered Leo, and that same someone may want to kill me. Until I have answers, I can't promise you a future. I can't even promise you a tomorrow.'

If she didn't love him so much, she could hate him for speaking that way. Didn't he know what a toll this constant anxiety took on her state of mind? There could be no peace for her, if this continued.

'Let me make this easier. Out there'—she nodded toward the square, and the city beyond—'there is danger, mystery, violence. And maybe . . . just maybe . . . an elusive answer or two. Meanwhile, in here'—she gestured behind her, toward the door of Harcliffe House—'I am offering you love, pleasure, comfort. A home. And perhaps, one day, a family.'

The cool night air took his sigh and made it a coil of vapor. A visible expression of his hesitance.

She grabbed the lapels of his coat and pulled him close, pressing her brow to his. 'Choose me,' she said, in a tone that she feared was too close to pleading. 'Choose *us*. I can't go on like this, bidding you farewell over and over, not knowing what will become of you once you've left my sight. If you desert me tonight, Julian . . .'

Dear God, was she really saying this? In principle, Lily abhorred ultimatums. They made a woman look desperate and manipulative. But she *was* desperate, no denying it. And since reasoning, arguing, and outright begging hadn't convinced him, manipulation seemed her only option left.

Before she could lose her nerve, she said, 'Walk away from me right now, and I don't want to see you again. Ever.'

Then she pulled away to wait for his answer. It was a lonely, unbearably quiet wait.

Everyone assumed that because she was deaf, her world was silent. But that wasn't the case. She lived with a steady, cycling murmur of sound—much like the effect she'd experienced as a girl, pressing a seashell to her ear. A muted roar, forever washing and ebbing at the edges of her consciousness. For one hideous summer, a high, shrill whistle had lodged just inside her left ear drum, and its ceaseless whine had nearly driven her mad. She'd wept with relief the morning she awoke to find it mercifully gone. But even afterward, total quiet was something she'd never known.

Until now.

There was absence of sound—and then there was *silence*. Julian's pause fell into the latter category.

After a long, soul-wrenching minute, he kissed her. So lightly, her lips trembled under his. As they ended the kiss, he cupped her chin in his fingers and stared deep into her eyes.

218

'God be with you, then.' His thumb stroked a tear from her cheek. 'Good night, Lily.'

Chapter Sixteen

Julian ordered the hack driver to return to the assembly rooms, and be quick. He was back on the same street corner where he'd met Lily in less than ten minutes' time.

Incredible. Had that entire blissful interlude really lasted less than ten minutes? He would make the memory last a lifetime. Her hot, sweet words sliding over his neck. The heady scent of her body, an intoxicating blend of citron and rosemary and feminine musk. Her fingertips, gliding along his . . .

Not now, he told himself. Not now.

The pistol he'd dropped was, as expected, gone. Vanished into the night—or rather, into the hand of some lucky passerby. Something that valuable and shiny wouldn't lie about unclaimed on a London street corner for more than a minute or two. Down the street, carriages were jostling for space, preparing to accommodate the departing guests. The immediate vicinity, however, was quiet and deserted.

So here he was. Alone, unarmed, and late for his appointment with Death. What happened now?

He stood there for a few minutes, just waiting to see if anything would occur.

When it didn't, he started to walk.

He walked back to his house along his usual route, ambling down the streets and avenues. He was honestly surprised when he arrived before the

219

modest Bloomsbury façade unchallenged. He then sat on his front stoop for a good quarter-hour. Try as he might to keep his attention sharp and scan the darkness for threats, his thoughts kept returning to Lily.

For Christ's sake, he was a marked man.

But even a marked man was a *man,* and he was a man irrevocably marked by Lily, branded by her touch. The way she'd moaned for him . . .

Why hadn't he called for the hack driver to circle the block? Another minute, and he could have had her coming again. He could have experienced the strength of her climax from the inside, felt her womanly flesh grasp his fingers tight. Her breathy cries, combined with the light touch of her fingers— all together, it probably would have brought him off, too. His loins stirred, just at the thought.

Not now, he told himself. Not now.

He rose, brushed off his trousers, and started to walk again.

He walked back to Mayfair, back toward the neighborhood of the assembly rooms, this time working a serpentine route down smaller streets and back alleys. Aside from the occasional sleeping beggar, some early carts on their way to market, and a few passing cabs, he met with no one.

And he found himself back on the same damn corner, still alone and undisturbed.

He walked some more. Through the straggling whores still haunting Covent Garden, by the cheap gin houses in the rookery of St. Giles, passing back along the Strand. He walked streets he normally wouldn't walk alone at night, for any reason. No one in his right mind would. But he walked them anyway, daring his unknown enemies to strike. Or if those enemies eluded him, simply tempting fate.

The hours passed. His feet went from sore to aching to numb in his boots. But Julian kept walking.

He found himself in St. James's Park at the first glimmer of daybreak, in the meadow that was the site of so many illegal, infamous duels. Here, in this field, a gentleman's honor could be redeemed by the firing of a single shot into the air. Julian had never understood it. Duels seldom amounted to more than a show of false courage. One ball sent whizzing skyward, and everyone went home mollified. England's 'best' men were preserved to live another day, clutch their gold more tightly to their breasts, and get more children on their wives and chambermaids. Sounded rather nice, didn't it?

But no one came to duel with Julian, and he'd lost his pistol anyhow. He would find no satisfaction here.

He could find satisfaction with Lily, a sly voice inside him whispered.

Not now, he told it. Not now.

So he walked some more, pondering other things. What did it mean, when a man planned his own funeral and no one came?

Lily and Morland had insisted from the beginning that Leo's murder was a senseless, random act. Could it be that they were right? Perhaps he'd missed his opportunity due to Lily's interruption, or he'd simply failed to lure his enemy to action. But the other possibility was equally strong: that there was no enemy to lure. No would-be murderer, at any rate.

It would have been easier to accept, if he didn't want to believe it so damn much.

221

Julian didn't have his destination in mind—rather, it seemed to draw him like a lodestone. Before he knew it, he was there—in Whitechapel, navigating a cramped district stacked high with warehouses until he stood in the alley where Leo had died. He'd walked here at night, several times. It was full daylight now, and the place looked narrow and dirty, not threatening. It smelled of filth and rotting fish.

Julian stared around him, wondering what the hell he was doing. He'd come to pay respects to Leo, he supposed, but any respect was wasted here. Leo had mercifully left this place behind, in body and spirit. Julian should do the same.

So he turned north and walked to Spitalfields. He traveled against the flow of the working poor, who streamed *en masse* toward better neighborhoods, on their way to work as scullery maids, chimney sweeps, rat catchers, and the like. Perhaps he would meet with one of his errand boys if he looked sharp.

The bells of Christ Church greeted him, ringing in the new day with familiar peals. *Welcome home,* he could imagine them to say. He'd spent his first nine years of life within earshot of these bells.

For the first time in decades, he entered the church. The devout were at their morning prayers, and Julian had no wish to disturb them. He lingered at the rear. Tilting his head to view the arcade, he was transported back to his boyhood, when these soaring arches and stately white columns made this the grandest building he could imagine ever being permitted inside.

And now, with stern-faced saints to chaperone, he loosed the reins on his thoughts. They went straight to her.

Lily. Just her name inspired in him more breathless awe than any psalm or choir could do. He might never learn who killed Leo, and whether or not that same person wished to kill him. But he knew that Lily loved him. And he knew that made him the luckiest bastard in England. Assuming she would even speak to him this morning, that was. He wanted to believe she was too generous to hold true to her ultimatum, but he couldn't be sure. Her will was strong. But perhaps her love was stronger.

What would it take, to make a real future with a woman like that? Not just a night of stolen passion, but a life worthy of her?

He would have to commit a small murder of his own. Mr. James Bell would need to die a quiet, sudden death, and Julian would have to sell off the business concerns discreetly. A lady of Lily's rank could not have a husband who dirtied his hands with trade. Julian would mourn the loss, no question. He'd been working for years toward the new mercantile scheme, and this would mean abandoning the idea entirely. And then, there were his employees . . . hundreds of mill workers and their families depended on his wages for their livelihood. Unlike most other owners, he paid them enough to live well. If he sold the mills, who could say what their fate would be?

But this was so much more than a business decision.

To be with Lily, he would have to *be* with Lily. Live in her aristocratic world, with no daily escape into his offices and no anonymous walks through the city at night. He would have to comport himself with dignity—no more wild antics or bacchanal

223

evenings at the club. The *affaires*—those, he would never miss. They hadn't been about pleasure in the first place, but merely revenge. So disgusting and degrading. It was a wonder he could stand in this holy place and not burst into flames.

Damn, there was no way around it. He was completely unworthy of her. If he did go to Lily, he would have to live with the knowledge that he'd betrayed Leo's friendship by taking his sister for himself.

And he would have to accept uncertainty, where Leo's murder was concerned. He would never know whether he'd unwittingly had a hand in his friend's death, or whether someone had wished to kill *him*. He would always worry. Always feel that little prickle of fear as he walked down the street, fearing that one day someone would recognize him, and Lily would suffer as a result.

What would he be forced to give up, to be with Lily? Only his trade, his principles, his possessions, his identity, his loyalty to Leo, and his very peace of mind. Only everything, forever.

Right. There really was no choice.

Before he left the church, Julian bent his head. He said a prayer for his mother and a prayer for Leo. And then a prayer of forgiveness for what he was about to do.

*　　　*　　　*

Lily's sitting room boasted a floor-to-ceiling bookcase, filled with volumes she'd collected from her girlhood on. Since Leo's death, she'd spent many a sleepless night rearranging its contents. She might pass one evening alphabetizing the books

224

by the author's last name. Then the next night, by the author's first name. Another night, she would sort them by genre: poems, plays, novels, essays. She'd invented dozens of ways to or ganize these books. Chronologically, by date of publication. Chronologically, in the order she'd acquired them. Chronologically, in the order she'd read them. By size. By color of the binding. By the number of pages.

One particularly melancholy night, she'd ranked them by how many characters died in each.

Last night, after Julian so heartlessly left her crying on the doorstep, Lily had marched upstairs, removed all the books from the shelf, and packed them away in trunks. When dawn came, she greeted it with fresh resolve. That was the last night she spent rearranging bookshelves. She'd only just emerged from months of mourning her brother. She would not lapse back into helpless grief today.

She took a light breakfast in her chambers. With her maid's assistance, she dressed in a cheery pink day dress and adorned her neck with a single strand of pearls. As the maid twisted her hair, Lily stared at herself in the mirror. Weary, red-rimmed eyes stared back at her from a pale, drawn face. She looked horrid, no question. But she couldn't improve her aspect by sitting about the house moping.

She dismissed the maid and considered the possible activities. She could pay calls, Lily supposed. But then, whom would she visit? Amelia would want to hear all about last night, and Lily didn't feel up to discussing it. As for others . . . it might be best to wait and see the scandal sheets today. She and Julian had departed the assembly abruptly, then vanished together into a coach. Who knew what the gossips might have concluded? She didn't especially care, but neither did she wish to face the rumors unprepared.

Shopping? Maybe it would boost her spirits to purchase something frivolous and pretty. Several somethings, at that. On credit. But while she knew such a strategy worked for other ladies, Lily had never experienced similar success. Her mathematical bent would not allow her to stop mentally tallying expenditures and balancing them against the pleasure accrued. Quite spoiled the whole exercise.

Exercise. Now there was an idea. Perhaps the park should be her destination. Yes, a nice long stroll along the Serpentine would be just the thing. She could ask Holling to accompany her. The house keeper would appreciate a chance to show off her new winter cloak.

'Oh. That cloak.' Lily sniffed back a tear, thinking of that lovely, luxurious garment. It was just like Julian, to be so inappropriate and so thoughtful at once. 'Even Holling has a cloak to remember him by, and what has he left me? Two ruined gowns and an intact maidenhead.'

A bright flutter caught her attention.

'I'm sorry, Tartuffe. I didn't mean to discount you.' She crossed to his cage and put one finger through the bars. The parrot nipped it playfully. 'You're right. I suppose I can't say he didn't leave me anything.'

But the bird would not be soothed. He bounced about his cage, flapping with agitation. Something must be happening downstairs.

Lily left her suite and padded down the corridor.

She descended the front stairs and stopped three risers from the bottom. There was Julian, standing in the entrance hall, dressed in morning attire and clutching a rolled paper in his hand. His face was unnaturally pale. She thought he looked like he might swoon again.

'Good morning,' he said.

'No,' she replied. 'No, it's not. It's a wretched morning, as you well know. I thought I told you if you deserted me last night, I didn't want to see you again.'

'You did.'

'Then what are you doing here?'

'I'm hoping you'll reconsider. Obviously.'

She gripped the banister, trying to steel herself. Yes, she was relieved beyond measure to see him alive, if not completely well. But she couldn't go through this same torment, over and over again. The books had already been packed away. 'Julian, I don't—'

'Wait.' He approached, coming to stand at the bottom of the staircase. 'Let me have my say. Please.'

Lily held her ground. If she was going to make it through this conversation without losing her nerve, she needed some space between them. Not to mention, the advantage of an extra eighteen inches' height.

'I'm sorry for leaving you last night,' he said. 'But I just couldn't do it. All threats and mysteries aside . . . You're a woman of remarkable character, Lily. Your brother was my very good friend. I couldn't soil your reputation and disrespect Leo's memory by taking your virtue that way.'

This? This was the reason he'd come here?

227

Just to reject her to her face, all over again? Lily couldn't believe it.

'However . . . ' He made a beckoning motion to the side. A man emerged from the drawing room. He was youngish, with thin brown hair and an earnest mien. Tucked beneath his arm, he carried a formidable tome. Swift and Holling followed close behind.

'However what?' Surely Julian didn't mean to present this poor fellow as a substitute? There was matchmaking, and then there was . . . well, she didn't even know the word, that's how unthinkable it was.

'I mean to do this properly. The way you deserve.' Julian gestured toward the man and said, 'Curate.' With a nod in Swift and Holling's direction, he added, 'Witnesses.' He unrolled the paper he'd been holding and raised it for her inspection. 'Special license.'

'Julian, what are you on about?'

He went down on one knee.

The room made a sudden twirl. She clutched the banister. 'Julian, do get up.'

'Marry me.'

She stared at him. 'What did you say?' She couldn't rush to conclusions. She had to be sure. Although, there weren't many other phrases that resembled 'marry me.' Except 'bury me,' perhaps. But given his sickly pallor—and the fact that the presence of a curate might be required for that activity, too—she thought it best to make absolutely certain.

'Lily Elizabeth Chatwick,' he said, slowly and solemnly, 'I am asking you to become my wife.'

Oh. There was no mistaking that word, *wife.*

228

'Here?' she finally managed to ask. 'Now? This very morning?'

'Yes.'

That extra eighteen inches of altitude was suddenly a dizzying height. She sank to the stairs, landing on her bottom with a jarring thud. Now she understood why he looked so pale.

'I'm no marquess, but I have the means to support you. I swear to be faithful, all my days. You may rely upon it.' He leaned forward and took her hand. His fingers were so chilled.

'What about Leo's murderers?'

'They're still out there, somewhere. I wish to God they weren't. But if I have to choose between finding the killers and holding on to you, there is no contest. I choose you. I choose us.'

The words sent hope spiraling through her. 'You're done with it then? The searching?'

'Yes.'

'Truly? You'll leave off all the late-night walks, the blood sport, the suspicion?'

'Yes.' He gripped her fingers tight. 'I see the skepticism in your eyes, and I know I've earned it. But believe me, Lily. Leaving you last night was the hardest thing I've ever done. I doubt I have it in me to ever do it again.'

His assurances should have been enough, but he just looked so miserable about the whole thing. 'Tell me this isn't because you think I'm ruined now, and no one else will ever have me. I can't bear to think you're here just because you feel obligated.'

'You don't want me to feel obligated? Well, I'm sorry, Lily. I *am* here because I feel obligated.' He brought her hand to his chest, pressing her

229

palm flat against his rapidly thumping pulse. 'I'm obligated by my heart. It's decided you're essential to my existence, you see. And it's threatening to go out on labor strike if I don't make you mine this very day. So yes. I am here on bended knee, acting from a deep, undeniable sense of obligation. I am, quite simply, yours.' He swallowed hard. 'If you'll have me.'

If? *If* she would have him? Her own heart pounded in her throat, making rather stern demands of its own. Did the man honestly think she could turn him away?

Yes, she realized suddenly. Yes, he did. This was why he was so pale. He was terrified. Even after all the love she'd confessed last night, he thought there was a goodly chance she'd refuse him this morning—or that if she did accept him, she might change her mind in the time it took to secure a license and curate.

Oh, Julian. She saw it all in his eyes—the vulnerability, the hurt, the years of perceived rejection and scorn. After a lifelong quest to take success, steal pleasure, and wrangle admiration from the world, it didn't occur to him he might actually deserve those things, freely given. Now the task of correcting this misapprehension fell to her.

She could not imagine a happier or more rewarding life's work.

'Yes,' she said, keeping her words simple and few, so that they might be absolutely clear. 'Yes, I will marry you.'

When he made no discernible reaction, Lily put her free hand to his face. 'Julian, breathe.'

He did, with sudden and apparent relief. Color rushed back to his cheeks.

She touched her thumb to the corner of his mouth, attempting to tease it into a smile. 'We are going to be so happy.'

He looked unconvinced. 'We'll be together.'

'Yes. Precisely.'

Chapter Seventeen

There was astonishingly little to a wedding.

Julian was surprised. He'd never attended any actual wedding ceremonies. Oh, he'd been invited to dozens, but he preferred to save his appearance for the celebration afterward. Somehow, he'd imagined a sacrament with such eternal implications would be accordingly lengthy and dry.

But even with the curate speaking slowly and every so often handing his liturgy to Lily so that she might read and respond, it took less than a quarter-hour to bind Lily Chatwick and Julian Bellamy in the eyes of God and man, for the remainder of this life and—with some outrageous luck—beyond.

The ceremony took place in the morning room. After vows were exchanged, he produced a pair of simple gold bands. They were unadorned, but weighty in both substance and significance. He thought nothing in his life would thrill him more than sliding that ring on her slim, elegant finger— until a half-minute later, when she slid the matching band on his. The first was the triumph of claiming his bride. The second was the poignant, bone-deep relief of being claimed.

It had been so long since he'd belonged to

anyone.

They all signed the register: Lily, Holling, Swift, the curate. Julian went last. He hesitated, wishing the name he prepared to sign was actually his own.

But it was too late for attacks of conscience now.

He scrawled the signature. There, it was done.

He looked to his bride—his wife; good Lord, she *belonged* to him now—and she gave him a wide, gracious smile. She'd seemed genuinely shocked by his proposal this morning. On close inspection of her appearance, however, he wondered if she hadn't expected it all along and dressed expressly for the occasion.

She looked timeless in her beauty, as a bride should be. Fifty years from now someone could say the name 'Lily,' and Julian knew his sieve of an octogenarian memory would still retain *this* image, from *this* day. No matter what changes time wrought on her aspect, he would always think of her thus. Looking not only lovely, but so very much herself. Straight-spined and resolute, but soft and feminine in that cherry-pink dress and pearls. Dark, gently curving tendrils of hair framed her milk-white cheeks and burnt-sugar eyes. So tempting and sweet.

Positively edible.

'Well,' she asked, clasping her hands behind her back and bobbing on her toes, 'what now?'

What now? Oh, he would show her what now.

With his thanks and a generous donation for the parish, Julian dismissed the curate.

To Swift and Holling, he directed, 'Give the staff a feast and good wine, then the remainder of the day off. Place a tray for us at the top of the staircase. After that, no one, and I mean no

232

one, is to venture above stairs unless we ring. No lady's maid, no footman, no chambermaid, no boy carrying coal for the grate. Not today, not tomorrow. I don't care if it's been three days and you've given us up for dead, do you understand? We are not to be disturbed.'

'But sir, the—' Holling began.

He cut her off. '*Not* to be disturbed.'

The house keeper curtsied. 'As you please, Mr. Bellamy.'

Once the servants had cleared out, Julian crossed the room until he stood about an arm's length from Lily. He didn't trust himself any closer just yet. 'I very much wish to kiss my bride.'

Her rosy lips curved in a smile. 'Your bride very much wishes to be kissed.'

'But there's a problem, you see. If I kiss you here, there's a fair chance we'll never make it upstairs.'

'Well.' Dark lashes fluttered as she surveyed the room with mock seriousness. 'There is always the divan.'

'Some other time.' He moved toward her, laying a hand on her shoulder. 'Do take pity on poor Holling's nerves, and try not to shriek.'

With that, he scooped her straight off her feet and into his arms. And she did shriek, but only a little. She clung to his neck with surprise—and perhaps a touch of playful desperation. The bite of her fingernails against his nape sent desire rippling down his spine. She weighed next to nothing, and rationally, he knew lifting her was no great feat of strength. But hefting her compact frame in his arms, fitting her tight against his chest . . . making a Julian-shaped bundle of Lily's precious angles and curves . . . he felt protective. Powerful. And just a bit savage. His male pride swelled. Other parts of him swelled, too.

He carried her through the entrance hall and up the stairs. Visualizing the windows as he'd so often viewed them from the street, he set off down the corridor, counting doors until he arrived at her apartment.

'How do you know which one is mine?' she asked, as he shouldered open the door to her sitting room.

'Lucky guess.'

He covered the carpet in three paces, swept her into the bedchamber, and fell with her onto the bed. A heap of white pillows and downy quilts sucked them in like a snowdrift. Julian sputtered at a bit of lace in his mouth and rolled onto his side, facing her. What with all the white, and the hour of noon approaching, the room was wild with sunlight.

'Oh, it's dreadful, isn't it?' she said, batting away clouds of white bedding. 'I had it done up this way when I was seventeen, and it's never been redecorated.'

He huffed at a tiny feather floating between them, then gave her a wolfish grin. 'Very virginal.'

All the better to ravish you on, my dear. This bed was like his most depraved adolescent fantasy come to life. Taking a well-bred lady on a cloud of white lace; pushing his crude, baseborn cock into her immaculate, tightly guarded virtue. And this was even better than the fantasy, because Lily belonged to him. She was his wife. Her immaculate, tight . . . God, he just *knew* she would be so tight . . . virtue was his. Not for the taking, but for the keeping. Forever.

It was the most heart-tugging, frightening, and

234

flat-out arousing notion he'd ever contemplated. His trousers pulled snug over his groin.

'Then it's still appropriate, I suppose. I mean ... that is to say ... ' Her face went pink against the white linen. 'You know there haven't been others.'

Dear, sweet Lily. He smoothed the hair from her brow, forcing himself to rein in his lustful impulses for the moment. 'Are you anxious?'

'No. Well, only a little. But it's a pleasant sort of anxious.'

'You needn't worry. This is going to be amazing. Spectacular.'

She laughed. 'Perhaps I should fault the arrogance of that statement, but I'm rather comforted by it, truthfully.'

'It's not arrogance, it's a promise. This is going to be wonderful,' he insisted, 'and I will tell you why. Because if at any time, you are feeling something less than indescribable bliss, you are going to tell me so, and I will stop at once. Do you understand? I would never hurt you.'

She nodded. 'What a very husbandly thing to say.' With a little gasp, she bolted straight up in bed. As if she'd just now received an express notifying her of the fact, she grinned down at him and said, 'I'm your *wife*, Julian. I'm Mrs. Bellamy.'

Her eyes sparkled with delight, sending bright shards of happiness to pierce his heart. She'd never looked so beautiful.

'No,' he said, struggling to sit up next to her, 'you are still the daughter of a marquess. You are Mrs. Nothing. You are, and will always be, *Lady* Lily Bellamy.'

'Heavens.' Her hand went to her brow. 'Another L sound in my name. That's four now.'

'Too late. You can't take it back.'

'Are you sure?' She toyed with his cravat. 'You still haven't kissed me, you know.'

He slowly leaned in, giving her ample time to retract that teasing smile to a soft, luscious pout. Their noses touched. She inhaled a quick breath. And just the instant before he pressed his lips to hers, she whispered, 'I love you so.'

He covered the precious words with his mouth, needing to drink them in. Sipping at each of her lips in turn, then delving lightly with his tongue. She reached for him, curling her fingers in his hair, and as he deepened the kiss, she moaned in the back of her throat.

Desire swept him like a flame through dry bracken. It took everything he had to hold to that promise he'd just made, and not simply push her back against the counterpane and sink into her at once. But he was determined to make this every bit as good for her as it was doubtless going to be for him.

He left her mouth and began a thorough investigation of the spot beneath her ear. Nuzzling first, then tasting with lips and tongue. She was so delicious, he couldn't resist a playful bite.

She gave a sharp cry.

He pulled away. 'Have I hurt you?'

'No.' She looked puzzled. 'Why do you ask?'

'You . . . you made a noise.'

'Oh, did I?' She smiled sheepishly. 'I suppose because I liked it.'

Right. He needed her *under* him, now. His hands gathered fistfuls of billowing white lace.

'Now who's anxious?' she asked, skimming a teasing touch along his jaw. 'Last night in the hack,

I'm positive I was making all manner of sounds. You weren't so concerned then.'

'Last night was different.' Last night, *he* was different. Julian wasn't sure how to explain it. In that carriage, he'd been a thief, taking what didn't belong to him under cover of night. Today, he was a bridegroom, who'd just pledged to cherish and protect this woman all the days of his life. The difference was so profound, it was . . . well, it was night and day.

'Let's settle on a signal,' she suggested. 'A word. If I'm uncomfortable or in pain, I'll say that word. With all other noises, you can assume the best. Do you agree?'

He nodded. 'What word?'

She considered. 'How about "spider"?'

'Spider?' He couldn't help but laugh. 'Who wants to think of spiders in the throes of passion?'

'No one, of course. That's why it's ideal.'

He shook his head. 'Something else, if you please, with fewer legs.'

'Very well.' Her eyes wandered past him, toward the connecting parlor. 'What about "armchair"? Perfectly harmless, and only four legs.'

'That won't do. What happens when you beg me—and no mistake, someday you *will* beg me—"Julian, make love to me right here in the armchair"? The moment will be ruined.'

Her eyebrow arched to a reproachful angle. She knew she was being teased. But here was a tried-and-true test of temperament—when confronted with sharp wit, did a person retreat or parry? Julian could never be friends with people who fell into the former category.

And Lily's response was the reason he adored

her, beyond expression.

'Well, then,' she said, working loose his cravat. 'If that's the case, we rule out so many options. Armchair, sofa, carpet, bathtub, dressing table, dining table, wardrobe. No good, any of those.' She pulled the unknotted cravat free, and the slow glide of linen against his neck made his body pulse with need.

Her fingers went to the buttons of his waistcoat. 'Nor can we use coach, carriage, hackney, landau, or anything of that nature. Oh, and nature! We must rule out grass, meadow, hillock, haystack, grotto, lake . . . Really, Julian, there are very few words left.' Her hands slipped inside his open waistcoat, and she skimmed her palms over the thin lawn of his shirt. She was teasing him, with words and touch, and he couldn't have loved it more.

'Turn around,' he said hoarsely, adding a hand motion for clarity's sake.

She obeyed, and he applied his fingers to the column of fabric-covered buttons chasing down her slender back.

'What about "mirror"?' she said, smiling into the floor-length looking glass across the room.

'Minx.' He caught her gaze in the reflection. 'Absolutely not.'

She laughed as he returned to the task of undoing her many, many tiny buttons. There might have been a hundred, and he wouldn't have complained. With each closure he eased free, he kissed the patch of newly revealed skin. When he ran his tongue down the valley between her shoulder blades, she shivered and moaned.

'Bedpost?' she gasped, gripping the same as he drew the bodice down her shoulders, revealing her

238

stays and tissue-thin chemise.

He let a swift yank on her laces serve as his curt refusal there. After undoing the tapes of her corset, he put his hands on her bared shoulders and turned her back to face him. Her loosened bodice gaped at the neckline, and he slid a hand inside to cup her breast, rubbing his thumb back and forth over her hardened nipple. He bent his lips to the creamy expanse of her décolletage.

She threw her head back, tilting her face to the ceiling as he kissed and nibbled her throat. 'I am,' she breathed, 'almost afraid to suggest "chandelier."'

He chuckled against her skin.

'Plaster,' she blurted out, pushing on his shoulder. He straightened. 'What?'

'Plaster.' Her eyes rolled to the ceiling. '"Plaster" is the perfect word. Not offensive, not suggestive.'

'Plaster,' he repeated. 'Very well.' He cupped her cheek in his hand. 'Lily, I adore you.'

Julian had to admit, he'd harbored worries in the dark recesses of his mind, about how to make *this* different. As in, the actual act. He felt the need to mark this time apart from every sexual experience he'd ever had before. He'd even searched his imagination for an as-yet-untried lovemaking position, much as he thought it prudent to begin with the basics.

But with her teasing, Lily had given him exactly what he needed. He could safely say he'd never discussed spiders and plaster in bed before, not with anyone.

And as he kissed her again, taking her mouth with possessive, unrestrained passion, he realized it wouldn't even matter if he had. They'd filled this

239

moment with so much genuine affection, there was no room for his sordid past to intrude.

This was different because this was Lily.

This was different because this was *love*.

And he needed to love her, *now*. Then again later. As many times as she'd permit. He tugged down her bodice and chemise to expose one breast, dipping his head to tongue the plump globe and taut, berry-red nipple. Drawing the nub into his mouth, he suckled with steady intent. *Moan for me, Lily*.

'Oh,' she sighed. 'Oh, Julian.'

'Oh, Juuuuuuulian,' Tartuffe squawked.

Startled, Julian jerked back his head. Unaware of the interruption, Lily picked the same moment to seek a kiss. They bumped noses, then recoiled from one another in pain. Deuce it all, now he'd truly hurt her.

'What is it?'

'Damned bird,' he grated out, pressing his fingers to his nose to check for blood, at the same time surveying her face for swelling. 'Where is he?'

'In my sitting room,' she answered ruefully, flopping back onto the mattress and covering her face with both hands. 'Perhaps he's jealous.'

Julian scrambled from the bed and darted through the connecting door into Lily's private parlor, gathering the birdcage with one hand and scooping up a stray lap blanket with the other. How he rued ever gifting her with the ridiculous creature. With determined haste, he shouldered open the door and marched the parrot down the corridor toward the staircase.

'There you are,' he said, setting the cage on the top step. 'Holling will find you eventually.'

240

The bird chided, 'Guilty, guilty.'

'Yes,' he said through gritted teeth. 'Yes, I know. Stop reminding me.' He shook out the blanket and prepared to drape it over the cage.

'Oh, Juuulian,' the parrot shrieked. 'Guilty, guilty! Mr. James Bell.'

His heart stalled. His hands froze in place, suspending the flannel drape in midair. 'What the devil did you just say?'

Blue and green wings stretched. 'Thank you, that will be all.'

'You miserable feathered . . . ' Julian growled with frustration and tugged at his hair. It was that or pluck the parrot bare, plume by impertinent plume.

Mr. James Bell. Who'd taught the bird to say 'Mr. James Bell'? Tartuffe must have been nearby when he came to escort Lily to the theater. Bloody hell.

What a fool he'd been just a minute ago, thinking there was no room for his past to intrude. He hadn't even been married an hour, and already the perfect future he'd imagined for himself and Lily threatened to crumble around him, all thanks to a loose-beaked, decrepit bird. Panic closed in, clammy and oppressive, sending rivulets of cold perspiration down his back.

'Now you listen to me,' Julian said, crouching low and leveling a finger at the impudent creature. 'You're going to forget you ever heard that name. Otherwise for tomorrow's dinner, I will specially request parrot fricassee.'

The bird cocked its head and regarded him with an accusing eye.

'I mean it. I will endanger you and your entire species.' The parrot turned away in indignant

241

silence.

Julian threw the blanket over the cage. 'Wise bird.'

As he made his way back to Lily's chambers, he tried to convince himself this was no cause for concern. So the parrot had learned the name 'Mr. James Bell.' It signified nothing. Lily couldn't even hear it. None of the servants would ascribe any meaning to it. The bird had been passed from gentleman to gentleman for years now. He might have picked up the name anywhere.

Julian paused with his hand on the bedchamber door latch, letting the cool brass calm his nerves. He would not allow the ravings of a deranged parrot to ruin his wedding day. This was what he'd been waiting for all his life.

This was *love*. This was *Lily*.

Resolving to banish all worries, he flung open the door. And halted mid-step.

Because this was Lily, *naked*.

*   *   *

Lily paused, one foot propped on the bed steps, arrested in the act of rolling her stocking over her knee.

Aside from that half-unrolled stocking, and its untouched counterpart on her other leg, she was bare to the skin. And Julian was standing in the doorway, utterly entranced.

Oh, drat.

'You . . .' she stammered. 'Er, that was fast.'

He didn't respond. Merely . . . tilted his head a fraction. His gaze roamed every part of her *except* her face. Fortunately, her bent leg and a fall of

242

unbound hair served to conceal her most private places from his view. She didn't dare move a muscle, for fear of exposing herself completely. Her hastily discarded gown, stays, and shift lay in an unhelpful heap on the floor.

'I meant to finish undressing before you returned,' she explained, 'and wait for you in bed, under the covers. To surprise you.'

He remained silent, considering.

Lily blushed from head to toe. Now that she'd explained herself, she hoped he would do her the courtesy of ducking back into the corridor, counting ten, and allowing her to finish. But he showed no sign of moving at all.

'This is better,' he finally said, nodding in agreement with himself. 'Much better.'

Still, he made no move.

'Are you just going to stand there staring at me?'

'Not for long.' He stayed her with an open palm. 'Hold right there.' Then he leaned against the doorjamb and began to work at removing his boots.

Hold right there, indeed. Wherever would she go? She could act missish, she supposed. Blush, squeal, and grab for her chemise. Make an ungainly scramble up these low steps and dive under the bedclothes.

But as vulnerable as she was in her nakedness, she wasn't afraid. She had power over him. The evidence was prominent indeed, where it pressed against his trouser fall. His obvious arousal told her he had needs. And the determined look in his eyes told her he had plans.

She wanted to learn what they were.

So she remained still, foot propped on the step and torso arched over her bent knee, watching him

243

as he set his boots aside and shrugged out of his topcoat and waistcoat. Stripped down to shirt and trousers, he crossed to her in smooth, confident strides. Her skin prickled with gooseflesh as he advanced.

He stopped at her side. 'I've wanted this for a long time.'

The stark hunger in his gaze revealed the truth of his statement. And that unsettled Lily. He'd wanted this for a long time. Perhaps imagined it in vivid, shocking detail. What if the actual experience didn't live up to his expectations? She wanted so much to please him. To reward his patience.

'Do you trust me?' His touch grazed her cheek.

'Always.'

Cat-like, he slid around her body, coming to stand behind her. She felt the flutter of linen against her back, then caught sight of his discarded shirt as it joined her garments on the floor. A moment later, his trousers topped the pile. She closed her eyes on a smile, knowing better than to wait for smallclothes.

His hands smoothed over her shoulders and came to rest on her upper arms. He tugged, drawing her torso upright and pulling her back flush against his naked chest.

Ah, warmth. Delicious heat slid over her chilled skin and sank deeper, permeating muscle and bone. He ironed her back with the hard planes of his chest, while his hands stroked up and down her arms. He bent his head, and his breath warmed her ear. His hips nestled against her backside, and she felt the springy hair on his thigh tease against her smoother flesh. He held her surrounded, captive. The heat of his body relaxed and aroused her, all

244

at once. She was melting in his arms, becoming languid and wet.

She started to pivot in his arms and face him, but he held her fast, forbidding her to turn.

He trailed one hand up her arm, then across, skimming his fingertips along her collarbone. Then his touch dipped, tracing the line of her sternum and continuing around to caress the underside of her breast. She felt his breath catch. Lily looked down, entranced by the way he balanced the soft, slight weight in his palm and circled her areola with his thumb. Her nipple puckered to a taut peak, seeking his touch.

He didn't oblige, the teasing cad. Instead he drew his fingers back up her chest. She stretched her neck, reclining her head against his shoulder as he feathered light touches up her throat, surrendering to the lovely ripples of sensation.

Now she knew why he wouldn't allow her to turn. If they faced each other, he would be the focus of her concentration. *Was he saying something?*, she would continually ask herself, scanning his expressions. Had she missed some important direction or cue? But standing like this, he freed her from incessant questioning and allowed her to simply respond.

His tongue flicked and swirled against her neck, raising the little hairs on her nape. He cupped her jaw, pressing his thumb to the corner of her lips. Her mouth fell open, and she panted as he traced the shape of her lips, then insinuated his thumb between them. He rubbed her tongue, and Lily knew a moment of uncertainty. Did he wish her to lick his thumb? To suckle it?

Obeying the urges of her own desire, she let

245

her tongue flicker against the tip of his thumb. His growl of approval rumbled through her. But before she could continue, he withdrew his thumb from her mouth. In the next instant, he pressed that moistened pad against her erect nipple, shocking her with the brisk sensation.

Who could have suspected bliss to be so cold? With every frosty lick of his wet thumb over the sensitive bud, she envied the intimate lives of seals and Laplanders. The exquisite chill had her shivering with desire, and growing ever more aware of the hot ridge branding the small of her back.

His manhood ground against her, hard and insistent, as he plucked at both her nipples now, cupping and shaping the mounds of her breasts. He nuzzled and kissed her neck and ear. The air surrounding them grew rich with musk, and Lily dragged it in and out of her lungs in open-mouth gasps. She writhed her hips, hoping to lure those talented fingers lower. She needed his touch *there,* down between her legs.

When he brought his first and second fingers to her mouth, this time she opened for them readily, sucked them hungrily. Another surprise, how the simple act of suckling aroused her beyond measure. She pulled his fingers deeper into her mouth, tracing their full length with her tongue and thrilling to his palpable groan.

She fought his retreat, pursing her lips tight and whimpering around his fingers as they slid from her mouth. But all complaining ended when he applied the wet tips to her intimate flesh, parting her folds with one confident sweep and centering on the sensitive nub at their crest.

She cried out. Nearly faltered, but he held her

fast with one arm cinched just below her breasts, binding her to him as he worked that needy, aching bit of flesh. Her posture, with one foot propped on the step, eased his exploration. Just a few skillful swipes of his fingertips, and he had her on the brink of ecstasy. Her thighs quivered as she approached release.

Suddenly, she felt him shift behind her. The hard, muscular thigh that had bracketed hers now moved between her legs, spreading her wide. And the erection that had pressed against her back now sprang up snug between her legs. His hardness worked back and forth against her aroused flesh, stroking in delicious counterpoint to the steady motion of his fingertips.

She was so close. Teetering on the edge of bliss. 'Julian,' she gasped. 'I need . . .'

But he knew what she needed. He pressed the tip of his arousal against her opening, nudging just inside. Not so much as to hurt her. Just enough to give her that full, tight sense of completion she craved. Her inner muscles stretched around his girth, and his fingers made feverish circles over her pearl.

She came apart, wracked by blissful shudders and inarticulate cries. He thrust, allowing her body to draw him in, steadily sheathing himself in her climax. The invasion hurt, but the pain dimmed in comparison to the bright, overwhelming pleasure. In the same way the cold against her nipple had only made her more aware of his heat.

She was aware of all of him now. Every hot, hard, powerful inch. He was *inside* her. He was *hers.*

After a few motionless moments, his grip on her waist slackened. He withdrew from her body, then helped her up the bed steps and onto the mattress, rolling her onto her back. Pillows bunched beneath her head as he arranged her limbs to his satisfaction and knelt between her thighs. After all this, she still had her stockings on. He didn't seem to care. If a man could drink a woman in with his eyes, then Julian was taking great, thirsty gulps of her bosom.

His body fascinated her, too. His small, flat nipples and smooth chest, the trail of dark hair that led down to his groin.

He balanced his weight on one arm and angled her hips with the other, preparing to enter her again. His every muscle and tendon tensed.

'Wait.'

He waited. Reluctantly. She looked up, into a gaze razor-sharp with yearning. His eyes let her know just how much sanity this delay would cost him. But he waited, because she'd asked.

His erect, ruddy manhood lay heavy on her stomach. At last, here was some facet of Julian she could fully *know*. When it came to this most elemental expression, a man could have no disguises, no complexities. This part of her husband was simple, honest, and currently very straightforward. She wanted to explore and understand him, from tip to root.

So, just as a lady should do with any new acquaintance, Lily began by offering her hand.

She brushed a fingertip against his swollen, dusky crown. The entire organ flinched. Startled, she pulled her hand away.

He retrieved it, curling her fingers around his thick, veined shaft and showing her how to slide down to the base, then up again. His breath heaved in his chest as she cautiously stroked, testing his

248

girth and length with her fingers, swirling her thumb around the broad, plum-like head. Her hand came away wet with an iridescent shimmer and streaks of her virgin's blood. So raw; so wildly arousing. She felt unhinged from this pristine, white-linen world.

'Go on.' She stretched her arms above her head, lifting her breasts and offering herself for the taking.

And he took.

Spreading her thighs with his own, he sank into her in a slow, powerful glide. He set a steady rhythm, working a bit deeper with each thrust. As he stroked into her again and again, he covered her body with hot, desperate kisses, interspersed with words. Lily wished she could catch them all. She recognized the double flicker of her name, a few phrases here and there. Comprehension came and went in little thrusts of carnality.

'You feel,' she glimpsed. A bit later, 'Can't help—' Then 'beautiful' and 'so wet' and 'God' and 'I love.'

'I love this,' she told him, running her hands over the straining muscles of his back and pulling him close. 'I love you.'

His tempo increased, and she felt him growl against her neck. Then he shuddered, stroking into her deep—once, twice—and was still.

He lay spent and heavy atop her. And that was a good thing, because without his weight, Lily thought she just might float away. Such happiness.

I am a wife, she thought. *I am Julian's wife.*

After a moment, he rose up on his elbows, smoothing the hair from her face and pressing tender, breathless kisses to her brow and cheeks.

249

'Are you well?'

She nodded. 'Very well indeed. And you?'

'Never better.' He touched the corner of her lips. 'And I say that with all honesty, Lily. Never better.'

Joy lifted her heart.

He withdrew from her and rolled aside, wrapping his arm about her midsection to keep her close.

She turned on her side to face him. 'Will you teach me to converse in signs, the way you spoke with Anna at the coffee house?'

He blinked at the abrupt change of topic.

'I mean,' she went on, 'I only ever learned the finger alphabet and never practiced it much at that.' Although, after her night at the coffee house, she'd excavated the crumbling pamphlet from her bureau drawer, practicing the signs for each letter until she could recall them from memory.

He rose up on his elbow. 'Of course I'll teach you, if you wish. Bear in mind, it's rather like a dialect. The signs I use are one part my mother's local language, and one part learned at the coffee house. Finger-spelled English is more standard, if you ever mean to use it with anyone else.'

'Perhaps we could practice both.' She trailed a finger down the center of his chest. 'We are married now. We have a lifetime ahead of us, and I hate the thought of missing a single word you say.' She pushed herself to a sitting position, folding her legs under her bottom and pulling the counterpane over her lap.

Carefully, and embarrassingly slowly, she signed letters with her hands.

I . . . L . . . O . . . V . . . E . . . Y . . . O . . . U

Smiling, he took her hands and kissed them each in turn. Then he sat up beside her and said, 'There's

250

a way to signal the end of a word. Watch carefully.'

She stared intently at his hands, noting the subtle wrist motion and slant of gaze he used to separate each cluster of letters.

I. L-O-V-E. Y-O-U.

And then, *T-O-O*.

She blinked furiously, her eyes misting with tears.

His hand cupped her chin, tilting her face to his. 'For God's sake, Lily. Don't cry. Is it such a terrible thing?'

'No. It's wonderful.' She wiped her eyes with her wrist. 'I'm sorry. I don't mean to weep. We love each other. We're husband and wife. It's the happiest day of my life, truly. It's only . . . I wish it hadn't taken us so long to figure it out.'

He stared at her for a moment. Then he threw back his head and laughed.

'What?' She sniffed. 'What's so amusing?'

'Lily. You have no idea.' He scratched the back of his neck, still grinning. 'Answer me this. Do you know that you rub your left ear when you're vexed?'

'I do? No, I don't. Do I?' Suddenly self-conscious, she pulled her fingers away from that same ear he'd just named.

'Yes, you do.'

He began signing along with his speech. She couldn't decode the rapid motions just yet, but she adored watching them, in much the same way she loved watching him play the pianoforte so masterfully.

'The night we met,' he said, 'it was your twenty-fifth birthday. A pleasant Wednesday evening, warm for April. You wore a gown of violet silk with gold braid trim. White gloves. Your hair was lovely. It was twisted into a knot at the center, with a smaller coil and ribbons encircling the chignon. You used to wear that style often, but I haven't seen you do so of late. Have you changed lady's maids?'

She nodded numbly. 'This past May.'

'I thought so.'

'But how did you . . .' Lily frowned, not understanding him. 'Last week, you said you didn't even remember the night we met.'

'Your menu was inspired by Indian fare,' he went on. 'All these exotic curries and chutneys and spiced lamb. I remember marveling at the fact that you'd ordered a birthday meal of entirely unfamiliar dishes, when most would ask for old favorites. It told me you have an adventurous spirit.'

'Me? I don't have an adventurous spirit.' Lily wasn't an adventurer. She was a keeper of lists and ledgers. She only *wished* she possessed an adventurous spirit.

'Not adventurous?' He teased her with a look. 'In the past week, you've danced in assembly rooms and crude taverns, attended the theater in outrageous disguise, flung yourself at me in carriages and dark alleys. If that's not proof of an adventurous spirit, I don't know what is. But back to that first night. You took us all on a culinary adventure to India. Our place cards had little elephants drawn on them. I still have mine, somewhere.'

'Leo didn't care for it.' She chuckled, remembering the way her brother's face had flushed beet-red after one bite of the spicy curry. 'He declared an end to Hindu sympathies and asked the footman to bring cold roast beef.'

'He did. And though he'd just thrown over all your hard work, you smiled and said nothing. The conversation floated on to something else, and you rubbed your left ear. And then, for some reason, your eyes sought mine. In that moment, I knew three things. First, much as you loved your brother, you occasionally found Leo a bit trying and dull.'

She gasped. 'No. *Leo?* I never—'

'Secondly,' he went on, undeterred, 'I knew that a band of vicious outlaws could storm the dining room and hold you at knifepoint, and you would deny that fact to the gruesome end. Just as you're doing now. But thirdly, and most remarkably, I knew you couldn't hide it from *me*. Didn't even wish to. I can't explain exactly how or why, but I understood you, Lily. And I felt certain, somehow, that you would understand me.'

She knew exactly what he meant. Lily had recognized their connection too, even when she'd called it nothing more than friendship. She'd always felt safe baring her emotions to him.

'I was in love with you by the time the third course was served. I've been in love with you ever since.' His lips quirked in a little smile. 'So you see, it did not take *me* so very long to figure it out. Perhaps an hour, all told.'

Truly? He'd known himself to be in love with her all this time? She hardly knew how to respond. A lump rose in her throat, and the taste was bitter. If he'd been in love with her, how could he have wasted so much time—so much of himself—on all those others?

W-H-Y, she signed with halting motions. 'Why did you never say anything?'

He gave a defeated shrug. 'I'm a bastard. Isn't it

obvious?'

If that was meant to be a joke, Lily wasn't laughing.

'I don't know,' he finally replied. 'Why do you rub your left ear when you're vexed? Out of pain at first, or perhaps fear. After a while, it just became habit.'

He went still for a moment. When he began again, his signs were expansive, animated. Deeply felt, she supposed.

'I've spent so much of my life wanting. As a boy, wanting food, wanting warmth, wanting shelter. Wanting my mother back, for even just one day. Then as a man, wanting wealth, wanting esteem, wanting revenge. By that night of your birthday party, I'd accomplished everything I'd set out to do by entering the *ton*. And as much as I'd taken for myself, I still wasn't satisfied. Always, I wanted more. That insatiable hunger . . . I reveled in it. I pretended to enjoy what I could not control. Let it become my life, my identity.'

He paused a moment before continuing. 'I saw you that night, and we had that moment of understanding over chutney and whatever else. And a little voice in my soul said, "This. If I had this— if I had *her*, I would want for nothing. She would be enough." And I think it scared me witless.' He gestured around them, at the rumpled bed linens and their naked limbs. 'This was something I never dreamed could happen. Not with you.'

Lily could hardly fault him for that. She'd never encouraged him to dream of it, and she'd kept her own imagination tightly laced—always so careful to label their connection as friendship, affinity. Never attraction or love.

254

Perhaps she'd been scared witless, too.

A question danced on the tip of her tongue. She shouldn't ask it. They'd been married all of an hour, after all, and it wasn't fair to put him on the spot. But she couldn't help herself. 'So, now we're here. Together. And am I enough?'

He stared intently into her eyes. 'You're everything.'

Oh, dear. Thrilling and romantic, those words, but also intimidating. Being a man's everything was no small task. Especially when that man was Julian, with his fathoms-deep capacity for passion and devotion.

'Am I doing it right?' she asked, raising her hands and spelling, *I. L-O-V-E. Y-O-U* . . . Feeling the need to lighten the moment, at the last instant she added an *R*.

He chuckled and gave her a naughty look. 'You love my what?'

Your heart, your mind, your complex, wounded soul.

She took her time with the letters, teasing him. Arching her back to thrust her breasts for attention and forming the signs just below her right nipple.

B . . . I . . . G.
H . . . O . . . T.
H . . . A . . . R . . . D.
S . . . T . . . R . . . O . . .

She could have gone on all day and all night, stringing adjectives together. But before she could start on the fifth, he had her tipped flat on her back, pressing his big, hot, hard, strong body to hers.

She didn't fault him for interrupting.

Chapter Eighteen

Bells.

Bells, bells, bells. More bells. Church bells.

Jesus God, no.

He was late. Mother was late. He'd fallen asleep when he should have been listening for the bells, and now it was too late for them both. The man with the ginger hair had wagged his finger at them Tuesday last, shouting himself bright red. If Mother was late to her post one more time, he'd said, she would be sacked.

They would have no more money. They would have to leave this rented room, which, even without a hearth, had been a far sight warmer than huddling under the steps. And perhaps their place under the steps was taken now. It was a plum spot. This was all his fault. He hadn't been listening, and now it was late, too late. Where would they go? What would they eat? The Italian butcher's scraps would all be claimed by this hour, gone to feed the dogs of noblemen. He couldn't risk nicking bread from the market again, not so soon after—

Something grabbed his arm. Julian lashed out in panic. He kicked, only to find his leg restrained, too.

He opened his eyes. Daylight blinded him momentarily before revealing his enemy . . . the tangled nest of bed linens. He was not in a barren, rat-infested rented room in Spitalfields, but a richly appointed bedchamber in Mayfair. He was, undoubtedly, late to wake his mother—by more than twenty years.

He took deep, rasping breaths, struggling to calm his racing heart.

'What is it?' His wife of two blissful days turned to him, rubbing her eyes and rising up on one elbow.

'Nothing but church bells.' He hastily wiped the sheen of sweat from his brow. 'Go back to sleep, love.'

'Bells?' She smiled. 'Perhaps they're tolling in celebration of our wedding.'

A nervous laugh rattled free of his chest. 'I doubt that.'

Her brow creased with worry, and Julian scrubbed his face with his palm. They'd sent a brief announcement of their marriage to the newspapers yesterday, thinking it best to get it over with before the gossips did it for them. Over dinner, they had joked and teased, imagining the shocked reaction of their friends and peers. They'd even devised an imaginary screed from Aunt Beatrice. Despite all their concerted effort at levity, however, Julian worried that *she* worried about public reaction. Hell, he was worried about it himself.

She put a hand against his rapidly thumping heart.

'A bad dream,' he admitted. 'That's all.'

She laid her cheek to his chest. 'It's Leo, isn't it? Are you thinking of him? It's five months today.'

'Oh, sweetheart.' Evidently it wasn't scandal weighing her brow this morning, but a much more serious concern. Reclining against the headboard, he pulled her to his chest and hugged her close, wrapping his arms around her willowy body and stroking her long, dark hair.

'I know it's hard for you,' she said. 'Giving up the

257

search. But just because you haven't found them, it doesn't mean Leo's killers will go unpunished. Men who are bad will end badly. I have to believe in that.'

Julian understood why that thought might comfort her. But he didn't find it especially reassuring, since he knew he fell into the 'men who are bad' category himself.

He stroked her back in a soothing rhythm, in time with the distant still-tolling bells. *Yes, darling. You believe in that. Just don't stop to ask yourself why it is I'm here with you, and not jailed or worse.*

Holy Christ.

Jailed.

The word was a blow to his skull, and his whole mind reverberated with the meaning. How stupid he'd been. How utterly, unbelievably dim. Where had Julian himself been, the one time in his life his friends and family had searched for him with no success? He'd been jailed, of course. Forced to spend a putrid, shivering month in Bridewell Prison, with all the other bad men—and boys— who had ended badly. Perhaps this was the reason his hunt for Leo's killers remained fruitless all these months, even after an exhaustive search of London's streets. Because they weren't on the streets. They'd been incarcerated for some other crime.

God, it was all so clear to him now. So bloody obvious.

He would write to Levi Harris, reopen the investigation. Tell him to search every court record, every jail and prison log in England, and quickly. They may have been already released, or they may have gone to the gallows—who could say?

258

The prospect of answers dangled before him, shining and seductive.

But he'd promised Lily he'd stop looking. He'd done more than promise. He'd made *vows*.

'Justice is in God's hands now,' she said, petting the line of dark hair down the center of his chest, 'as it should be. We shall find retribution in sheer happiness. Don't ever lose sleep over those men again.'

He gently dislodged her from his chest and sat up. 'What is it?' she asked.

'Those bells,' he said, frowning at the low, mournful peals. 'So strange. It's been minutes now, and they haven't stopped.'

*   *   *

With those bells, married life was off to a rather unusual start.

Lily had steeled herself for a certain measure of scandal, once their marriage became common knowledge. Had either one of them married, it would have been a source of great excitement and gossip within the *ton*. For Lily and Julian to have married each other—and in such hasty, unexpected fashion—well, this would be a story responsible for many a tongue wagging over many a cup of cooled tea.

But on that morning, when the bells roused her husband from sleep and failed to cease tolling even after some time, Julian ventured downstairs to investigate and returned with shocking news.

Princess Charlotte had died in the night, some hours after giving birth to a stillborn babe.

With that, all England plunged into deep, formal

mourning. The papers were filled with news of funeral arrangements and the relayed condolences of the world's royalty. Parties were canceled, theaters closed. London emptied of laughter. No one paid any attention to the nuptials of a gently bred lady and an infamous rake.

It was all so very ironic. The world was too busy mourning to care about them, and behind the drawn shades of Harcliffe House, Lily and Julian were celebrating life.

Naturally, Lily shared the country's shock and grief at Princess Charlotte's untimely passing. After learning of the tragedy, she spent a stunned morning in her husband's strong embrace. And as a vaguely connected relation of the royal family, she would of course attend the funeral. But she'd spent the past five months in mourning for Leo, and she seemed to have exhausted her reserve of melancholy. This was her honeymoon, and happiness would not be held at bay.

With every day—every hour—that passed, their bond strengthened. They talked of nothing new. Most of their conversations were reminiscences of old events, or a reprisal of some topic they'd discussed years before. But they went over them again with new perspective and a sense of serendipitous wonder. Like thieves who'd dug up a treasure chest by night and were only now examining its contents in the light of day. Their fingers worked constantly as they spoke, sifting through the precious gems and heavy strands of gold.

They mostly kept to the house, some days never even venturing downstairs. Julian's valet had delivered his full wardrobe to Harcliffe House, but

260

the dozens of topcoats and felted hats remained untouched in the closet. He lounged about in a silk banyan and loose trousers, when he dressed at all. No shirt beneath, to Lily's infinite delight. She loved sitting across the breakfast table from him, letting her gaze stray to his unshaven throat and studying the muscular definition of his bared chest.

So she was shocked indeed to wake late one morning after a deliciously sleepless night and find him already starched and stuffed into a somber gray suit.

She blinked at him, rubbing the sleep from her eyes, and he noted her confusion.

'It's Sunday,' he said, pairing signs with his words. 'Church.' He came to the bedside and offered a hand. 'Out of bed with you, then. We'll have to make haste.'

She accepted his help in rising from the bed. 'I wasn't aware that you attended church regularly.'

'*I* didn't.' He emphasized the 'I' with a jab to his chest. '*We* do.'

'Very well.'

So they did. They attended church, and they attended the royal funeral, and they did it all looking appropriately solemn and composed. She wasn't certain Julian's old friends even recognized him as the man sitting at her side. There was no cracking jokes. For heaven's sake, he never so much as cracked a smile. No matter the wild cries he wrenched from her by night, by day he seemed determined to present an eminently civil face to the world. She didn't want to complain, but neither did she want him feeling he must change his personality for her.

'Julian,' she said one evening at dinner, almost

261

two weeks into their marriage, 'you needn't stay at home with me every night.'

He put down his fork. 'Why would I want to be anywhere else?'

'I don't know,' she said, blushing at the implied compliment and digging a furrow in her peas. 'But if you did wish to visit your friends some evening, or go round to the club, I want you to know it's perfectly fine with me.'

'Do you *wish* me to go out?'

'No, not at all. I mean . . . I wish for you to do as you please, that's all. Simply because you're married doesn't mean you must give up all your fun. Other gentlemen don't.'

He didn't reply right away, but took his time finishing his roast duck and red wine. With thoughtful precision, he folded his linen napkin and set it aside.

'Do you know,' he said, 'I think I will go by the club tonight.'

A few hours later, Lily sat up alone in her private sitting with a roaring fire, a book, and a pot of coffee to keep her company. Well, all these and her regrets. Why had she ever suggested Julian spend an evening out? She missed him terribly.

Lifting her cup, she took a scalding sip of coffee and grimaced at the bitter aftertaste. She hated the brew, but she'd requested Holling to bring it especially for its stimulating properties. She wanted to be awake when Julian returned. Even if he stumbled in at half three, reeking of brandy.

Or cheap perfume.

She shook herself, feeling a twinge of dismay. That had been a jealous, spiteful thought unworthy of them both. After all his displays of tender devotion over the past weeks, did she really think one night at the gentlemen's club would have him reverting to his old, rakish ways? Julian was her husband now, and he deserved her trust and good faith. But it was more pleasant to imagine him surrounded by bare-breasted opera dancers than skulking down dark, dangerous streets.

Lily tried to plant her nose firmly in her book, but her mind insisted on wandering, tracing through every gentleman's haunt and shadowed alleyway in her mental map of London. She was still stuck on the first page of her novel—the first paragraph, really—when she looked up to check the mantel clock yet again. She saw that barely an hour had passed. And she saw that Julian had already returned.

He brought with him no odor of brandy or perfume. But he was festooned with several yards' worth of vibrant ribbons and satins in every color of the rainbow, tied end to end and yoked about his shoulders.

So this was the infamous billiard-room garland.

If he noticed Lily reclining there on the sofa, feet curled under her dressing gown, he paid her no greeting. Instead, he went straight to the roaring fire and began feeding it the gaily colored garters, an arm's length at a time. He paused every so often to take up the poker and prod an errant swatch of silk into the flames.

She looked on in silence as he methodically destroyed his colorful amatory past. The string of old lovers vanished into the flames, occasionally flaring in hot protest, but ultimately leaving behind no more lasting legacy than ashes and the acrid scent of singed fabric. When he was finished, he replaced the poker in its holder and brushed his hands clean of the task.

He shrugged out of his topcoat and came to sit at her side. After a pause, he asked, 'What are you reading?'

'I don't even know. I've spent the past hour staring stupidly at the first paragraph and wishing you were here. I've made no progress at all.'

'Good. I should hate to miss anything.' He swiveled sideways, then reclined backward, propping his boots on the arm of the sofa and laying his head in her lap. He closed his eyes and signed, 'Carry on.'

Clearly he didn't want to talk about what he'd just done, and Lily decided not to press. The actions spoke for themselves in this instance. Words were unnecessary.

Kisses, however, were imperative. She teased her fingers through his hair and pressed a lingering kiss to his brow. Then the tip of his nose. Then his mouth. 'Julian, I love you.'

He exhaled deeply, then finger-spelled in response, 'Can't imagine why.'

'Can't you?' Her heart squeezed, but she kept her words light. 'I shall have to draw you a very explicit picture.'

Chapter Nineteen

Julian stared at the letter in his hand, reading it for the third time in as many minutes. His eyes raced over the preliminaries, then tripped to a halt when he reached the names.

'Horace Stone and Angus Macleod. Apprehended this seventh of June,' he read aloud. Somehow it seemed more real when read aloud. 'Charged with drunkenness, vandalism, and breaking and entering with the intent to commit robbery. Sentenced to sixth months' hard labor on the prison hulk *Jericho*.'

There it was. The truth, laid down in black ink on white paper, in Levi Harris's neat penmanship.

Horace Stone and Angus Macleod had been apprehended the morning following Leo's death, not a mile from the murder scene. Charged with smashing the window of a cookshop, with the intent to rob the place. According to Harris's inquiries of the prison guards, the two matched Cora's basic description.

These men were Leo's killers. Julian knew it in his bones. He read through the letter again, though by now he could have recited it from memory.

'The *Jericho*,' he said wonderingly. 'I'll be damned.' He'd spent months searching, trudging down every gutter and lane in the county of Middlesex and beyond, and here they'd been floating on a decaying ship in the middle of the Thames, less than ten miles downstream. Virtually under his nose the whole time.

From his perch by the drawing room window, Tartuffe stretched his wings and squawked. 'Jericho!' he trilled merrily. 'Jericho!'

Ridiculous bird. 'What is it with you and names that start with J?'

'Oh, Julian,' the parrot sang. 'Mr. James Bell. Oh, Juuuulian.'

'Yes, don't tell me. Guilty, guilty. Thank you, that will be all.' Julian shook himself. He was conversing with a bloody bird. For once, the blasted creature's nattering shouldn't even disturb him.

He did feel mildly guilty for pursuing the matter after he'd promised Lily he wouldn't. But she'd been concerned for his safety, and he hadn't done any of the investigating himself. He'd merely written to Harris and let him do the work.

And now, less than a week later, Julian held deliverance in his hands. True liberation from fear and doubt, in the form of two names. After attacking Leo and Faraday, this Horace Stone and Angus Macleod had gone on to commit more criminal acts the same night. Impulsive ones, by Levi Harris's account. Acts like those didn't suggest the behavior of two paid assassins. Wouldn't hired assailants have fled the area and reported back to their employer, rather than bruising about the same neighborhood, indiscriminately smashing windowpanes? The pattern of events pointed to two drunken louts on a petty crime spree. Nothing more.

Lily and Morland—and he had to face it, pretty much everyone else—had been right all along, it would seem. Leo's murder had been a random act of violence. The death was no less tragic, but the implications for Julian were markedly less profound. Of course, he would always regret not being there that night. Leo was a good friend, and his death cast a long, sorrowful shadow. But if Julian could see the killers punished—if he could feel certain, once and for all, that Peter Faraday was wrong and those men actually *hadn't* intended to murder Julian—his future with Lily looked three shades brighter, instantly.

Julian folded the letter from Harris, jammed it

266

in his breast pocket, and crossed to the escritoire, withdrawing two sheets of paper and taking up a penknife to sharpen a quill.

He needed to send an express to Ashworth at once. If the brutes were sentenced to six months' hard labor, they were due to be released within weeks. Both witnesses to the killing were in points far West, out Ashworth's way—Cora Dunn, the prostitute, had stayed on in Devonshire, and Peter Faraday remained convalescing in Cornwall. If Ashworth could deliver one or both of them to London before Stone and Macleod were released, they could bring the men up on murder charges before they ever tasted freedom. Leo would finally have justice.

And Julian could feel some measure of peace. 'Julian?' Lily's voice, from the doorway. 'Are you ready? The property agent will be waiting.'

Deuce it. With the arrival of Harris's letter, he'd forgotten all about their appointment to look at houses for lease. She was excited; he could hear it in her tone. And now, with this news from Harris, Julian was excited, too. He didn't dare tell Lily about this latest development, not yet. No benefit in raising her expectations or anxieties until he could be sure.

He looked up. Spied his wife, a vision in sage-green muslin and frothy lace. Promptly dropped the penknife and quill, as if they burnt his fingertips.

'What is it?' she asked, laughing at his clumsiness.

He smiled. 'Beautiful,' he signed expansively, putting face and shoulders into the gesture. 'Beautiful.' Because sometimes, spoken words just

267

wouldn't do.

She looked to the clock and finger-spelled, 'Late.'

'The property agent will wait.' He readied his hands and waited for her attention. Feeling mischievous, he decided to test how her comprehension was improving. In swift finger-spelling, he described in explicit detail what he planned to do with that sage-green dress when they returned, and then what he planned to do with the body beneath it.

Her cheeks burned crimson as he went on. When at length he concluded his indecent proposition with the words, 'five times,' she laughed and put a hand to his cheek.

She said aloud, 'Finally. There's the infamous scoundrel I know and love. I wondered where he'd been hiding these past few weeks. I was beginning to wonder if I'd truly married a boring, stuffy clerk.'

He dropped a playful kiss on her brow before offering his arm. 'Shall we, then?'

Lily, Lily. The things she must never know.

* * *

'Oh, I like this one.' Lily's face lit up as they stepped over the threshold of the third house that afternoon. She gripped his arm. 'I have a good feeling about this house, Julian.'

'We've only seen the entrance hall.'

'Yes, I know. But it's a very fine entrance hall.'

Julian thought it looked rather shabby. The paper on the walls was faded and peeling, and cobwebs shrouded the far corners of the ceiling.

'It's been vacant for some time,' the property

268

agent said. 'The owners have only just decided to let it out.'

'The proportions are lovely,' she said, turning into what he supposed to be the dining room. With no furniture, it was difficult to tell. 'And there's so much air and light.'

True, for a town house, it did have a pleasant, open feel. Something about the number of windows and the harmonious arrangement of the rooms, he supposed. Julian would have liked to build her a lavish mansion from the ground up, surrounded by acres of green, rolling park. But such houses weren't built in a matter of weeks, and a matter of weeks was all they had before Leo's heir arrived from Egypt. Julian's old house in Bloomsbury was out of the question, for a host of reasons. So they would choose from the available homes for lease in Mayfair. If Lily was pleased with this one, Julian was pleased.

She asked the property agent, 'Is there a garden?'

'Yes, my lady.' The man led them down the corridor to the morning room at the rear, pulling back the dusty drapes to reveal a stone terrace and an overgrown jumble of weeds.

'Needs a great deal of work, doesn't it?' Julian said.

'I'm not afraid of work,' she replied, giving him a cheeky smile. 'Are you?'

He shook his head. No, he wasn't. He dearly missed work, truth be told. Somehow he needed to find an excuse to visit his offices this week. They would only just now be expecting Mr. James Bell back from his journey north to visit the mills. He needed to settle his business affairs and quietly

269

talk to his solicitor about selling off the whole concern—properties, mills. The thought left him feeling gutted and empty, not unlike this house.

Lily is worth it, he reminded himself. *Lily is everything.*

Surely he would find something to do with his time. Buy farmland and manage it, he supposed, like other gentlemen of leisure did. What he knew about agriculture could balance on the razor-thin edge of a scythe, but he could learn. He'd tutored himself in the principles of trade once. He would just start all over again. And if he occasionally woke in the night, roused from nightmare echoes of clacking looms and tolling church bells and scratching rats . . . well, Lily would be there next to him, her pale, slender arms and rosemary scent, ready to soothe his pounding heart.

'Tartuffe will love these high ceilings,' she mused, tilting her head.

The property agent led them on a tour of the second and third floors. With each bedchamber they toured, Julian found himself becoming oddly aroused. Since the object was to decide whether this house could be *their* house, it only felt logical to picture himself and Lily in every room. Dining in the dining room, sitting in the parlor . . . and now bouncing off the walls of each and every bedchamber.

Viewing the nursery gave him a very queer feeling indeed. A feeling that was not quite arousal, but extremely compatible with it.

'There's the kitchen below, of course,' the property agent said as they descended the staircase once again. 'And we haven't yet properly seen the hall, but . . .' He checked his timepiece. 'I'm afraid time is drawing short. I've an appointment back at my office in a quarter-hour.'

'Why don't you leave us here?' Julian suggested. 'We'll show ourselves around the rest, then lock up. I'll send a man round to your office later, to return the keys.'

The agent happily complied, no doubt sensing that the deal was within reach. He dropped the keys into Julian's waiting palm. 'Very good, sir.'

After Julian had seen the man out, Lily wandered into the hall. He followed her. She stood in the center of the large, open room, flanked on one side by a row of high windows. On the opposite wall, dark ovals and squares marked the spaces where portraits and mirrors had once hung.

'Oh, Julian. They don't build houses with halls like these anymore, not in Town. We could have the grandest parties, with an orchestra and dancing.'

He smiled at her excitement. 'Happy thought, indeed.'

Yes, they would throw grand parties, the two of them. With exotic foods and outlandish amusements and coveted invitations. Place cards engraved with whimsical creatures would live in the keepsake boxes of debutantes, for years and years to come. Lily would sparkle at the center of it all, joyous and carefree, surrounded by friends and admirers. And right there, it would be enough. Julian would know he'd lived his life to good purpose.

Yes. This house was going to be *their* house.

'We'll need to replace the paper on the walls and give all the trim a fresh coat of paint.' As he moved forward, his boots clomped noisily over the parquet. The report echoed off the vaulted ceiling.

'The flooring feels sound. Only needs a bit of wax.'

'Look, there's even a pianoforte.' She went to the far corner, where the large instrument sat hidden under a dust cover. 'I wonder why they left it here.'

'Couldn't make it fit through the door, I'd wager.' Julian slid the canvas cover from the piano and let it drop to the floor. 'It's a great beast of an instrument.' He touched a few keys and winced at the discordant result. 'Horribly out of tune.'

'I don't care about that,' she said, leaning against the piano. 'Do play something for me. I love watching you play. Love feeling it, too.' Her breasts plumped atop the closed case, like two silk-covered pillows sitting on a shelf. His mouth watered, and sensual excitement gathered in his groin.

'I have a very wicked idea,' he told her, rounding the enormous instrument to stand before her.

She shifted her weight onto her back foot. 'Do you?'

'I warn you, I won't be dissuaded.'

'Oh, dear.'

He slid his hands to her waist and lifted her straight up, then deposited her atop the pianoforte. He pulled at the fabric of her petticoat and gown, yanking her skirts out from under her, so that nothing but the thin lawn of her chemise would come between her intimate flesh and the surface of the closed instrument.

'You say you love watching and feeling me play?' he asked, walking back around to the keyboard. She nodded, clearly breathless from her sudden change of altitude. 'Then you're going to adore this.'

He touched a finger to one ivory key, then tapped it with a firm stroke.

'Oh.' Her hand went to her throat. 'Oh, my.'

Grinning, he played a quick arpeggio with his right hand, skipping up and down the high range of the keyboard.

'Julian,' she said in a shocked tone, her cheeks flushing with color. 'The vibrations, they're . . . You were right. This is wicked indeed.'

'Shall I stop?' He held up his hands.

'Heavens, no.'

He teased her a bit longer, with light, discordant scales. Just as he would trace tantalizing caresses up and down her bared thighs. She closed her eyes, and her lips fell apart. A husky moan eased from her throat.

Enough with the études and foreplay.

He put both hands to the keyboard and coaxed from it a full-bodied, if ill-tuned piece of music, with dark, powerful chords and a lilting melody.

'Oh.' She squirmed atop the pianoforte. 'Oh, *Julian*. Is that . . . Is that our waltz?'

God, how he loved her. He nodded in affirmation. 'It is indeed our waltz. And this'— he paused—'is our country dance.' He gave her no time to adjust before launching into the brisk, vigorous, pounding rhythm.

She made a sound that was half shriek, half delight. 'Have mercy, please,' she laughed. Her throat and chest were blushed crimson, and he could see the points of her taut nipples pressing against the bodice of her dress. 'I can't take anymore. Julian, do stop, or I shall speak of plaster.'

He stopped.

Her breath heaved in her chest. Strands of her hair had fallen loose, floating about her face. 'Goodness,' she said, putting a hand to her brow.

273

'I'm perspiring. I must look as though I've been tumbled.' Her eyes accused him merrily. 'You truly are wicked.'

'Brace yourself, my dear wife. That was just the prelude.'

He reached for her over the keyboard, buffing the polish with her skirts as he pulled her toward him and spun her legs around. Now she sat perched just before him, sitting directly above the keyboard. Her knees grazed his chest. He pushed up her skirts and spread her legs wide, so that her feet dangled over opposite ends of the piano keys.

Lust surged through him, and he took a moment to adjust his trouser fall. He'd gone hard as marble, just watching that erotic display. He probably could tap out a tune with his engorged staff, if he freed it from his clothing.

But first he needed to free her from hers.

She was spread out before him like a luscious feast, her trim, stocking-clad legs converging in a shadowy valley of bare skin and dark curls and intoxicating feminine musk. He removed her left slipper and let it fall to the floor, skimming his hand up the enticing curves of her leg—from the high arch of her instep, to the gentle curve of her calf, over the knob of her knee, and further.

'Julian,' she said frantically, as he yanked at her garter. 'We can't do this. Not here.'

'Why not here? It's our house.'

'No, it isn't.'

'Oh. Did you prefer one of the other homes we toured?' He pulled the garter loose, then deftly rolled the stocking down her leg.

'No, you impossible man. You know I want this house, but—'

274

He shucked her other slipper. It hit the floor with a softly echoing thud. Then he ceased his attentions, momentarily devoting his whole body to communication. 'You want this house, and you shall have it. I want you, and I shall have you. Right here. Right now. There will be no further discussion.'

Then he went back to removing her other garter and sliding her leg free of its delicate silk sheath. Once he'd pulled the garment free and exposed her dainty, wriggling toes, he kissed his way up her leg, tracing every smooth ivory contour with lips and tongue. As he reached the quivering slope of her inner thigh, her foot slipped to the keyboard in disharmonious protest.

'Be still,' he told her, shushing against her skin. He picked up her foot and braced it on his shoulder. Pushing aside the white, gauzy folds of her chemise and petticoat, he bared her most intimate places to his view. The petals of her sex were flushed deep red and dewy with excitement, and the sight alone drove him to a new peak of arousal.

Rather then dipping to taste her directly, he schooled himself to be patient. Instead, he licked a winding path up her inner thigh, giving her time to grow accustomed to the idea. Even so, her hips bucked with surprise when he made that first teasing pass with his tongue.

He kept a firm grip on her ankle, holding her bare foot braced against his shoulder. With his other hand, he clutched her hip. She wasn't getting away from him. Oh, no.

He pressed his open mouth to her sex, just lightly. No kisses or fancy work with his tongue.

He merely settled there, hovering near. Feeling her maidenhair tickle at his freshly shaven cheek, letting his ragged breath warm her aroused flesh. With devilish intent, he lifted his gaze and made eye contact with her over the heaving horizon of her bosom. Her brown eyes were glazed, her lips dusky and flushed.

He licked, once. In a reflexive move, her leg tensed against his shoulder, as if she would push him away.

He licked again, this time making a long, slow slide along her cleft, parting her. Her eyes fluttered closed, and she slumped back with a moan.

Eye contact ended. Her leg relaxed. Now he could tend to business.

He slid his hands up to frame her hips. She was so slender, he could curl his fingers over her waist and still reach toward her center with his thumbs, spreading her open for his pleasure and hers.

Damn, but he loved this. The teasing, the tasting, the tonguing of her every delicate contour and crest. Having explored every secret part of her, he swept his tongue to the pinnacle of her cleft and found her swollen bud.

Above him, she gasped and moaned. Her hand tangled in his hair, twisting and grasping. But she made no effort to wrench him away.

Needing to get closer, he lifted one knee to the piano keyboard. The incidental chord faded as he slid one hand up to knead her breast, tweaking her hardened nipple through the fabric. She inched closer to him, splaying her legs with shameless abandon and pressing her heat against his mouth. He began a swift series of experiments, running through his repertoire of kisses, nibbles, and licks until he found just the precise flicker of his tongue that set her thigh aquiver.

There, her body told him. *Just like that.*

So he did it again. And again. And again, refusing to slow or stop until she cried out in ecstasy, arching off the pianoforte with the force of her climax.

And still he did not relent.

Her fingers relaxed their grip on his hair, and she stroked him instead, raking her fingernails lightly over his scalp. A little sound escaped her throat. He doubted she was even aware of making it. A whimper, raw-edged with yearning. It was a sound of sensual satisfaction, and yet—it was an unmistakable plea for more.

Something in him snapped. She'd wanted a return to the wicked Julian, and she was going to have her wish. Turning his head, he kissed her inner thigh. Then he bit it, drawing on the fragile skin with firm suction until he pulled from her a sharp hiss of pain.

Widening his stance to brace his lust-weakened knees, he stood, pulling at the buttons of his trousers with desperate fingers. Within moments, he'd freed his rampant erection. He stroked himself a few times, gazing hungrily upon the plump, rosy display of passion so con veniently positioned at eye level. Staring at the way he'd marked her with that bite just at the top of her thigh. The tiny bruise was a violet petal fallen on fresh snow.

She was wet and hot and glistening. She was *his*.

'Beautiful,' he muttered, giving his aching arousal one last squeeze. 'So damned beautiful.'

From the pianoforte, she rose up on her elbows. She gave him a sleepy smile, looking drugged with satisfaction. She would not wear that look for long. He was determined to rouse her, in more ways than one.

Grasping her by the hips, he dragged her down from atop the pianoforte. Her backside landed on the keyboard with a discordant crash, her legs on either side of his. Giving her no chance to prepare or protest, Julian guided himself to her entrance and thrust deep, encasing himself in bliss.

Sweet . . . *heaven.*

'Your legs,' he demanded, 'wrap them over my hips.' He demonstrated his wish, lifting her thigh to aid her in compliance. Soon her ankles were linked at the small of his back.

'Arms, too,' he said.

She laced them tight around his neck.

With her clinging to him, he slid one arm around her waist. He braced his other hand against the pianoforte, to protect her from taking the brunt of his thrusts.

He worked her hard and fast, and beneath them, frenzied music played in an ungodly key, building to a quick crescendo. This was not tender lovemaking, but a claiming. This was *his* beautiful wife. This was *his* beautiful house. And this bright, elegant, glittering future . . . all of it, his for the taking.

She felt so good against him, under him, surrounding him. He threw back his head, and she chased him, pressing her lips to his throat. His whole body hummed with anticipation as he raced toward completion. She beat him to the finish, seizing around him in a second climax. He heard himself making harsh, guttural noises—shouting, almost. And why shouldn't he shout? This was his house, his wife. No need to hold back.

So he didn't. He came into her, losing himself in a clamor of bucking hips and strange, groaning piano chords, and clashing, open-mouthed kisses.

And life was very, very good.

For now.

Chapter Twenty

'Well, it appears someone's feeding the beast. Grooming him, too.' Rhys St. Maur, Lord Ashworth gave the stallion's withers a brisk rub. 'Osiris, you look a damn sight better than when I saw you last.' The former warrior looked to Julian. 'For that matter, so do you. Marriage must be suiting you.'

Julian shrugged. 'Funny how that works, isn't it? Where's Lady Ashworth?'

'Merry?' Ashworth's eyebrow lifted, splitting in the middle where a thick scar divided it. 'Left her at the hotel. She's fatigued from the journey, or so she says. Too enamored with the scented soaps and bed hangings, is more like it. But she sends her regards.'

'Bring her by Harcliffe House later, if you will. My wife will be glad to make her acquaintance.'

'Your wife.' Ashworth chuckled. 'And just think, six months ago you were so determined to marry Lily off to some other man.'

Julian knew he was being ribbed, but he didn't take offense. These days, so little seemed worth getting upset about. 'I was only following the code, you know. A member of the Stud Club needed to marry her. Once you and Morland married elsewhere, the duty fell to me.'

'Duty, my arse. You've been in love with that

279

woman from the start. Don't try to deny it.'

Very well. Julian wouldn't. He pulled a stub of carrot from his pocket and offered it to the horse.

Ashworth scratched the stallion behind his ear. 'What would Leo think, if he could see the remaining members of his fast, subversive club? We're all old married men now, settled and sedate.'

Osiris snorted, sending a little cloud of vapor into the brisk December morning.

'This stallion's none too youthful, either.'

Ashworth asked, 'You think Morland will agree to your plan?'

Julian nodded. 'I have my ways of convincing him.'

The duke himself arrived at that moment, approaching the mews astride a stately bay gelding. He dismounted smoothly and handed his reins to a waiting groom.

'Ashworth,' he said, catching his breath as he removed his gloves. 'This is a surprise. When did you arrive in Town?'

'Just now.'

'I hear you've married.'

'Aye. My lady's resting at our lodgings. But I hope to introduce her to you and Her Grace while we're in London. She and Amelia will get on well, I think.'

'We'd be delighted. Where are you staying in Town?'

'At the Pulteney.'

'You're at a hotel?' The duke's brow wrinkled with disdain. Odd, how Morland's superior expressions used to enrage Julian. Now he just found them mildly irritating. Not nearly worthy of a punch to the jaw, at any rate.

'Don't stay at a hotel,' the duke continued. 'You're more than welcome at Morland House. We've plenty of rooms, and Amelia loves nothing more than guests.'

'That's generous of you, but Merry had her heart set on the Pulteney.'

'Trade research,' Julian explained to the duke. 'The new Lady Ashworth is the proprietor of Devonshire's finest coaching inn. Only natural she'd want to investigate the London hotels. Anyway, Morland, you'll be needing your guest rooms for someone else.'

'Who?'

Ashworth took his cue and went over to his waiting coach, opening the door and reaching inside to help Peter Faraday down. Yet another man Julian had once been desperate to pummel. Christ, had he truly walked around irate for so much of his adult life? It all felt so foreign and far away now.

Faraday slowly advanced, unaided by Ashworth but relying heavily on the assistance of a walking stick. The man looked to be in better health than he had in Cornwall, but that wasn't saying much. He was still pale, still obviously in a great deal of pain. If he hadn't healed after six months' time, it was unlikely he'd ever walk unaided again.

'Mr. Bellamy. Your Grace.' Faraday inclined his head. 'Forgive me if I don't bow.'

'Peter Faraday,' Morland said, returning the man's nod of greeting. 'I almost didn't recognize you.'

'Last time we met, your attention was on the cards.'

'What are you doing here now?'

281

'Let me explain,' Julian said. He summarized the progress—or lack thereof—of his investigation into Leo's death. Then explained how last month, the idea had finally occurred to him to check the prison and court records. 'My investigator explored that angle in the first weeks after Leo's death, but at that time we had no real description. A few weeks ago I received these names. Angus Macleod and Horace Stone. They match Cora Dunn's physical description of the men. They were jailed the morning after Leo's death, apprehended not a mile away from the scene of his beating. Sentenced to six months' hard labor for breaking and entering.'

Ashworth whistled low. 'Has to be them. Too many coincidences not to be.'

Julian nodded. 'They're serving on a prison hulk, due to be released in just over a week. We'll ride out that morning and meet them on the docks. As lords, either one of you'—he indicated Morland and Ashworth—'can easily have them rearrested. With Faraday's testimony, they'll swing by the turn of the New Year.'

Faraday gave a heavy sigh. 'I told you in Cornwall, I don't recall a thing about the attack itself. I don't know that I'll be able to identify them.'

Julian said tightly, 'Well, I'm positive that seeing them will jog your memory. If not, we'll send for Cora.'

'Sorry I couldn't bring her along,' Ashworth said. 'But someone has to mind the inn. Besides, it felt cruel to pull the girl away from her honeymoon.'

'The comely Miss Dunn's married, too?' Faraday gripped his walking stick. 'What a shame. It's a veritable plague of matrimony. Stay far clear of me, all three of you.'

With that, he hobbled to the side and lowered his weight onto a bench. Julian sensed the man's loud decrial of marriage was merely an excuse to take a much-needed rest. After the exertion of standing upright all of five minutes, the poor soul needed a rest. Julian almost felt bad for him.

Or he would have, if he felt certain he could trust the man.

'Morland,' he said low, 'I need you to keep a watchful eye on Faraday.'

'You want me to take the man under my protection?'

'I want you to take the man under your roof.'

'Now hold just a minute—' the duke began to object.

'You just said you have plenty of rooms. Your wife loves hosting guests.' When Morland's face didn't soften, Julian lowered his voice to a whisper and added, 'Not to mention, you're already hiding one invalid.'

Morland's eyes flared. 'How did you learn that? Did Amelia tell—'

'No, no. Your wife is the soul of discretion. It's your ward who can't keep herself concealed.' He clapped a hand on Morland's shoulder. 'Listen. Do me—do Leo—this last favor, and you can have the horse. I'll relinquish all interest in him. You and Ashworth can work it out from there.'

Morland stepped back. 'Really. You'd surrender your share in Osiris?'

Julian nodded.

'In exchange for me housing Faraday for the next week?'

'Yes. Just until this is all settled. But you'll be

283

guarding him, not just giving him a bed.' He cut a glance over his shoulder to make sure the man himself wasn't listening. 'I can't shake the feeling there's still something he's not telling us. Maybe he's afraid, and that's why he's resistant. We can't risk him running off again, to Cornwall or God-knows-where. Ashworth can't host him, and I certainly can't bring him home to Lily. She knows nothing about this.'

'How long do you think that will last?' Ashworth asked. 'I mean, here we are making plans for our wives to get acquainted. Do you honestly think they won't talk amongst themselves?'

'So don't tell your wives, either.'

Morland gave a bark of laughter. 'If Faraday's staying in my house, Amelia's going to know.'

'And my own wife just traveled all the way from Devonshire with the man,' Ashworth put in. 'She knows all about the attack and Faraday's role in it.'

'Besides,' the duke said, 'I don't lie to Amelia. We tell each other everything.'

'As husbands and wives should,' Ashworth concurred. 'Merry and I, we're the same.'

Julian cursed under his breath. This was becoming far too complicated.

'Here, then. You each tell your wives the truth.' To Morland, he said, 'You tell Amelia that Faraday is a former Stud Club member, stricken by illness and fallen on hard times. You're hosting him as a favor, but she's to keep it very discreet because Mr. Faraday wouldn't want his difficulties widely known. There, all of that's true. Isn't it?'

The duke shrugged. 'I suppose.'

Julian turned to Ashworth. 'And you ask Meredith to keep what she knows to herself, for

284

Lily's sake. We don't want to raise Lily's hopes or anxieties. For all we know, this will come to nothing.'

'Fair enough,' Ashworth said. 'So what are you planning to tell Lily?'

'Nothing,' Julian answered. A marriage without secrets sounded lovely for others, but it wasn't in the cards for a man like him. 'Nothing just yet.'

*   *   *

'Oh, how lovely!'

At Lily's exclamation, Amelia and Meredith perked up. The two ladies wandered over from across the gallery, eager to investigate the object that had inspired such delight.

'It's just a desk.' Lily opened the top of the vast mahogany piece. The hardwood panel swung easily on its hinges, flattening to a sturdy writing surface. Inside, she found neat drawers for paper, ink, and quills, two locked compartments, and an entire regiment of pigeonholes for the sorting and filing of bills and receipts. The sight filled her with an absurd sort of joy.

The gallery owner, a meticulous man in a pale pink waistcoat, appeared beside them. 'An antique,' he said. 'Belonged to . . .'

Lily missed the name completely. No matter. Whichever magistrate or dignitary had owned the thing in the first place, it didn't belong to him anymore.

'Are you thinking of this for Mr. Bellamy?' Meredith asked, running her fingers over the smooth veneer.

Lily had to confess no, shaking her head. 'For

285

myself. We're making adjoining studies in the new house. One for him, and one for me.'

It was high time she had her own space for recordkeeping, rather than always using Leo's study. She'd already agreed with Julian that she would take responsibility for the household accounts, as well as the investment of whatever funds she brought to the marriage. For all her teasing, it seemed *she* was the stuffy, boring clerk in their relationship.

'I'll take it,' she told the gallery owner.

He bowed with obsequious gratitude. 'Very good, my lady. An excellent choice.'

Yes, she rather thought it was. With a grand new house to furnish, Lily was discovering a new appreciation for shopping. The company of friends increased her enjoyment. Over the past week, the three of them had spent part of every afternoon wandering the shops. Obviously Lily had known Amelia all her life, and even though they'd only been introduced to the new Lady Ashworth a week ago now, the three of them got on well indeed. Meredith was a sensible, plainspoken woman, with a heart for hospitality and head for business, which gave her something in common with Amelia and Lily both.

'Adjoining studies,' Meredith said, examining the hinges of the desk as Lily closed the top. 'I like that idea. I'll talk to Rhys about such an arrangement for the new Nethermoor Hall. He plans to meet with some architects while we're in Town.'

When Meredith walked away, Amelia caught Lily's attention. 'I've been meaning to ask, are you and Mr. Bellamy attending the Carstairs' party Wednesday next? Spencer is reluctant, as ever. But if the two of you attend, I might be able to convince him. Or at least I'd be assured of having someone to talk to after he disappears to the card room.'

Lily hesitated. 'The Carstairs' party?'

Amelia nodded.

'I . . . I'm not certain. We hadn't yet sent our reply.'

In actuality, they had not received an invitation. Lily told herself she shouldn't be surprised. She'd expected this might happen when her hasty wedding to Julian became known. Obviously Mrs. Carstairs wished to communicate her disapproval of Lily's marriage, or perhaps her envy of it. Lily was almost ashamed to realize how it annoyed her, being cut by a woman who last year would have counted it a coup to host any Chatwick in her home. Even Tartuffe.

She shook off the irritation. No matter. Slights like these would serve to teach her who their true friends were. And Lily had two very good ones right here in this gallery.

She followed the gallery owner to the back counter, to sign off on the expense and arrange for delivery of her new desk. While he prepared the bill, her eye wandered to the soaring expanse of paintings behind him. They were mostly the standard decorative scenes: pastoral landscapes of ruined castles, still-lifes with vases of flowers and bowls of fruit. Nothing particularly caught her interest. Disappointing. She and Julian needed *something* to hang on the walls, after all. She noted a curtained doorway leading to another room.

Once the bill of sale had been signed and settled, and the address of the new house given, Lily asked, 'Have you another gallery?'

287

'There is another room, my lady.'

'May we see it?'

The man's cheeks flushed pink to match his waistcoat. 'My lady . . . I'm afraid that gallery is for gentlemen only.'

Lily thought she must have misunderstood him, but then Meredith appeared at her side. 'What do you mean, for gentlemen only?'

'The paintings there are of a . . . shall we say, earthy nature. Not suitable for ladies.'

'What's all this?' Amelia joined them.

'He means to protect our delicate female natures from scandalous paintings,' Meredith informed her. To the shop keeper, she said, 'We are all married women, sir.'

'Nevertheless.' The man tugged at his cravat. 'Your husbands are not present. Without their express permission, I am sure I cannot—'

Meredith laughed. 'Must we send for notes with their signatures?'

'Ridiculous,' Amelia said, squaring her shoulders and lifting her chin. 'My husband, His Grace, the Duke of Morland, would be displeased indeed to be troubled on such a trifling matter. Do your worst, sir. We shall ready our vinaigrettes.'

Lily laughed. She thought they stood a decent chance of deviling him into capitulation. But in the end, it wasn't necessary. Amelia and Meredith suddenly wheeled to face the door, clapping with excitement. Lily followed their gaze.

Ah. Julian had finally arrived. He'd promised to meet her here after his day's business was done.

All three ladies rushed to greet him at the door. Lily, however, was the only one to claim the pleasure of a kiss on the cheek.

288

'What's this? I haven't known such a rousing female welcome since—'

'Since the last time you entered a room full of women,' Lily said. She cut a playful glance at her friends. 'Your timing couldn't be better. There's another gallery—a naughty gallery, apparently— and the owner won't let us view it without our husbands present.'

'Hm.' Julian surveyed the hopeful trio. 'I don't suppose I can pose as a sheik with my harem of wives, can I?'

'Why not?' Amelia asked slyly. 'You do have a certain reputation.'

Meredith linked her hand through Julian's free arm. 'Let's have a go.'

'Why, Lady *Ashworth,*' he said, pretending shock.

Or perhaps not pretending. On closer inspection, Lily thought he might actually be blushing. How very sweet.

With good-natured charm, he extricated himself from Meredith's grasp. 'I'm a confirmed monogamist now, I'm afraid. And even if I weren't, both your husbands are confirmed barbarians, whom I know better than to cross. I've just come from meeting with them. We made plans to go out early tomorrow for a ride in open country. Shouldn't like to make it a daybreak duel.'

'You're going riding?' Lily asked. It had been ages since she'd been out riding. 'Where to? May I join you?'

'No, you may not. It's a gentlemen's excursion.' He paused. 'And I'm not precisely sure where to. Down the Thames a bit, I think.'

'Down the Thames? Whyever—'

'Morland's looking at property down that way.'

289

'He is?' Amelia asked. 'First I've heard of it.'

'Yes, well.' Julian's smile was strained. 'Perhaps I misunderstood.'

Lily could tell he was uncomfortable. Uncomfortable with the entire outing, most likely. Julian's horse manship was nowhere near the level of Morland's and Ashworth's, and he was probably a bit worried about being shown up by them. But he was going to ride out with them anyway, and that pleased Lily no end. She was so gratified to see the three of them becoming close friends. Leo would have been happy, too.

Meredith spoke. 'Well, if you've just come from meeting with Rhys and the duke, where are they? We can all view the naughty paintings together.'

'I'm afraid they stayed at Morland House.'

Amelia rested one hand atop her pregnant belly and rubbed her lower back with the other. 'Then I should go home, too.' She looked to Meredith. 'Care to join me in the carriage? You and Lord Ashworth are welcome to stay for dinner.'

Out of habit, she extended the invitation to Julian and Lily as well, and they politely declined.

Once they'd left, Lily and Julian were the only remaining customers in the gallery.

'I bought a desk,' Lily said.

'Did you?' But he didn't ask about it. He simply offered her his arm and walked her straight back to the gallery owner, whose buttoned pink waistcoat scalloped like the edge of a seashell as he bent to arrange some books.

When he noticed Julian, the man stood and bowed. 'Good afternoon, sir. How may I be of service?'

'My wife would like to see the nudes.' Her

290

impossible husband grinned down at her, daring her to contradict.

Scoundrel. Lily introduced the sharp point of her elbow to his ribs.

Although she was certain her cheeks were twin banners of crimson, she faced the owner and hoisted them high. She wasn't about to demur. She wanted to be able to crow about this to Amelia and Meredith tomorrow.

And atop that, she *did* want to see the nudes.

The gallery owner tugged on his waistcoat. 'As you wish, sir.'

With all the élan of a carnival barker, he swept aside the heavy velvet drape. Feeling a tingle of excitement, Lily nestled closer to her husband.

Together, they entered the forbidden room.

*   *   *

The 'secret' gallery was rather a disappointment, as forbidden things all too often turned out to be. Julian was well-acquainted with the phenomenon.

But it did serve as a welcome diversion.

He carefully watched Lily's expression as they entered the narrow room. She seemed to have no care for anything but the pictures on the walls, which put him somewhat at ease, after their conversation about tomorrow's ride. He hated lying to her. Despised it with a dark, unwavering passion. After today, never again.

Tomorrow morning, he, Morland, and Ashworth would ride some ways out of Town, down to Woolwich, where Stone and Macleod were due to be released. The brutes would never even be freed of their chains. Once the men were hauled back to

Newgate, Julian and Morland would bring Faraday to identify them. Charges would be pressed. The courts would carry the matter from there.

It would all be over tomorrow.

Calming at the thought, Julian began to take some notice of the art. On either side, the walls were lined with framed paintings. High clerestory windows lit the space, sending down trapezoids of watery light to frame the works at odd angles, making them look askew. There were a few of the expected boudoir portraits, naked women lolling about on unmade beds, their nipples blazing unrealistic shades of cherry and plum. But the quality works outnumbered these.

The owner followed them down the row, rattling off information about each work. Artist, provenance, and such. The way he nattered on so industriously, Julian deduced the man had no idea of Lily's deafness. Lily paid him no attention, of course, but shop keepers were accustomed to being ignored.

She wandered thoughtfully from one picture to the next, then paused before a nude study of a man. Her foot slid back, as she retreated a pace to better take it in. Julian briefly considered teasing her, but decided against it. He loved the seriousness with which she approached the art. No missish giggles or blushing.

'The model was a laborer,' he said, when she turned to him.

'How do you know?'

'Look at the tan on his forearms and face, the roughness of his hands.'

'I suppose it must be difficult to find gentlemen of leisure willing to pose for such studies.' As

292

though it were a connected thought, she added, 'I was thinking of commissioning your portrait.'

He laughed, startled.

And now she blushed. 'Not like that, of course. Fully clothed. But we should have a large one, for the house. And I would like a miniature for my dressing table.'

Ah. Sweet thought, that.

They moved on to a lovely painting of a mother bathing her young child. Julian wondered at its placement in this 'gentleman's' gallery, as there was nothing at all erotic or prurient about the composition. It was a domestic, maternal scene. The two stood before a roaring fire, the child with his feet in a basin and the woman crouched beside. The woman's plaited hair dangled as she bent to sponge her naked cherub. She herself was dressed in a thin shift, the linen wet and clinging to her rounded breasts and hips. The artist had done a remarkably fine job of rendering the damp, translucent fabric stretched over pink skin.

'Who is the artist?' Lily asked, turning to the gallery owner.

'A Mr. Conrad Marley,' the man answered.

Lily frowned as she turned back to the painting. Julian touched her arm, raised his eyebrows in question.

She hesitated, throwing an apprehensive glance toward the owner. Then she signed, 'Spell it for me.'

Julian smiled. He reached for his wife's hand and brought it to his lips, ignoring the curious stare of the gallery owner. The man would never understand the small victory he'd just witnessed.

He and Lily had been practicing signing in

293

private for weeks, but this was the first time she'd used signs with him in the company of someone else. Julian understood why she hadn't until now, and he never would have pressed. To begin with, excluding anyone from a conversation offended her natural sense of etiquette. She would no sooner sign with him in friendly company than she would converse with him in Hindustani, for the sole reason that it alienated their companions from the discussion. But in front of servants and hackney drivers and shop keepers, he knew she had an entirely different reason for hesitating. By signing, she openly declared herself to be deaf. She made herself vulnerable to the curiosity and even cruelty of strangers.

Julian knew better than most the courage that required. He'd grown up watching his mother make this calculation in so many interactions—at what point would she break down and sign to Julian, asking him to explain? When did her need to understand trump the perpetual cause of caution?

Thankfully, Lily would never know the sort of treatment his mother had endured. She was wealthy and highborn, and no shop keeper with sense would slam a door in her face. No street urchins would throw bits of refuse at her back. Still, she faced subtler forms of prejudice and disdain. And always, that backhanded 'concern' from the imbecilic, self-righteous Aunt Beatrices of the world, who to preserve the fragile peace of their feeble minds would insist the defect resided not only in Lily's ears, but in her very soul. *If you cannot be like the rest of us,* their subtle shaming implied, *at least do not call attention to your differences.*

Just now, Lily might as well have signed,

294

'Bollocks to that.' With her question, she'd asserted her right to receive information on her own, understandable terms. Even if it made those around her suspicious or uncomfortable.

Julian wanted to catch her in a tremendous hug. Instead, he carefully spelled the artist's name and waited for her reply.

'Mister?' she spelled back.

He confirmed with a nod.

She looked at the painting again, then signed, 'No. A woman painted this. I can tell.'

'How?'

She pointed to the babe's plump arm. 'Perfect. Men always paint babies too fat or too thin.'

He considered. He'd never spent much time thinking about the relative corpulence of infants, in life or art—which, he supposed, was rather Lily's point. 'Perhaps you're right.' Though gently-bred ladies were encouraged to draw and paint, a female artist would have to assume a man's name if she wished to be taken seriously. Or to earn any decent money for her work.

Lily stared at the painting for a minute longer, tilting her head. Julian stared at Lily, because lovely as the picture was, his wife was lovelier. Besides, he was obviously going to buy the thing, and he'd have plenty of time to gaze upon it later. The only question was whether to purchase it now or come back in secret, to make it a surprise. Perhaps a Christmas gift.

But before he could decide, Lily surprised *him*.

'I think I'm pregnant,' she signed.

And with that, his world stopped. Went still as a painting.

It was as though some invisible, divine hand had

295

forced him, and this moment, into a small, square frame. He didn't feel hemmed-in or constrained. No, never that. Just . . . put into perspective. Within the borders of this picture, this precious vignette, resided everything of true meaning: the two of them, and the promise of a child. The world outside it was just noise, nothing but meaningless distraction.

At a loss for words, he laid a hand to the small of her back.

She didn't turn to him, but her cheek dimpled with a shy smile. 'I can't be certain yet.'

Julian was certain. He *knew*. Within a year's time, the world would include another plump, squirming, rosycheeked creature, and that infant would be part him and part her, forever intermingled and impossible to separate. Looking at the domestic Madonna in the painting before him, Julian felt he understood why God had introduced His greatest miracle to the world in the form of a helpless infant. He couldn't conceive of a more humbling, awesome thing than a child.

Not just *a* child. *Their* child.

This was his chance to start fresh and do everything right. For so long he'd chased revenge. Now true redemption was in reach. He wasn't a bastard child any longer. He was a grown man, a husband, soon to be a father. *His* family would have every advantage Julian had never known. *His* wife would never be driven to sacrifice her own comfort or nourishment for the sake of their child. *His* son would be tutored in Latin and Greek, would never even learn the signs for 'hungry' or 'cold' or 'frightened' or 'penny.'

'We'll take this one,' he told the gallery owner.

Once the purchase had been settled, they left the shop together and began strolling aimlessly down the crowded street. Lily suggested they walk the short distance to their new residence before returning to Harcliffe House.

'I'd like to see how the blue toile is working in the parlor.'

Julian was thinking of the house, too. But he wanted a look at the nursery. He needed to check it for draughts. Had there been enough bars on the window? 'Just wait until it's all done,' he told her. 'It's too dusty right now.'

'And what is a touch of dust?' Lily shook her head. 'I knew I shouldn't have told you. Now you'll be insufferably protective.'

Of course he would be protective. And if she thought he was insufferably so today, she ought to wait for tomorrow. Once Leo's killers were brought to justice, safeguarding Lily would become his paramount purpose in life. Ridiculous as he knew it to be, part of him wanted to wrap her in cotton wool and confine her to bed for the next eight months.

With one arm draped around her shoulders, he steered her through the river of humanity, banked by shop fronts on the one side and carriages on the other. He was unbearably anxious she might be jostled by a passerby or jabbed in the eye with a parasol spoke.

Wham.

Julian was broadsided. An anonymous shoulder and elbow conspired to give him a firm, swift shove that sent him careening off-balance. Despite his best efforts, he stumbled against Lily, slamming her into a shop's display window. She cried out in

297

surprise, and no doubt some measure of pain.

Julian righted himself and took Lily by the shoulders, assessing the soundness of her arms and wrists. 'Are you hurt? I'm so sorry. There was a—'

'I'm fine,' she said, patting down her dress. 'Just a bit rattled.'

Rattled. The word made him see red. Julian was going to find the man who'd pushed him so rudely and rattle him to the bones.

As Lily adjusted her cape, he wheeled to search the crowd. No one figure particularly leapt out. It had happened so fast. He'd formed no impression of the arm that shoved him, much less the man to whom it belonged.

Frustrated, he clenched his hands into fists.

Something crumpled in his left palm.

He opened his hand. There, on his gloved palm, lay a crunched card with writing on it. Someone must have slid it into his hand during the confusion. With a quick glance around, he grasped the card in his fingertips and pulled the creases straight.

Hold your tongue, if you wish to keep holding your lovely bride.

A clanging Bell will be silenced.

The ground buckled beneath his boots. The words on the card fuzzed, as though grown over with black mold. *A clanging Bell will be silenced.*

Someone knew. Someone knew everything.

298

Chapter Twenty-one

That card . . . it was more than a blow to the stomach. More than a shot to the heart. More than a lightning strike, or even a grenade. It was a split-second deluge of ten thousand tons of snow. The obliteration of everything. Life as he knew it, replaced by cold, blank, oppressive silence.

For a fraction of time, Julian's world ceased to exist.

And then it rushed back, in a million crystalline facets. His senses opened like floodgates, taking in every available stimulus. The myriad sights and sounds and smells that typically melded into a patchwork of 'city street' sorted themselves out, announced themselves one by one in his consciousness. Especially the sounds. He heard everything. The clop of each individual horse shoe against the cobbled street. Rats scrabbling in the gutter, their tiny claws shredding through autumn's last few desiccated leaves. The cries of street merchants hawking apples, posies, herbs, newspapers, snuff, and 'Ink, black as jet! Pens, fine pens!'

Across the street, some dozen doors down, hinges creaked. An old man coughed and spat.

Julian's heart pounded through his whole body, beating down the encroaching panic with grim, steady blows. With frantic composure, he scanned the vicinity. *Who? Who knew? Who'd done this?*

'Goodness,' Lily said, leveraging his grip on her arm to steady herself. 'That was unexpected. Are you well?'

No. No, he wasn't well, and this was hardly unexpected. How could he have ever relaxed his guard? He was a fool. A bloody goddamned fool. He'd wanted to believe, so badly, that Leo's death was mere coincidence and he had no mortal enemies. That he'd escaped his squalid past and left it behind to embrace a bright future with Lily. But he'd been wrong, all wrong.

'Julian?' She tugged at his sleeve. 'Really, I'm perfectly well. Let's just go on.'

They couldn't continue to walk in the open street like this, with Devil-knows-who following them. He needed to get her home, but could he even risk a hackney? The drivers perched atop their boxes peered down at him, vulture-like, their necks sunken into their high, black collars.

Threat menaced from every direction. The wrinkled old fellow with his box of doubtless tainted fruit. The gray clouds looming overhead, squashing them all. Even the wind's cold bite made him want to snap back.

He trusted no one.

He put one arm about Lily's shoulders, bent to slide the other under her thighs, and with a small grunt of effort, swept his wife into his arms. As he made his way down the street, he barked at the people before them. 'Make way. My wife is ill. Let us pass.'

'Julian,' she insisted, 'I tell you, I'm fine. No injury whatsoever.'

He paid her no mind, simply continued striding down the center of the walk, forcing all others to scramble out of his path. It was unreasonable. The behavior of a madman. He didn't care. This woman was his responsibility, placed into his keeping by

300

sacred vows, and he'd exposed her to danger. Now he was going to personally rescue her from it, if it exhausted all the strength in his body.

If it killed him.

*   *   *

He carried her all the way back to Harcliffe House. After the first quarter-mile, Lily gave up protesting and concentrated on being portable. None of her objections had any effect. Her husband was a man possessed. He didn't even seem winded from the exertion. His heartbeat thumped against her body, almost preternatural in its unflagging, deliberate rhythm.

Goodness. As they finally approached the square, she made a mental note to save the news of her next pregnancy for a location closer to home.

He carried her up the steps of the house. A footman opened the door, and Julian swept her inside, barely acknowledging the servant or Swift, who stood slack-jawed in the entryway.

'I'm fine,' Lily called out to the butler, as Julian carried her straight past and mounted the stairs. 'Don't be concerned.'

When they reached the door of her suite—now *their* suite—Julian temporarily transferred her full weight to one arm and opened the latch with the other. Off-balance, he lurched through the open door, kicked it shut, and collapsed against it, still holding her fast against his chest.

She felt his lungs expand with a deep, gasping breath. His knee shook, fluttering her draped skirts. Her hand flew to his face, and she found his skin clammy to the touch. He was so pale.

301

He looked as though he'd come face-to-face with Death.

'Julian, truly. I understand a bit of male protective impulse, but this is nonsensical. Women have babies every day. It's hardly cause for alarm.'

He swallowed hard and gave a little nod. 'I know. I know.'

Seeming to recover a bit of his strength, he stood once again and carried her into the bedroom, laying her gently on the bed. Straightening, he shrugged out of his coat and paced back and forth, patrolling the bedposts.

'Julian?'

He pushed a hand through his hair and continued pacing, mumbling something to himself.

'*Julian.*'

He halted mid-step, still staring straight ahead, glaring a hole in the wainscoting.

Lily rose to her knees, pulled off her cape and tossed it aside. Leaning forward, she took him by the wrist. 'Come,' she said, tugging firmly.

He gave in with numb resignation, sitting on the edge of the mattress and reclining to join her on the bed halfway, wrapping an arm about her waist. Even in this moment of emotional upheaval, she could tell he was trying to keep his boots off the counterpane, unwilling to muddy the lace. A pang of tenderness wrenched her heart.

'Never mind it,' she said, pulling him down beside her. 'Just be with me.'

At last, she had his full surrender. He stretched out alongside her, and they tangled together, holding one another tight.

She tried to calm him, stroking her fingers through his dark hair and pressing kisses to his temple. 'It's all right,' she said. 'I understand. Parenthood *is* rather overwhelming to contemplate, isn't it? I'll admit to being a little scared, too. There's so much to be anxious about. Not just the pregnancy and birth, but after. What if our . . .' Her voice faltered. Perhaps she should have held her tongue, but the words came out anyway. 'What if our baby needs me, and I can't hear his cries?'

With a quick flex of his arm muscles, he drew her close and tight.

Lily took refuge in his strong, secure embrace, allowing herself a few private teardrops. There were so many fears, more than she could possibly express. Fears she'd been tamping down for years, preferring to remain unmarried just so she wouldn't have to face them. What if she inadvertently neglected her own child, when he was in pain? What if she needed to call out in warning, and her voice failed? There was already deafness in Julian's family; what if their baby was born deaf, too? What if he wasn't, and he grew to be ashamed of his mother?

Julian's arms released her, and he maneuvered back, putting just enough space between them to sign. His leg remained thrown over her hips, holding her close.

'Never think,' he said, his eyes fierce with sincerity, 'that I doubt you. You will be the kindest, best, most capable mother to ever live. I am certain of it.'

She nodded. If Julian's mother could give birth to him in a vacant warehouse and raise him alone in the streets, surely Lily could cope with this. She had a comfortable home; she would have nursemaids to help. Most of all, she had a husband who would always understand, as few people could.

'I tell myself it will all be fine.' She tried to sound braver than she felt. 'Of course it will be. I have you.' His face drew tight.

'That's it, isn't it?' she said, suddenly understanding his distress. She smoothed the hair from his brow. 'That's what has you so concerned. What if something happens to you?'

He nodded, closing his eyes and resting his brow against her hand.

'Will you tell me what happened before? With your mother, when she fell ill?'

She recalled his heartrending emotion when he spoke of being jailed and letting his mother die alone. Perhaps if he talked about it, he would feel more at ease. He would see how different matters were now, and how unlikely it was that something similar would happen with Lily.

'Please,' she urged. 'I'm your wife, Julian. You can tell me. You *should* tell me.'

'Yes,' he finally agreed. 'You should know.'

He helped her to a sitting position, and they separated, folding their legs and facing one another. Carefully, he undid each of his cuffs and rolled his shirtsleeves up to the forearm.

'You told me you were jailed,' she prompted. 'You ran afoul of the wrong aristocrat.'

'It starts before that.'

She recognized him settling into his lengthy-discussion posture. Arms and hands at the ready; facial features relaxed, ready to lend nuance or emphasis to his words. He went slowly with his story, using both spoken words and signs, repeating himself or offering clarification at her slightest frown.

'The coffee house,' he began. 'You already know it was entirely staffed by the deaf. That was the establishment's draw. Gentlemen met there to feel charitable and noble, ostensibly. But other times, to discuss matters they didn't want overheard, not even by a serving girl. The place offered private meeting rooms for that purpose. Since I worked there and signed with the others, the clientele just assumed I was deaf. I was careful to never contradict their assumption.'

'So,' she said, 'you heard things you weren't meant to hear.'

He nodded. 'Honestly, most of the time I paid no attention. I was a boy. Their political intrigues and business affairs didn't interest me. But one day, when I was fourteen, I brought a tray up to a private meeting room, and I heard a group of noblemen celebrating their scheme to fix a horse race. They were in collusion with the jockeys and several gaming lords. A certain horse was set to win over the favorite, at very long odds, and these men would rake in a fortune.'

'That sounds terribly unethical, if not illegal.'

'Probably both, but I didn't care. I just wanted my cut.' A wry smile touched his lips. 'I knew my mother kept money stashed beneath a loose board in the garret. I went and pried up the board. I found two pounds, three shillings. I took it all, stuffed the coins in a purse, and hurried off to place a wager on the race. The odds were twelve to one. Can you imagine? That meant I'd win five-and-twenty pounds. More than my mother earned in a year. Poor as we lived, I saw this as our chance to taste luxury. For myself, I wanted shoes that fit. At that age, I was growing an inch a month, it seemed, and

305

my shoes forever pinched my feet. So it was shoes for me, and a warmer cloak for my mother. Then something pretty. Perhaps some combs for her hair.' Moisture gathered in the rims of his eyelids. 'I planned to surprise her.'

'And what happened?'

'Stupidity happened. Greed happened. There I was, on my way to place this bet. I had two pounds, three. And I thought to myself . . . why not try for two pounds, four? Before we found Anna's coffee house, I used to beg pennies in the street. I have this ability to reproduce voices, you know?'

She nodded.

'It was how I learned to speak,' he explained. 'Since my mother could not. I would listen carefully to well-spoken men and mimic what I heard. Once I hear a voice, I never forget it. As a boy, I would go down on the Strand with the West Indian minstrels, and imitate overblown, pompous men as they passed. People would laugh and toss me a coin or two.' He paused, finding his place in the tale.

'But that day something went wrong?'

'Everything went right, for a while. I'd amassed a bit of a crowd and a smattering of coins in my hat. Then I became too cocksure, and I picked the wrong target for my mimicry. He was a lord, with a bloody enormous manservant who appeared out of nowhere. When he challenged me, I tried to joke my way out of it. He only took more offense. He told his man to take me in custody, said they'd show me down to the Fleet and bring charges of mendicancy.'

'Charges of begging?'

He nodded. 'It's unlawful. But here is where my stupidity reached its pinnacle. I pulled out my

306

purse, shook the coins into my hand. Said, "Look here, I have two pounds, three. Why the devil would I be begging?"'

Lily's heart sank to the pit of her stomach. 'Oh, no. You didn't.'

'Oh, yes. I was that foolish. I'll never forget the smug jubilation on that man's face when I proudly whipped out those coins. Of course his reply was that I must have stolen it, and unless I handed the purse over to him, he would bring me up on charges of thievery.'

'But you didn't steal it!'

'I know that. But what judge would believe a smart-mouthed guttersnipe over a lord? This whole world is arranged to value the word of a man like him over that of a man like me. Even with the truth on my side, I had no chance.' A vein pulsed angrily on his temple. 'I was a fool, but not ignorant. I knew stealing anything over a pound was a hanging offense.'

'So what did you do?'

'The only thing I could.' He shrugged with defeat and obvious frustration. 'I gave up the purse and let him charge me with mendicancy. My sentence was a month in Bridewell. I couldn't even send word. And during that month, my mother took ill again. Perhaps a doctor could have helped her, but I'd left her with no money . . . '

He broke off. Lily impatiently dabbed her tears with her sleeve. Julian's eyes were moist and rimmed with red, but he refused to wipe them or even blink. As if ignoring the tears might make them go away. After a prolonged, stoic struggle on the brink of his lashes, one drop shook loose and plummeted to the counterpane.

Lily longed to embrace him, but she could tell he wasn't finished speaking.

'I will never know,' he said at length, 'what my mother thought of me when she died. I'd argued with her earlier that week. Over everything and nothing, much as we'd argued many times before. Just as any young man argues with his mother when he chafes against the leading strings. I was sorry for it. It was one reason I hoped to surprise her with a gift. But then I vanished, by all appearances having made off with her savings. I tried to get word to her, by sending a message with a boy released from jail the week after I arrived. But who knows if he relayed it, or even if he did, whether she was able to understand.'

He inhaled deeply. When he continued, his manner was listless, resigned. 'I have to live with it now. Knowing she may have gone to her grave believing I'd left her alone. That I didn't care.'

There was no stopping the tears now. Not his, not hers.

'Perhaps . . . ' He stopped to swipe angrily at his eyes. When he continued, his signs were rich with pathos, tugging at her heart. 'Perhaps the money could have saved her. Perhaps she would have battled harder against her illness, if she'd known the truth. What if she succumbed because she felt I'd abandoned her?'

'No,' Lily said firmly, not even bothering to sign. 'I cannot believe that.' Her beginner's finger-spelling was too slow and clumsy for this. Besides, she needed to touch him.

She raised her hands to his face, wiping his tears with her thumbs. He wouldn't look at her. 'Your mother was so brave and strong. She sacrificed so

308

much for you. A woman like that would never just
. . . succumb. She would never lose faith in herself,
or in you.'

'Lily.' His features twisted with emotion. 'Lily, no
matter what happens, you must never doubt that I
love you.'

'I won't.' She kissed his brow. 'Oh, darling. I
could never.'

'If something should happen to me—'

She clapped her hands over his, stopping him
mid-sentence. His fear was palpable. She wasn't
sure she could vanquish it completely, and yet she
had to try.

'If something should happen to you,' she began,
'I would be inconsolable. Devastated. I would not
want to go on.' Her fingers tightened reflexively
over his. She hated even talking this way, but
she knew it was what he needed to hear. 'I would
not *want* to go on, but I would. After my illness, I
learned to live without hearing. When Leo died, it
was as if my right arm had been cleaved from my
body. And yet I adapted, found a way to make do.'

She leaned close and pressed her forehead to his.
'If you were taken from me, I would feel as though
I'd been cracked apart and a piece of my very soul
removed. I would never be the same. But I would
go on. For you, for our child. For myself. I am
stronger than you know, Julian. Stronger than even
I know. Life has proved this to me, time and again.'

She spoke the words with certainty, determined
to convince him. And as an unexpected benefit, Lily
managed to convince herself.

They sat there together, legs crossed on the bed.
Both leaning forward, her brow pressed to his.
From the side, they must have resembled a gothic

arch. But the space between their bodies was hardly empty. It seethed with passion and anguish and love and heated breath. As they slowly leaned in, the space grew smaller, compressing all that emotion into a tense, volatile coil, ready to spring.

They were breathing so hard. Almost in unison. Lily was sure she'd never been so fully *aware* of another person, another body, another soul in her life. And as one half of twins, that was saying something.

Want, he signed.

Or was it *need*? They were almost the same gesture, he'd taught her. A flick of the wrist, drawing the hand down the chest and then slightly away. The difference between 'want' and 'need' was subtle, and mostly in the intensity of expression.

He repeated the sign. Her breath caught.

Need. This was definitely need. *I need.*

And she knew exactly what it was he needed, because she needed it too.

Buttons. The next minute was all about buttons. The carved horn buttons on his waistcoat, the silk-covered buttons chasing down the back of her dress. The closures of his fall. True nakedness was an unattainable goal—for he still wore his boots, which meant his pantaloons were going nowhere below the knees. They had no patience for the knotted tapes of her stays, and so her corset and chemise remained on, as well.

But they were bared enough. Enough to kiss. Enough to taste. Enough to press skin to skin and feel each other's heat, each other's need.

He rolled atop her, hiked her shift, spread her thighs—and thrust home with no further preliminary. She was tight and not quite ready for

310

him, but she didn't complain. She knew how badly he needed this, to join with her. To feel surrounded and safe. To get *inside*.

She wrapped her legs over his hips, and he stroked harder, deeper, as though he would lose himself in her embrace. Or dig a trench for them both in the mattress ticking, whichever came first. Moisture dripped from his brow, splashing her chest. Tears, sweat, or some mixture of both. His movements were desperate, tortured. Pained, and a bit painful, too.

She took it all, ignoring the sharp pinch of pain, wondering if he meant to test her resiliency by doing his devil's best to break her apart.

Take this, he challenged with brutal digs of his hips. *And this. And then more.*

She would hold together. She could take whatever he gave. But she also had needs of her own, and truth be told, Lily was growing a bit weary of being the object of concern. If it was proof of her strength he desired . . .

On his next deep thrust, Lily cinched her legs around his and rolled over, reversing their positions and coming to rest atop him. The pantaloons tangling about his knees restricted his ability to retaliate. Even if he wished to, and from the look on his face, she would wager that he didn't. She had her captive well and happily pinned.

She sat tall, straddling his hips and centering herself on his monumental erection. With a little smile, she told him, 'Be still. I'll take matters from here.'

Obviously bewildered but not at all displeased, he reached to stroke her thigh. 'Lily . . .'

'Now, now.' She flicked his touch away. 'I said,

311

be still.'

Placing her hands flat atop his chest, she lifted herself in a slow, torturous glide before sinking onto him again. His resonant groan tickled her palms.

He clutched her hips, nudging himself even deeper.

'Naughty.' Lily tsked, stopping midstroke to remove his hands from her backside. 'Don't you want to see that I'm strong? That I can manage without you?'

His eyes flared with lust, and she knew he'd finally understood.

A thrill of power surged through her. 'Hands out to the sides,' she demanded. 'Flat against the bed.' He complied, stretching his arms to either side. 'You won't move?'

'I won't move.'

'Promise. Or I shall have to tie you down.'

Oh. Part of him leapt at that idea. How very interesting. Well, perhaps another time.

'I promise,' he said, arching his back. 'Anything. Just hurry.'

She grinned. This posture gave her a beautiful view of his chest and arms. His muscles and tendons were taut with the effort of restraint. A sculpture of sensual agony.

Devouring him with her eyes, she began to ride him once more, rolling her hips in a steady rhythm. Each downstroke sent delicious friction just where she needed it. His deep moans of pleasure resonated in her bones.

'Do you see?' she said coyly. 'I know what you need. And I know how to take what I need, too.'

With a curse, he squeezed his eyes shut.

As her arousal gathered and built, she increased her pace. She let her hands wander over his chest, tweaking his flat nipples and sinking her fingernails into his skin.

He gritted his teeth. 'Lily,' he said, lifting his head just a bit. His gaze dropped to the place where their bodies joined. 'I want to touch you. Let me touch you.'

'No.' Then with a sweet smile, 'I'll do it.'

She raised her hands to her breasts, long since popped free of her stays, cupping and lifting the globes through the thin covering of her chemise. They were tender and swollen, no doubt because she was with child. Her nipples were so sensitive, just the chafing of the thin muslin shift sent sharp ripples of pleasure to her core. She gave the dark, turgid peaks an experimental pinch.

'God.' Julian bucked beneath her. 'You'll kill me.'

His desperation pleased her beyond measure. Yes, this was what she wanted. To tower over him, rounded and feminine and merciless as a heathen fertility goddess. She was creating a new life inside her. What could be more powerful than that? Never mind protected. She deserved to be worshipped, feared.

Flattening her hands, she slid her palms down her belly, down to where their bodies joined, sending her fingers to burrow beneath the gathered fabric of her chemise. She found that swollen, sensitive nub, covered it with a fingertip.

Then she stilled, resting her pelvis to his, savoring the feeling of having him so deep inside her as she touched herself, circling her finger over her needy pearl. The joy spiraled and spread, and again she began to move her hips, moving up and down on his hard length. She couldn't look away from his face. And his gaze was riveted to her hand where she pleasured herself. If he'd ever been more transported by lust, she had not witnessed it. His fingers twisted the bed linens as he thrashed beneath her.

Close as she was, she held back. She wanted more. She wanted him to acknowledge her control, beg for his own release.

'Lily,' he pleaded. 'God, Lily. I can't—I'm going to—'

'Yes. *Yes.*' Her peak came in a hot, dizzy rush. It came, and it stayed, going on and on as he broke form, reaching to clutch her hips and pump his release into her depths.

In the aftermath, she collapsed atop him, panting and shivering with bliss. His arms wrapped her snug against his chest.

'We'll be fine,' she told him, blanketing him with her body and pressing a kiss to his parted lips. 'Just fine. Believe me, Julian. Trust in this. I love you, and you love me. All the hurting is in the past. We have our whole future ahead of us, and it will be wonderful.'

Never had she believed her own words more. And never had she been more wrong.

Chapter Twenty-two

She found the letter in the morning.

My dearest Lily,

I can only imagine your reaction when you find this. You will wish you had made good on your threat last night and tied me to the bed. I rather wish it, too.

Dear, darling Lily. Where do I begin?

I have an enemy. Ever since Leo's death, I have suspected that attack was meant for me. I explained to you yesterday how, as a youth, I became privy to sensitive information at the coffee house. Although my attempt to place a wager on that horse race went disastrously wrong, I eventually found other ways to use the information to my material advantage. And if I were ever brought to a reckoning in those cases, neither the law nor the truth would be on my side.

These past six months, I've feared someone had discovered my true identity, finally connected Julian Bellamy with the deaf-mute errand boy. I thought this unknown person had tried to silence me permanently that night of the boxing match.

Lily, you must believe how ardently I hoped my suspicions were wrong. For a while, I managed to convince myself that you were right, and Leo's death was nothing but a random, senseless tragedy. Then yesterday, both my brightest hopes and my worst fears were realized. You blessed me with the news of our child, and within the same hour I received incontrovertible proof that I am a marked man. My life is in danger—and, as long as I remain near you, so is yours.

315

I cannot risk harm to you or the babe, nor can I live with the specter of fear overshadowing our joy. I ride out this morning with Morland and Ashworth, with plans to confront Leo's killers and hopes of identifying my enemy. From there, I will do whatever I must to protect you and our child.

Believe this: I will do my damnedest to fix this and come home to you. However, I cannot ignore the possibility that I may not return. If I fail to come back, look for my solicitor to discreetly make contact. There are funds set aside. You will never want for anything.

Lily, by leaving you like this, I break a promise. And thus, I behave in a manner completely unworthy of you. The plain truth of it is, I have always been unworthy of you. You don't know the half of what I've done. But no matter the shame in my past, these weeks with you have been the happiest and proudest of my life. Had we shared only one night together, it would be worth all this and more to have called you 'wife' just once and to wear your ring to my grave. I could cover this paper with 'I love you's, and still they wouldn't be enough.

I love you.

There, kindly read that a thousand times over. Then pause to take tea, and read it a thousand times more. Daily, if you will.

Be faithful to those vows you made last night. You must never doubt my love for you, and no matter what occurs, you must find a way to carry on. The irony is not lost on me, that even as I break my own promises, I'm insisting you must keep yours. Unfair of me, but true to form. I'm a bastard, a scoundrel, and as you've said, an unmitigated ass. Even the damned bird knows it's true. But above all

316

these, I remain
   Yours, always,
   —J.

'No!' Lily shouted, stepping back from the letter where it lay on her dressing table. 'No, no, no! How could you?'

She pressed a hand to the thin lawn of her shift. They'd spent a magical night together. Had she somehow dreamed it all? No. The supper tray was still there, not even yet cleared. He'd made love to her so sweetly, all night through, scarcely allowing her to rest between bouts of passion. She'd thought his exuberant ardor meant he'd finally moved past all his fears and reservations.

But no. It meant he'd been saying good-bye. Making love to her as if last night could be their *last* night, ever. And now he'd rushed out to meet some unknown danger, leaving her behind to helplessly fret.

Damn him. *Damn* him. Lily seldom swore, but if ever there was an occasion to merit blasphemy, this was it. He must have been planning this. Hadn't he said so yesterday in the gallery? The three gentlemen had made plans to go riding.

'Damn you, Julian,' she said aloud. 'And damn your noble words. I'll be damned if you'll leave me like this.'

She looked to the clock. Already half nine. Damn, damn, damn. Who could say how long he'd been gone?

Her lady's maid came rushing in, no doubt drawn by the angry shouting.

'I want a traveling habit, and a warm cloak,' Lily told her. 'And I want them now. Don't bother with

317

pressing.'

While the maid was still curtsying her agreement, Lily rushed past her and wrenched open the door, sticking head and shoulders into the corridor. 'Swift!' she bellowed, putting her whole body into the effort.

Within moments, the butler's silver head appeared at the top of the stairs.

'The carriage, Swift. I want it readied immediately.'

Without even waiting for his acknowledg ment, Lily slammed the door shut and went to the washstand, swabbing herself with tepid water and yanking a brush through her love-tangled hair. By the time her maid appeared with a fresh chemise, stays, and petticoat, Lily was read to don them. She grabbed the stockings and garters for herself. 'Get the dress,' she told the maid.

The stockings were uncooperative, and the garters were downright incorrigible. 'Damnable stockings,' she grumbled, perversely wishing she *did* swear more often, so she would have a broader repertoire of profanity to draw from. 'Damnable garters.'

As the clock ticked toward ten, she was fully dressed and simply coiffed. Presentable, if not a picture of elegance. She took one last glance in the mirror, smoothing her damp palms over the pleated amethyst superfine.

'Gloves,' she called. 'I need gloves.'

Her maid was right there beside her, holding a pair in either hand for her selection.

Lily took the buff doeskin gloves and ran with them, working her fingers into their tight sheaths as she hurried down the stairs. 'Is the carriage ready,

318

Swift?'

'Nearly, my lady.'

'Tell the driver to pull around front. I'll wait on the steps.' Honestly, Lily had no idea where she intended to go. She just knew she had to go *somewhere*. She could not sit in this house, poring over ledgers and alphabetizing books while Julian was out in the world, courting danger.

She went to the front door and grabbed hold of the handle. *Amelia,* she thought. She would start with Amelia and Meredith. Since all three men had gone out together, perhaps the other ladies would have some clue where they'd headed.

Lily wrenched open the door and bolted through it, only to pull up short on the threshold. Amelia and Meredith themselves stood on the front stoop. Amelia's hand was arrested midair, as though she'd been preparing to ring the bell.

'Good morning.' She smiled brightly. 'That was speedy of you. Did you see us coming up the walk?'

Lily shook her head. 'No.'

Meredith said, 'We thought with the men gone out for their ride, we ladies deserved some amusement of our own. What do you say to a stroll in the park?'

'Damn the park. That's what I say to it.'

Both ladies blinked with surprise.

'I'm so sorry,' Lily said. 'But come in, come in. I'll explain.' She ushered her stunned friends through the door and shut it behind them. 'Our husbands haven't gone out for a leisurely ride. They've gone out to confront Leo's killers.'

Amelia and Meredith looked to one another.

'You must believe me,' Lily said. 'Julian left me a letter this morning.'

'We do believe you, dear.' Amelia put a hand on Lily's arm. 'We already knew.'

'You . . . You *knew*?'

Meredith nodded. 'Our husbands told us. But Mr. Bellamy asked us not to say anything to you. I gather he didn't want to raise your hopes or anxieties until it was all over.'

Lily went numb with anger and disbelief. She didn't know what to think. Her husband, her friends, her friends' husbands . . . Was the whole world conspiring to deceive her?

Amelia tightened her grip on Lily's arm, guiding her into the drawing room and helping her into a chair.

Sitting down across from her, Amelia said, 'There's nothing to fear. Let me explain. Through the work of an investigator, Mr. Bellamy was able to find the two men believed to have attacked dear Leo. They've been imprisoned these six months for another crime, and they're due to be released today. The men have gone to meet them, bring them to London, and swear out a new charge of murder. There is no danger, and it will all be over soon.'

'But . . . but that makes no sense.'

If there was no danger, why would Julian leave a letter saying he might not return? He said he'd received a threat on his life yesterday. Lily's memory flashed back to that moment on the street, when she'd been shoved against the windowpane. Could that have been the incident? It would certainly explain Julian's behavior of the subsequent half-hour, carrying her more than a mile home before collapsing with relief.

She reached for Amelia's hand and clutched

it tight. 'I believe you, Amelia. I believe that as recently as yesterday, their plan was as you describe it. But something changed. That's why Julian wrote me that letter. He spoke of not only confronting Leo's killers, but identifying an unknown enemy. He spoke of violence, and the possibility he will not return. I believe our husbands may be in true peril. Or at the very least, mine is. We must do something. Do you have any idea where they've gone?'

Amelia and Meredith exchanged guarded looks.

'Lady Lily,' Meredith began, 'I know you are anxious. But even if there is danger, our husbands are better equipped to handle it than most men.'

Lily ignored her. 'If they went to meet prisoners being released . . . How many prisons are there? The Fleet? Newgate? Bridewell? And so many more, just in London alone. Oh, but a London jail makes no sense. Why would they ride out on horse back? It must be somewhere further away.'

Amelia touched her wrist, then waited for her attention. 'Lily, my dear—'

Lily cut her off. 'I know what you're going to say, Amelia. That our husbands have the situation in hand, and we can only make a muddle of things by interfering. But I know you're wrong. I can't tell you how I know, but I *know*. Julian would not have left me that letter if there was no reason to fear.' She took a deep breath. 'Now, the two of you can either help me find him . . . or you can leave, and I'll do it myself.'

Meredith sighed. 'Rhys gave me no details about their destination. He said only that they were riding into the country.'

'I'm afraid I don't know any more than that,'

321

Amelia said. 'I confess, when Spencer's talk turns to horses and riding, I don't always listen so closely as I ought.'

'We need a list,' Lily said. 'A list of prisons and jails within easy riding distance.'

'Even if we obtain such a list,' Amelia asked, 'what will you do with it? We can't possibly go searching in every direction at once.'

Lily dropped her gaze and blinked back the tears of frustration stinging her eyes. Crying wouldn't help matters.

Her attention was jerked upward by a flurry of rainbow-hued feathers. Tartuffe swooped the length of the drawing room, circling back to perch on the chandelier.

'Damnable bird,' she cursed up at him. 'How did you escape your cage?'

Amelia clapped with astonishment. 'Is he yours?' Lily nodded.

'He's lovely,' said Meredith. 'And he seems to share your distress over Mr. Bellamy's fate. He keeps singing his name. "Oh, Julian," he says. Over and over. "Oh, Julian." ' She chuckled. 'And now, "Guilty, guilty." '

'He belonged to a barrister once,' Lily explained. 'And yes, he has quite a fondness for Julian's name.'

Something pecked at her memory. A line from Julian's horrible, heartbreaking letter.

I'm a bastard, a scoundrel, and as you've said, an unmitigated ass. Even the damned bird knows it's true.

Just what did this damned bird know about Julian? Guilty, guilty indeed.

'Don't . . . you . . . move,' she warned the parrot,

322

slowly backing away. Once she'd reached the room's exit, she darted into the corridor and found two footmen standing there.

She snapped her fingers at the first. 'You—bring quill and paper.' She swung her gaze on the second. 'Run and ask Cook for a dish of minced fruit and nutmeats. And both of you, be quick.'

They dispersed as ordered, and Lily returned to the drawing room. It was a wild, likely futile idea, but it was the only idea she had.

'Amelia,' she said, retaking her seat and keeping her eyes trained on the feathered menace overhead, 'I know you are a duchess, and this task is horribly beneath your station in life. But I must ask you to do it anyway.'

'Whatever can you mean?'

The footman arrived with paper and quill, and Lily waved him toward Amelia, saying, 'I must ask you to take dictation from a bird.'

*   *   *

'What time are they set to be released?' Ashworth asked.

Extricating his boots from the squelching marsh, Julian climbed a small ridge and squinted toward the Thames. In the deep center of the river, the prison hulks floated at anchor—skeletal, rotting corpses of ships, stripped of masts and sails. Retired from their work as sailing vessels, now serving as overflow prisons for convicted felons.

'After the day's work,' he answered. 'This time of year, labor ends at four o'clock.'

'Odd, isn't it?' Ashworth mused. 'That they put convicts to work around all those weapons and guns?'

'I reckon the officers watch them close.'

Longboats ferried the prisoners back and forth from the shore, where they spent their days laboring in the Woolwich Warren, England's largest armory. To the south of where they stood now, a large wall rose up from the marshland, enclosing the Warren—a maze of shipyards, weapon foundries, powder magazines, and more.

'Four o'clock?' Morland consulted his timepiece. 'It's not yet noon. We have plenty of time, then. Let's take a meal at the inn beforehand.'

They'd ridden out from Town before dawn, tracing the Thames some distance on its journey toward the sea. Around daybreak, they'd come within sight of Woolwich and the fleet of hulks. They'd stabled the horses at a nearby inn and set out on foot to scout the area.

'Let's go over the plan again,' Julian said.

'Again?' Ashworth groaned.

'It's not as though it's complicated,' the duke said. 'We enter the Warren. Before the two brutes can be released, we'll intervene. Explain matters to the officer, take them into our custody. We arrange for transport to Newgate, where I see them charged with murder. End of plan.'

'Wrong,' Julian said. 'The plan has changed.'

'Oh, really?' Ashworth asked. 'How so?'

'We have to enter the armory on false pretenses. Then let them be released. I'll follow them for a bit before taking them into custody. My custody.' He opened a satchel at his side and removed a pistol, a horn of powder, and a pouch of lead shot.

'*Your* custody? At gunpoint? Why?'

'Because I need to know who hired them.'

324

In matter-of-fact terms, Julian told them about the shoving incident in the street yesterday, and the card pressed into his hand. He didn't repeat the words of the message, only the gist.

'It was a warning,' he said. '"Don't interfere, or you'll be silenced."' He paused for a moment, concentrating as he measured black powder. 'It's just as I've always suspected. That attack on Leo and Faraday was meant for me. If these two brutes go to the gallows, I'll never know who put them up to it. Lily will never be safe. My only chance is to capture them and force them to lead me to their employer.'

'And you propose to do that alone?' the duke asked.

'It's kidnapping,' Julian said. 'And torture, if they need some convincing to talk. I wouldn't ask you to be a part of that.'

Ashworth said, 'You've asked me to do worse.'

'That was in the past. You both have wives now, responsibilities. Morland here has a child on the way.'

Morland countered, 'And what about you?'

A swift pang caught him in the chest. He ached for Lily. Would she be awake yet, he wondered? Was she already cursing his name, ruing the day they wed?

'Just leave,' Julian told the others, 'I'll go it alone.' Ashworth and Morland exchanged glances. Neither man moved to depart.

'We're not going to leave you alone, man.' The duke kicked at a loose stone. 'We think too highly of your wife, for one.'

'And we both owe you our assistance,' Ashworth added.

Julian shook his head. 'Forget the Stud Club. It was nothing more than a joke on Leo's part. I only puffed up that honor and fraternity and "Code of Good Breeding" nonsense to prod you into action when he died. Neither of you owes me anything.'

Ashworth snorted. 'I owe you my life. Or don't you remember?'

Julian tilted his head, considering. Well, he supposed there was that. He'd hauled Ashworth up from a cliff in Cornwall. At the time, however, the man hadn't treated it like a favor.

The duke added, 'And I seem to recall your assistance in a midnight search for my runaway ward.'

'That hardly counts. I didn't want to help.'

'For God's sake, you stood up for me at my wedding,' Ashworth said. 'We're friends, Bellamy. And you're stuck with us, whatever fool plan you've cooked up.'

'But at least give us some explanation first,' Morland said. 'Why the devil does someone want so badly to kill you?'

Julian hesitated, unsure whether to tell them. Were they friends, truly? He looked from the stern, aristocratic duke to the formidable, battle-scarred warrior. Well, he supposed, these were two men he would rather have as friends than enemies.

'I know things,' he said. 'Things I was never meant to know. I overheard secrets as a youth, working at a coffee house. I was an errand boy. My mother worked in the kitchen.'

'And your father . . . ?' Ashworth prompted.

'Not in the picture,' he said tightly. Julian couldn't imagine that news would come as a shock to either man. It didn't.

326

Morland frowned. 'What do you mean, "you know things"? Such as . . . ?'

'Such as that horse you're so fond of? Osiris? You know, the reason for this whole club?' At Morland's nod, Julian continued, 'I happen to know the first race he ever won was fixed.'

Morland's chin jerked in surprise. 'His first win? That would have been . . .'

'At Doncaster. He was a three-year-old colt. His jockey had been purposely holding him back all year. The gaming lords kept increasing the odds. By Doncaster, they were twelve-to-one, and all bets were on—'

'Mariner,' Ashworth finished. 'He'd been running strong all year. I remember it well, the general shock when he ran third.'

'Not everyone was shocked. There were ten members of the Jockey Club in on the plan. I heard them discussing it myself, at the coffee house where my mother worked. I didn't know their names at the time, but I remembered their voices. Repeated them over and over to myself, so I wouldn't forget. Over the next few years, I learned their identities, and then . . . And then I blackmailed them, each and every one.'

There was an awed silence in response to this. Julian found himself enjoying it a bit. Even he could hardly believe he'd possessed the stones to do it.

Once he'd learned the identities of each conspirator, he'd posed as—well, as himself, as those men knew him. A deaf-mute ruffian. Through gestures and written cards, he'd demanded a private audience with each man in turn. In each interview, he'd handed over a block-lettered note.

327

It was the first missive he'd ever penned, each word collected separately over a span of weeks; the whole copied and recopied with painstaking care.

Give one hundred guineas to the deaf-mute, and send him back forthwith. If both guineas and boy do not arrive by sunset, tomorrow's papers will blaze the truth of Doncaster.

They might have shot him where he stood, and no one would ever have been the wiser. There would be no one left to tell the newspapers the truth. Even if Julian had gone to the scandal sheets himself, it was unlikely they would have believed his tale.

But with his mother gone, he'd had nothing to lose. So he played this bluff ten times in all, and in each instance it worked. Almost sad, how none of the men even thought to suspect him. They saw that deaf errand boy from the coffee house, and they assumed him to be a simpleton. Ten times, he'd walked away with his heart pounding in his throat and a hundred guineas testing the seams of his pockets. He could have asked for more money; he knew that now. As a youth, he simply hadn't been able to conceive of a greater sum. A thousand guineas, all told. From it, he'd purchased new shoes and a proper suit of clothes. And then he'd gone about building a fortune.

Years later, when Osiris was retired to stud and Leo started the Stud Club . . . ah, the irony had been too sweet. At last, he was one of the ten. Not the boy scraping mud from their boots.

'Blackmail.' Ashworth whistled low through his teeth. 'And you think someone's recognized you?'

Julian nodded. 'I'm sure of it.'

'But I don't follow,' Ashworth said. 'It was just a horse race, and years ago now. Why would they kill to protect that secret?'

'It wasn't just a horse race,' the duke said. 'Fortunes were gambled and lost. Men were ruined. If the plot were ever known, the conspirators would be permanently barred from not only the Jockey Club, but most of polite society.'

'So they'd commission a murder just to save face?' Ashworth shrugged. 'I suppose men have killed for less.'

'It could be something else,' Julian said. 'This coffeehouse where I learned of this race-fixing scheme . . . gentlemen came there every day to discuss their secrets. Political secrets, business secrets, *affaires* of the heart. If someone has recognized me, who knows what else he thinks I *might* have overheard. That's why it's impossible for me to identify my attacker. I need Stone and Macleod.'

'That's assuming Stone and Macleod are actually the men who killed Leo. Shouldn't we at least have Faraday identify them first?'

Julian leveled his pistol toward the riverbank, checking the sight. 'We leave Faraday out of this. I'm not sure he can be trusted.'

Chapter Twenty-three

'Today,' Claudia vowed, 'victory will be mine.'

'Perhaps.' Her opponent did not look up from arranging the backgammon board. 'Your play has seen moderate improvement.'

'*Moderate* improvement? I nearly won yesterday.'

He nudged the last group of black markers into a precise line. 'Do you know the difference between "nearly winning" and defeat, my dear?'

She shook her head.

'There isn't one.'

Claudia pretended to pout. 'The dice, if you will.'

Feigned petulance aside, Claudia liked Peter Faraday. She liked him a great deal. He'd been a most welcome addition to the household. Amelia and Spencer were always busy with their obligations, or each other. Now she had a fellow invalid, a captive companion. Like her, Mr. Faraday was confined to the sitting room and scarcely able to move without a servant's assistance. They spent most of the day together, and typically part of the evening too. They played backgammon and cards. When they tired of games, he read aloud from the newspaper whilst she worked on a baby quilt or simply rested her eyes. Claudia didn't care much about the content of the newspaper articles, but she enjoyed listening to his witty commentary.

She enjoyed listening to him, in general. He had a very pleasant voice, Mr. Faraday did, with a rich, soothing timbre and an accent that bespoke education and good breeding. He was very handsome, in a way that recalled Mr. Bellamy, but with less flash and more refinement. A true gentleman, Claudia thought. Quick to jest, but never belittling.

He asked her questions, about everything from her childhood to her pregnancy. Not that Claudia was unused to being questioned, but it

was a rare pleasure to have someone truly *listen*
to her answers. She'd told him all about Amelia
and Spencer, and what she could remember of
her late parents. She'd even talked honestly of her
foolish tryst with that horrid tutor in York, and
Mr. Faraday hadn't been the least bit judgmental
or cross. Just interested. She could talk to him of
anything.

They got on well, indeed.

She rolled the dice and moved her tokens
accordingly. 'Would you like to marry me?'

Poor man. He'd spent a week at Morland House,
and this was the first time Claudia had seen him
stunned speechless.

'I beg your pardon?' he finally said.

'Did you not understand me? I thought I made
myself rather clear. I'm asking if you'd like to marry
me.'

She sensed him mulling over a response, and she
sipped at her glass of tepid lemonade, giving him
time.

When he still didn't reply, she tried to put his
mind at ease. 'Don't be concerned, Mr. Faraday.
I'm not so foolish as to imagine I'm in love with
you. But we get on well, don't we?' She patted the
squirming mass in her belly. If this babe's behavior
in the womb was any indication, Claudia was in
for trouble years down the line. Still, she loved
the bothersome, soon-to-be squalling lump. 'Any
day now, I shall give birth. And I want to keep my
baby.'

'Then keep it you shall.' He frowned. 'Don't tell
me the duke is insisting you either marry or give the
child away?'

'No, no. Spencer and Amelia say they'll support

331

me, whatever I decide. But there's no denying our lives will go easier if I do wed. And I thought perhaps you might like to be a father. You seem well-suited to fatherhood, and this could be your chance to have a child without . . . you know, the nuisance of impregnating a wife.'

'The nuisance,' he repeated, incredulous. 'The *nuisance* of impregnating a wife? Just how miserable a lover was this music master, anyway?'

'Bad indeed. But that's not my point.' With a glance to the corridor for servants, she leaned toward him as much as her pregnant belly would allow and whispered, 'You *are* a molly, aren't you?'

He was very careful not to react. Instead, he unstoppered the decanter of lemonade and freshened her glass.

'It's all right,' she assured him quickly. 'I'm very good at keeping secrets. And no one else has noticed, I'm sure. You know how it is, being homebound. I don't have anything else to do with myself, but sit and notice things.'

'But how . . . ?'

She smiled. 'Easy. Your eyes follow the footmen, not the maids. And you fancy the tall one with the square jaw, don't you? So do I. He has perfectly lovely calves. And that arse . . .' She propped her chin on her hand and released a languid sigh. 'Sad for us both, my lady's maid says he's devoted to his sweetheart. She's a seamstress, I hear. Still, that's no reason we can't look. We must contrive to drop a great many objects when he's about, so he will have to pick them up.'

'Why, Lady Claudia.' He sat back in his chair and studied her. A bewildered smile slowly crooked his lips. 'You are a truly remarkable young woman.'

Claudia allowed herself a small moment of satisfaction. It was high time someone noticed that. 'Does that mean you'll marry me?'

'No, my dear,' he said gently. 'I can't marry you. But I think I would very much like to be your friend.'

'A friend can't give my baby a name.'

'No. There, you will be on your own. But you will do splendidly.'

She slumped back in her chair. 'I don't know how I'm going to care for a child. I can't even keep myself out of trouble, most days.'

'Claudia, listen to me. I've spent the past week learning all about you. Would you like to know what I've learned?'

She shrugged.

'You are intelligent, forthright, curious. Extraordinarily perceptive. Unafraid to take risks. You will not be bound by nonsensical rules. These qualities may have made you an awkward girl, but mark my words—they will one day make you an exceptional woman. And a good mother. Of that, I am sure.'

A welling tear made her vision wavy, and Claudia dabbed at it with impatience. 'You're the only one who's kind to me.'

'That's not true. Your cousin and his wife are very good to you, indeed. They love you, even if they don't always understand you. And someday, you will meet the man who both loves *and* understands you. If there's any justice in the world, he will also possess a square jaw and well-turned calves. Don't settle for less.'

'Settling is the best I can expect. An unwed

mother of a natural child? I won't have the opportunity to be choosy. I can't even have a season.'

His eyes were kind. 'Oh, I think you will. Years from now, you will return to London as a strong, independent, beautiful, and deliciously scandalous lady. Believe me, the men will be powerless to resist.' Collecting the dice, he said, 'I shall make it a point to attend your first ball, just to gloat over my accurate prediction.'

'Truly?' She cast a glance at his hobbled leg, thinking it rather brave of him to contemplate attending balls. 'Then you must be my partner for the first dance.'

'It's a bargain.'

They shook hands over the backgammon board. A mild cramp seized her abdomen, and Claudia winced.

'Are you well?' he asked.

'Yes, yes.' She took a deep breath, then released it slowly. 'I have these twinges most every day now. False labor, the doctor called it.' She rubbed her domed belly in small circles until the tightness eased. This was nothing, compared to those frightening episodes in her early pregnancy. The pain and blood . . .

'What about you, Mr. Faraday?' she asked, trying to distract herself with a change of subject. 'Have you been in love?'

His gaze cut away. 'Yes.'

'But it didn't end well.'

'No, it didn't.' He rolled the dice, then stared at them. 'It ended very badly indeed.'

There was a deep, unsettling sadness in his mien. It made Claudia want to comfort him, but she

334

didn't know how. She took a long sip of lemonade instead. 'But you're certain it's worth waiting for?' she asked, wiping her mouth. 'Love?'

'Yes,' he said firmly. 'It's worth waiting for, Claudia. It's worth living and dying and killing for. It's everything.'

'Ah!'

Pain, sudden and excruciating, clamped down on her womb like a vise. It robbed her of breath for a moment. Just when she thought it would ebb, it returned with even greater force, wrenching a scream from her throat. The room looked washed in orange and red, the color of alarm. This wasn't false labor; this was something very *wrong*. She instantly rued every instance in which she'd disregarded the doctor's orders or ignored Amelia's advice. Perhaps she shouldn't have climbed the stairs that morning. Perhaps she shouldn't have eaten that rich pudding last night . . .

Please, she silently prayed. *Please let the bothersome lump be unharmed.*

'Mr. Faraday,' she panted, 'I . . .' Another surge of pain. She gritted her teeth. 'Something's wrong. I need help.'

But Mr. Faraday—injured, hobbled Mr. Faraday—was already out of his chair . . .

And striding quickly from the room.

* * *

'Give it here, if you will.' Lily took the paper from Amelia's grasp and scanned it quickly. A half-hour's cajoling and several dozen nutmeats had resulted in a full page of avian ramblings. 'It's all the usual,' she noted with disappointment.

335

Oh, Julian. Guilty, guilty. Thank you, that will be all. Endless permutations of the above, interspersed with whistles and squawks.

Then, toward the bottom of the page, she noted something new.

"'Mr. James Bell,'" she read aloud. 'Now that's amusing. I wonder how he picked that up.'

'An acquaintance of yours?' Meredith asked.

'In a way.'

Lily was momentarily transported back to that darkened theater pit, seated on a cushioned bench aside her bookish, bespectacled beau. She'd been so amazed at his ability to transform his appearance and seem an entirely different man. Now, after these weeks of marriage, it amazed her that no one else saw him as she did. Society recognized Julian Bellamy as a collection of wild hair and wilder clothes and loud, brash behavior, never taking note of the man beneath. A quietly handsome man, with sincere blue eyes and a passion for fairness. Keen intelligence, and a thoughtful, tender way.

That man was her husband.

> *The plain truth of it is, I have always been unworthy of you. You don't know the half of what I've done.*

'I think,' Lily said slowly, 'Mr. James Bell may be more than a mere acquaintance.'

Amelia jumped on her chair. 'Oh. He just said something new. Just now.' She beckoned for the paper, and Lily gave it quickly.

Craning her neck, she watched over Amelia's shoulder as her friend inscribed a single word.

'Jericho,' Lily read aloud. 'Well, that's not

336

terribly helpful. Is it?'

'Could mean anything,' Meredith agreed. 'Perhaps one of his previous owners was fond of scripture. It could be a servant's name, or even the bird's name.'

'Or a ship,' Amelia said. 'That was Michael's first assignment in the Navy. I'll never forget it, having written him so many letters that year. He sailed from Plymouth on the HMS *Jericho*. The vessel's been retired now. I remember he pointed it out to me once when we traveled to—' She grabbed Lily's arm, and her eyes went wide. 'To Greenwich. The *Jericho* is now moored in the Thames, near Woolwich. It's a prison hulk.'

'A prison hulk?' Lily's heart jumped into her throat.

'Now wait. That's a very big leap,' Meredith warned. 'And we could be making it in the wrong direction entirely.'

'I know. I know you're right,' Lily replied, the gears of her mind clicking at a furious whir. 'But it's the only direction we have.' How many miles was it to Woolwich? Ten? Fifteen? How fast could the carriage take her there? 'We must leave immediately. There's not a moment to waste.'

But before she could even rise from her chair, Swift entered the room. The aging butler extended a salver, on which lay a haphazardly folded note.

He bowed deeply. 'Forgive the interruption, my lady. But an urgent message has just arrived for Her Grace.'

Amelia took the note and opened it. Her blue eyes shuttled back and forth as she scanned the lines of text. 'Oh, no. It's Claudia. She's in labor. I must go to her at once.'

337

Lily was surprised indeed to learn of the note's contents. But she was stunned immobile by the envelope's reverse, where the words 'Her Grace, the Duchess of Morland' had been hastily inscribed in black ink.

Lily knew that penmanship. Knew it as well as she knew her own.

'Oh my God.' Without even thinking, she leapt from her chair and ripped the note straight from Amelia's hand. 'Who sent this?' But she didn't lift her gaze to receive a reply. Rather, she read the brief missive for herself.

Your Grace,
  Lady Claudia has entered her labor pains. I have taken the liberty of sending for the doctor.
—P.F.

'P.F.? Who is P.F.?'

Amelia gave an answer as she tugged on her gloves. Lily couldn't catch it.

'Write it down,' she insisted, urging the quill and inkpot toward her friend.

'I can't right now,' Amelia said, gathering her shawl. 'Claudia needs me. I must go at once.'

Lily slammed the inkpot on the table, ignoring the spatter of ink, and thrust the quill in Amelia's face. She trembled so violently, the feather quivered in her grip. '*Write*. Write it down.'

While Amelia addressed the footman, Meredith took the quill and quickly scrawled something on a scrap of paper.

Lily read it. 'Peter Faraday. Who is Peter Faraday?'

'Amelia's house guest,' Meredith explained.

338

'Rhys and I brought him from Cornwall, and he's been staying at Morland House. He's injured. He . . . He was with your brother, the night he was attacked.'

A wave of dizziness dropped Lily back into her chair. She was completely disoriented. This bit of information . . . it both explained so much, and opened up entirely new questions.

One thing was clear. She had to get to Woolwich, and quickly. Julian had no idea what he could be facing.

Meredith touched her hand. 'I'll go with Amelia now. She needs help.'

'Yes, of course,' Lily said, pushing to her feet. She helped her friends to the door. 'I pray all goes well with Claudia.'

'Thank you.' Amelia put a hand to her brow. 'I only wish there were some way to get a message to Spencer.'

'Don't worry, dear. He'll learn of it soon enough.' Lily intended to deliver the news herself.

*   *   *

'There they are. Those two, on the ridge.'

From their sentinel post atop the scaffolding, Julian followed Ashworth's gaze. Two convicts labored on a rocky breakwater, some yards distant from the riverbank. The men, dressed in standard-issue buff breeches and brown coats, were shackled to one another at the ankle. Under the watchful eye of a cutlass-wielding officer, they passed and piled massive rocks, building up the breakwater. Julian noted with satisfaction that the prisoners' tattered, soiled garments hung loose on their frames.

Good. They'd known hunger these past six months. 'You're positive it's them?' he asked.

Ashworth nodded. 'Had a chat with the officer down at the dock. He confirmed the names. Nasty sorts, the two of them. Hardly—'

The boom of cannon fire forced him to break off. Between the clanging of heavy machinery and the occasional blast from the artillery range, the armory wasn't a quiet place.

'Hardly model inmates,' Ashworth finished at length. 'That's why they're working in shackles. When their day's labor is finished, a guard will be striking the irons. An officer will give them each ten shillings and their papers, and then they're on their way.'

'And so are we.'

Once Stone and Macleod left the warren, they would follow and bide their time. No doubt the convicts' first order of business would be a pint at the local tavern and a visit to the closest brothel. With any luck, they'd apprehend the men once they were well into their cups, trousers tangled at their ankles. Three against two, and pistols in their favor. No contest. Perhaps they'd wrangle a name from the brutes then and there, and Julian would at least have a direction for his efforts. He wouldn't be able to go home to Lily quite yet, but he would feel as though he were journeying in that direction.

Until then, they would wait and observe from here. 'Here' being an unused bay in the dockyard. This small inlet for the repair and rigging of ships was flanked by high platforms on either side, accessed by rough-planked stairs.

By revealing himself to be the famed Lieutenant Colonel St. Maur, Ashworth had easily talked their way into the armory and dockyard. No one suspected. They were just a friendly group of gentlemen out for a ride, curious to have a look at things. Their greatest struggle had been shaking free of the many officers angling to tour them around.

Light footsteps clattered on the wooden steps. The men frowned at one another before turning to see who would join them. Another starry-eyed young officer, likely, hoping to trade battle tales with Ashworth or curry the favor of a duke.

But it wasn't an officer who emerged on the platform.

It was Lily. His wife, clad in a violet traveling dress and dark winter cloak, rushing straight for him. Her heel caught on a board, and his heart plummeted, only sputtering back to life when she caught and righted herself.

'Jesus Christ,' Julian blurted out, taking his wife by the shoulders. He couldn't help but give her a little shake. To be sure she was safe. To be sure she was *real*. 'Lily, what the hell are you doing here?'

'I'm chasing you.' She panted for breath. 'You unmitigated ass.' Her eyes blazed with fury, and she trembled in his arms. He'd never seen her in possession of such intense, evident rage and fear.

But she wouldn't be here if her love didn't surpass both of these.

His heart rolled in his chest. 'This much, Lily? You truly love me this much?'

'Of course I do, you hateful man. Damn you.' She clutched her side with one hand and raised the other in a fist. Lowered it. Raised it again. Then

341

punched his shoulder, hard.

He kissed her full on the lips. She struggled for a moment, having stockpiled all that nervous energy for the cause of defense. But he would not be pushed away. He held her tight with his arms and cherished her lips with the softest of kisses, tasting the sweetness of her skin and the salt of her tears. 'I love you,' he murmured against her lips. 'I don't know how it's possible to love you so much. I will die of it.'

The platform trembled beneath their feet. A powder explosion in the armory, perhaps. Or maybe just this kiss, shaking the foundations of the earth.

'See here!' the duke called.

With reluctance, Julian lifted his head, ending the kiss.

Morland waved them over, jerking his head toward the breakwater. 'Looks as though they're slowing work. Perhaps they'll be released early.'

Julian turned to Lily and signed, 'Go. You must go home. Now. This is men's business. Dangerous.'

'No,' she said, still holding her side. 'You don't understand. It's Peter Faraday.'

Peter Faraday? How the devil had she learned of Peter Faraday?

'He was with Leo that night,' she huffed. 'They were . . . They were lovers.'

'What?' he signed. Julian was certain he'd misheard her.

'*Lovers?*' Ashworth and Morland echoed.

So. It would seem he hadn't misheard.

She nodded, looking around the group. 'Yes, lovers. I'm sure of it. I have letters from Faraday to my brother. They leave no doubt.'

342

For a prolonged moment, the armory was strangely silent. He and Ashworth and Morland looked from one to another. To their boots. To the horizon. Looking around in vain for explanations, he supposed. Or maybe just escape.

Considering Julian's own history of debauchery, he'd never felt himself in the position to judge others' sexual affairs. And to be sure, he'd known his share of mollies. His own tailors, for a start. It was no secret Schwartz and Cobb were more than just business partners. In his youth, there'd been a molly house just a block from Anna's coffee house. And even within the *ton,* there were always those 'confirmed bachelors.'

But those were *other* men. They weren't Leo. Lovers. Leo and Faraday, *lovers.*

Julian briefly considered reconstructing his mind to accommodate the concept. Then he pushed the idea away. Renovations on such a grand scale took more time than he could spare right now. 'We already knew Faraday was there. He took the attack meant for me. I was supposed to be with Leo that night.'

'But you weren't,' Morland said. 'Faraday was. And if they had some kind of relationship . . .'

'A crime of passion?' Ashworth put in. 'Is that what you're thinking?'

'Wait a minute. You're forgetting Cora Dunn. You know, the *female* prostitute Leo picked up that evening?' Yes, Julian reminded himself. He'd been with a woman. Lily had to be wrong. 'Cora saw two men attacking them, and the brutes she described looked like Stone and Macleod down there. They were apprehended in the same neighborhood, on the same night. We're here for a reason.'

343

Of all the untenable notions, that would be the most impossible to accept—that they were here for nothing. That after all this, no answers awaited him. No future.

Morland swore. 'I have to leave. Jesus Christ, that man is in my house.'

'Faraday had nothing to do with it,' Julian insisted. Lily tugged at his sleeve, but he pulled his arm free and gestured toward the two convicts on the breakwater. 'If those men killed Leo, we can't let them walk free. He was our friend.'

'He was my *brother*,' Lily argued. 'I'm his closest kin. If there's a question over how to deal with this, shouldn't it be mine to say?'

Click. The sound of a gun being cocked, uncomfortably close.

'I loved him. It's mine to say.'

Julian wheeled around to see another man had joined them on the platform. Peter Faraday—standing tall and fit, armed with a double-barreled flintlock pistol.

Hatred flickered in the man's gaze as he raised his gun. 'No one move.'

344

Chapter Twenty-four

A shot cracked the air.

Julian had no time to raise his own weapon. No time to do anything, save throw his body in front of Lily's. Faraday fired again, and a ball whistled past Julian's ear.

After a split-second inventory of his vital organs to assure himself he was alive and unharmed, Julian whipped his head around, following the shots' trajectory. Through the acrid cloud of black powder, he glimpsed Stone and Macleod reeling on the breakwater. The two convicts made slow, insensate dives into the Thames, shackles and all. If they weren't already dead from their gunshot wounds, they would drown within the minute.

'No!' Julian cried. He surged toward the edge, in his desperation thinking to leap straight off the shipyard platform. How many feet down to the riverbank? Fifteen, perhaps? If he survived the jump with no broken bones, maybe he could fish the men out of the river.

But Lily wrapped her arms about him, holding him back. 'No, don't! There's nothing you can do.'

Julian froze, swearing with helpless rage. He had no choice but to stop. It was that, or drag Lily over, too.

'It's done,' Faraday said, coming to stand beside them. 'It's over.'

Yes, it was over. And Julian was done for. God damn it to hell. With those men went his only hope of identifying his enemy. His future was sinking to the bottom of the Thames like a lead weight.

Nothing was left to mark Stone and Macleod's presence on this earth, save a few ripples. The officers seemed not to have noticed a thing. It had all happened so fast, and what was the sound of two gunshots in the midst of an armory?

He choked on a sob. What did he do now? Numbness struck him in the knees. Feeling hopeless and doomed, he turned, took his wife in his arms, and held her. This was what he would do. He would hold on to Lily for as long as he could.

No one knew what to say.

Finally Morland said to Faraday, 'I thought you were an invalid.'

'I was for a time.' He lowered his still-smoking weapon. 'I got better.'

No doubt about it. Julian scarcely recognized Faraday as the same person they'd visited in Cornwall. Aside from his miraculous physical recovery, the man's whole demeanor had changed. The Peter Faraday of Julian's recollection had been vacuous, irreverent, shiftless. This Faraday was collected and sure. Ruthless, in a strangely professional way.

'Rot in hell,' the man said through gritted teeth, glaring hard at the breakwater.

Morland said, 'You seem certain they were the right ones. Thought you said you couldn't identify them.'

'I lied. I'd know them anywhere,' Faraday said. 'They were the ones. They killed him.'

Another prolonged silence.

'Impressive marksmanship,' put in Ashworth at length, in some absurd attempt at small talk. 'From your form, I would have marked you as military trained. But I'd know if you'd served in the army.'

346

'No. No army,' Faraday said, finally standing back from the edge. 'My service to the Crown was in . . . shall we say, an unofficial capacity.'

'A spy?' Julian blurted out. 'You're a bloody spy?'

Faraday sighed and glanced around. 'Yes, well. Generally, we avoid shouting that out in public.'

Julian could only stare at the man. Peter Faraday, a secret agent? In a dozen years, Julian never would have suspected him of espionage. But then, he supposed that was rather the point.

'What?' Faraday quirked a brow. 'Did you think yourself the only man in England with a double life . . . Mr. *Bell*?'

'*You.*' Stunned, Julian allowed Lily to slide from his arms. He leveled a finger at Faraday. 'In the street the other day . . . It was you.'

Faraday nodded. 'It was me.'

'So when you said in Cornwall that the attackers had meant to kill me . . . you—'

'Lied. Yes. Men in my line of work tend to do that.'

Dizzied, Julian put a hand to his temple. From the beginning, everything that had led Julian to believe the attack was intended for him . . . all of it came from Faraday. And if Faraday had been lying to him the whole time, that meant no one wanted to kill Julian at all. He'd spent the past months seeing phantoms in shadows and tilting at windmills. 'But why?'

'I wanted to keep you out of this.' He looked around at Morland and Ashworth. 'Bloody amateurs, all of you.' He gestured toward the breakwater with frustration. 'I had plans for them, damn it. To be sure, you're all a bit slow, but it didn't take *me* six months to learn who and where they were. I have connections, you know. I could have had these men killed at any time. Fallen overboard. Beaten to death in a prison fight. Shot during an attempted escape. Easiest thing in the world. No one would ever question their deaths, just like no one will question this. Stray shots from the firing range, the report will say. Happens all the time.'

He stared out at the river, toward the spot where the men had disappeared. 'This is not what I had planned, damn it. I wanted to deal with them myself. Slowly, and at close range. I wanted them to suffer. I wanted them begging for mercy, and then I wanted the pleasure of denying their sniveling pleas. I wanted my face to be the last thing they ever saw.'

In a sudden fit of rage, he rushed to the platform's edge and heaved the pistol out into the river. 'Bastards!' he called after it, his voice breaking. 'Goddamned filthy blackguards. That death was too good for you. I will hunt you down in hell.'

Julian looked to Lily. Her face was a blank mask of shock. How much of all this had she understood?

'Are you well?' he asked his wife, touching her arm.

'I'm not certain.'

Fair enough. At the moment, Julian wasn't certain of much, either. He swiveled Lily to face Faraday and spoke and signed, 'You owe us a great many explanations.'

Faraday nodded slowly. 'You'll have them. The two of you.' He turned to Ashworth and Morland. 'As for you two, it's none of your damn business.

348

Morland, go home. Your ward is in labor.'

'Claudia?' The duke paled. 'She's giving birth?'

'May have done so already. When I left her, the doctor was already there. I couldn't wait for your wife, but I sent word.'

'Amelia's there with her,' Lily said. 'She and Meredith both. They went back to Morland House straightaway.' To Faraday, she added, 'They were at my house when your note arrived. That's how I knew. I recognized your penmanship.'

'Ah.' Faraday's eyes warmed. 'So he saved the letters, did he?'

Lily nodded. 'He did.'

A bittersweet smile curved his lips. 'Incorrigible romantic. I expressly told him to burn them all.'

Leo had apparently disobeyed Faraday's instructions, but to Julian's eye the man wasn't displeased. There was no denying it. It would seem the two had been more than mere lovers.

They'd been in *love*.

Lily took a step toward Faraday. 'Mr. Faraday . . . ' She sniffed. 'May I hug you?'

Faraday blinked with surprise. His red-rimmed gaze slid sideways, and he gave a slight nod. 'I'd welcome that.'

Lily moved forward and embraced the man, wrapping her arms about his shoulders and resting her cheek to his lapel. 'I'm so sorry,' she said, starting to cry. 'So terribly sorry. I miss him, too.'

'There, there,' Faraday murmured, patting her on the back. 'Aren't you a dear soul? And very much your brother's sister, so much is clear.'

The two huddled together, drawing consolation from their shared grief. Julian felt a stab of ridiculous jealousy, but he forced it away. Far be it

349

from him to deny Lily comfort from any source.

He would have his turn to hold her later. All night long. And for the lifetime after that.

Bloody hell. Belief hovered nearby, and his mind stretched to grasp it. Was it truly over?

'Go on,' Julian told Morland and Ashworth. 'Go see to Lady Claudia and your wives. We'll meet again soon.' As his friends started to leave, he impulsively added, 'Oh, and thank . . .'

Both men halted mid-stride, turned, and stared at Julian as if he'd grown a third eye in the center of his brow.

' . . . you,' Julian finished self-consciously. This had been so much easier to say when they were faced in the opposite direction. But there they were, patiently listening, and it did need saying. 'I, uh, just wanted to say'—he cleared his throat and made the next words almost part of the cough— 'thank you. You know. For . . . not leaving. Earlier.'

The duke's discomfort was plain. 'Don't go getting emotional, Bellamy. We aren't going to hug.'

'I should hope not.' Ashworth threw a glance in Lily and Faraday's direction. 'Er . . . not that there's anything wrong with that.'

Julian laughed. The awkwardness was so thick between them, there was just nothing else for it. 'For God's sake, leave off, the both of you. Go play midwife. Thanks for nothing.'

'That's more like it.'

'And send us word of the babe,' he called after them.

After they'd gone, Lily pulled back from Faraday's embrace. The man offered her a handkerchief from his breast pocket, and she used it to dab at her eyes. 'Will you both ride back with me in the carriage?' she asked, looking from Faraday to Julian. 'We have just enough daylight remaining to talk along the way.'

They agreed and made their way to the Warren's gatehouse. On the other side of the gate, Lily's driver and coach waited patiently. On their way out of town, they stopped at the inn to make arrangements for Julian and Faraday's mounts.

Back in the coach, Julian pushed back the drapes from the window glass to let in as much light as possible. He and Lily situated themselves at opposite ends of the front-facing seat, and Faraday sat across from them. In this manner, they formed a triangle, so as best to facilitate conversation.

'So if you rode out here on horse back,' Julian began, 'you must not have been so gravely injured.'

Faraday replied, 'I was gravely injured indeed. No deceit there. But I worked hard to recover from my wounds. I was determined to regain my strength.'

'But you led us to believe you were still an invalid.'

'I was planning to return to London anyway. When your friend Ashworth showed up in Cornwall, I reckoned I might as well ride with him.'

'And stay at Morland's house?'

Faraday shrugged. 'There's been some curiosity about the duke amongst my superiors. He wasn't raised on English soil, you know, and he's always been a recluse. I couldn't pass up the chance to stay in his house. If I'd uncovered something shocking, it surely would have meant a promotion.' He sighed. 'As it turns out, Morland is the furthest thing from shocking. He's rather a bore, and quaintly devoted

351

to his wife. Now his ward, on the other hand . . . *she* is interesting.'

'Can we please go back,' Lily said, 'and begin at the beginning? I want to understand what happened.'

'The beginning.' Faraday rested his head against the tufted seatback and sighed. 'Yes. The beginning was lovely.'

'How did you meet?' she asked.

'The club, of course. Back during the war, I was given interesting assignments. Lately, it's all stuff and nonsense. What's this "Stud Club" about, my superiors wanted to know. An elite membership, open to anyone with luck? It sounded suspicious to them. They thought there must be something more behind it. So I won a token, gained entrée to the club. And I learned there was nothing behind it, except the best, most kindhearted man I've ever known. Divinely handsome, to boot.'

Julian glanced at his wife, amazed by how she was taking this all in stride. His own thoughts were still cycling through a sequence that went much like this: *Leo, a molly? No. Surely not. But it must be. Lily says it's so. Truly, though. Leo?*

So shocking, this new intimation of his friend's private life. He didn't want to let it change his high opinion of Leo, but Julian couldn't help but wonder if he'd ever truly known the man.

'Did you know?' he asked Lily. 'Of Leo's . . . ?' God, he couldn't even finish the sentence.

'That he preferred men to women, romantically? Yes, I've known since we were youths. We never really discussed it, but he was my twin brother. How could I fail to notice something like that? I wish I'd been brave enough to talk to him. I . . . I just had no

352

idea what to say.'

'He struggled with it, too,' Faraday said. 'Living outside the rules comes easily to a man like me. But it didn't come as easily to Leo. He was a very honest, loyal sort.'

'I worried about him so,' Lily said. 'Always surrounded by friends, but isolated at the same time.' She looked to Julian. 'For the longest time, I thought you must know. You didn't even suspect?'

'No,' Julian answered numbly. No, he hadn't. He'd been too busy guarding his own secrets to wonder about Leo's. But he understood well the strain of presenting one face to the world while living a different life entirely. Under that burden, Julian had grown bitter and vengeful. But Leo was a better man than he. Perhaps this explained his friend's endless quest to make everyone around him feel accepted and at ease.

His hands clenched in useless fists. He wanted to go drag the river for Stone and Macleod's corpses, revive them, then kill them all over again.

'Let me guess,' Lily said to Faraday. 'It started more than two summers ago. That's where Leo was that July. With you, not his Eton classmates.'

Faraday nodded in confirmation. 'He hated lying to you, but it seemed the only prudent course. We went to—'

'Cornwall,' Julian finished, finally piecing it together. 'That house. You said you'd spent a pleasant holiday there once. With a . . . with a blond.' And he'd never said that blond was a woman. Faraday had just let them assume.

'Very sharp, Mr. Bellamy. High marks to you. After Leo's death, I returned there to convalesce. And to grieve. My bones healed faster than my

353

heart, as it happened.' His eyes slid to the window. 'That particular organ is still not all of a piece.'

'But the letters,' Lily said. 'They made it sound as though you'd ended it.'

'Leo ended it. Last spring.'

'Did you have a falling-out?'

'No. Not exactly.' He tossed his hat aside and pushed a hand through his hair. 'He'd learned the truth of my . . . profession, as it were. Leo was always scrupulous about discretion. He wanted to protect you from scandal, Lily, and he was doubly concerned about exposing you to danger. Too ironic, in the end.'

'So the attack in Whitechapel was related to your profession?' Julian asked. 'Enemies of yours?'

Faraday shook his head. 'No. Nothing so logical as that. Stone and Macleod were just a pair of bloodthirsty brutes, riled up on liquor and violence after the boxing match. They weren't out to get me specifically, nor Leo, nor you. They were just bullies looking for amusement, and they found it. It's a time-honored pastime, roughing up the mollies.'

'Oh, God,' Lily said. 'That's so horrible.'

Horrible, Julian silently agreed. Also despicable, cowardly, and nauseating. But all too believable. He'd grown up on the streets. He'd seen such beatings before.

Faraday tapped the flat side of his fist against the carriage wall. 'Such a stupid reason for a good man to die. That's the hardest part to move past, the senselessness of it all.'

He'd taken the words from Julian's mouth. Others had insisted all along that Leo's death was the result of random violence. Julian just hadn't been able to accept it. Not only because of his own

354

secrets and fears, but because he hadn't wanted to believe Leo was taken from this earth for no earthly justification, save some brigands' drunken sport. He wanted a *reason*.

But there wasn't one. There never would be. Damn it all to hell.

Faraday sighed. 'I can only imagine you must blame me. I blame myself. When Leo ended it, I didn't take it well. First I lost my token to Morland, out of spite. I heard the two of you making plans for the boxing match. I don't even know why I came that night. I just couldn't stay away. When I found Leo with a woman . . . I went a little mad. We argued in the alley. I stupidly accused him of lying and cheating and a slew of other unfair things. When I finally gave him a chance to explain, he told me he'd decided to finally marry. Do his duty to the title and produce an heir. He'd picked up the whore with hopes of warming to the idea, but so far he wasn't warming in the least.'

Faraday looked away for a moment. 'He couldn't stop thinking of me, he said. Didn't think he could marry anyone while he was still in love with another. So we ceased arguing and began . . . reconciling. And then those two brutes came out of nowhere.' He punched the cushion in earnest. 'Damn it all, if only I hadn't been caught so off-guard. Ordinarily, I can hold my own in a brawl.'

Julian didn't doubt it. He'd watched Faraday dispatch those two convicts with cold, ruthless ease. And now that the man had stopped feigning injury, he moved with unquestionable strength.

'Leo was knocked senseless almost instantly. That left me outnumbered. You saw them. They

355

were big. By the time Miss Dunn rounded the corner and screamed, I'd given up fighting back. My only goal was protecting Leo's body with my own. We were down and defeated, and still the bastards kept kicking.' Faraday wiped his eyes. 'I hated leaving Leo there, but there was nothing I could do to save him. Vengeance was my only thought. I needed to follow his killers. Learn anything I could, even if only which direction they'd run. You can both understand, I hope, why there could never be a trial.'

They nodded in response. If Stone and Macleod had been brought to answer their charges in court, they would have exposed the truth of Leo and Faraday's relationship. All England would have learned of their *affaire*.

'Leo valued his privacy. I couldn't do that to him. No, I needed to mete out justice myself. And I did. Though not in quite the way I'd hoped.' Faraday sighed heavily. 'It will have to be enough.'

Lily began to cry. Julian pulled her into his arms. He drew her to his chest and held her as she wept, stroking her back and pressing a kiss to her crown. Her hair smelled like home.

'It's so tragic,' she said after several minutes. 'And so horribly, horribly wrong. You're right, the senselessness is the hardest thing to accept. But it's some comfort to have answers at last.'

Yes, Julian silently agreed. Yes, that was some comfort.

She sat up straight and said to Faraday, 'Those men were vermin. Villains. The Devil's own spawn. You mustn't blame yourself for what they did. I don't blame you, and neither does Julian.'

Faraday looked to Julian, eyebrows rising in

unspoken question. *Don't you?*

He shook his head. 'See here, I've only just stopped blaming myself.'

'Yes. About that . . .' Faraday leaned close. 'You do understand, it was my assignment to investigate all the club members thoroughly.'

Julian narrowed his eyes at him. 'How much do you know?'

'Everything.'

'Who else knows?'

'No one.' Faraday's voice was firm. 'I didn't include it in my report. But no one's out for you. If someone were, I would know it. What's more, I would take care of it. You were a good friend to Leo.' His gaze slid to Lily. 'And you, my dear. Even though we've only just met, I can't help but think of you as a sister.'

Lily gave him a tearful smile. 'I've missed having a brother.'

'Well, now. That's an unexpectedly lovely end to this day.' Clearing the emotion from his throat, Faraday shot a glance out the window. 'We're coming up on Charing Cross. I'll get out there. After today's events, I'll need to see to some paperwork.'

He signaled to the driver with a rap on the carriage roof. As the coach slowed to a halt, he rose from his seat. 'Oh, yes,' he added, pausing in the open door. 'Do send my regards to Lady Claudia, and kindly send me word of how it goes. I've grown quite fond of that girl.'

And then he was gone, having disappeared into the crowd. The man was rather good at that—disappearing.

The carriage thrust into motion again, and Julian

357

let his head fall back against the tufted leather. What a day. He had answers to Leo's murder. He had the assurance that no one was trying to kill him.

He turned his head, letting his gaze slide to his wife. Fading daylight gilded her delicate profile. A dark tendril of hair caressed her pale cheek.

And he had her. Beautiful, generous, brave, intelligent Lily. His dearest friend. The mother of his child. How could he ever want for more? Tenderness unfurled in his chest as he reached for her, brushing the lock aside. She turned to him, her eyes dark and sweet.

'Let's go home,' he signed, before reaching to draw her close.

'No.' With a firm touch, she pushed him away. 'No, Julian. I can't go home with you.'

Chapter Twenty-five

'What?'

Julian's shock was evident. It was *so* evident, Lily found it mildly annoying. How could he fail to understand what he'd put her through today?

Transferring to the opposite seat, she said, 'I can't go home with you and just pretend that nothing's happened. Only to wake up to another tragic letter the next time you've decided your unstarched cuffs make you unworthy of me, and thus you've exiled yourself to the Arctic Circle.' She tried to mimic a gruff, masculine voice. '"Farewell, Lily. You must be strong."'

All the pain and betrayal of the early morning caught up with her, smothering her like a wave. She fought through tears to continue speaking. 'You abandoned me, Julian. You lied to me, withheld information that I had a right to know. I was so desperately afraid. And now I'm furious at you for making me feel that way. Why does Peter Faraday know more about your life than I do? Why didn't you tell me about him in the first place, let me know he was in London? If I'd known of his role in Leo's attack, we might have pieced together the truth months ago.'

'Yes, but . . . you were keeping secrets, too,' he replied. 'You might have told me Leo had a lover.'

'I did. Or at least, I asked you if he had someone special, that night of the play. When you made it clear you knew nothing . . . ' She shrugged. 'It wasn't my secret to divulge. If Leo had wanted you to know, he would have told you.' She paused to calm herself and take a deep breath. 'And then this morning, Julian. Really. You left me with a *letter*.'

'A letter that said how much I love you. How dearly I hoped to fix this madness and come home to you.'

'A letter that tells me I don't even know the half of your life,' she countered. 'A letter that says you're unworthy of me.'

'Lily . . .' He threw up his hands in frustration. Then blew out a breath and began again. 'The thing of it is, I just am. But I'm determined to make myself worthy. I promise you, I will devote my life to making you happy. You are everything to me.'

'I don't want to be your everything!'

He actually recoiled, as if she'd shot him. His gaze was wounded, bleeding out hope in rich shades of blue.

'Julian.' She softened her expression and signs,

trying to make him understand. If there was one thing she'd learned from losing Leo, it was the danger of depending on another person for *everything*. 'I love you. But I don't want to be your reason for living. I want to share your life. There's a difference between the two.'

'There are vast chasms between the two. Worlds between them. Whole galaxies and nebulae.'

'So?'

'So we should stay in your world. Where it's all bright and rich and dazzling.'

Oh, yes. A bright, rich, dazzling pack of *lies*. 'I thought we already had this conversation. You were going to stop treating me like a child who can't know her own mind.'

'Of course I know you're not a child. You're so clever, Lily. Your mind is one of the things I most admire about you.'

'Well, you certainly don't trust my judgment. Not enough to tell me the truth. Can you possibly understand how lowering it is—how abjectly humiliating—to beg a bird for information as to your husband's whereabouts? A *bird*.'

'That's how you found us? Did Tartuffe mention the *Jericho*?' He stared at her with open admiration. 'I'm sorry I called you clever just now. It was a profound understatement. Obviously, you're a genius. A brave, beautiful genius.'

'I'm a perfect simpleton, judging by your treatment of me. Again and again, I've told you I love you. I *wanted* to marry you. I am carrying your child. And you continue to insist you're unworthy of me. How is that not an insult to my intelligence? Am I so stupid, I can't even know who's worthy of my love and who isn't?'

360

He clearly had no idea how to respond to that.

'When we married,' she went on, 'I was so foolishly full of my own emotion. I thought, if I only held you very, very tight and whispered enough words of love in your ear, you would move past the hurt in your past. But kisses don't truly heal wounds. It's just a fiction nursemaids pass along.'

He was still for a long moment. Finally, he signed, 'You're right. If we go on like this, I'm always going to feel a fraud.'

It was what she'd suspected. And his admission was a small victory in itself. Even so, Lily couldn't help but wither in her skin. He seemed to be telling her they couldn't be happy together, or apart. That didn't bode well. 'So where do we go from here?'

He turned to the window and was silent. Lily tried not to stare at him. She didn't want to seem as though she was desperately hanging on the hopes of his reply. Even though she was.

Suddenly, he swore. 'Fine. Let's do this.' He rapped smartly on the carriage roof, calling for a halt. Gesturing for her patience, he opened the window to call up to the driver. With his head turned, she couldn't make out what he was saying.

But he resettled in his seat, and the carriage resumed its journey. Lily watched out her window. Where they normally would have turned on Oxford Street, the coach continued straight. She considered asking him their destination but then decided against it. Wherever he was headed, she was along for the ride.

They rattled on past Mayfair and turned into Bloomsbury. She recognized the street name instantly from addressing so many invitations and notes to Julian over the years.

361

'We're going to your house?' she asked.

He lifted one shoulder in a shrug. 'We're going to Julian Bellamy's house,' was his cryptic reply.

The carriage rolled to a stop, and Julian opened the door himself, reaching to hand her down. Day was quickly dwindling, giving way to a cold December night. Lily shivered in her traveling cloak as she followed him to the doorstep of a nondescript row house. The home was largish, but not especially grand.

From his breast pocket, he withdrew a pair of keys and fitted one into the lock. She watched with absurd fascination. In all honesty, she could not recall ever locking the front door of her home. There was always a footman standing at attention, waiting to open or close the door for her.

He used the second key to turn another lock, down near the bottom of the door. And then he used his shoulder to push the panel inward.

The entry was cold and dark, and stairs loomed directly before them. They climbed the steep flight, then emerged into a spacious corridor. From what she could see, peering into adjacent rooms, the furniture had all been covered with Holland cloth.

'Wait,' he signed. He ducked through a door and returned a minute later, candelabrum in hand. Two lit tapers burned in the holder, casting flickering light around the room. He offered the candelabrum to her, and she took it, holding it between them to throw warm illumination on his face.

'So,' he said. 'This is Julian Bellamy's house. Here on this floor, we have library, drawing room, dining room, parlor.'

With the exception of a pile of correspondence in the library, there was little evidence of

362

habitation. No half-read books with ribbon markers or unfinished letters lying about. No cozy rug to throw over one's lap while sitting by the hearth. In fact, the hearth was so absent of ashes and soot, she wondered if it had ever been used.

Perhaps this *was* Julian Bellamy's house. But no one lived here.

She followed him up an even narrower staircase, her sense of unease mounting with every step. What with the encroaching darkness and the flickering fingers of candlelight and the eerie desolation of the place, Lily began to feel as though she were living some horrific legend, like Bluebeard. Perhaps he would show her upstairs to his private room of horrors, where on the wall were mounted the severed heads of his first six wives . . . soon to be joined by her own.

Don't be ridiculous, her practical nature chided.

Her heart, on the other hand, drummed a repetitive two-beat warning: *Beware. Beware.*

When she reached the top of the stairs, turned into a small antechamber, and spied a vaguely human shape on the settee, heaped over with newspapers . . . Lily gasped.

When the heap of newspapers suddenly moved— she screamed.

A man bolted upright, shoving papers to the floor. 'What's all this, then?'

It took all Lily had not to drop the candelabrum. She plastered herself to Julian's side.

'My valet,' he explained for her, spelling out, 'Dillard.' To the man, he said, 'What are you still doing here? Didn't I pension you off with the others when I married?'

The slovenly heap of a manservant shrugged,

363

sending one last sheet of newsprint sliding to the floor. 'I like it here. And I reckoned there was an even chance it wouldn't work out. And here you are, back.' He gave Lily an insolent, appraising leer. 'Very nice, guv. A step up from your usual. Whose wife is this one?'

'*Mine,* you lackwit.' Julian shook his head, obviously disgusted. 'Useless clod. Get out.'

Dillard blinked at him, the very embodiment of inertia.

'Oh . . . just go back to sleep.'

That much the valet could manage. Leaving him to his settee and newspapers, Julian ushered Lily through the antechamber and into the next room.

'So this,' he said, gathering the candlelight and her attention with a tug on her wrist, 'is Julian Bellamy's private suite.' He gestured toward their immediate surroundings. 'Dressing room.'

Most of the shelves and racks were bare, their contents having been exported to Harcliffe House some weeks ago. Lily's eye went to a row of hats on a high shelf. She recognized some of them from years past, though she had not seen them in recent memory. Out of fashion now.

'For bathing and such,' he said, pulling her through another small chamber, equipped with washstand, mirror, and copper tub.

'Bedchamber.'

Well. And so it was.

Lily lifted the candlestick high, taking a good look around. The room was twice as large as Harcliffe House's largest bedchamber. Surely some hapless, well-meaning walls had been sacrificed for its creation. It was furnished in an eclectic frenzy of Oriental, Egyptian, and Continental décor. An obelisk here; a rounded bowl there. Sensual shapes, all. Rich color saturated the room, and ornate patterns danced on every surface.

In the center lounged a bed. No, not a bed. A monstrosity of velvet draping and sturdy posts and firm pillows and mattresses of no doubt specially-ordered size. Not much sleeping went on in it, she would wager. It looked more like an erotic gymnasium. She cringed, hoping he didn't wish to make love to her here.

But he skirted the bed entirely, heading for a bookcase in the far corner of the room.

He beckoned her close. 'So you've seen Julian Bellamy's house. Now I'm going to show you where I live.'

'What? What do you mean, where you live?'

In lieu of an answer, he put his hand into the bookcase, stretching to reach the hidden recesses of the third shelf. He gave a swift pull on whatever it was he'd grasped, and Lily felt a change in the room, as if the wall had released a gust of breath. When Julian stepped back, the bookcase swung out from the wall, revealing a dark space. She lifted the candelabrum but could make out nothing within.

She blinked and tried again. This time she discerned a few faint curving glimmers in the dark. Perhaps . . . a row of brass hooks?

Lily swallowed hard. Her Bluebeard fancies returned with a bloody vengeance.

'It's only a closet,' he said, stepping backward into the newly revealed space and extending her his hand. 'You live in a closet?'

'No,' he said, smiling. 'There are more rooms on the other side.' His fingers crooked to beckon her. 'You did say you wanted to share my life.'

So Lily accepted his hand, screwed up her courage, and followed him into the dark.

They went through the closet and emerged on the other side, into a modest, humbly furnished apartment. If two small rooms with a closet could be called an apartment. There was a narrow bed, made up for one. It displayed no more signs of actually being slept in than the grandiose Mount Mattress in the other room had done. But the rest of the space showed signs of life. On the desk blotter, a penknife and quill lay yearning for one another, separated by an expanse of blank paper. A discarded cravat was draped over the back of a chair. The grate had some ashes in it, and a scorched rag hanging on a hook by the kettle suggested someone rather inexpert at the task had recently been making tea.

A new light source flickered to life as Julian lit a lamp and placed it on the table. He went to the small mirror on the wall and began pushing his hair flat against his scalp.

'You live here?' she said.

He nodded, shrugging out of his coat.

'You. Live *here*.' She gestured first at him, then around the place, still not comprehending.

'Until we married, I did.'

'Why?'

'It's convenient. My offices are just below.' He frowned at his waistcoat, seemingly displeased with it.

But evidently he and waistcoat reached some kind of truce, for he let it alone. He reached for a new topcoat, this one from the hidden closet.

'Your . . . your offices?' She finger-spelled the word to make sure she'd understood him correctly.

366

'Yes.'

He donned spectacles and a brown felt beaver, and the transformation was complete. Here was her theater escort—the boring, overworked clerk. Mr. James Bell.

'Come downstairs. I'll show you.'

This time, he carried the lamp. Lily followed him out of the small apartment and down the narrowest staircase yet. This one folded in half on itself on its journey downward. It ended at a nondescript brown door.

Julian seized the handle, paused for a second, and then thrust it open wide to reveal . . .

Offices. He'd been true to his word.

Though it was growing dark, it was only late afternoon. People were still at work, in shops and factories all over the city.

This establishment was no exception. From two orderly rows of desks, two orderly rows of clerks jumped up, snapping to attention. They made a chorus of greetings, which Julian acknowledged with a nod. The clerks all retook their seats, but they kept stealing glances at Lily. They peered at her as though they'd never seen a woman before. Or at least, not one on their employer's arm. Comforting, that.

A man in a brown suit hurried toward them. Lily thought he looked vaguely familiar.

'Mr. Bell.' He bowed. 'Sir, how very good to see you. We weren't expecting you in today.' The man's gaze slid to Lily. He was visibly squirming with curiosity, but his employer did not indulge it.

'Enough, Thatcher. I'll call if you're needed.' Lily's husband—she wasn't even certain what to call him anymore—steered her toward a partitioned office at the back of the room. She barely had a chance to read the lettering on the door's frosted window: *Mr. J. Bell. Manager, Aegis Investments.*

Once inside, he directed her to sit at the large desk. From here, a large plate window gave her a view of the two rows of clerks seated at their desks. She looked out at them. In unison, they jerked their gazes away and dipped their quills.

Before her, her husband worked to clear away a haystack of papers and envelopes.

'Sorry,' he said, sifting through the papers and piling them in a neat stack. 'It's not usually so disorderly. I haven't been in much of late, and I'm behind on my correspondence.'

'What is this place?'

'It's . . . mine.' His chest rose and fell. 'You're now the only soul alive who knows that. Except Faraday, apparently, and a very discreet solicitor. Thatcher and the clerks—they all believe I'm the manager of Aegis Investments, reporting to wealthy investors. But in truth, the investments are all mine. I own it all.'

'You own what, precisely?'

He began pulling ledgers from the wall and plunking them on the desk before her. 'Various properties,' he said, plunking down a black leather-bound volume, 'including most of the immediate neighborhood. Several textile mills.' A green ledger joined the first. 'Miscellaneous investments.' This one was bound in a reddish brown.

'Have a look at them,' he said. 'Better yet, here—' He yanked a folio from a high shelf and opened it, spreading the contents on the blotter before her. 'This is last year's report. Income and

368

expenses.' He pulled one sheet apart from the rest. 'Total assets are listed here.'

Lily didn't look at it. She looked to him, agape.

He took a seat in a straight-backed chair across from her. 'Mainly, I produce and sell cloth, wholesale. That's the reason behind Julian Bellamy's striking style. I've been setting the fashion trends to benefit my trade.' He gestured toward the papers and ledgers. 'Go on, have a look.'

Lily couldn't deny that she was curious. So she did as he suggested. First, she flipped through each of the ledgers. Of all people, she could appreciate a well-kept ledger, and these were meticulous. In every case, the income eclipsed the expenditures. In the Miscellany volume, she found several pages of charitable donations in astounding sums. Then she turned to last year's summary, where she had to peer at the 'total assets' portion for a solid minute, performing calculations in her mind to check the arithmetic before she could completely believe the final balance was correct.

He was worth a fortune. And not a small one. He was worth far more than Leo had been, if one discounted the entailed property that came with the marquessate.

'How did you amass all this?' she asked, lifting her head.

'Investments. I did have some seed money. A thousand guineas.'

'Where did you get a thousand guineas?'

'Blackmail.'

'*Blackmail?*' He said the word so baldly, with no equivocation.

'Yes. You recall the fixed horse race. I bled the

369

ten conspirators for a hundred guineas each. A small fraction of their ill-gotten gains.'

'And from that, you did all this?' She gestured around at the ledgers.

He gave a modest nod.

Lily marveled at him. To think of all he'd accomplished, entirely on his own. A boy raised in the gutters, orphaned in his youth. All this, and yet he didn't flash his wealth around for amusement's sake, and certainly not for pride's. No one had any idea. She couldn't even bring herself to be angry with him for the deceit. She was too overwhelmingly proud. If only his mother could see her son now.

She dabbed away a tear. 'I always knew you were a remarkable man, and I've long suspected there was more to you than the world supposed. But I'm ashamed to say even I could not have imagined *this*. Julian, I—' She broke off, biting her lip. 'Do I still call you Julian?'

'I don't know.' He shifted in his chair, looking serious. 'I have been living two lives, under two different names. Neither one is precisely my own. My mother was Mary Bell, but you already know I'm uncertain of my Christian name.'

'Surely you could find out, if you went to the church.'

'I'm not certain I want to know.' A smile tugged at his lips. 'What if it's something dreadful, like Jedediah or Jehosephat?'

She cringed. 'I see your point there.'

'My solicitor tells me my legal name can be whichever I choose. All I need to do is settle on one identity, and then transfer everything to that name.'

'Which name?'

'That's for you to decide.'

'I think you should choose James Bell,' she said. 'Don't you? It honors your mother.' Although secretly, she would find it difficult to call him anything other than Julian. And she hated to admit, Lady Lily Bell sounded unbearably precious.

'That may be. However, I married you as Julian Bellamy. Changing to Bell now . . . I worry it could invalidate our union.'

Secretly relieved, she said, 'Well, we can't have that.'

'Are you absolutely sure?' His brow creased. 'You wouldn't prefer it that way?'

What? She sat back, stunned. How could he even say such a thing?

'Come now, Lily. A noblewoman of royal lineage, married to a man in trade? You know as well as I, it just isn't done. When I proposed to you, I planned to sell it all. I've been making arrangements to do just that, but it takes time.'

'Really? You meant to sell off everything?' The magnitude of the sacrifice pained Lily, even in the abstract. Not the wealth or possessions, but just the sheer accomplishment represented by the documents on this desk. This was his life's work.

'You deserved a gentleman. So I meant to play at being one for the remainder of my days. But I've come to realize—and I think *you've* come to realize—living like that, I will always feel something of a fraud. If I'm to prove myself worthy of you, it must be on my own terms.' His gaze made a slow circuit of the busy office, then came home to hers. 'I'm good at this, Lily. It's what I'm meant to do. I don't want to give it up.'

She nodded, understanding.

371

'So it's come to this. Your choice. Part ways with James Bell, or stay married to Julian Bellamy.' He held her response at bay with an open palm. 'Understand, you'll be a tradesman's wife. Think about what that means, Lily. Think long and hard. Your social standing and connections will suffer. Our children will not be accepted to the same schools and circles of friends you and Leo enjoyed. People may be cruel. You'll be spitting in the face of social convention.'

She stared at him.

'That is, if you were the sort to spit.' He shifted uneasily. 'I know you're not.'

'Social convention,' she said musingly. 'The same social convention that left you a penniless orphan? The same social convention that made my brother the target of violence and scorn? I'm not keen on social convention of late. If I *were* the sort to spit, that should be my first target.'

She touched a hand to the stack of papers and folios. 'I adore ledgers, Julian. I love sitting in the pit at Drury Lane. And I wasn't joking that evening. I find spectacles wildly attractive.'

Smiling, she reached across to trace the rim of one lens with her fingertip, then follow the earpiece back to where it plunged into his thick, dark hair. Tenderly, she framed his cheek with her palm.

'I think I was born to be a tradesman's wife. Or perhaps I was just born to be yours.'

For a long moment, he seemed incapable of reply. 'I'm certain I was *not* born to deserve you,' he finally said. 'But I vowed long ago to never accept the limitations of my birth.'

'I'm so glad of it.'

They stayed that way for the longest time, lost

372

in one another's loving stares. Sitting across a desk crowded with paperwork, in the midst of a busy office, under the curious gaze of several clerks. Elegant ballrooms, nothing. Lily couldn't imagine a more romantic scene.

'We're going to be so happy. You told me that, the day we wed.' He pressed his hand over hers. 'I confess, I didn't believe you then.'

'But now you do?'

'I do. Heart, mind, and soul. We are going to be so happy.'

The words alone filled her with joy. Heart, mind, and soul. 'We're going to be *unstoppable*.'

She reached to slide the spectacles from his face. As she slowly teased them free, his gaze flicked to the window and the curious clerks beyond.

'They're watching us.'

She folded the spectacles and carefully set them aside. Leaning toward him over the desk, she asked, 'Isn't there a curtain for that window?'

'Yes,' he said, closing the rest of the distance. 'There is.'

And then he kissed her, long and slow and deep. In plain view, without drawing any curtains at all. Because they weren't hiding anything anymore. Not from each other. Not from the world.

Well, and because beneath the clerkish spectacles—her husband remained, at heart, a scoundrel.

She wouldn't have it any other way.

Epilogue

'She's grown up well.' Julian propped his elbows on the fence rail. 'Pretty thing, isn't she?'

Morland and Ashworth turned to him, surprised. 'Where did you come from?' the duke asked. 'We weren't expecting you until tomorrow.'

He doffed his hat and hung it on a fencepost. 'I finished my business in York early.' To the duke, he said, 'Remind me. How old is she now?'

'Turned three this past spring.' Morland's voice was rich with pride.

'And the dark one?' Julian pointed. 'He's yours, too?'

'No, no,' the duke said. 'He's Claudia's. Note the intractable spirit. Take care with him around your little ones. He's been known to bite.'

He chuckled. 'Why am I unsurprised?'

'What took you to York?' Ashworth asked. 'Another mercantile venture?'

Julian nodded.

'How many does that make?'

'Eleven, all told. Our twelfth opens in Liverpool this autumn.'

He'd just come from the grand opening of the latest Aegis Emporium, a shop selling quality, ready-made clothing for the working man. The idea had come to him back during the war, when the military contracts were rolling in faster than he could fill them. Rather than custom-tailor each coat, they'd begun producing them in advance,

375

based on the most common measurements. In recent years, Julian had adapted the process to civilian attire, making above-average clothing affordable to the average man.

It was honest trade, and worthwhile work. And thus far, a very lucrative venture.

He squinted. 'Which one is yours, Ashworth? The big one under the tree?'

Ashworth nodded. 'Only a yearling, but fast as a demon. I plan to sell him for racing, but Morland's training him here for another year first.'

'Osiris left quite a legacy,' Julian mused.

Collective silence served as agreement, as the three of them stood there, leaning on the paddock fence and watching the ponies graze. The grand old stallion had died this past winter, but Osiris was survived by several colts, a good many fillies, and a lasting circle of friendship.

The summer sun warmed Julian's face, and a light breeze lifted his hair. He was tempted to stay and rest, enjoying the fine Cambridgeshire afternoon and the simple pleasure of not talking with old friends.

Another day, perhaps. It had been two weeks since he'd last seen his family, and he didn't want to wait two minutes more. He pushed off from the fence and retrieved his hat. 'Where are the ladies and children?'

*   *   *

'Kiss it.'

Mary crossed her arms. 'Absolutely not.'

'It's the game,' Hugh insisted. 'You have to kiss it.' He thrust the foul, squirming creature in her face and smacked his lips noisily. Behind him, Philip and Leo doubled with laughter.

Mary gave a little growl. *Boys.*

It was bad enough she had to share everything with Leo, but at least in Town, she had her own friends. Here on holiday at Braxton Hall, her choice of playmates was limited to boys or babies. Mary didn't want to play with the babies. She wanted to play in Hugh and Philip's splendid play house. It was built like a castle, with real doors and windows and furniture. But it was Hugh and Philip's play house, which meant she had to pay for the privilege of enjoying it by playing along with the boys' games.

On good days, they would let her play scullery maid to their Arthurian knights or galley wench to their pirates. In the little kitchen, she could spend happy hours weaving reeds into trivets and arranging flowers, whilst the boys dashed about with wooden daggers, looking ridiculous as anything.

Yesterday, they'd even crowned her Queen. But she must have enjoyed her power a little too much, for today she'd been demoted to Imprisoned Princess and confined to the hot, dusty turret. Hours now, and still they hadn't rescued her. She'd all but decided to head back to the Hall to find a book, when up the ladder the boys clambered, red-faced and laughing.

And in possession of a toad.

'I will not kiss that thing. I'd rather stay imprisoned forever.' In other words, until dinner, which could not be far off. Her stomach rumbled.

'Beg for your freedom, then,' Hugh said. 'Say, "Prithee, my lord."'

She rolled her eyes. Hugh would never let them forget he was a duke's son, and already Earl of Something-or-Other.

'See here,' said Philip. 'Kiss the toad. Or we shan't let you back in the play house again.'

Mary dug in her heels. That was one thing about always having to play with boys. A girl learned to be tenacious. 'Go right ahead. My father will build me my own play house. Ten times grander than this old heap.'

Philip said smugly, 'Your father's not even here.'

'At least I *have* a father,' she shot back.

'My godfath—'

'Your godfather what?' she said, teasing. 'Flew to the moon Thursday last?' Philip was always spinning wild, unbelievable tales about Mr. Faraday.

Don't, her brother signed at her, his shoulders tight with anger. *He's my friend. It's not kind.*

A glance at Philip's face told Mary she'd gone too far. *The toad*, she signed apologetically. *Take it away.*

Over the loud objections of his friends, Leo grabbed the toad and shoved it through the narrow turret window. She and Leo weren't supposed to sign in front of those who couldn't understand—it was rude, Mother always said. But at times a secret language came in useful.

'What's this?' came a deep voice from below. 'An Egyptian plague? Toads, falling from the sky.'

Mary and Leo's gazes met. 'Father!' they cried as one.

There was a mad scramble to climb down the ladder, which Mary won. She then set herself the task of climbing her father.

378

'Papa.' She clutched his neck and hugged tight, not even minding his rough whis kers. Even unshaven, he was much nicer to kiss than a toad. 'The boys are horrid. They locked me in the turret.'

He laughed. 'Well, and so I've come to rescue you.'

Leo stood close. He was a year younger, but he considered himself too grown up now for hugs and kisses, especially in front of his friends. He did accept a brisk rub on the head.

Mary wormed her hand downward, to her father's side pocket. But before she could reach her prize, he set her on the ground. She and Leo had to do three sums each and correctly spell 'hypotenuse' before he finally withdrew the packet of sweets.

'One last question,' he asked, holding the tantalizing treats just out of reach. 'Where will I find your mother?'

*   *   *

'Oh, take care, darling!' Amelia rescued a chubby finger from a near miss with a thorn. She kissed the plump little hand in apology and herded her daughter back toward the mums. 'Just the daisies, Claire. Only pick the daisies. Leave the roses to Mama.'

'I think I see someone coming.' From her seat beneath the canopy, Meredith looked up from fanning the blond infant slumbering in her lap. She peered into the distance. 'Just there, over the rise.'

'Well, I know it won't be our husbands.' Amelia snipped another rose. 'I'd bet my last crock of winter pears, Spencer will keep Rhys at the stables all day. Perhaps it's Claudia and Mr. Faraday, back from their walk.'

'No,' Meredith said, raising one hand to shade her brow. 'I don't think so. I only see one. But I'm glad to know those two are still fast friends.'

'So am I,' Amelia replied. Claudia had grown into full womanhood now, tall, curvaceous and—as ever—bold. Mr. Faraday seemed to have a gentling influence on her. 'They exchange a great many letters. And Mr. Faraday takes his role as Philip's godfather very seriously. He's already planned out the boy's schooling, from tutors to Eton to Oxford to a tour of cathedrals on the Continent. Both Philip and Hugh are terrifically fond of him.'

A thin wail rose up from beneath the canopy. With reluctance, Amelia put away her shears. Nap was over.

In Meredith's lap, baby Charlotte squirmed, squalling and red-faced.

'I'm so sorry,' Meredith said, rising to her feet.

'Don't be,' Amelia reached to gather her crying child. 'It's high time she awoke. Come to Mama, darling.'

She thought she glimpsed a flicker of emotion in Meredith's eyes as her friend relinquished the fussing babe. After eight years of marriage, she and Rhys still remained childless. 'It will be your turn soon,' she said softly, patting Charlotte on the back. 'I'm certain of it.'

'I'm reasonably certain of it, too.' Meredith smiled. 'It will be my turn in November, if the midwife can be believed.'

Amelia's startled cry of delight set off another round of baby Charlotte's wails. And the little one was most displeased to be squashed in the middle of a hug.

'I'm so happy for you. Why didn't you tell us earlier?'

The corner of Meredith's mouth tugged. 'So many times, we've thought . . . we've hoped . . . only for naught in the end. Don't tell Rhys I've told you. He's so oddly superstitious.'

'But you're certain now?'

'I think so.' Meredith's eyes misted, and she pressed a hand to her belly. 'Does it feel like a little frog? Kicking around inside?'

'Yes. That's precisely how it feels.' Amelia hugged her again. 'I'm so happy for you. You and Rhys will be wonderful parents.'

'You're expecting? That's brilliant.' The deep voice startled them both.

'Why, Julian,' Meredith said, releasing Amelia and stepping back. 'So it was *you* I saw coming over the ridge.'

'I suppose it must have been.' After tipping his hat, he reached for Amelia's hand, bowed over it, and kissed it lightly. 'Your Grace.' He then went through each of the others in turn, kissing hands. 'Lady Ashworth. Little Lady Charlotte.' Then, crouching beside a clump of daisies with all seriousness, 'Lady Claire.'

'We weren't expecting you until tomorrow,' Amelia said.

'I was able to conclude my business a bit early. I met with your husbands over by the stables.'

She laughed. 'I could have guessed that you would.'

He turned to Meredith. 'Ashworth didn't let on a thing about your good news, however.'

'It's meant to be a secret yet,' Meredith said. 'Don't tell him you know.'

381

Julian's mouth tipped as he considered. 'I'll keep your secret if you give me an answer.'

'Oh?' Meredith's brows arched. 'To what question?'

He spread his arms wide. 'Where, on this grand, magnificent, sprawling estate is my wife?'

* * *

Lily took a cautious step to her right. Her bare toes squelched in spongy mud, and the knotted hem of her skirt swirled atop the rushing stream.

Bending at the waist, she grasped a handful of watercress and pulled by the stems. She shook the leaves free of excess water before adding them to the basket threaded over her wrist. Just a few more bunches, and she would call it enough.

A brilliant blue dragonfly zipped past, darting from one patch of sunlight to another as it hovered above the creek. Lily watched, delighted with the creature's iridescent beauty and graceful speed. The dragonfly made a sudden streak to the left. She turned her head to follow its path—

And spied her husband standing on the riverbank, one shoulder propped against a beech tree. She was stunned. She hadn't expected him until tomorrow.

'How long have you been standing there?' she asked.

'Not long.'

She turned to face him. Lord, he was dangerously handsome. Unshaven, rumpled, bronzed from a day of travel in the sun. He'd stripped off his coat and wore it slung over his shoulder on the crook of one strong, talented finger. His cravat, if he'd been

382

wearing one, was gone.

The stream's brisk current lapped at the backs of her knees. Her mouth watered.

He tossed his coat over a branch and advanced toward her. 'You,' he signed, 'are very hard to find.'

She swallowed hard. Then lamely lifted her basket. 'I'm gathering watercress.'

'So I see.' He came closer, plunging right into the stream, boots and all. As he neared, he drew a deep breath. 'You smell of it, too. Green and peppery and fresh.'

'I've missed you,' she told him. And she had, every hour of every day.

'Nowhere near as much as I've missed you.' His throat worked as he swept her with a hungry gaze, from her loosely plaited hair to the froth swirling and eddying about her bare legs. 'I'm going to kiss you, right here in the water. And then I'm going to make love to you on the riverbank.'

'That sounds lovely.'

He reached for her basket of watercress and unthreaded it from her wrist, stretching to place it safely on the riverbank. Then his hands went to the ribbon ties of her straw hat. He unknotted the bow beneath her chin and tossed the whole business aside.

Then . . . at last . . . he reached for *her*.

He touched one hand to her cheek and released a deep, full-body sigh. 'Lily.'

A shiver swept her, all the way from the cool stream's surface to her sun-warmed nape. She trembled. So absurd. He was her husband of more than eight years. Most days, she felt she knew him better than she knew herself.

Still, she trembled.

They smiled at one another as they slowly leaned forward, taking their time easing into the kiss. Because by now, they both knew better than to rush. It was drudgery, being apart for long weeks. But it was magic, reuniting after long weeks apart. A mere glance was exciting. The first brush of skin against skin was pure exhilaration. The first taste of each other was an exquisite blend of the familiar and the wild.

And wherever they were—be it London, or York, or the middle of a stream in Cambridgeshire—this first kiss meant they'd come home.